The
CHARMED FRIENDS
of TROVE ISLE

Also by Annie Rains

Through the Snow Globe

ANNIE RAINS

The CHARMED FRIENDS *of* TROVE ISLE

KENSINGTON
PUBLISHING CORP.

www.kensingtonbooks.com

KENSINGTON BOOKS are published by

Kensington Publishing Corp.
900 Third Avenue
New York, NY 10022

All Kensington titles, imprints, and distributed lines are available at special quantity discounts for bulk purchases for sales promotion, premiums, fund-raising, and educational or institutional use.

Special book excerpts or customized printings can also be created to fit specific needs. For details, write or phone the office of the Kensington Sales Manager: Kensington Publishing Corp., 900 Third Avenue, New York, NY 10022. Attn. Sales Department. Phone: 1-800-221-2647.

KENSINGTON and the K with book logo Reg US Pat. & TM Off.

ISBN: 978-1-4967-4087-8
First Trade Paperback Printing: June 2024

ISBN: 978-1-4967-4088-5 (e-book)

10 9 8 7 6 5 4 3 2 1

Printed in the United States of America

For Sarah Younger.
Thank you for believing in this book, and in me.

For Trisha and Susan.
Childhood BFFs live on forever, if only in our memories.

To: Bri Johnson
From: Liz Dawson

Subject: I might be losing my mind

Bri,

I had a dream about the charm bracelet last night. Funny, I haven't thought about it in ages, but I guess some memories just creep up on you like that.

Do you ever wonder where we'd all be if we hadn't lost it? Would we all still be the kind of forever friends we'd promised to stay, passing the bracelet back and forth like we'd said we would? I'd like to think so. I'd like to imagine the links would be full by now, telling a story of adventures, friendship, and maybe even love. That Alyssa would be alive, probably singing somewhere on Broadway. Melody would have stayed on Trove Isle, bossing us all around, like she's good at. And you would be here too.

Anyway, e-messages are fine, but I miss seeing your face. I'll come visit soon!

xx,

Liz

P.S. Little sisters are not meant to be roommates. Having Rose stay with me while my parents are in Ecuador might prove to be the longest six weeks of my life. Then again, you've been away for four years now, and that has felt like a lifetime. I can't wait for July when you finally come home. It's too bad it can't be all three of us, but I'm 99.9% sure Melody will never return to Trove Isle.

CHAPTER ONE

MELODY

Melody Palmer pulled up to the address in her GPS and parked along the curb. The sign above the awning read HIDDEN TREASURES in large golden block letters. The word *treasure* brought visions of jewelry or fancy clothing to mind. It conjured images of special knickknacks or mementos that one might find in a fancy gift shop, which was what Melody had assumed she'd inherited. This store and its sign, however, reminded her of a pawn shop.

She swallowed past a tight throat and reached for a bottled water in the center console, taking several long sips. She was meeting with a lawyer here in just a few minutes to sign the papers and make this place hers.

When Mr. Lyme had called last week to inform her that—*surprise!*—she was the new owner of a store that her Great-aunt Jo had willed to her in Trove Isle, North Carolina, Melody's first remark had been, "I thought someone had to die to will you something."

After a long pause, the lawyer had cleared his throat and responded in a thick southern accent, "My condolences, Miss Palmer."

So Great-aunt Jo was dead. The realization that her father's aunt was gone still knocked the breath out of Melody when she thought about it. She hadn't seen Jo in nine years, but the fact that she never would again stung. After Melody's mother had died when Melody was eleven, Jo had picked up the slack on the things that moms did, like teaching Melody and her sister Alyssa, who was one year younger, about boys and puberty, having at-home spa days that were unconventional to say the least, and making butterscotch tea when they'd had a bad day.

When Melody had left her small ocean isle town at eighteen, she'd left everyone behind, including Jo.

Pushing her car door open, Melody stepped out onto the sidewalk of Seagull Street. She'd been impressed when she'd heard the address. This was prime realty in the little isle town. Unlike the other beachfront towns nearby, Trove Isle wasn't a touristy hot spot. It was too small to accommodate many out-of-towners, and most people had never heard of Trove. For those who lived here though, Seagull Street was the place to be. It had everything a town might need, and maybe a little of what it didn't need.

Melody looked at the storefront again. Jo hadn't owned this place before Melody left town. Instead, Melody's great-aunt had worked odd jobs, scraping money together to barely make ends meet. When Melody had heard Jo left her a store, she'd assumed her great-aunt had finally found success. Melody had envisioned a nice storefront with good business.

That's not what this was. Melody should have known better. Jo was what one might call a hoarder. There was an untold story in everything that Jo was drawn to—an unlived life. Melody used to disappear into her aunt's closet for hours, opening boxes, and pulling things out to try on.

"Those shoes will lead you to one of your very best friends," Jo once said when Melody had tried on a pair of

shiny black ballerina flats. Melody had been twelve. The very
next day, she'd gone to school, wearing her shoes that Jo had
salvaged from some unknown place, and she'd sat down beside the new girl, Brianna Johnson—Bri—who soon became
one of Melody's closest friends. Well, up until the accident.

Jo had been right. She was always right about things like
that.

Melody glanced in each direction up the sidewalk before
walking to the store's window and pressing her hands against
the cold glass to peer inside. There was wall-to-wall clutter.
Clothes, toys, books, handheld appliances, everything one
could possibly want—to get rid of.

Along one wall Melody spotted a fluorescent sign that
read STUFF A BEACH BAG FOR $1.

Is this a thrift store?

"Miss Palmer?" a deep voice asked.

Melody jumped back from the window and whirled to
face a balding man with dark brown skin and a neatly
trimmed silver beard. "Mr. Lyme?"

He held out his hand for her to shake. "Nice to see you
again, Melody. It's been awhile, hasn't it?"

Melody slipped her hand into his, finding his grasp firm
and warm. She didn't exactly recognize him though.

"I think the last time I saw you, you might have been
ready to graduate high school," he said in a friendly manner.

She stiffened at the reminder of her senior year. It was supposed to be the launching pad for the rest of her life, and it
had been. It just hadn't launched her where she'd expected to
go. Back then she'd been eager to travel, yes, but she'd never
intended to forget her roots. She was feeling claustrophobic
by her tiny hometown and wanted to go and do and see all
that the world had to offer. It was as if the world was her
oyster and she was destined to find her pearl. By the time
she'd ended up leaving though, it hadn't been in the spirit of

adventure, but more of a desperation for escape. Now here she was, back in the little town that had once felt like her prison.

Melody avoided the lawyer's gaze, pretending to observe the storefront again. It had brick facing, and it was painted a creamy white color, chipped in a way that made it look both old and quaint—unlike that blaring sign above their heads. "Thank you for meeting me."

"Of course, of course." He took a pair of keys from his blazer's pocket and jingled them in front of her with a wide grin. "Let me show you Jo's pride and joy." He opened the shop door and gestured for her to go in ahead of him. The aroma was what hit Melody first. Did dust have a smell? The air was stale, reminiscent of a closet that had been closed for too long, its shelves lined with moth balls and bricks of cedar meant to offset the musty scent.

Melody coughed once and then another time, finally deciding to breathe more shallowly while she was in the confines of this space.

"You okay?" Mr. Lyme asked, following behind her. "Jo has been gone a couple weeks now and no one has been in here to care for this place. This store meant everything to Jo," he said. "Every time I stopped in to see her, she had an ear-to-ear grin. Then again, that was Jo. Always spreading cheer wherever she went."

Melody turned to the lawyer, finding his kind words about her great-aunt interesting. "You and Jo were good friends?"

Mr. Lyme looked down for a moment, which Melody also found intriguing.

Oh. Apparently, he and Great-aunt Jo were more than good friends. That shouldn't have made Melody sad, but it did. She didn't know her great-aunt anymore. She hadn't known about this store or the man Jo had been involved with. She hadn't even known Jo was gone until two weeks after the fact.

Melody's father had been calling and she'd been ignoring him. Was this what he'd been trying to tell her? If she had taken the time to call him back, perhaps she would have known. Turning, Melody let her gaze roam over the items on the shelves. There were knickknacks, costume jewelry, racks of shoes, books, clothing. "Where did all this stuff come from?" she asked.

"Donations mostly. Jo was a bit of a dumpster diver too," Mr. Lyme admitted. "She'd wake up before the birds were even singing and go out looking for her treasures."

Melody didn't dare ask how he knew her great-aunt's early morning habits. "Dumpster diving?"

He looked a little embarrassed on Jo's behalf. "Going through other people's trash. One man's junk is another woman's treasure. That's what Jo loved to say," he said with a deep belly laugh.

Melody could feel her expression tighten. She couldn't help it. Between the smells and the idea that some of this stuff had come from the bottom of a dumpster, her senses were misfiring.

"I know it's probably not your dream to own a place like this," Mr. Lyme went on, "but breathing life into lost things was Jo's passion."

Melody felt the tickle of another cough threatening in the back of her throat. "I don't understand. Why did Jo leave Hidden Treasures to me? Surely there were other more deserving people in Jo's life."

Mr. Lyme looked around. He wasn't grimacing. Instead, his distant gaze appeared to be more of a walk down memory lane. "As you know, she didn't have any living kids and was never married. Jo knew your father wouldn't appreciate this place. That's why she left Hidden Treasures to you."

Melody wished she could say she felt appreciative. Right now, she was more overwhelmed with guilt and sadness. And disappointment. This store wasn't at all what she'd imagined, and it certainly didn't appear to be the answer to her prayers. She'd been hoping any inheritance would serve as a down payment for her own place in Charlotte, so that she could finally lay down roots somewhere. "I don't live in Trove Isle anymore and I don't plan to ever again," she told the lawyer honestly.

"Oh, Jo knew that. She was a special woman, your great-aunt. She didn't make this choice lightly." He stepped up to a glass counter full of costume jewelry and laid his leather briefcase down. "I'm sure you'll figure it out, Melody." He pulled out a stack of paperwork and handed Melody a pen. "Just need your signature on a few lines to make this official."

Melody's breaths began to quicken. She rubbed a hand behind her neck. "What if I don't sign the papers?" she asked, her chest feeling tight as a slow panic wrapped around her. This store suddenly seemed like a lot more responsibility and work than she'd bargained for. Maybe she didn't want it after all. How much money could she even get from selling a place as run-down as this?

Mr. Lyme's smile wobbled. "Why wouldn't you sign?"

Heat torched her cheeks. "Well, I, um, I don't know if there are expenses attached to this property. Will I owe money on it? I don't have the means to pay any outstanding bills." For many years after leaving the isle, Melody had barely been able to pay her own bills. But now she was doing well for herself. She lived in a modest one-bedroom apartment in Charlotte, paid her rent on time, and could afford to get her hair cut at a place that cost way too much. A cut was a cut, but her hair had never looked so stylish. It was worth every penny.

Melody wished she had more to her name, but she liked at least having a little more than enough, and she never wanted to find herself just scraping by again. Especially not over a musty thrift store that she didn't even want—or deserve.

Mr. Lyme gave her a reassuring smile. "Jo owned this place free and clear. You'd be inheriting the shop and everything inside. You would need to cover the utilities and the annual taxes, of course, but that's it." He waved the pen in front of Melody again as he waited for her to move.

Finally, she took the pen, her hand slightly shaking, and she started signing until she got to the bottom of the stack. She didn't give herself time to second-guess what she was getting herself into. She owed Jo at least this much.

"All right then. You are the new owner of Hidden Treasures Thrift Store," Mr. Lyme said. "I know Jo would be relieved that this place is in your capable hands. I'm sure I'm not alone when I say I can't wait to see what you do with this place."

Do with the place? Other than sell it?

Melody cleared her throat, feeling another tickle that threatened to turn into a cough. "Thank you, Mr. Lyme."

"You're welcome. I've been waiting on you to return home, per Jo's wishes. She didn't want a funeral. Instead, she planned a celebration of life for herself."

"Oh." Some part of Melody had thought she'd missed Jo's funeral. "When is the celebration?"

"This Friday night. It was Jo's final wish that you'd attend."

Melody really didn't want to be thrown into a social event with the entire town. She was just hoping to get in and out and see as few people as she could get away with. But she couldn't deny her great-aunt's dying request. Jo had meant more to her than a distant relative. Once upon a time, Jo was as close as a mother to Melody. "Of course, I'll try to attend." *Try* being the operative word. If she could come up with a decent excuse not to, she'd choose that route. Saying goodbye was a personal thing. Melody didn't need to do it with a group of people whom she hadn't seen in ages. Or worse, strangers.

"Good." Mr. Lyme seemed to exhale as if he'd been worried that she'd refuse. "It's going to be at Sunrise Park."

"The park?" That was an odd place to hold a celebration of life.

"Right on the water," Mr. Lyme confirmed as if the detail made perfect sense. "I'll see you there," he said as he walked back to the door.

Melody followed him. Once he was gone, she turned and inspected the somewhat claustrophobic space, all her hopes crashing down around her. What was she going to do with a thrift store? It wasn't even the high-end kind. This place was messy, unorganized, and quite possibly a safety hazard.

Melody walked the aisles, tried not to breathe, and avoided touching anything. Finally, she ended up at the glass case where the register sat. She peered down at a display of costume jewelry. Some of it was surprisingly kind of fun. In the far corner was a handwritten sign in Jo's looping penmanship: NOT FOR PURCHASE. That was odd. Why display something in a secondhand store that wasn't available to buy?

She inspected the items more closely. There was a crystal frame with a baby picture inside. Melody didn't immediately recognize the baby, but she guessed it might have been Jo's son who'd passed away when he was less than a year old. Next was a pink cameo broach that Melody vaguely recalled Jo wearing to special events. It clashed with her favorite lime-green pantsuit. The last item made Melody suck in a startled breath, forgetting momentarily that she was trying not to breathe in too deeply.

There, on a plastic jewelry display, was a charm bracelet that looked impossibly familiar. The piece was a mixture of rose, yellow, and white gold, braided together loosely like the one she and her friends had once shared. Except the bracelet she remembered only held one heart-shaped friendship charm. This one held several charms.

Melody blinked the sting from her eyes. There was no way that this was the same bracelet Alyssa had gifted their little quartet of friends right before high school graduation. Once upon a prom night, that charm bracelet was lost in a car accident—along with so much more.

Melody turned the key that poked out of the case's lock and slid the glass door open. Then she reached for the jewelry, picked it up, and inspected the dangling charms. A house, a car, a muffin, a tiny camera, and . . . a friendship charm.

The breath whooshed out of her so hard that she had to brace her hands on the glass case to keep from sinking to the floor. The charm was dented on the top left bend of the heart. A defect that identified this charm as the very one that Melody and her friends had all shared. But this wasn't possible. This bracelet was lost in the car accident that had killed Alyssa, who'd been wearing it that horrible night. No one had ever seen the piece of jewelry again. How had it gotten here?

Melody blinked the bracelet into focus, her breaths coming out fast and shallow. The idea was that they'd take turns wearing the bracelet. When it was their turn, they had to do something amazing. Something that scared them. That made their heart race.

"In a good way," Alyssa had said with that wide, perfect Broadway smile that Melody missed every day. "That's how we'll know we're alive and not just zombies like our parents and a few teachers who shall not be named," she'd said dramatically.

Melody and Alyssa's father had led the pack of so-called

zombies, ever since their mother died. Principal Blevins was also suspect, barely mustering a smile most days despite Bri's best attempts to make him crack one.

The charm bracelet had belonged to Jo first. That was where Alyssa had gotten it. Had the piece of jewelry somehow returned to Jo and she'd kept it safe? Jo always had a talent for finding lost things and putting them right back where they belonged. Just like that time she'd found Melody's favorite doll that she'd lost after their picnic in Sunrise Park. Melody's mom had given her that doll, and Melody had been distraught, crying herself to sleep night upon night. Then one morning Melody had woken up with the doll in her arms.

"Where did you find it?" Melody had asked Jo as she hurried down to her great-aunt's sewing room, which was really a room full of old things. Lost things. Found things. Treasures, according to Jo.

"I found it on the Isle of Lost Things," Jo had said, all wide-eyed and full of dramatic flair, which was Jo's style. Alyssa had been a lot like her.

The Isle of Lost Things was as real to Melody back then as Santa Claus and the Tooth Fairy, and the idea that her mother was sitting on a cloud in heaven with angel wings, looking down on her.

Melody didn't believe in such things anymore. So where had this bracelet been all this time? There were so many unknowns that would probably never find answers now that Jo was gone.

Melody swallowed, her throat the consistency of sandpaper. She thought about flinging the bracelet back into the case, but this wasn't something to keep on display. It felt private, off-limits. So much so that Melody hadn't even allowed herself to look on these memories for the last nine years. Yet here they were, threatening to suffocate her. Her next impulse was to walk out of this store, get back inside her car, and drive over the bridge and away from the tiny town of Trove Isle. She'd left all this pain behind once. She could do it again.

Not knowing what else to do with the bracelet, she slid it onto her wrist for safe keeping. As she looked down at it, unshed tears burning her eyes and blurring her vision, the home charm seemed to catch the light. It reflected so brightly that she had to blink. When she did, one of those tears finally fell free.

No. She didn't want to cry. She didn't want to be home in Trove Isle. Or to be the owner of a store full of stuff retrieved from the bottom of a dumpster. If the Isle of Lost Things was in fact a real place, she was standing in the middle of it. And maybe that was the reason Jo had brought her here. Maybe she was the most lost thing of all. And if that was the case, she didn't want to be found.

To: Liz Dawson
From: Bri Johnson

Subject: Deep Thoughts by Bri

Liz,

I've been reading a lot of poetry in the prison library lately. Have I mentioned that? I'm not sure why, but reading a poem gives me a sense of accomplishment, you know? I'm not one of those people who finishes books. Even the ones I like. But I can read dozens of poems in one sitting. I have the beginning, the middle, and the end all in a matter of minutes.

I'm in a mood today. My daughter is on the other side of the country for the immediate future, and even though I'm not allowed to see Ally as often as I'd like, I miss her more just knowing she's so far away. It's good for her to spend time with her dad in California. She needs that. The old Bri never would have admitted it, but it's true.

It's amazing how four years can change a person. Honestly, I know this sounds flippant, but in some ways, prison has been a bit like high school. There are cliques and rules, mean girls and meaner ones, and it feels like you want to scream at these people who seem to be running your life. But you can't. And, in this analogy, I'm in the last leg of my senior year, which was great in real life—until it wasn't. So, as I prepare to blow this joint, honestly, I'm a little scared. Okay, I'm freaking out. Because I can see a light at the end of this tunnel, and last time that happened, my whole world got body-slammed against an oak tree.

I know I've always been the tough one. At least that's what I've projected to the world around me. You want to know the truth, though? You're the toughest one of us all. While Melody skipped town and I got hooked on pain meds to deal with all my crap, you stayed. You were clean and sober, and you have been my steadfast friend through it all. So, thanks for that. I owe you.

B

CHAPTER TWO

LIZ

Liz Dawson blew out a breath and tried not to panic. Her younger sister Rose was only a couple of minutes late. Sixteen was too young to have a driver's license, in Liz's opinion. Too young to have a car. Why did their parents agree to let Rose have one, especially before deciding to leave the country?

The bell on the bakery's door chimed. The Bitery closed at six in the evening, but Liz hadn't locked up because she was waiting for her sister. The story of Liz's life, starting with when she was twelve years old and her parents had sat her down to tell her they were pregnant. Since that time, Liz had been waiting for Rose in some form or fashion.

"Hey, thought I saw you in here," Danette Rhodes said. Danette owned The Book Whore next door. She was pushing ninety years old, walked with a cane, and shook like a bobble-head doll when she spoke. "Saw you didn't park your bicycle out front today. Need a ride, Lizzie?"

Liz smiled as she weighed the risks of that offer. Danette had less business driving on the streets of Trove Isle than Rose did. "No, thank you. My sister is actually supposed to be driving us home today." *Supposed to* being the key words.

Danette frowned, which only made the deep lines of her face contort and twist like unruly rivers on a desperate search for their ocean. Liz understood that search. Her entire adult life she'd been twisting and curving on her path, looking for something. Her path seemed to be one big loop though, keeping her in the familiar. In safe territory. At least it had felt safe until her parents had dropped everything to spend the summer in Ecuador where Liz's maternal grandmother, Mami, lived.

Mami had what doctors called a transient ischemic attack. In layman's terms, a ministroke. That had necessitated her parents leaving the country three weeks ago to visit a place Liz had never known her parents to go. Liz's grandmother had come to the states in her twenties and she'd had Liz's mother here in Trove. Liz had grown up with her mom always wishing out loud to return to her mother's homeland, especially after Mami had moved back, but between family and running her own business, there'd never been time.

It wasn't exactly the perfect time now, either. Not with Rose still in school. But illness didn't make appointments. Inconvenient or not, Liz's parents had left Rose in Liz's care. Liz was an adult after all. And Rose could take care of herself—in theory.

Her mom had also left the bakery under Liz's care. It was a huge responsibility and a lot of pressure that Liz wasn't sure she could shoulder. Not that she had a choice in the matter. So here she was, babysitting a teenager and tending a bakery, when all she really wanted to do was disappear behind the lens of her Canon and spend her evenings editing her photographs.

"Is Rosie old enough to drive?" Danette asked.

"According to the law," Liz said in as cheerful a voice as she could muster. Liz, on the other hand, had her doubts about a sixteen-year-old hormone-ravaged teen girl operating a motor vehicle.

A horn beep-beeped beyond Danette.

Liz blinked the bright-red car into focus. Expelling a breath, because *yes*, she'd been slightly worried that Rose was upside down in a ditch somewhere, she glanced at her watch with a touch of annoyance. Fifteen minutes late. She guessed she should be grateful because, by teenager standards, that was practically early.

"Looks like your ride is here," Danette said, her head wobbling with each word. "I'll see you tomorrow, hon. Stop in The Book Whore if you have time. I'm having a sale." Danette liked to work in her store name as often as she could. For shock effect, Liz suspected.

"I will. Goodnight, Danette."

"Night, Lizzie."

The horn honked again. With a sigh that bordered on a growl, Liz collected her purse from below the counter and headed toward the door, her gaze moving to the latest black-and-white photograph that she'd taken of the south isle pier, framed and hanging on the bakery's wall for sale.

The walls were full of Liz's monochrome photographs, all for purchase. The money they brought in was good, but not enough to support Liz as a full-time photographer. That would require that Liz be able to take jobs working various functions and celebrations that took place outside of Seagull Street. And that would require that Liz have access to a reliable form of transportation.

A bicycle with an oversized front-hanging wire basket didn't count.

Liz locked up the shop, cut across the sidewalk, and dipped into the passenger seat of the sporty red car. After pulling her seatbelt across her body, she faced Rose. "Why isn't your seatbelt buckled?"

Rose's brown eyes narrowed slightly. While Rose had gotten their mother's dark brown skin, Liz's skin tone was lighter like their father's. It blushed too easily and far too often. Liz had also inherited her father's mousy brown hair and his nearsightedness. Thus, the rounded glasses she was wearing. "Seriously?" Rose muttered. "We're just going down the road. Your house is, like, three minutes away."

"Ten. And accidents happen." Liz pushed her glasses up on her nose. "Mom and Dad always say—"

"Mom and Dad are in Ecuador. And they left me in sister-jail with you." Rose jerked the steering wheel and swerved the car onto the street. And *no*, she didn't buckle up first. Liz wasn't even sure Rose had checked to make sure there wasn't oncoming traffic before she'd pulled out.

"Put your belt on." Liz stiffened the way she always did inside a vehicle in motion. "And slow down. The speed limit is forty-five."

For spite, Rose pressed the gas pedal a little heavier. The little car's motor roared louder and the speedometer climbed to forty-eight. Forty-nine.

Liz loved her younger sister. She really did, but their parents couldn't come home soon enough.

Liz turned to look at Rose in the driver's seat, noticing the glint of something shiny on Rose's eyebrow. "Is that . . . is that a piercing in your brow?"

Rose glanced over, one side of her mouth quirking upward.

"Eyes on the road!" Liz practically yelled. Once her sister was facing forward, she continued her lecture. "Who told you that you could get your eyebrow pierced?"

"No one," Rose said with a shrug. "I didn't ask." She appeared to press the gas pedal harder, effectively silencing Liz as Liz white-knuckled the door handle.

As the speedometer reached fifty, an oncoming car veered into their lane. Rose screamed, yanked the steering wheel right, and swerved onto the roadside. But not in time to clear the path of the other vehicle. It scraped along the entire driver's side of their mom's car, the sound screeching in Liz's ears.

Rose slammed the brakes and the car jerked to a halt, sending them both lurching forward. Liz's body jerked to a stop after a couple inches, secured by her seatbelt, and then slammed back against her seat. Rose's body, however, sprawled across the steering wheel.

The air whooshed out of Liz's lungs. She stopped breathing for a moment, clutching the side door so hard that her nails were pulling off the flesh at her fingertips. Memories of a night long ago crashed into her mind. Metal screeching and then an eerie silence except for the ringing in Liz's own ears. Were her ears ringing now or was this a flashback?

Rose peeled herself off the steering wheel, seemingly unfazed and unharmed. "The nerve of that jerk!" she screamed as she slammed her hands against the dash. "That was not my fault! You saw that car come into our lane, Lizzie! Not. My. Fault!"

Liz still didn't say a word. Maybe she was like one of those animals that died from sheer terror.

"Liz?" Rose poked the side of her arm. "They barely touched us. I mean, the mirror and the paint job are probably jacked, but . . . Liz? Are you okay?"

Liz finally exhaled. Inhaled. Exhaled. Okay, she was still alive. She hadn't died of fright.

She turned to look at her sister and blinked. This was why she didn't drive and rode her bike whenever and wherever possible. But Rose was a new driver and among her mom's many requests before leaving the country was that Liz supervise Rose when she was driving.

It was a poor decision on her parents' behalf. Liz had gotten her own license when she was seventeen, but she'd barely driven before the accident that made her hang up her keys forever.

"I didn't mean for that to happen. Are you about to have one of your freak-outs?" Rose asked.

Liz pulled a hand to her chest where her heart was hammering twice as fast as Rose had been speeding. One of her "freak-outs" as Rose had called it wouldn't help things right now.

"Do you need, like, a bag to breathe in or something?" Rose looked more alarmed by the second.

This made Liz smile just a touch. Rose was a brat, but there were times—not often—when she let on that she actually cared. "Don't worry. I'm not going to hyperventilate."

Rose gave her an unsure look. Then her gaze flicked to the road. "Oh, the driver is coming. I am going to have some major words with that woman."

Liz touched Rose's shoulder. "No. I'll talk to her." Liz was the adult after all. Technically, Rose was still a child. They had twelve years between them, but that might as well have been a universe.

Liz pushed the car door open and stepped out on wobbly legs. Her body was still shaking as she walked to the front of the car and approached the woman who'd driven them off the road.

"I'm sorry," the woman said as she walked toward Liz. "That was totally my fault."

"Damn straight it was your fault!" Rose called from the rolled down window.

The driver continued to ramble. "My bracelet got caught on the gear. I'm not even sure how that happened." She shook her head, her dark hair tossing around her shoulders.

Liz was speechless for a moment. Unable to believe her eyes, she blinked several times. When she had one of her panic attacks, her vision sometimes got distorted. For a moment, she thought she was staring at Alyssa Palmer. But that couldn't be right. Alyssa had red hair. And Alyssa was dead. Nine years ago this June.

Instead, Liz was staring at Alyssa's older sister Melody. Melody had rich brown hair. She was taller, thinner, and she'd been Liz's best friend from third grade until their senior year of high school. Melody might as well have been dead too. Liz hadn't seen or heard from her since that same June. One night. One swerve. One dead.

"Melody?" Liz's first inclination was to run over and throw her arms around her long-lost friend, but something kept her feet cemented to the road. She couldn't even muster a welcoming smile. Her heart and her brain were at war on how to react right now, and it seemed her brain was winning. "What are you doing here?"

Melody was wearing black Capri pants and a form-fitted cotton top. It was simple, but she wore it well. In some ways, she looked exactly like she had in high school. In other ways, Liz could see the imprint of the past decade in Mel's hazel eyes and slightly rounded posture. Her shoulders hung by her sides as if she was carrying a heavy backpack.

"I just found out about Jo," Melody explained. "I would have come sooner, but I didn't know."

Liz had heard Melody was living in Charlotte, about four hours northwest of Trove Isle. Liz had tried to reach out many times that first year after Melody had moved away. All of Liz's calls had gone to voicemail though. All her texts were unanswered. Melody didn't even have a Facebook or Instagram account that Liz could find her at. Melody's only online footprint was a website for Memory Lane Events, a Charlotte-based business that Melody appeared to co-own with another woman.

Guilt swirled around in Liz's chest. Maybe she should have tried to reach out to Melody after Jo's passing, but Melody's lack of contact over the years had made it obvious she'd forgotten this town and everyone in it.

"Apparently, I inherited a store," Melody said.

Liz had wondered who Jo would entrust her business to. "Jo left Hidden Treasures to you?"

"That's the one. I just met with Mr. Lyme to make it official."

A horn honked as it approached the small collision even though there was still a lane the driver could use to bypass the scene. Liz and Melody stepped further out of the way. A moment later, a deputy sheriff's cruiser pulled up and parked behind them.

Perfect. Today had promised to be a smooth, uneventful, maybe even boring day. The kind Liz liked best. But it had derailed with Rose's reckless driving and was ending with a bang, literally, an old friend, and an encounter with Deputy Matt Coffey.

Matt lived down the street from Liz. She'd known him her entire life. They'd kind of grown up together, although he was about five years older. He was already working as a deputy sheriff when she was a senior in high school. He'd worked her accident. Not this one. The first one that had also involved Melody. And Bri. And Alyssa.

Matt stepped out of his vehicle and headed toward them, looking at Liz first. "Everything okay?" His dark brown eyes hung on her too long, concern knitting his brows. "You were driving, Liz?"

Liz shook her head, which made her feel a little dizzy. Her ears were still ringing too. "Rose was driving."

"Not my fault!" Rose hollered out the window again.

"It was, um, my fault," Melody explained. "I was trying to change the radio and my bracelet caught on the gear. I'm not even sure how it happened," she told him, just like she'd done with Liz.

Liz thought Melody seemed a bit dazed and confused too. Perhaps she'd hit her head in the accident.

"Your bracelet?" Matt glanced down at her wrist, but Melody didn't show them the piece of jewelry that Liz assumed she was wearing under her sleeve.

Instead, Melody nibbled at her lower lip and looked at Liz. "I'm very sorry. I hope you're okay."

Physically, Liz was fine. Emotionally, that was a different story. How often did you see the ghost of your long-lost friend and that ghost's sister who was once your very best friend? "Rose and I aren't hurt."

"Good." Melody looked as unsure about what to do right now as Liz felt. There hadn't been this horrible fight between them. Melody had just left, cutting off all contact, as if her friends and family meant nothing. Maybe it would have been better if there had been a nasty blow-out. There'd been nothing though. Not even a goodbye.

Matt seemed to suddenly recognize Melody. "Mel? Is that you?"

Melody half grimaced, half smiled as she turned her attention back to him. "Guilty."

"When did you get back in town?"

"This afternoon." She glanced at Liz who quickly looked away. "I was hoping to make a quiet entrance."

Liz suspected Mel had wanted a quiet exit as well. There really was no hope in entering or exiting Trove Isle without someone noticing though. There was only one way into the small isle town and one way out—the bridge.

Matt looked around as if to make that very point. "No such luck. There are people around here who act like it's their job to know all the goings-on in Trove Isle. The welcome wagon should arrive at your place within the hour. You staying with your dad?"

"I tried to get a room at the Seagull Inn, but it was booked. So, I guess I'll be at my father's. Just for two weeks. I have to get back to Charlotte as soon as possible." Melody looked at Liz with something akin to apology in her eyes. Was she sorry for slamming into their car? Or sorry because she'd had no intention of even saying hello to Liz while she was here? Probably both. "I'll fix your car."

"It belongs to my parents." Liz shrugged as if the tiny bang up were no big deal. Her mom would probably flip out over the damage, but it served her right for leaving Liz here to watch over her sister.

Liz could feel Matt inspecting her, undoubtedly deciphering if she really was okay. "Want me to drive you home? I can come back and get the car for you."

Liz shook her head, making it spin again. "It'll still drive. It's just the paint." She knew that wasn't why he was asking though. Everyone in town was aware that she hadn't been comfortable in cars since the accident. Driving with her sister right after a fender bender might send her into a full-fledged panic attack—something else that most people knew about her. Liz was always one heartbeat and one breath away from letting her anxiety win. She'd always had anxiety, ever since she was a kid, but it had gotten so much worse since the accident. "It's just down the road. We'll be fine."

Matt nodded, uncertainty playing on his expression. Then he looked at Melody. "Welcome home, Mel."

"Oh, I'm not home," Melody said a little too quickly. "Just visiting."

"Right. Well, it's good to see you. I'll let you ladies work out the details of this little scrape-up." Matt looked at Liz again. Liz wanted to reiterate that she was fine, but she wasn't sure that was the truth. Instead, she offered a wobbly smile and waved, still keeping her eyes a notch above, below, beside, anywhere except his warm brown eyes which seemed to see right through her. They always had.

Matt was a good friend and possibly, in another life, he and Liz would have been more than that. She couldn't see dating a guy who reminded her of one of the worst days of her life though. It wasn't his fault; he was actually her hero that day.

Liz watched him walk to his cruiser. Then she looked at Melody. They stared at each other awkwardly for a moment.

"So, you still work at The Bitery with your mom?" Melody finally asked.

"Yep," Liz said of the bakery, which specialized in bite-sized treats. Thus, why it was called The Bitery. Liz had been working there since she was sixteen. Back then it was a part-time afterschool job. She'd never intended for it to become her career. "But it's just me and sometimes Rose at the moment. My parents are out of the country." Which Melody didn't need or deserve to know. She and Liz weren't even friends anymore. They were barely acquaintances.

"Great. I'll stop in sometime this week and we can work out the details of fixing your car," Melody offered.

Liz felt conflicted. She didn't want to see Melody again. Part of her thought her old friend should get in her car and drive right back over that bridge. Another part of her was glad that she and Melody had run into each other. Liz had missed her friend—even if she wasn't sure the friend she'd known in high school still existed. That friend would've left, yeah. Running away from hard things was classic Melody Palmer. She was the girl who made herself sick during an Algebra test in ninth grade because she didn't know the answers. She'd also run away the night before her mom's funeral because she didn't want to say goodbye. But she came back just in time. The friend Liz knew and loved always came back—no matter what. She didn't stay gone for nine years.

"Don't worry about the scratch. One of the bakery's customers works on cars. He's traded his services for our coffee in the past."

"Hey, that's not a bad arrangement," Melody said with a shaky smile.

They stared at each other for a long moment. Then Liz lowered her gaze and it caught on something shiny on Melody's wrist. For a moment, she thought it was the charm bracelet. *Their* charm bracelet. But it couldn't be. Another thing about anxiety was that it played tricks on the mind. Not exactly hallucinations, but when she was anxious, Liz thought she saw things that weren't there. People. Objects. Oncoming cars when she sat in the passenger seat.

"Okay, well I'll see you around," she said, still flustered from the wreck, Melody's return, and Matt Coffey. She didn't wait for Melody to say goodbye. Instead, she turned and walked back to her car where Rose was leaning out the window, watching her. Once Liz was seated in the passenger seat, she blew out an extended breath. "Let's go."

Rose was quiet for a moment, as if weighing what to do.

"Please," Liz added, actually hoping her sister would learn from today. Accidents happened, even in a short ten-minute drive.

Without a word, Rose pulled on her seatbelt, put the car in motion, and drove the exact speed limit for the entire way home, which was progress. But she didn't slow down as she whipped their mom's sporty red car into the driveway of Liz's tiny home.

Liz had purchased this place with the money she'd had in savings for college. After the accident, she'd been too much of a mess to go. So she'd stayed in Trove Isle, worked at her mom's bakery, and she'd found this modestly sized brick house that was within walking distance of her job, the market, and church. Her father had helped her renovate the place, which had been labeled a fixer-upper, and her mom had painted the shutters and front door a pale shade of blue.

Over the years, Liz had planted azalea bushes out front, which added a cheery splash of vibrant color that she loved to take pictures of, although she always developed them in black and white for a reason she couldn't explain. She guessed black and white was how she viewed the world around her now. Right or wrong. Whole or broken. She was the latter.

Liz focused on her house and the deep-pink color of the azaleas for a long moment as she took deeper breaths and began to relax.

"You're sure you're not going to have one of those episodes of yours?" Rose finally asked.

"Panic attacks," Liz corrected, uncurling her fingers from the door's handle. "No. I think I'm okay."

"Good." Without any more hesitation, Rose pushed the driver's door open, got out, and headed toward the porch, leaving Liz sitting in the passenger seat, her chest lifting a little too high and too rapidly with each breath. Liz guessed that Rose was distancing herself in case Liz brought the lack of seatbelt or the speeding back up. Or the brow piercing. Liz wasn't in the mood for arguing right now though.

After several long minutes, Liz stepped out of the car and followed suit. "I'll start dinner," she called as she headed through the front door. Rose was nowhere in sight, which wasn't unusual. Since Rose had come to stay here, she'd mostly kept to Liz's guestroom when she wasn't out with friends.

Liz had kind of hoped she and Rose would have time to grow closer during their parents' absence. Since Liz was a good bit older, it'd been a long time since they'd actually lived in the same house. Becoming friends with her sister was a fantasy though. They were too different. They were practically strangers who shared the same parents, only together when they were forced to be during the holidays. Any of the other times that Liz went to her parents' home to say hello, Rose made her presence scarce.

Liz walked into the kitchen, turned on the stove light, and removed the ground beef she'd put in the fridge to thaw this morning. A yawn stretched her face. Since her mom had been gone, Liz had been getting up at four o'clock most mornings to begin baking for the morning rush at The Bitery. The rush didn't stop after ten. There was cleanup and then the lunch time wave of customers. After that came the afternoon snackers. Then the evening bingers.

Liz's mom had other employees, of course, including Danette's sister, Sissy, who often worked on the weekends. It was Liz's mom who kept The Bitery afloat though, and without her, Liz felt like she was sinking.

"I'm going to the mall to meet Blake and Devin," Rose announced, coming back into the kitchen. She'd changed from her ripped jeans to a short jean skirt and a yellow sleeveless top cropped at her midriff.

"Just you and two boys?" Liz was responsible for Rose's welfare right now. Would her parents allow Rose to leave looking like that? With not one, but two boys.

Rose lifted her pierced brow. How had she managed to get a piercing without adult permission? Now Liz had a visual reminder every time she looked at Rose that she was a miserable babysitter.

"They're girls, if you must know," Rose huffed.

Liz frowned. "But I'm making dinner."

"I'm not hungry." Rose's gaze flicked around the kitchen, seeming to notice Liz's efforts. Liz could almost see the guilt creeping in on Rose's expression as her gaze skittered around the room and her smile faltered. She blew out a frustrated breath. "I'll eat it for breakfast, okay?"

Liz hesitated. She didn't want to say no, but Rose was never here. The door was revolving for her. Had she even gotten a full meal since she'd come to live with Liz temporarily? "Maybe you should stay in tonight. After what just happened."

Rose's lips puckered into a pout as she folded her arms over her chest. "You're acting like we almost died. I thought you said you were fine."

"I am fine." Liz forced a smile as proof. She was being ridiculous. She could feel it, but it was hard to help. "Okay. Just make sure you wear your seatbelt. And be home by eight o'clock. It's a school night."

"Nine," Rose countered. It wasn't a question; it was a demand.

They stared at each other in a semi standoff of wills.

"Fine. Nine." In a battle of wills, Liz was usually the loser, even with a sixteen-year-old. *Especially* with a teenager.

"Sister-jail is the worst," Rose muttered as she headed out, slamming the front door behind her.

Liz couldn't agree more. She closed her eyes and took another cleansing breath like Dr. Mayer, her therapist, used to suggest. She hadn't seen Dr. Mayer in a while. Her panic attacks had become less frequent and she had every stress-relieving and calming technique there was in her arsenal.

Her photography was perhaps the best therapy. Since her parents had left the country, there had been less time for that and more time for stress and worry. Caring for Rose for six weeks combined with Melody being in town might just be Liz's unraveling. Maybe she should squeeze in a session with Dr. Mayer sometime soon.

Liz walked over to the dining room table and plopped down, not caring about dinner anymore. She'd only wanted to make it for Rose's sake. She'd had some weird fantasy of the two of them actually eating a meal together and maybe even talking. Yeah, that wasn't going to happen anytime soon.

On a sigh, she reached for her laptop, centering it on the table in front of her. She typically ended most days by e-messaging Bri through the prison's ConnectNetwork system before messing around in Photoshop for an hour or two. Emails were a poor substitution for seeing her friend in person though. Maybe Liz would ride up to the women's prison in the next couple weeks. However, that would require a bus trip or asking Rose to do the honors of driving her over the bridge and out of town. And neither of those options was all that appealing.

Liz positioned her fingers over the home keys and began to type.

To: Bri Johnson
From: Liz Dawson

Subject: Liz Dawson's Very Bad, No Good Day

Bri,

Today was miserable for so many reasons. Long story short, there was a car accident. Don't worry, it was just a fender bender. Rose was driving under my inadequate supervisory capabilities. Really, what were my parents thinking? I saw my life flash before my eyes, which I know is ridiculous because it was literally just a scratch on the side door. I appreciate that you think I'm the strong one, but I'll remind you that I never drove again after our accident. I ride my bike everywhere I go and consequently, I'm working a job that I don't love. Oh, and I have panic attacks more frequently than I do orgasms. Do you still think I'm the strong one?

Anyway, these awful things are not the worst of my very bad, no-good day. The wreck wasn't Rose's fault. It was the other driver's, who you wouldn't believe it turned out to be. Want to guess? You'll never guess. I think I'd like to see your face when I tell you though. I'll come visit soon.

xx,

Liz

CHAPTER THREE

MELODY

Melody's heart was still pounding. Of all the people to wreck her car with, she'd run into the one person in town she was hoping not to see during her time here. Jo used to say that was how things worked.

"If you're trying to avoid someone, best bet they'll be the first person you see today."

Jo had been right the last time she'd said those words to Melody. Melody had been avoiding a boy at that time. She'd broken up with him, like she always did soon after beginning a relationship. Melody never stayed with anyone for very long. Some things never changed. That same day, after Jo had said those words, Melody had run into the boy at least three times.

As she drove, Melody tried and failed to remember the boy's name. At least she'd been successful in wiping some of her memories away.

She turned her car onto the street where she grew up and headed toward the end, pulling into her father's driveway. She didn't blink or breathe for a moment as she stared out her windshield at the one-story brick ranch-style house where she'd grown up. She hadn't seen her dad in nine years, although they'd spoken infrequently on the phone.

A dozen raw emotions whirred inside Melody's belly as she retrieved her luggage from the trunk and headed up the porch steps. She rang the doorbell before seeing the folded note clinging to the glass-paneled window, her name neatly printed on the front. She pulled it out from where it was wedged between the panes and carefully unfolded the paper.

> *Melody,*
> *I'm at work until six. The door is unlocked. Feel free*
> *to go inside and settle into your old room.*
> *Dad*

A frown tugged at the corners of her mouth. She'd called her father after hearing about Jo's passing, and he'd invited her to stay here. She would have expected him to meet her at the door. But no. After all this time apart, he'd chosen work instead. She guessed she should be happy she didn't have to greet him with a forced smile and polite hello. The reunion promised to be awkward at best. Having a little time to collect herself before facing her father was probably for the best.

Swallowing past the growing lump in her throat, Melody twisted the doorknob and then flipped a light switch to her left. Before stepping inside, she inspected the front room. It was exactly the same as it had been when she'd left. Neat, orderly, and as sterile as a hospital.

She crossed the threshold and took her time as she wandered through the living area. It smelled like lemon, a sign that Mrs. Chavis was still cleaning this place as she'd been doing since Melody's mom had died. Melody had always liked the sweet-natured housekeeper, probably because she'd left candies on her and Alyssa's pillows on the days she'd come to clean.

Melody headed down a dark hallway toward her old bedroom. A few posters were pinned to the pale-pink walls, unchanged since Melody's middle school days. The twin-sized bed on the left side of the room still had a quilt featuring hearts and flowers. And there on the pillow was a caramel-flavored hard candy from Mrs. Chavis.

Melody's gaze swept to the bed on the right side with polka dots in pink and purple. There was no candy on that pillow because Alyssa wouldn't be coming home again.

Melody sucked in one breath and then another, suddenly finding it hard to pull air into her lungs. How was she going to stay in this room with her sister's memory? With *all* the memories here. The Seagull Inn would have been a more neutral place to stay. But here? Melody blew out a long breath. *This is just for two weeks.* At least that was what she'd told her business partner, Julie. Maybe Melody wouldn't even need that long though. She'd already signed the paperwork for the store. She just needed to put it on the market and then go to Jo's celebration of life on Friday. Perhaps she'd be crossing that bridge out of Trove by Saturday.

Melody set her bags on the bed and reached for the caramel candy on the pillow. She peeled off its wrapper and popped it into her mouth, the taste reminiscent of her childhood. Then she let her gaze fall to the charm bracelet she was still wearing. She was half surprised that she hadn't taken it off yet. She didn't like reminders of her past, and this was a pretty big one. In some way, it made her feel close to Alyssa though.

Melody lay back in bed, entertaining random memories from this room. Alyssa on the neighboring bed chattering endlessly about the boy next door, Christopher West, whom she'd had an enormous crush on. He was a skinny boy with large, dark-rimmed glasses and deep-set blue eyes. Melody had never understood what Alyssa saw in him, but Alyssa would lie on her stomach, propped on her elbows, with a pen and her diary—the one she kept wedged between the box spring and her mattress—scrawling her name with his and surrounding their names with little hearts and flowers.

In Melody's opinion, Christopher really wasn't that much of a catch and yet, he'd never returned any romantic feelings toward Alyssa. He'd even broken Alyssa's heart when she'd asked him to go with her to junior prom. Alyssa had been devastated for weeks.

Alyssa had deserved a chance at first love. She'd deserved a chance at life. So much had been taken from her, and some part of Melody would always blame herself—in addition to the boy next door who'd broken Alyssa's heart.

At some point in her memories, Melody drifted off to sleep. She was awakened by the sound of the front door opening and closing.

Her father was home. She didn't breathe for a moment. Maybe she should step out and say hello. Then again, he hadn't been home to welcome his prodigal daughter when she'd arrived. Instead he'd left a note. In turn, she was going to stay inside the confines of her childhood bedroom and go back to sleep.

Melody waited to leave her room the next morning until she heard the front door close. Then she showered, dressed, and headed outside to her car. She was hoping her second impression of Hidden Treasures Thrift Store would be better. When she arrived, however, she decided that it was maybe worse.

She'd thought she was being overly dramatic in her reaction yesterday. She'd had high hopes in coming to the store, and they'd taken a sharp dive once she'd realized what she'd actually been gifted.

Melody leaned against the glass case full of costume jewelry and tried not to cry. She needed air. A coffee would be nice too. After that, she'd return and figure out her next steps. Or get into her reliable Honda Accord and pretend like none of the last forty-eight hours had ever happened.

Melody collected her purse and walked quickly to the store's front entrance. She stepped outside and locked up behind herself, using the set of keys that Mr. Lyme had jingled proudly in front of her yesterday. A quick glance down the street told her that Liz's family bakery was the only viable option for coffee.

In contrast to Melody's thrift store, The Bitery was inviting. The awning above the door was bright pink with white polka dots and the store name was written in teal script. From the outside looking in, it was quaint and cheery.

Melody didn't want to avoid Liz the entire time she was in Trove Isle. They'd probably never be best friends again, but maybe Liz could tolerate Melody's presence. She certainly hadn't looked happy to see her yesterday.

Without giving herself time to second-guess, Melody headed up the sidewalk, distracting herself by taking in the detail of the downtown area. It was the picture of a small coastal community without the tourist mobs that overran nearby towns. Seagull Street was scenic with black cherry trees and bald cypress lining the two-lane street. There were as many bikes in the sidewalk racks as there were cars. And just like its name, seagulls squawked overhead, on their way to the ocean and pier two miles away.

Melody stopped in front of The Bitery, hesitating before pushing through the entrance door. *You can do this, Melody. One foot in front of the other.* A little bell chimed overhead as she stepped inside.

"Be with you in a minute!" a voice called from the back.

"No rush!" Melody headed to the glass display case full of delicious-looking treats. The only thing that didn't appear to be small portioned were the cinnamon twists, which had always been Liz's specialty. She used to make them during the sleepovers they'd had together while growing up. Melody, Liz, and Bri. That's how it had started.

Alyssa had somehow inserted herself into the mix, the way that younger siblings tended to do. Melody used to object to Alyssa manipulating her way into their slumber parties, but then Melody had started inviting her. Alyssa brought an element of fun to the group. She could make them laugh so hard that orange soda came out of their noses. In truth, Alyssa became Melody's best of the best friends.

"Just one more second," the voice in the back room called again.

"Take your time!" Melody looked around the shop, finding it mostly the same as she remembered from the days when she and her friends would gather here after school. One thing that was different were the framed photographs that decorated the walls. They were all black-and-white snapshots of places Melody recognized around Trove Isle. The bridge that crossed over the Atlantic Intracoastal Waterway. Sunrise Park. The old drive-in theater on Cameron Street two streets from the oceanfront. Melody and her friends, including Alyssa, would catch a movie and then get ice cream cones and walk the beach until curfew.

"Can I help you?" Liz stepped out of the back kitchen and froze when she saw Melody. She wore an apron that matched the awning outside, pink with polka dots and teal writing across the chest that read *Bite Me.* "Oh. Hi."

Melody waved, feeling slightly awkward. "It's just me."

"What are you doing here?" Liz's tone wasn't mean or even rude. It was more surprised than anything.

"I was hoping to get a coffee. And maybe something to eat."

Liz seemed to hesitate for a moment before nodding. "Yeah, of course. What would you like?"

"A cinnamon twist." Melody hadn't had breakfast yet and she needed more than one or two bite-sized foods.

"Sure." Liz rang her up for the order, her gaze flitting up to look at Melody behind her glasses, but never sticking. She wasn't smiling either. When they were growing up, Liz always had a smile on her face. There were different versions of the smile though, that only those closest to her understood. The happy smile. The anxious smile. The heartbroken smile. The smile of despair. Liz smiled to make everyone around her feel better. But Melody was the only one here right now though, and apparently Liz wasn't concerned with how Melody felt.

Liz tapped the register and read out the price in a monotone voice.

Reaching into the front pocket of her purse, Melody pulled out a ten-dollar bill and slid it across the counter. A second later, Liz handed back four single-dollar bills.

"Take a seat and I'll bring your breakfast to you in just a moment," Liz said curtly. Liz had always been the sweetest of their little group of friends. If she didn't like someone, they must have been a horrible human being. So, it was official. Melody was decidedly horrible.

Melody turned and looked around. A few tables were occupied by folks she recognized. Hopefully they wouldn't notice her. She wasn't in the mood for socializing this morning. Keeping her head down, she walked toward the front of the store and slid into a corner seat. Then she watched as Liz retrieved several items from the display cases for incoming customers.

Melody had hoped that she and Liz could take a moment to talk, but now she realized that was a foolish fantasy. She couldn't just reappear after nine years and expect to be welcomed with open arms. Melody had bailed. In the face of so much pain, she'd decided to turn her back on everyone and everything in Trove Isle. Even her best friends.

A few minutes later, Liz headed over to where Melody was

sitting. She slid a plate of treats onto the center of the table along with a to-go cup of coffee.

"I hope you haven't changed the way you like your coffee." Liz pulled out the seat across from Melody and sat down, propping her elbows on the table and using her hands to cradle her chin.

Melody was surprised. She was starting to think it would be lucky if Liz didn't pour salt in her drink instead of sugar. Melody pulled the cup to her and took a sip, practically sighing because it was freshly roasted and so smooth. Much better than the gas station variety she usually grabbed on the go. "You remembered that I like hazelnut?"

"Of course I remember. I'm not the one who left and seemingly forgot everything and everyone in her life." Liz's gaze was pointed.

Melody put her coffee down, her hand trembling slightly.

Liz shook her head and placed her hands flat on the table. "I'm sorry. I shouldn't have said that."

"Yes, you should have. I deserved it." Melody looked directly at Liz and offered a give-it-to-me gesture. "Keep going. Tell me everything you want to say. I'll sit right here and take it. I won't even say a word."

Liz frowned. "Why? So you can feel better, and I can still feel abandoned by my best friend? It wouldn't be any fun if you didn't fight back anyway."

"I'm not here to fight." When Liz didn't say anything, Melody switched topics. "I can't believe Jo didn't have a funeral."

Liz shook her head stiffly. Everything about her was rigid and guarded. "She wanted a celebration instead. Mr. Lyme has been waiting for you to come home. Jo's wishes. Honestly, I thought we were going to be waiting forever."

"Right." Melody looked away for a moment. "Jo never did like funerals." Jo had always said yes to a good party, but she'd opted out on memorial services, saying they weren't how she wanted to remember that person. The only funerals Melody could remember her great-aunt ever attending were for Melody's mother and Alyssa. She hadn't worn traditional black though. Instead, she'd put on her favorite lime-green suit with her pink broach and she'd wrapped a soft silk scarf around her neck. It was her attire for all special occasions.

Melody brought her cup to her lips and took another sip. "I don't deserve to have her store. I haven't even seen her in years."

"You're a busy woman," Liz said. "A successful event planner."

Melody furrowed her brow. "Hmm?" she asked, partly confused by the concept of success. By whose definition did her career define anything remotely successful?

"Your dad told me."

"He did?" Melody didn't hide the shock in her voice.

"That's how he explains you not coming home during the holidays. You have other people's events to run," Liz said, raising a skeptical brow over the rim of her glasses.

Melody bit into the cinnamon twist instead of responding. She didn't want to lie, but she wanted to admit the truth even less. She barely did enough jobs each month to pay the bills. If she was lucky, she got enough business to afford a nice haircut some months. Other months, she stuck to cereal box dinners.

Liz lowered her gaze to Melody's wrist where the charm bracelet had slipped out from under her sleeve. "What's that?"

Melody practically choked on her bite of cinnamon twist. Then she pushed her arm forward for Liz to get a better look. "I found this in the glass case of Jo's thrift store." Melody pulled the bracelet off and slid it over.

Liz's eyes were wide as she moved the piece of jewelry across her fingers the way Melody had done yesterday, no doubt looking at the random charms that had nothing to do with them. Then Melody heard the sharp intake of breath when Liz found the heart-shaped friends forever charm. The one that was bent at the top corner just like theirs. Liz looked up. "Where did Jo get this?"

Melody shrugged. "I have no idea. That's the same brace-let though."

"Yes, it is," Liz agreed, looking at it again. Melody saw the small tremor of Liz's hands as she held onto it. Melody imagined all the memories barreling back, the same way they had for her yesterday. Liz's eyes grew shiny, and then she tried to hand the bracelet back.

Melody tucked her hands below the table. "No. You wear it for a while. We were supposed to share it after all. Wasn't that Alyssa's rule?"

Liz frowned. "How can we share something when we never see each other anymore?"

Melody swallowed past the guilt. "Well, I'm here through next week. The thrift store is right down the street from the bakery. We can pass it back and forth . . . Or you can just keep it." Melody didn't really want to get rid of the bracelet, but Liz deserved it more than she did. "Go ahead. Put it on."

Liz hesitated. Then she shook her head and slid the piece of jewelry across the table anyway.

The bell chimed above the bakery's door again and an-other customer walked toward the front counter.

Liz looked at Melody. "I've got to get back up there. You're not the only busy one." She scooted back from the table. "It's nice to see you, Melody. Really. Will you be at Jo's Celebration of Life?"

Ouch. The fact that Liz even had to ask that question spoke volumes.

"Yeah. Of course. Friday night at Sunrise Park. On the water." Melody assumed, knowing Jo, she'd arranged for some kind of raft to be pushed off from the waterway's shore, carrying pictures or mementos from her life. Jo was sentimental to her core.

"Good. See you Friday." With a small wave, Liz stood and hurried back behind the counter. The smile she gave the waiting customer was much fuller. More real. Less guarded.

Melody reached for the bracelet and slipped it back over her wrist. Then she sat there for a moment before collecting and discarding her trash. She waved as she exited the bakery and returned to Hidden Treasures, wondering what in the world she was going to do with this place. She headed toward the register that sat above the glass case where she'd found the charm bracelet. That was maybe the most valuable thing the store had to offer, and Melody shouldn't even have that after the way she'd left her friends. They'd promised to always be there for one another, and she'd bailed at the first sign of pain.

It was her sister who had died though. Melody was the one who'd lost the most. Yes, Liz had suffered with anxiety. So much so that she'd never gone to college like she'd planned to. And Bri had struggled with pain following the accident. She'd gotten addicted to pain meds and had spiraled into self-destruction, leading her down a path that had ultimately led her to a low-security women's prison.

And yet . . . Melody had lost her very own sister. The one she was supposed to look out for. Alyssa was younger and her father was counting on Melody. After the accident, her father could barely look Melody in the eyes, even though she hadn't even been the one behind the wheel. That was Liz—not that it was Liz's fault.

It was just an accident. There was no one to blame. Unless you asked Melody's father. Then the accident fell squarely on Melody's shoulders.

To: Bri Johnson
From: Liz Dawson

Subject: Okay, I'll tell you

Bri,

Me again. I wanted to wait until I could tell you in person, but I might combust and you don't like surprises anyway. Here goes: Melody is back. I wish I could see your face. She's the one I had that fender bender with. How's that for coincidence? Jo would have said there are no coincidences. That everything that happened was orchestrated by something bigger than us.

Anyway, Melody is just here because she inherited Jo's thrift store on Seagull Street. Not because she wants to catch up or hang out. When I saw her, it was all I could do not to run up and hug her, but then I remembered that Melody is a traitor. She left us.

In the next moment, I felt awful for having these thoughts, knowing that Melody lost more than we did. She lost a sister. Maybe that should give her a pass on forgetting about her friends all these years. I don't know. It's all so twisted and complicated, I'm not sure how to feel.

So, imagine me standing there, face to face with our long-lost friend, wanting to hug her, and hating the fact that I did. What would you have done? You get in a wreck, you step out, and come face to face with your former BFF who turned her back on you when you needed her most. What do you do?

xx,

Liz

CHAPTER FOUR

LIZ

It's not a heart attack.

The first time Liz had a panic attack, that's what she'd thought was happening. And this wasn't even a full-blown one right now. She just had sharp pains in her chest, right above her heart. Angina was the medical term. She wasn't getting a good supply of blood to her heart because she was in fight-or-flight mode—for no good reason.

She sat on the wooden stool in the kitchen of her mom's bakery and closed her eyes, sucking in a cleansing breath that was thick with the swirling aroma of cinnamon, melted sugar, caramel, chocolate, and butter. She still loved her long-lost friend, but so many memories had come rushing back at the sight of her yesterday and again this morning. Too many memories. And then there was the charm bracelet which had appeared out of nowhere, almost like a ghost.

Everything was suddenly fast and loud. Liz needed to shut it out for just a moment. She focused on the steady, mind-numbing hum of the vent like Dr. Mayer had once taught her. She breathed as she listened to the flow of the air conditioning.

She used to pray for amnesia, thinking it would fix everything that was wrong in her life. It would be amazing to wake up one day, to open her eyes and not have that wave of reality come bearing down on her. It started with a heaviness on her chest. And then, even though it'd been nine years, she remembered that Alyssa was dead. Her friends were gone. And she was left here on her own, with her mountain of fears.

Liz blew out another breath and then opened her eyes as the oven's timer went off. She stepped over to check on her baked goods. Then she turned as the bell on the bakery's front entrance dinged, announcing yet another customer.

Without thinking, Liz put on a smile that was far from sincere and stepped into the front area of her bakery. She looked up at her customer and her breath froze for just a moment.

"Hey there," Matt said with an easy smile like he did every day.

She loved seeing Matt. She did. There was also this little part of her, though, that wished he could go somewhere else for his breakfast. That's because the little flutter he caused in her heart was in direct contradiction to the stutter in her brain whenever she saw him. The past collided with the present and, for a moment, she was that terrified girl again, staring up into his eyes and wondering if she was having a nightmare.

The problem with small towns though—or at least Trove Isle—was that there was only one bakery. This one. "Um, hi, Matt. You need a muffin bite?" she asked. He came in every day and always got the same thing.

"Please," he said. "And an extra strong coffee, if you don't mind."

"Long day already?" She glanced at the clock as she busied herself preparing his beverage. It wasn't even noon yet.

"I've had a few calls for minor things. No big deal."

"Keeping the town safe is a huge deal," she said. And that's another thing that made her feel so conflicted. He'd kept her safe. He was the one who'd pulled her from the vehicle all those years ago. She should be grateful to him. There should be a welcome mat with his name at the entrance.

A slow grin formed on his mouth. "Trove Isle isn't exactly running over with crime, Liz. The most action I've gotten on the job lately was breaking up a Bunco fight at Pearl Lauderdale's house."

Liz laughed, her heart winning the good fight against her mind, which didn't like any stressors or reminders of the accident. Her mind looked for calm. But Matt made her laugh, and that had its advantages. "Sounds pretty dangerous to me. Pearl Lauderdale can be feisty when she wants to be."

"Don't I know it? I barely escaped that house with my life."

Liz pressed the lid on the to-go cup and then slid his coffee across the counter. "Here you go. No charge. Just keep on protecting the citizens of Trove Isle."

"You sure?" he asked.

"My treat."

"Thanks." His dark brows lowered and formed two lines between his brown eyes. "I was worried about you after the run-in with Melody yesterday. You sure you were okay?"

Liz met his gaze. She always had this feeling that he could see right through her. "Yeah. I mean, it was a shock to see Melody, of course, but I'm glad she came back. I just wish she would have gotten here before Jo . . ." Liz trailed off.

Matt frowned. "Jo's illness was quick. Melody might not have even gotten the word."

"No, I don't think she did." Liz shook her head. "Anyway, back to your original question. Yes, I'm fine."

"Well, I was talking about the accident. You were pale and I was halfway tempted to follow you back to your house and check on you again." He held up his hands. "But you said you were okay, and I didn't want to be one of those guys."

Liz tilted her head to one side, watching him. "One of which guys?" she asked, feeling the corner of her mouth turn up.

"You know. The ones who women get irritated with just for being alive."

Liz laughed, a bigger, harder laugh.

Matt smiled as he watched her. Then he reached for his drink and brought it to his lips. "Your coffee is just as good as your mom's. I'm glad you're okay. And that Melody made her way back to Trove Isle for a visit. Thanks again for the coffee, Liz." Turning, he headed toward the door.

She watched him go, her chest light and airy. There was nothing like a good laugh. Or a run-in with a handsome man who engaged her in flirty banter. Her cell phone pinged from below the counter. Lowering her gaze, she picked it up and groaned at the text from her sister, the light and airy feeling dissipating immediately.

Rose: I'm sick. I need your permission to check out of school.

Sick? Rose had looked fine last night when she'd come in from the mall. "Fine" meaning she had a tight scowl and went straight to the guest bedroom.

Liz tapped her fingers along the screen.

Liz: I'll call the school nurse and see what she thinks.

If Rose was throwing up or had a fever, then she could go home. If not, she needed to stay and learn. That's what Liz's parents would do if they were here. Right?

A quick reply pinged from Liz's iPhone.

Rose: Don't bother. You are the worst.

It was a quarter after six when Liz finally left the bakery that evening. Rose was supposed to help after school, but unsurprisingly, she was a no-show. Liz was getting used to Rose's flakiness when it came to helping out at their mom's business. Were all sixteen-year-olds this way? Liz didn't remember shirking her duties at the bakery back then when it'd just been a part-time gig to fund going out with her friends.

Liz flipped the sign on the door to CLOSED and stepped onto the sidewalk of Seagull Street. Her arms were tired from reaching inside the glass case and the oven. Her legs were tired from standing and walking to and from the kitchen. Even her face was tired from the constant smile she offered customers. Even so, she couldn't wait to take a few pictures while there was still a little bit of daylight left.

Looping her camera around her neck, she headed over to the community bike rack. After unlocking her vintage Schwinn from the metal bars, she swung her leg over the crossbar, straddling it while she shifted back and forth to gain her balance. As she did, she appreciated the cool salty air on her bare arms. It was the peak of spring. The surrounding trees and flowers were blooming with bright purples and deep pinks. Crimson reds and flashy oranges.

Liz pushed her right foot forward on the pedal and the bike propelled forward as she navigated to the far edge of the street, moving with traffic. She never felt scared on her bike, even with cars whizzing by. The fear came from being inside one of those cars, specifically behind the steering wheel.

She pedaled faster, racing against the slow-setting sun. The evening's destination was the town fountain. She could get there, spend fifteen or twenty minutes taking pictures, and then head home to upload them to her computer while eating a microwave dinner. That was the plan at least.

As she rode, she waved at several familiar faces that she passed. There was no time to stop and chat. And even if there had been, she was all talked out. That was the hazard of working a full day at one of the town's favorite hangouts.

Up ahead, Liz spotted the fountain and her heart lifted. She was eager to feel the familiar click of the camera's shutter button beneath her index finger. Once she reached the fountain, she got off her bike and walked it to a safe spot. She used her foot to push the kickstand into place. Then she excitedly turned to look around her. She'd photographed the spray from the fountain a dozen times already. The cement wall that encircled the fountain too. She'd also snapped photographs of the flowers and the trees. And the memorial plaque on the nearby bench in Alyssa's honor.

The plaque had been paid for by Liz's family. Melody's father had shut himself off after the accident and Melody had left town. Bri's parents were never too involved in her life to begin with. They never had been from the moment Bri arrived in Trove Isle during third grade. It was Liz's parents who carted Bri off to afterschool activities. Bri had become an honorary member of the Dawson family. Even though Bri's real family was physically available and usually on a couch in their living room when Bri arrived home. Even when Bri had been injured after the accident and had gotten addicted to alcohol and prescription pain medication, her family had seemed unconcerned as her life had spiraled downward for years. It was Liz's family who'd staged interventions. Who'd offered to pay for rehab and even sent her once.

Bri's grandmother was the only one who supported Bri. She took care of Bri's daughter Ally, sharing custody with Ally's father in California. Liz's family went to visit Bri, month by month, year by year, for four years now. It went to prove that blood didn't make a family. You got to choose who you were loyal to. Who your family was. And in Melody's case, she'd chosen who it wasn't anymore.

Liz stepped in front of the bench memorial and lifted her camera to peer through the viewfinder. She'd taken this exact shot many times before, but it looked different today. Maybe it was the exact location of the sun in the sky, but the metal plaque seemed to shine. The shutter clicked beneath her finger as she pressed down.

Click, click, click.

She stepped back and forth to photograph from different angles, fascinated by how bright the silver plate looked through her lens this evening.

Click. Click. Click.

"Liz?"

Liz lowered her camera and spun around to face Missy Lyons, an old classmate of hers. Missy was a teacher at the elementary school these days and a mom of three. The kind of mom who was perfectly put together with matching everything including her nails.

"Oh, it is you," Missy said with an energetic smile.

Liz gave a small nod. "Hi, Missy."

"I thought I spotted your bike over there." Missy gestured behind her. "Dave took the girls on a daddy-daughter date this evening so I have some rare free time. I'm just out for a walk," she explained as if she needed an excuse to be out by herself on this beautiful evening.

Liz always felt a little awkward when she ran into classmates who were married with kids. Maybe she was imagining it, but it felt like her former classmates looked at her like she had three heads. Liz could practically hear their thoughts wondering why she lived alone and had no life to speak of. "I'm just out taking pictures."

Missy looked around with an appreciative nod. "This place is perfect for that, isn't it?" She faced Liz again. "Hey, do you photograph small events by chance? My parents are having a vow renewal ceremony and their photographer suddenly backed out."

Liz's heart leapt in her chest. "Oh?"

Missy grimaced. "I don't know what price they had negotiated for. My parents can be quite the hagglers, I'm embarrassed to say."

"Well, I'm not exactly a professional photographer." Liz was several steps above an amateur though. She'd started taking pictures during a journalism class in high school. She'd fallen in love with the pastime and became self-taught on all the ins and outs of lighting and photography editing. The only reason she didn't consider herself a pro was because she didn't hire herself out.

"Don't sell yourself short. I've seen your work hanging in The Bitery. It's really good," Missy said.

"Thank you. Where is the event?" Liz didn't drive, and Rose wasn't exactly reliable for giving Liz a lift. But maybe if the event was within bicycling distance . . .

"Highland Forest," Missy said.

Liz's heart sunk. That was half an hour's drive away. And a cab ride would eat up any profits she might make on the job. But maybe it'd be worth it for the exposure. Then again, Liz would have to get someone to run the bakery in her absence. Those were all inconvenient pieces to an ill-fitting puzzle.

"How about I give your business card to my mom, and she can call you to see if it'll work for you to be their photographer?" Missy asked.

"My card?" Liz repeated, feeling completely unprepared.

Missy's smile faltered. "You don't have business cards?"

Liz wondered why she'd never thought of getting some made. "I have cards for The Bitery. Hold on." Liz dug into her bag and pulled out the business cards for The Bitery. She grabbed a pen and wrote her cell phone number and email address on the back. "You can contact me here."

"Perfect." Missy slid the card into the front pocket of her purse. "I'll give it to my mom when I see her tomorrow. It's all about connections, right?"

Liz nodded. Connections, transportation, time, and apparently, business cards.

"Well, it was good to see you," Missy said, her warm smile returning to her lips. "We'll be in touch."

Liz waved and watched Missy continue on her walk. She felt equal parts invigorated and deflated after that interaction. Just like she had with her earlier conversation with Melody. It'd been brief, but Liz had replayed the moments in her head for the rest of the day. Melody had found the lost charm bracelet. That was a surprise. And she'd tried to pass it to Liz.

Liz felt so rude for turning that chance down. Melody couldn't just waltz back into town like she'd never turned her back on them though, and try to pass their charm bracelet around like the silly teenaged girls they'd once been. They weren't those same girls anymore. A lot had happened, creating a wedge between them that couldn't be repaired in a thirty-minute time span.

Frustrated, Liz returned her attention to the plaque with Alyssa's name on it. She lifted her camera and prepared to take one more photograph. The sun had sunk lower, and she didn't like to ride her bike after dark. Plus, she couldn't wait to get home to edit these photographs. Taking and developing pictures to hang at the bakery was the extent of her photography career. A photographer who couldn't be available for gigs wasn't much of a photographer at all. Just like a friend who wasn't available for, oh, say, nine years, wasn't much of a friend.

To: Liz Dawson
From: Bri Johnson

Subject: You asked, so here's my answer

Liz,

When I get out of prison, I'll finally return to Trove Isle. I've thought about this day so many times over the weeks and months and years. I'm a little worried that it'll feel like I'm coming home with my tail between my legs. Part of me doesn't even want to go back for that reason. I don't want to show my face because that's going to be hard. I know it will be. I'm guessing Melody feels that way too. After all this time, being back and being the subject of gossip. All eyes on her. When it's me, I'll want to have a friend by my side. I hope it'll be you. In fact, I don't need to hope because I know it'll be you. Because you're the strong one (don't forget it).

B

CHAPTER FIVE

MELODY

Melody had spent the last several hours at Hidden Treasures, taking stock of what was inside and deciding on her next steps for putting it up for sale. Now, Melody stepped inside her father's house, intending to go straight back to her room. She and her father had barely uttered a word to each other since she'd arrived so why start now?

"Melody?" her father's voice called after her.

Melody froze but didn't turn. "Yes?"

"How are things going with the store?"

"Fine. I scheduled a meeting with Abigail Winslow for tomorrow. She's going to help me put it up for sale."

"Sell? You're sure that's what you want?" he asked.

"Absolutely. I have no use for the place." Melody waited to see how her father would respond. When he didn't, she continued down the hall.

"Melody?"

She stopped walking again. "Yeah?"

"Are you . . . okay?" he asked quietly.

She noted the hesitation in his voice. Why would he hesitate? He was her father. He had a right to ask how she was doing. And she was his daughter. She had a right to want him to care. To want him to ask her to consider keeping the store. To stay in Trove Isle. Not that she ever would, but it was nice to be wanted.

She turned now and took a few steps toward him, her breathing shallow. "Not really."

"Is there anything I can do?"

"Doubtful. Once I sell, I'll be out of your hair. As long as you don't mind me staying through next week." She hated to ask anything of her father, but it was that or live out of her car. Or she guessed she could use the foldout cot she'd noticed in the back room of the thrift store. The amount of dust inside might kill her in her sleep though.

"This is your home. Stay as long as you want."

Two things. This wasn't her home—not anymore. And he wasn't saying he wanted her to stay, just that she could.

She blinked past the threat of tears that stung her eyes, reminding herself to breathe. "Thanks. I'm leaving next weekend at the latest. I told my work partner that wrapping things up here wouldn't take longer than two weeks, but I'm hoping to be gone sooner."

"Of course," he said quietly.

She cleared her throat. "Right now, I think I just need to go to bed. Sleep always makes things new again," Melody said, the words rolling off her tongue the way they had all her adult life.

"Your mom used to say that. Do you remember?"

"No," Melody said, honestly. And she didn't want to remember. That's why she'd left Trove Isle. To forget. Being back for too long threatened to bring all the painful things right back to the surface. There was too much grief wrapped up on this side of Trove Bridge. Even more than she'd realized. "Goodnight," she called behind her, walking down the hall.

She stood in her bedroom doorway for a moment. There were two beds for two sisters who'd grown up as the worst kind of enemies. Not for any particular reason except that they were siblings vying for the same things and attention from their parents. Then suddenly one summer everything had changed and they'd become the best of friends. They'd shared secrets and stayed up late talking about their dreams and the boys they liked.

The boy next door, Christopher West—undeserving as he was—for Alyssa. A dozen different guys for Melody.

A deep ache settled over her heart. She needed to get out of here, the sooner the better. First thing tomorrow, she'd meet with the real estate agent and begin the process for listing Hidden Treasures. Who knew? Maybe by the end of next week, it would even be sold. Either way, she had to head back.

Her business partner Julie was holding down the fort at Memory Lane Events. Melody was the business brain, and Julie had all the creativity. Thus, it was fine that Julie was organizing and running things while Melody was gone. Melody could still run numbers from a distance, pay bills, make orders, and stuff like that. Melody was still keeping up with everything and she didn't want to let her partner down.

Lying back on her bed, she stared up at the ceiling now. After the accident, Melody had packed her bags and driven to the bridge several times, ready to cross over and leave. She'd forced herself to turn back, however, telling herself that Alyssa wouldn't want her to disappear on her dad and her friends when they needed her most. On Melody's final night in this house though, right after the funeral, her father had finally broken what had felt like an insufferable silence. They'd wordlessly sat at the dinner table like they'd been doing every night since Alyssa's death. Then he'd looked up at her. For a moment, she'd thought he was going to offer some words of comfort. She was grieving too after all.

"Why Alyssa? There were four of you in the car, but she was the one taken. Why her?"

Melody had interpreted that question as *Why not you?*

They had been on their way to prom. It was senior prom for Melody, Bri, and Liz. And junior prom for Alyssa. They'd decided to go stag because what could be better than attending prom with your very best friends? Well, okay, Alyssa had wanted to go with Christopher, but he'd turned her down. Melody couldn't figure out why. Her sister had been beautiful, so sweet, and hilarious. Who wouldn't love her?

"Forget him anyway," Melody had said in the car ride on the way to prom, bumping her shoulder against Alyssa's.

Alyssa's smile, stained with fiery red lipstick, had lifted at the corners, but Melody caught the brief flicker of sadness in her eyes. "We're going to have the best time tonight." Alyssa was the optimist of the group with Liz being a second runner-up.

"You bet we are!" Liz called from the driver's seat. "Everyone's buckled up, right?"

"Yes, Mom," Bri said sarcastically, sitting in the front passenger seat.

Liz sighed dramatically. "Is it really a crime for me to want us to make it to prom in one piece?"

"You sound like my dad." Alyssa laughed quietly.

"You sound like my grandma," Bri added, making them all laugh harder—even Liz.

"Okay, let's make a bet," Melody finally said. "We're going stag, but I bet Bri is going to be the first one to hit the dance floor with a guy."

"Nu-uh. My money is on Alyssa back there." Bri glanced over her shoulder to look in the back seat. Bri looked beautiful tonight without a single dab of make-up on. It was a small miracle that Bri had even worn a dress. "The guys are going to go nuts when they see Alyssa walk in. She looks like a Hollywood actress."

Bri wasn't wrong. Alyssa was the most outwardly beautiful.

"Well, it definitely won't be me." Liz kept her eyes on the

road and her hands at two and nine. She was a responsible driver—the only one of them to never have gotten a ticket. "I bet it's Alyssa too," Liz said. "She's going to ditch us first."

Alyssa shook her head. "I think you guys *want* me to ditch you. I'm Melody's younger sister and I'm not supposed to be here. Three's a charm and four is a crowd."

Melody jabbed her elbow into Alyssa's side again, harder this time. "You're only one year younger. And you *are* supposed to be here. You're one of us."

"Agreed." Liz looked away from the road momentarily to meet Melody's gaze in the rearview.

"For sure," Bri said. "Three's a charm and four is the whole dang charm bracelet."

Alyssa grinned, rubbing the spot where Melody had jabbed her with her elbow. "Well, I plan on dancing with you all tonight. No guys."

"What if Christopher asks you to dance?" Melody asked in a teasing tone.

Alyssa's cheeks flushed darker than the blush she'd put on for the occasion. "Doubtful?"

"Okay, new rule," Bri said, taking hold of the conversation. "We all dance with each other, *but* we each get one exception."

"What kind of exception?" Melody asked.

"Like, my grandparents are committed to one another, but they have some agreement that if they run into their favorite movie star, they get a free pass to . . . you know."

"Your grandparents have a free pass agreement?" Liz asked in shock, her jaw dropping.

Bri shrugged. "They talk about it all the time. They don't think I know what a free pass is."

"You're suggesting that we get a free pass dance?" Melody clarified. "Just a dance?"

Bri rolled her eyes. "None of us are getting laid tonight, okay?"

Melody gave a resolute nod. "Yeah, I like that idea. Okay, Alyssa's free pass is obviously Christopher. Mine is Harmon."

"Harmon Lambert?" Liz flicked her gaze to the rearview mirror again. "Really?"

Melody leaned forward in her seat to talk to Liz more easily. "Who's yours?"

"I don't have a crush on anyone." Liz returned her eyes to the road. "But I'll choose David Pierce as my free pass."

Bri cackled. "You *would* choose him. He is destined to become a mall cop one day."

"Nothing wrong with mall cops," Alyssa said, happily. "Bri?"

Bri hummed thoughtfully. "I choose—"

Before Bri could answer, Liz gasped loudly as something darted into the road. Melody didn't get a good look. Everything happened so fast. Liz yanked the steering wheel and swerved to avoid hitting the shadowed creature—a small deer maybe—as it darted toward the woods.

Alyssa's body fell against Melody's with the car's quick movement. Why wasn't Alyssa wearing a seatbelt? No doubt she didn't want to wrinkle her dress.

As the car righted, Alyssa straightened to an upright position and let out a startled laugh. "Well, that was scary."

Melody was about to chastise her sister for not wearing a seatbelt when Liz slammed the brakes, sending the tires screaming into the night. The car hit the roadside and then they were spinning. Or maybe it was Melody's mind that was spinning. She pressed her eyes closed, momentarily reminded of that ride at the fair, the Gravitron. The one where you could barely open your eyes against the pressure inside the small enclosure. That's how she felt in this moment. Her eyelids were heavy, as if little lead anchors were weighing them down.

When her lids finally lifted, she looked out the front windshield and saw a huge tree coming at them at fifty miles an hour. Time slowed. Melody sent up what she thought would be her final prayer.

Please don't let us die. Please protect us.

The details of what happened next were filled in by the emergency services who showed up on the scene after the accident.

Alyssa was ejected. The air bag broke Liz's nose. Melody banged the side of her head against the window. She had a concussion. Bri broke her spine in three places. Three days later, Melody and Liz were sitting somberly in the front row at Alyssa's funeral while Bri lay in a hospital bed. She'd been devastated that she couldn't go, but Melody thought maybe Bri was the lucky one. The funeral made it all real. Alyssa was gone—forever. She wasn't coming back.

Melody's father didn't cry during the service. He didn't comfort Melody either. He didn't say a solitary word to her until hours later when they were leaving the burial ground. Then he leaned in and looked at her with lost eyes. *"You were supposed to watch over her."*

Melody blinked past hot tears that stung her eyes. She was surprised she hadn't run out of tears by now, but they kept coming; they wouldn't stop. Had she heard her father correctly?

"This is your fault," he said before standing more upright, turning, and walking back toward the black Town car that the funeral home had driven them in.

Melody hung back, speechless. Law enforcement had deemed what happened to be an unfortunate accident. Melody's father, however, had found her guilty. He blamed her for the simple fact that she had lived.

At dinner that night, he'd reiterated that sentiment when he'd asked, *"Why Alyssa? There were four of you in the car, but she was the one taken. Why her?"* How could a father think, much less say, such a thing?

Melody set down her fork and retreated to her bedroom—the one she used to share with Alyssa. But Alyssa wasn't coming back and, as Melody packed up her belongings that night, she promised herself that neither was she.

"I can't sell this place as is," Abigail Winslow said the following day, standing in the center of Hidden Treasures. The real estate agent kept her arms close to her sides as if she was afraid to touch anything.

Melody guessed that Abigail didn't want to dirty her neatly pressed pantsuit. "I'm really sorry, Melody, but you have some work to do before anyone will want to buy Jo's store," she said in a thick New York accent. She was a city transplant who'd moved South and had settled on the isle for fresh air and a lower cost of living. "If I put it up now, you'd maybe get half of what it's worth, and that might be months from now. Real estate on Seagull Street isn't as coveted as it once was. Sandpiper Street is much hotter territory."

"I see." Melody felt a little sick. "I thought people liked a good fixer-upper."

Abigail chuckled. "They like it because they can get it for a steal. If you're looking for fair market value, like you said, then you need to clean this shop out. No one wants to buy a dusty old thrift store. Sorry to be so blunt," she said with an exaggerated grimace.

"No, I want your honest opinion." Melody wanted to get fair market value too. The money would help her during the tight months. It might even afford her a house, which was something she'd dreamt of owning for a while now. An apartment felt like a temporary dwelling. By this point in life, she'd always thought that she'd own her own place. She'd thought she'd be successful and married too. Instead, she was living in a one-bedroom apartment and she was so single that she couldn't remember when she'd been on her last date. She wanted to finally put down roots in Charlotte. Maybe she'd create a dating profile online when she got back.

"My honest opinion is that you need to toss the junk and do a few renovations. You can hire someone to help if you need to."

"I don't have money to hire someone," Melody countered.

Abigail looked sympathetic. "Then start watching HGTV, honey." She shrugged. "We've completed most of the paperwork. I'll come back when you're ready, and I'll sell it any way you want. I'm only advising you on what I think would be the best strategy."

"Thank you." Melody walked Abigail to the door. She knew what Abigail said was true. But clearing out this shop meant that she'd have to stay at least a couple weeks longer than planned, and she wasn't sure she could agree to that. Her business partner, Julie, would definitely object. Maybe she should take whatever money she could get and run. But the possibility for more money was too tempting.

The bell over the door rang as Abigail walked out of the store which would be more appropriately named Hoarder's Delight. Then Melody turned and headed to the glass case where she knew there was a notebook by the register. She loved organizing and making to-do lists, which was one reason she'd been drawn to event planning. She grabbed a pen from a nearby drawer and plopped down on the stool to plan her next steps.

For the next two hours, that's exactly what she did. Then she left the store midafternoon to get ready for Jo's Celebration of Life at Sunrise Park. As much as Melody loved her great-aunt, and missed her, no part of Melody wanted to attend this function. She'd barely seen anyone since returning to Trove Isle, which was how she preferred things. The entire town was likely to come out tonight to give Jo the send-off she deserved. Jo was beloved in Trove and for good reason.

Melody doubted Jo had a single enemy here, and if she did, it was only because she spoke her truth unapologetically, which most folks respected.

Melody let herself into her dad's house and headed down the hall toward her bedroom. Jo deserved a lot better than she'd gotten. At least from Melody. Melody stepped into her bedroom and lifted her suitcase up onto her bed. She unzipped it and stared into its depths.

She hadn't packed anything appropriate for a funeral. Then again, this wasn't going to be a funeral. What did one wear to a celebration of life on the banks of the intracoastal waterway? Melody wasn't sure. One thing she was certain of was that people would be watching her tonight and whispering, looking for clues as to whether Melody was healthy and happy, on drugs, or whatever other story was circulating.

Melody lifted out a white top with a large, purple floral print from her suitcase. She pulled out a pair of black pants because, yes, she was mourning whether Jo liked it or not, and some fun black strappy sandals. *There.* Dress casual, appropriate for a barbeque or a celebration for the woman who'd meant a lot more to Melody than Melody had even realized. It was true, sometimes it took dying for people to appreciate you.

Melody stepped into the bathroom and freshened up, and then looked at the time on her cell phone's screen. If she didn't hurry, she'd be late. Then again, she was already too late to say goodbye.

She grabbed her keys and walked back out of the house, locking the door behind her. Her father wasn't home, but maybe he was going straight to ceremony from work. Or perhaps he wasn't attending at all. Melody wasn't sure how close he'd been to Jo in these final years. Maybe not very. In the past, Jo's very reason for visiting always seemed to revolve around Melody and Alyssa. With them gone, maybe Jo stopped coming over altogether.

Melody got into her car and hesitated behind the steering wheel for a moment before forcing herself to drive. She could do this. She could face the town she'd run away from so long ago. How hard could it be to put on a smile and pretend to be happy and successful, like her father apparently told everyone she was?

It was a short drive to Sunrise Park, which was conveniently located near the bridge if Melody decided to skip town when the night was over. She parked and watched as folks headed toward the isle's waterfront. The sun was on its descent, blending into a mixture of bright pastels over the horizon. She didn't recognize most of the faces that crossed in front of her windshield. And they weren't noticing her while she sat there, breathing shallowly and entertaining fantasies of driving away. Perhaps she'd just stay on the outskirts of the crowd, watch from a distance, and leave without having to hold any conversations.

Yeah. Good idea.

With a plan in place, she swung open her car door and then winced as it hit a person with a heavy *thud*. "Oh! I am so sorry!" Melody jumped out of the car and onto her feet, apologizing profusely as she waited for the man to turn around and face her.

Tall. Black hair. Dark-rimmed glasses. She should have recognized him immediately, but right now her thoughts were scattered and she was concerned he might be injured. "Are you okay?"

"That might hurt tomorrow, but I know where you live so . . ." He trailed off.

Melody frowned. "You do?"

The man grinned. Where did she know him from? "Christopher?" she finally said. As in Christopher West, Alyssa's boy-next-door crush. The boy who'd broken Alyssa's heart.

A smile twitched at the corners of his mouth. "Hey, Melody. I heard you were back in town. I saw the car in your dad's driveway, and guessed this might be one of the rumors around here that's actually true."

"I'm just here temporarily. I inherited Hidden Treasures."

"I heard that too. Congratulations." Chris's face blanched with the realization of what he'd just said. "And my deepest condolences."

"Thanks." Her first inclination was to be polite to this man who'd been little more than a kid the last time she'd seen him. Her second inclination was to snub him the same way he'd done Alyssa when she'd asked him to prom. Alyssa's tear-stricken face flashed in Melody's mind. Her sister had deserved so much better in life.

Melody looked over at the crowd forming on the waterfront. She didn't want to make small talk with this man, but he was still standing in front of her, an expectant look on his face. "So, if you saw my car, I'm guessing that means your parents still live next door?" Melody asked.

"Just my mom." His gaze flicked down for just a moment. "My dad passed away last year."

Melody's heart dropped into the pit of her stomach. "I'm so sorry," she said for the second time in five minutes. And suddenly she felt guilty for feeling bitter towards him.

"It's okay. You didn't know. How would you?"

Burn. Maybe she should leave before she got any more comments like that. They were sure to come once she was out there, mingling among folks with questions and made-up answers of their own.

"I didn't intend any insult by that, by the way," Christopher said. "I just meant, we were never close. You wouldn't even give me the time of day, if I remember correctly."

"You hung out with my sister until she started liking you more than a friend. Then, if I remember correctly, you wouldn't give *her* the time of day," Melody said.

Christopher offered a pained expression. "I just didn't want to lead her on. Alyssa was an amazing person."

"Speaking to the choir," Melody said, determined not to like this guy, even though he'd always been likeable.

Christopher glanced over at the crowd by the water. "C'mon. I'm sure a lot of folks here can't wait to catch up with you."

He didn't give her a chance to slink back into her car like she wanted to. Instead, he reached behind him, pushed her car door closed, and gestured for her to follow him, leading the way to where someone was passing out candles up ahead. Everyone seemed to have one.

Melody kept her head down, her hand absently fidgeting with the charm bracelet on her wrist as she followed the uneven ground toward the small crowd, her heart pitter-pattering like a heavy-footed toddler having a tantrum in her chest.

"Melody!" Mr. Lyme turned toward the two of them as they approached and handed them both a candle. Then he pulled a lighter stick out of his blue blazer, the same one he'd worn when he'd met Melody at Hidden Treasures earlier in the week, and flicked a flame atop each. "I'm so glad you made it," he told her with a wide smile. "Jo really wanted you here. She mentioned you often."

Melody wished that Jo had reached out to her more recently, but Melody probably wouldn't have answered the phone anyway. In an attempt to truncate her gushing emotions, she'd left Trove Isle behind, shutting everyone out. Even Jo.

Mr. Lyme's eyes were shiny as he looked between them. He fanned a hand in front of his eyes. "I'm sorry. It's going to be an emotional night for me, isn't it?"

"We're all here for you." Christopher patted a hand along the older man's back. "My mom sends her love. She wishes she could be here."

Mr. Lyme nodded solemnly. "I know, I know." He released an audible breath. "I guess I need to mingle. Thanks for coming tonight. I'm sure Jo is smiling down on us."

"I'm sure she is," Christopher agreed.

As Mr. Lyme walked away, Melody turned and asked, "Why can't your mom be here? Is she okay?"

Christopher kept his gaze forward. "She's homebound these days," he said, matter-of-factly. "If you plan on spending any time at your dad's, you'll see a lot of me over there. I check on my mom daily. Complete her to-do lists, bring her groceries, stuff like that."

"Wow." Melody wanted to hold a grudge against this guy, but he was making it hard to have a single negative thought about him. She was about to ask more questions, but several people walked up. Christopher seemed to take on the role of her buffer, reintroducing her to the town while keeping her from standing alone awkwardly and stopping her from running.

"You remember Danette?" Christopher asked as an old woman with white curls grabbed Melody's hand.

Melody nodded, recalling the onetime school librarian. Why were the older woman's hands so cold?

"I own a bookshop now," Danette said proudly. "The Book Whore. It's right down from your thrift store. People can buy a book from me and I'll send them for a treasure from you. We'll be pals," she said conspiratorially.

The Book Whore? Melody wasn't sure she'd heard the store's name correctly. Surely this older woman wasn't referring to herself in such a derogatory manner. Unsure of how to respond, Melody glanced over and caught Christopher's amused gaze.

He turned his attention to Danette. "I need a book for my mom, Danny. How about I stop in next week?"

Danette's eyes lit up. "Perfect! What does Gina like these days?"

"She likes murder mysteries," he said. "Nothing too bloody."

"Of course. I'll prepare a stack for you to choose from."

The bookstore owner seemed wobbly and unsafe with her candle, especially when she got excited.

Christopher leaned in to give Danette a side hug and, if Melody wasn't mistaken, he blew out Danette's candle on purpose.

"Oh, no!" Danette's expression crumpled in disappointment.

"I'm sorry, Danny. My fault," he said, swiping his gaze at Melody.

Danette pointed a finger in his direction. "Yes, it was, and I'm not senile. I know you blew my candle out on purpose, you stinker. Which is good because I sneezed and nearly lit my hair on fire earlier." She grinned up at him. "I just didn't want to be disrespectful to Jo by having an unlit candle."

"I think Jo would understand, Danny." Christopher kept what Melody considered to be an impressively serious face. She was having a harder time doing that.

Danette reached for Melody's hand again. "Jo talked about you all the time, dear. I'm so glad you're home."

Melody held her tongue, and her heart, and the flickering candle in her opposite hand. She turned to look for more people she knew, spotting her father standing stiffly by a large cypress tree. He was wearing a suit and shifting his candle back and forth between his hands. Where was Liz? She had said she was coming tonight, and Melody had really hoped to get another chance to talk.

"Looking for Liz?" Christopher leaned in to ask.

Melody turned to look at him. "Are you a mind reader or something?"

"A high school history teacher actually."

Melody found this interesting. So, the boy next door was still a bit of a nerd, albeit a frustratingly handsome one. "Liz said she would be here, and the celebration is about to start."

Christopher glanced around too. "Her younger sister Rose

usually has to drive her. And sixteen-year-olds aren't the most punctual or responsible. Especially Liz's sister."

"Why does Rose have to drive her?" Melody asked.

Christopher furrowed a brow behind his dark-rimmed glasses. "You really haven't been back in a while, huh? Liz doesn't drive. She quit after the, uh . . ."

Melody swallowed and looked down, suddenly understanding. "I see."

"So, she's probably running a bit late." Christopher gave a small chuckle. "And she's probably not happy about it. I can fix this." He pulled his cell phone from his pocket, using one hand to bring up his contacts.

"Who are you calling?"

"Matt Coffey lives down the street from Liz. He's not here either. Maybe he can swing by and pick her up. Liz wouldn't want to miss this. She thought the world of Jo." Matt must have answered because Christopher grinned. "Hey, bud. Are you home? . . . Oh, that's great. Do you think you can pick up Liz? She's not here yet, so I'm guessing she must be waiting on Rose . . . Yeah . . . Yeah. Okay. See you in a few." He tapped his screen and shoved his phone into his back pocket. "Matt is on the case."

"Great," Melody said.

Christopher held out his open palm. "Can I see your phone?"

Melody felt her lips part. "Hmm? My phone?" She pulled it out of her pocket, but hesitated to hand it over. "Why?"

He wriggled his fingers. "Unlock it first."

"You're asking a lot from someone who barely knows you." And someone who was carrying a grudge from years ago.

Christopher tilted his head, his eyes subtly squinting. "You know me well enough to know I'm not going to steal from you."

That was true. She didn't have to like him to admit he didn't seem like a criminal. Unlocking her phone, she placed it in his palm, her fingers brushing against his skin accidentally. An electrical current zipped through her fingertips, traveling up her arm and into her chest. "What are you doing?"

He tapped along her screen with a quick hand. "I'm adding myself to your contacts. Just in case you need something while you're back on the isle. A friend, a ride, a burger."

Melody blinked. "Oh. Thanks."

He handed her phone back to her. "Don't hesitate to call or text for anything. I mean it. Your dad has helped my mom a lot over the years, especially after my dad passed away. I want to return the favor. I'm here for whatever you need."

She swallowed thickly. That was a really nice offer from someone who, as she mentioned earlier, barely knew her anymore.

Christopher started to step away. "Okay. I'll just go tell Mr. Lyme to wait on Liz."

Melody grabbed his arm. "Wait. You're leaving me?" She felt a sudden surge of panic. Grudge or not, he was her buffer. She didn't want to brave this crowd on her own.

"Don't worry. You won't be alone out here. I'm sure everyone is eager to speak to you tonight," he said as he continued forward, leaving Melody standing by herself. But not for long, which was exactly what she was afraid of.

To: Bri Johnson
From: Liz Dawson

Subject: I hate it when you're right

Bri,

Read the subject line because I'm only saying this once so that your head doesn't get too big. Melody does look like she could use a friend. I'm not sure I can go as far as being that to her, but I can be friendly, at least.

Tonight is Jo's Celebration of Life. I wish you could come. It seems wrong that you can't be here. She was like family to us all.

Remember her True Love's Pretzel Knot? Eat it with the one who has caught your eye and you'll catch that person's heart? I wonder if she used that recipe on Mr. Lyme. That man is still so smitten with her. It's adorable. Anyway, Jo confided the secret ingredient with me and that makes me feel like family. The way she always sent me a special card on my birthday did too. Jo was special, and I think my heart will always ache a little now that she's gone.

When you come home, we'll have to make butterscotch tea in her memory.

Anyway, thank you for your advice. Read the subject line again.

xx,

Liz

CHAPTER SIX

LIZ

Liz let the drapes fall back in place in her front window where she'd been waiting for over thirty minutes now. Where was Rose?

She'd called, but her sister wasn't answering. Liz supposed she should be worried, but this was typical Rose behavior. Tonight, of all nights, Rose needed to be on time. They couldn't miss Jo's celebration of life. It was important.

Tears gathered in Liz's eyes. She was dressed in a pair of pinstripe pants with a royal-blue top and a soft-cream cardigan sweater because it got chilly on the waterway at night, even this time of year. Now it looked like she might not even make it to the celebration after all. Maybe she should just put her pj's on and curl into bed. The thought was fleeting. She was a lot of things, but a quitter wasn't one of them.

She'd ride her bike. If she rode fast, she could be there in fifteen to twenty minutes, tops. She'd miss the mingling and the part where people said a few kind words about the dearly departed. But she'd be there for the main event. Over the years, Jo would talk about her grand send-off one day. She had made it sound like she was going on a cruise or something, instead of dying.

Liz grabbed her purse and keys and hurried to the garage, freeing her bicycle from its rack on the wall and pulling on her helmet. Then she straddled the seat and coasted out of the driveway. At its crest, she started pedaling with determination, mostly fueled out of irritation at Rose.

She made it to the STOP sign, looked both ways, and then pumped her right foot to go when a truck pulled up beside her. Liz glanced over into Matt's rolled down window. She felt her lips part a little because she wasn't expecting to see him at this moment.

"My instructions are to escort you to Jo's Celebration of Life. Hop in, my lady."

Liz blinked. She was still slightly out of breath from racing down her street.

Matt pushed his truck door open and stepped out. "Here, let me help you put your bike in the bed of the truck."

Liz swung her leg off and watched as Matt picked up her Schwinn like it weighed nothing. "Careful with it," she said, unable to help herself.

"Of course." He grinned at her over his shoulder and when he did, a million butterflies stormed her stomach.

She ignored the fluttering sensation in her belly and unsnapped her helmet, placing it into the bed of his truck next to her bike. Then she headed over to the passenger seat, opened the door, and ignoring her inner reservations, climbed in. "Thank you," she said once he'd returned to sitting behind the steering wheel.

"You could have called yourself, you know?" His gaze lingered on her a long moment before returning to the road.

Matt was ever helpful. And kind. She had his number programed into her phone, of course, but she didn't want to have to use it. No, she wanted her sister to be a responsible human being for once.

"You were running late too?" Liz asked.

"I got home later than expected. I was working a wreck on

Conch Avenue." He cast her an apologetic look. And there it was. The reason she didn't call Matt. They had a history that started with her very own wreck. Every time they were together, something happened or was said that created that very look he was giving her now. The concerned divot between his eyes, pulling his brows into a slight tilt. He'd pulled her to safety, held her as she'd cried—although that's just what she was told because she didn't actually remember anything. She was in shock.

He remembered though. She could see it on his face when he mentioned an accident or a scene. That was his job. It was what he did, day in and day out.

Matt lifted his foot off the gas pedal just a notch. Without thinking, she clutched the safety handle on the truck door. He continued to drive five below the speed limit all the way to Sunrise Park, where he pulled in at the end of a long trail of vehicles.

"Look at that," Matt said.

Liz followed his gaze to the turquoise and fluorescent-orange-colored horizon, melting behind the distant coastline. "It's beautiful out here."

"Jo had the right idea. You can be buried below the ground or you can have your ashes out there in nature's beauty."

Liz knew not to look at Matt right now. She was already feeling everything. Frustrated and irritated at Rose. Sentimental and mourning Jo. She didn't need to mix in anything else. Especially not anything romantic. Instead, she pushed open her truck door. "Thank you for the ride," she said. "I'm sure Rose can take me home afterward."

He stepped out too, meeting her on the other side of the truck. "You're sure Rose is coming tonight?"

Liz looked at him. "Rose knew Jo. I'm sure she'll be here."

"Well, you have my number and I have your bike. You know I don't mind giving you a lift if you need it."

Liz offered him a grateful smile. "Thank you."

As they approached the small gathering, Mr. Lyme stepped over and handed them each a candle. He pulled out a lighter stick and lit the wick on both. "You're just in time. I'm about to read the letter Jo wrote to everyone."

"Jo wrote a letter?" Liz asked, intrigued that she'd get to hear one or two more Jo-isms before saying their final goodbye.

"Oh, yeah. You know Jo always had to have the last word." Mr. Lyme wiped at a tear on his cheek.

Liz reached for his arm. "I know you miss her. I'm so sorry for your loss."

"Well, after tonight, every time I look up into the sky, I'll think of her."

Liz tried to keep her expression neutral. Jo was an unusual woman. She didn't do things the conventional way, and Liz would expect nothing less than what Jo had prepared for her own celebration of life tonight. Jo wouldn't want to be under the ground. She'd want to spend her eternity among the stars.

"Excuse me," Mr. Lyme said. "I need to collect myself before I read the letter."

"Of course." Liz watched him walk away. Her gaze connected with Melody's. Melody was surrounded by Tammy Flynn, Kiki Rogers, and Mr. Rodriguez, their old geometry teacher from middle school.

Matt leaned in and spoke in a soft whisper only for Liz's ears. "C'mon. You know you feel sorry for her. I'm not sure how long she's been stuck talking to them, but judging by her face, she could use a friend."

Liz remembered Bri's advice in her last message that she'd sent. Bri had always been the one with the attitude growing up. Quick to kick butt in her own words. But as she'd matured, she was the wise one. Whether Melody deserved her empathy or not, Melody did look a little over-whelmed, and Liz did feel sorry for her. Just a little. "Okay. Yeah. I'll go say hi."

"Great." Matt turned to go in the opposite direction. "I need to find Christopher. We're doing the honors of Jo's send-off tonight."

"Oh," Liz said, catching his eye. "You are?"

"Yep. We're taking Mr. Lyme's boat. Three miles from the shore is the ordinance. Though, I think Jo would appreciate a little bit of rule-breaking for her send-off."

Liz laughed. "Maybe go out two and three-quarter miles.

"My thoughts precisely." His smile could have lit up the night.

Liz caught herself staring and then looked away. "Good luck with that. Thanks again for the ride." She started walking toward Melody, forcing her steps until she was standing in the midst of the odd group. Tammy Flynn was a gossip. Kiki was nice enough, but Liz knew Kiki had never really liked Melody so her motivations for standing here were sus-pect. And Mr. Rodriguez couldn't hear when they were in middle school. He'd yelled even back then because he refused to wear his hearing aids.

"Liz!" Mr. Rodriguez yelled, still not wearing his aides.

Liz flinched and then accepted the hug he offered. Tammy hugged her too. Then Kiki.

"It's so good to see you," Kiki said, warmly. Kiki did like Liz, so Liz knew it was sincere. To be fair, Kiki probably didn't like Melody because Melody had professed her crush on Marcus Wilkes once. It was a middle school scandal consid-ering Kiki was already going to the spring dance with Mar-cus. Even though it was years ago, decades even, some grudges held on tight, especially in a small town.

Pulling back from the hug with Kiki, Liz looked at

Melody, the only one in the little group she was standing with that she hadn't yet embraced. Not hugging would send a message that Tammy, the gossip, would undoubtedly relay all night. So Liz dutifully leaned in. Reading the cues, Melody opened her arms. The hug was awkward at best. Liz wanted to squeeze Melody tightly and then wring her neck. She also wanted to hold onto her friend and not let go for a solid five minutes.

Liz felt her eyes well up. *Time to let go before actual tears start falling.* As she pulled back, her sweater caught on something. She and Melody looked down at the same time, bumping foreheads.

"Ow. Sorry," Melody said.

"Here! Let me take those candles!" Mr. Rodriquez yelled. "Before you two start a fire out here." His laugh was just as loud as his voice.

Liz handed her candle to him, twisting her neck to look at what was caught.

"My charm bracelet is caught on your sweater." Melody reached around and tried to free herself. "I think it wants you to wear it," she teased, a small smile playing at the corners of her mouth. "I can't get it free without snagging your top."

Liz twisted her neck again.

"Here." Melody maneuvered her arm and pulled her wrist from the bracelet.

Liz looked down at Melody's now bare wrist. "Where is it?"

"On your sweater." Melody gestured with a tip of her head. "It was your turn anyway."

Liz didn't know what to say. She hadn't taken the bracelet at the bakery when Melody had first offered it because it symbolized a friendship that she wasn't willing to give another chance. But after Bri's advice, Liz didn't know how to feel anymore. "I'll, uh, clip it free when I get home."

"And then wear it. You should." Melody offered back a soft smile.

"So nice to see you two friends making up!" Mr. Rodriquez yelled, gaining all the attention of those nearby.

Liz groaned under her breath. She couldn't help it. She needed to step away. She needed air, but she was standing outside. She couldn't get any more air than this.

Mr. Lyme tapped the top of his cordless microphone to gain everyone's attention as he stood at the front of the crowd. "Thank you all for being here tonight," he said.

The noise of the crowd died down as everyone turned to face him.

Liz listened as he talked about the woman he'd loved. His Jo. They'd never married, but they were as married as any two people could be in Liz's mind. Mr. Lyme was devoted, and Jo had loved him more than all the treasure in the world's treasure chest. That's what she'd always told Liz.

"Find you a man who makes you feel like you've happened upon your lost treasure of Atlantis."

Mr. Lyme handed off his candle to Matt who was standing nearby with Christopher. Then he opened a letter from Jo, explaining that she'd written it the night before she'd passed away and had instructed him to read it at this very occasion.

Without thinking, Liz glanced over and locked eyes with Melody, exchanging a meaningful look. They both seemed to be anticipating and dreading Jo's final words. Until Jo, the only person who Liz had ever lost was Alyssa. Alyssa's final words to her were, "Well, that was scary." It was after the small deer had darted in front of their car, causing Liz to swerve.

Hopefully, Jo had something more insightful to say with her final words.

Mr. Lyme cleared his throat and looked down at the paper in his hands. He began to read.

To the ones I love,
This is not goodbye, although it might feel that way.
And for that I'm sorry.

There's so much I want to say before I leave this
world—with a bang—but sometimes less is more, and
I'd rather you remember the most important things I
have to tell you. Because sometimes we forget to
remember. We're humans after all. But all those little
forgotten things, the lost pieces of us that we don't
even know we're missing, add up. If we're not careful,
we'll lose ourselves entirely.

So I'm keeping this short and sweet and simple.
Here goes . . .

Dreamers, don't let fear keep you from chasing the
desires of your heart. Some people think dreams are
just for sleeping, but I say the best ones are had when
we're wide awake. Hidden Treasures was my dream,
but I know owning a thrift store isn't everyone's thing.
God made us all different and I thank Him for that.

One thing I loved about Hidden Treasures was the
shoes! Have you ever put yourself in someone else's
shoes? It's an amazing thing, really. We don't know
what we'd do, or say, or how we'd act until and unless
we've walked to the market in their shoes. So, in
honor of me, try on someone else's Nikes for a time.
Just Do It.

Also, don't be too stubborn to forgive. But never
forget because forgetting can turn you into a fool. True
forgiving though, that lifts you to a level that few
achieve. Accept each other and love while you can.
Because life is fleeting, and sometimes the things that
are lost can't be found again.

Jerry, I'm waiting for you, over the horizon, out
among the stars, ready to be your Mrs. Lyme once you
join me. No rush. I'm in no hurry. You'll get here when

you get here. Until then, know that I'm not lonely. I'll
be here with my baby son, Jasper, and Alyssa.
  Yours Truly,
  Jo

  P.S. Melody, if you're home, welcome back. I valued
people more than material things in life, but Hidden
Treasures was the one thing I regret leaving behind. It's
true to its name. The treasure is there, waiting for you
to uncover. Look for it!

Liz looked over and saw Melody's eyes shimmering with
tears. Without thinking, she reached over and squeezed
Melody's hand. Maybe Melody had left when Liz had needed
her most, but that didn't mean Liz's heart was cold toward
her. She knew disappearing was always Mel's way of dealing
with hard things. Leaning in, Liz whispered, "You okay?"
  "Yeah." Melody wiped at her eyes and nodded. She didn't
look okay though.
  Mr. Lyme started talking again. "All right, men. If you'll
do the honors."
  Holding her hand, Liz felt Melody's body tense as Matt
and Christopher carried a huge rocket-shaped firework toward a boat that sat idling off the Sunset Park Pier.
  "What's going on?" Melody asked, watching the men.
"What are they doing?"
  "This is what Jo wanted." Liz had assumed Melody knew
what was about to happen. Jo was her great-aunt. They were
family. Wouldn't Melody's father have told her that Jo requested to have her ashes poured into a firework to shoot off
over the water? Jo wanted to light up the sky and go out with
a bang. And that's exactly what she was doing.
  Liz wasn't thrilled about the idea, but Jo was her own person. The thrift shop owner was unconventional, and Liz
loved her for it.

"Jo's wish was to be shot off in a firecracker?" Melody said, raising her voice. "They're going to shoot my great-aunt off in a piece of plastic?" Her eyes were wide as she looked at Liz now. "And you think this is okay?"

Liz shook her head. "It's not for me to think anything of. I have no say. She's not my family. Not legally."

Melody's cheeks were flushed the way they used to get in school when she got mad. Melody had never been one to anger easily, but when she did, the blood rushed to her skin. "No, Jo is my family. And I am not okay with this." She pointed down to the boat that Matt and Christopher were navigating out in the water. Two and three-quarter miles. "I'm not okay." Melody's voice cracked. Her gaze flicked around as she seemed to realize she wasn't whispering anymore. If possible, her skin bloomed an even darker shade.

"Melody, you need to—" Liz started to say, but Melody cut her off.

"Go. I need to go." Turning, Melody started a brisk walk up the hill, away from the crowd, and away from Liz.

Liz debated chasing after her, just like she had the last time Melody had run. But tonight was about honoring Jo's wishes. Jo wanted her loved ones to send her off with an incredible bang. So that's what Liz would do.

Facing forward, Liz held her breath and her tears. Minutes later, a squeal penetrated the night, high-pitched and shrill, followed seconds later by the brightest, most vivid display of colors that Liz had ever seen lighting up the isle's sky. It was a show worthy of Jo herself with all her thrifty flair.

Tears ran down Liz's cheek as she watched until the last color fizzled out in the dark sky. Then Liz blew out her candle, silently celebrating Jo, who had been right. It did feel like goodbye. But tonight also felt like the cuff of something new.

A hand tapped Liz's back. She whirled and faced Rose.

"Did you know you have a bracelet stuck to your sweater?"

Rose folded her arms at her chest. Her eyebrow piercing glinted in the moonlight.

Liz wiped at her cheek. "Yeah, I know. Where were you?"

"I forgot about this thing, okay?"

"I texted and called." Liz tried to remain calm. Dr. Mayer used to say that when she felt herself getting upset, she should focus on a small part of her body, like her toes. Liz curled them into the bottom of her shoes as she waited for Rose to explain.

"My cell phone was dead. Sorry." She didn't sound apologetic. Her tone sounded more annoyed than anything. "I'm glad you made it. Did you ride your bike?"

"Matt gave me a ride."

"Great." Rose took a step backward. "So he can give you a lift back home too?"

Liz knew that Rose hadn't had much of a relationship with Jo. Not like Liz. Even so, wouldn't Rose want to be here in support of Liz? Liz had loved Jo like family. Liz reached for Rose's arm before she took another step to leave. "Where are you going?"

"I have a social life, you know," Rose said.

"Not tonight you don't. Tonight, you're taking me home," Liz practically growled, suddenly exhausted and on the verge of tears. She softened her tone. "Please."

After a moment, Rose's pinched expression seemed to relax. "Fine." She shrugged. "I guess I don't really feel like hanging out with Devin tonight anyway. Maybe we can watch something on Netflix."

Liz blinked. We? "Yeah, I'm sure we could agree on something to watch."

"Doubtful. But when I spoke to Mom on the phone earlier, she said I had to be sensitive to your needs. Because of Jo and all. So . . ." Rose shrugged.

"Making me catch a ride to the celebration of life is being sensitive to my needs?" Liz asked.

"Look, as soon as I remembered what tonight was, I sped home and then raced here to find you. I'm sorry, okay?" Rose shrugged. "Truly."

Liz nodded, remembering the words of Jo's letter. Something about forgiveness and walking in another's shoes. She looked down at Rose's combat boots and back up at her sister, who had maybe needed more of her parents' attention than she'd gotten growing up. Their parents had been worried about Liz for a long time after the accident. Rose had probably gotten shorted the attention she was due. Liz probably hadn't been the best sister either. "Okay," Liz said, relaxing her curled toes. "Let's get out of here. I'm ready to go home."

To: Liz Dawson
From: Bri Johnson

Subject: Remembering Jo

Liz,

I don't need to be there tonight. I'll lie on my cot and think of her along with everyone else. I don't even know where to start. There's one memory I never shared with you, or anyone for that matter. But since we're celebrating our "Aunt" Jo, I went dumpster diving with her once.

It was dirty and smelly, but, oh wow, we had the best time. At the time, I was high on pain meds, but Jo was just Jo. I think we got some day-old bread that hadn't even been opened. We brought it back to her place and ate it with apple butter. We also found an old radio and a small cherub statue pouring a vase of water. Weird and random, I know, but it's my favorite memory of her so how can I not think on it tonight?

There are people in this world who are too afraid to be who they are because the world has taught them that who they are is not okay. Jo was everything that I imagine people tried to change along the way, and she bucked their efforts.

Rest in peace, Jo. May the dumpsters in heaven be gold-plated and full of fresh bread and little cherub statues that make your heart happy.

B

CHAPTER SEVEN

MELODY

Melody had watched the splattering of red, blue, and green light punctuating the sky through her rearview mirror as she sat in her parked car. She'd waited until the fireworks had fizzled, feeling somehow like she owed Jo at least that much. Then she wiped her tears and drove away from Sunrise Park.

Tears continued to blur her vision as she drove. Great-aunt Jo's send-off was a firework display? Not to be disrespectful to Jo's final wishes, but what kind of sick and twisted celebration of life was that? Melody was on her way to her father's house, but she didn't want to face her dad when she was this upset. Not tonight. He must have known about this. Couldn't he have at least warned her? Couldn't Liz have done so?

Melody changed directions, considering briefly driving over Trove Bridge and leaving town. But her bags were at her dad's, and she would need the items inside eventually. As much as she wanted to leave Trove Isle, she wasn't ready just yet. She needed to finish cleaning out Hidden Treasures and put it up for sale.

She drove the roads by memory, turning and navigating

her way to Seagull Street until she was parked in front of Hidden Treasures along the curb. She stepped out of her car, locked it behind her, and let herself inside the thrift store. She never would have expected to find comfort here, but tonight all she wanted was to be alone. Even if she was surrounded by junk.

She didn't flip the lights on as she walked toward the back, where she'd seen that Jo kept a fold-out cot. Melody unfolded it, holding her breath as dust plumed upward. Then she found some clean linens that she placed on the bed. When she was done, she climbed under a heavy quilt that she vaguely remembered from her childhood. It wasn't for sale. It was located in the tiny back room, the size of a walk-in closet.

Melody lay back and stared up at the ceiling, decorated with glow-in-the-dark stars. And she thought about Jo being sent off in a firecracker and the final lines of Jo's letter about meeting her late baby boy and Alyssa.

Melody swallowed past a sob that caught in her throat. Why was life on the isle so sentimental and sad? There were too many ghosts here, jumping out from every corner. She had no ghosts in Charlotte. There, she went about her day as an event planner, making everyone else's precious moments memorable while she barely felt anything at all. She didn't have family in Charlotte and she didn't keep close friends. That was what she preferred, even if the result was a lonelier, colder life.

She swiped past one tear, then two.

"Why did you bring me back here, Jo?" she whispered into the darkness. "I am not one of your lost things." Except she was. She'd been lost since the night Alyssa died. Maybe since seven years earlier when their mother had passed away. Like Jo's letter had said, she'd been losing pieces of herself here and there until she didn't even know who she was anymore.

Melody blinked up at the glow-in-the-dark stars and then shut her eyes. The next thing she knew, she was waking up to the sound of someone tapping on the storefront window.

Melody sat upright in bed, disoriented for a moment. *Where am I?* Then she remembered. She was in Hidden Treasures. It was Saturday morning. Last night Great-aunt Jo had been launched into the sky in a firecracker.

The knock came again.

Melody got out of the bed, her body achy from the thin, springy mattress. She peeked out of the back room, down the store, to see Liz standing outside on the sidewalk, her hands cupped to the front glass as she peered inside. Melody stiffened when Liz's gaze latched onto hers. Too late to hide.

On an exhale, Melody walked toward the front, smoothing her hair and clothes as she approached. She must look a mess. She was still wearing last night's clothing. She opened the door and looked at Liz.

"Here." Liz held out a coffee cup with The Bitery's logo on it. "I saw your car out front and figured you must have slept here last night. I thought you might appreciate this."

"I do. Thank you." Melody took the cup and gave Liz a sheepish look. "I'm sorry about last night." She pushed a lock of hair behind her ear, but it fell back along her cheek. "I was expecting a small raft with Jo's ashes. Or that we would all release lanterns into the sky. Something nice."

Liz lifted one corner of her mouth in a sideways grin. "You know Jo better than that."

Melody nodded. "Yeah. A firework makes more sense now that I think about it. It just shocked me, I guess."

"I get it." Liz held out her arm. "Do you, uh, want the bracelet back?" It was draped along her wrist, the friendship charm catching the light where it lay just below the back of her hand.

"No, it's your turn. It chose you last night," Melody said half-jokingly. "I hope your sweater is okay."

"It left a little snag, but it's fine." Liz looked at the brace-let. "If you don't mind then, I'll wear it for a while."

"No, of course I don't mind. I think that's great."

Liz nodded and then glanced down the street. "I have to get back to The Bitery. Rose is helping out today, but I can't really leave her alone for too long. She burns the croissants and puts out a tip jar. We don't accept tips at The Bitery."

Melody sipped from her cup of coffee as she listened. "Thanks for this. I really needed it this morning."

"You're welcome. So are you staying overnight at the thrift store now?" Liz asked.

"No. I'll go back to my dad's tonight. I just couldn't deal with things yesterday. I needed to be alone."

"I understand." Liz shifted from one foot to the other, looking nervous. "Well . . . I'll see you later then?"

"Yeah." Melody watched Liz turn to go, feeling something opposite of grief and sorrow. She hadn't allowed herself to realize how much she'd missed her friend until now.

"You open?" a voice asked, grabbing Melody's attention.

Melody turned to the middle-aged woman with two kids in tow. "No. I'm, um, not open this morning."

"It's nine o'clock though," the woman said impatiently. "The hours say you're open at nine. I need some shoes for these two. Jo always helped me find exactly what I needed." The mom looked past Melody into the store. "It won't take long."

Melody glanced back for just a moment. Before she knew it, one of the kids ran past her.

"Chandler! Come back here! . . . Sorry!" The mom fol-lowed with the other kid trailing behind.

Melody was at a loss for what to do as she watched them run around the store. Finally, she flipped on the store lights so that the mother and kids didn't hurt themselves. Next thing she knew, another customer walked in. "Oh, I'm not open for business," she told the older man.

He didn't even acknowledge her. Instead, he went straight to the rack of men's clothing and started perusing.

After that, another man walked in. Then a woman.

"Okayyy," Melody said to herself. "I guess I am open." She headed to the back room of the thrift store long enough to freshen up. Then she stepped up to the counter where the mom was waiting with two pairs of shoes for her children.

"So you own the store now?" the mother asked, lying a worn wallet on the counter and pulling out cash.

"Temporarily. I inherited it," Melody explained.

"Jo was so amazing. When I was pregnant with Chandler, she placed a hand on my belly and said that he would be a force to be reckoned with." The mom laughed. "She wasn't wrong."

The rest of the morning was filled with customer after customer and story after story. Melody greeted and listened to them all. At noon, she finally flipped the sign to CLOSED. At least some of the store's stuff was sold, which would help a little with cleaning the place out like the real estate agent had suggested. Melody really needed to stop the donations though. Every time Melody stepped back there, the donation box was full.

Melody grabbed a piece of cardboard that she'd seen in the back room and a Sharpie and wrote: NO LONGER TAKING DONATIONS! She searched through the drawers until she found some masking tape and carried the sign out back, stopping in her tracks. Since the last time she'd stepped out, she'd received even more donations. The bin was now overflowing onto the pavement. She couldn't just leave the stuff out here to get rained on or ruined.

After taping the sign to the metal bin, Melody grabbed a few boxes and took them inside. At a glance, it was full of clothing, toys, and a small wooden jewelry box that caught Melody's eye. It looked like one she'd had as a child with a pop-up ballerina that twirled when the lid was open. Curious, she pulled it out and sat it on the cot in front of her.

Music played as she lifted the music box's lid. There was a ballerina lying flat that should have popped up, but it was broken. Maybe she could fix it with some superglue later. She was about to close the jewelry box when she noticed something silver wedged between the crevices of the velvety inner casings. She pried the material back with her index finger and shimmied out a thin charm shaped as a burst of fireworks.

Goose bumps fleshed on Melody's skin. What were the odds of finding such a charm the night after Jo's Celebration of Life? It hit too close to reality to be a coincidence, but Melody's rational brain thought that was the only explanation. It certainly wasn't the work of Jo or Alyssa behind the scenes.

Melody ran the tip of her finger over the smooth surface of the charm. The bracelet was with Liz right now, but when Melody got it back, she was going to attach this charm, she decided. Coincidence or not, it held meaning and it deserved a new home on one of the golden links.

Still feeling the goose bumps, Melody walked over to her purse and placed the charm into a tiny pocket for safe keeping. Then she grabbed her keys, locked up the store, and got into her car to drive back to her dad's. Her father was asleep in his recliner when she arrived. Quietly, she closed the front door behind her and tiptoed toward her bedroom.

"Melody?" his deep voice called. He'd never been one to call her Mel like her friends.

She stopped in her tracks and turned back, halfway down the hall. "Hi, Dad. I'm sorry if I woke you."

"It's okay. I was up late last night," he said. "I thought maybe you'd left town."

She looked down at her feet. "No. I went to Hidden Treasures. I didn't mean to worry you." She winced because he probably hadn't lost any sleep over where she was. Maybe he was just a night owl.

"It's fine. Are you . . . okay?" he asked, his words stopping and starting.

"I'm not sure," she said honestly.

"Is there anything I can do?"

The question took her off guard. "I don't think so."

There was a long silence.

"It was nice. Last night. Jo would have liked it," he finally said.

Melody had already realized that he was right. Jo would have liked it. She probably did like it from wherever she was watching from. Maybe from the Isle of Lost Things. "Yes. She would have."

"I think when I die, I want to go out the same way," her father said, surprising her.

Melody let out a startled laugh. Her father was dry. Humorless. Boring even. She would expect nothing less than a funeral with only piano music. No singing. No guitar. Definitely not drums. "You're kidding."

"Absolutely." He turned to look at her. He wasn't smiling exactly, but there was a subtle twinkle in his eyes. "I'm glad you're here. It's good to see you."

She shifted back and forth on her feet, currently in the strappy black sandals she'd slipped on yesterday before the celebration of life. Her feet ached to take them off. Her body ached to climb into her childhood bed. She couldn't quite return her father's sentiment—not yet—but she was working on it. "Thank you," she said instead. "That means a lot," she added, meaning it.

To: Bri Johnson
From: Liz Dawson

Subject: Change is coming

Bri,

Sharing a house with Rose has reminded me of why I couldn't wait to leave my parents' place when I was eighteen. She doesn't pick up her things or respect mine. And she's a night owl even though she knows I wake up early to open The Bitery.

I turned down the photography job for Missy Lyons' parents. I don't have transportation or a responsible person to cover the bakery. Saying no took a little piece of my soul though. I wanted to say yes. Really wanted to. I've been thinking, ever since Jo's letter at her celebration of life. She said something about not being afraid to follow your dreams. I know this sounds crazy, but I think she was talking directly to me. There are things I want to change about my life, but for that to happen, *I* need to change. I'm just not quite sure how. I guess deciding what I want is the first step. Scratch that, deciding what I don't want is first. I don't want to work at the bakery for the next thirty years. I don't want to spend my whole life on Seagull Street. I don't want to be afraid of everything. I want to chase my dreams like Jo did. I'm tired of letting my fear hold me back.

Stay tuned. Liz 2.0 is coming.

xx,

Liz

P.S. I'm coming to visit next week. It's not as easy with my parents in Ecuador. I'll find someone else to drive me—just not Rose because her license should be revoked.

CHAPTER EIGHT

LIZ

Liz's gaze flicked to the clock on the wall. It was four o'clock. Rose was an hour late. She was supposed to take over the counter after school so that Liz could leave early and snap some photographs. But it looked like that wouldn't be happening today, no thanks to Rose.

Just as Liz had resigned herself to closing the shop for the sixth night in a row, the front door to the bakery opened and Rose breezed in, wearing a tank top and the shortest pair of shorts Liz had ever seen.

Liz sucked in a breath. "We had an agreement. You have to follow Mom's rules. You can't dress like that."

Rose stopped walking and thumbed behind her. "Want me to leave? I can go home and chill while you finish up the day here."

Liz was sure her sister would love that. "No. You're working. I have a spare pair of shorts in the back room on the shelf. They should fit you. I'll wait while you change."

Rose's face contorted in disbelief. "You're not serious."

"Oh, I am. Hurry, please. I'd like to leave while there's still daylight outside."

Rose turned on her heel and headed toward the staff rest-room, returning a couple minutes later wearing a pair of stone-washed jean shorts with a longer hemline. "Happy now?"

"Much better. Call me if you need anything." Liz collected her oversized purse from under the counter and headed toward the front door. "And don't put a tip jar out this time. We don't collect tips here. Mom's rule."

Rose huffed. "Mom doesn't pay well enough *not* to collect tips."

Liz sucked in a breath. "She pays better than most part-time jobs around here. Especially ones that are willing to hire irresponsible sixteen-year-olds who are consistently late. No tip jar."

Rose rolled her eyes. "Fine. But I'm quitting just as soon as I find a better place to work," she called to Liz's back.

Liz didn't respond. She wanted to argue that Rose had to stay indefinitely because Liz had done her time working at their mom's bakery. Liz was ready to move on to other things. It was her turn to branch out. She didn't want to quit the bakery completely. Not yet at least. But she was ready to decrease her hours after her parents returned from Ecuador and start focusing on her own career in photography. It wouldn't be easy, but chasing her own dreams was long over-due. Jo's letter had opened her eyes to that.

Instead of getting into more battle of the wills with Rose, Liz walked out and breathed in the crisp air tinged with salt and sea. She got tired of breathing in cinnamon and spice all day. She stood there on the sidewalk for a long moment, letting the afternoon sun beat down on her skin, soaking in its warmth and trying to let the frustrations of her sister roll off her.

She had her camera looped around her neck. Removing the cap, she lifted it off her chest to snap a picture of the wil-low tree beside the shop, its long branches swaying in the slight breeze. These photos seemed to be what sold the best at the café. Everyone on the isle liked a memento of the downtown street. Liz's other photographs, of a seagull swooping in the sky or an especially stunning sunset from the bridge, also sold decently.

Since she'd turned down the photography job for the Lyons' family, her mind had been swirling on what steps to take in order to say yes next time. It would have to be once her parents were back. Since she didn't drive, she'd need to be willing to spend all her earnings on a Lyft ride to and from photography locations though. What was the point of that?

She sighed. Liz took a few more pictures and then glanced down the way at Hidden Treasures, and headed in that direction. She didn't necessarily want to see Melody, but Melody had mentioned passing the charm bracelet back and forth. Liz had been in possession of it since Friday night.

There'd never really been any rules established about how long one of the friends was supposed to keep the bracelet. Just until they did something crazy to earn their charm. Maybe it was a weak plan that would've fallen apart if they'd ever really gotten started with it. None of them had the money to buy frequent charms, although they likely could have gotten what they needed from Jo, who seemed to have everything in spades.

Liz reached the outside of Hidden Treasures, pulled the door open, and walked in. Instead of cinnamon and spice like the bakery's scent, she breathed in the distinct smell of old things. It wasn't necessarily a bad aroma. It kind of smelled like Liz's paternal grandmother's home. Full of antiques and stacks of books, knickknacks, and a little bit of dust which always seemed to lightly coat her grandmother's most cherished items no matter how often she cleaned.

Liz looked around, not seeing anyone behind the counter. "Melody?" she called as she headed down the aisles, noting that things were looking a lot more organized in here since

Melody had taken over. When Jo was alive, there were times when Liz couldn't even walk through the aisles without stepping over a pile of random stuff. "Melody?"

Melody appeared from a small room in the back where Jo had kept the donations she hadn't put out yet. "Liz." Melody seemed to pull in a breath. "This is a nice surprise."

"Well, you've come to see me at The Bitery, so I thought it was my turn to stop by your place. It's looking great in here." Liz let her gaze roam the racks and shelves of things. "You've really been working hard."

"I have." Melody's hair was pulled back today and she had a few pieces of lint floating in her blond locks.

Liz stepped closer and plucked them off.

"Thanks. I got a lot of the dust and all the cobwebs. And I've laundered a lot of the clothes. There's a washer and dryer in the back, which has come in handy because I can't seem to get people to stop donating."

"That's a good thing, isn't it?" Liz asked, noticing Melody's frustrated expression.

"Not when you're trying to clean out a store. I put out a sign to stop donations, twice actually, but the signs keep disappearing and the stuff keeps piling up." Melody shrugged, then she gestured at her outfit. "It worked to my benefit today though. These were just my size. What do you think?" She angled her body back and forth to show off what she had on.

"You're wearing secondhand clothes?" This was not typical Melody Palmer behavior. At least not the Mel she used to know. The Melody she remembered had only liked name-brand items.

Melody looked down at her indigo-colored jeans and striped, cotton shirt. "I've shopped a lot of thrift stores in Charlotte. I'm not as picky as I used to be, I guess. When you start paying for things yourself, your ideals shift."

Liz's gaze dutifully traveled down Melody's body. "Well, I love the look. There's just one thing missing."

Melody frowned as she looked back up at her friend. "What's that?"

Liz slipped the bracelet off her wrist, immediately missing the feel of it against her skin. There was something comforting about having the cool metal brushing over her forearm, reminding her of days long ago. "Here."

Melody didn't take it immediately. "But you've barely had your turn."

"It's okay. I think you need it more than me right now. Go ahead. Put it on."

Melody reached for the piece of jewelry and slipped it over her wrist, her eyes suddenly shiny. Liz would have thought Melody held no sentimental value to anything or anyone on the isle anymore, but maybe she was wrong about her old friend who stood before her now in used clothes and tears in her eyes.

Liz looked down at the bracelet as well. The friends forever charm seemed to catch the light, bringing a flood of emotions and memories to the surface. Alyssa had been so excited about giving the bracelet to their group of friends.

"We don't need a charm bracelet to bind us together," Bri had said warily at first. *"We're not going to drift apart. We're best friends."*

Liz could still see the unshakable grin on Alyssa's face. *"Friends forever,"* Alyssa had said, referencing the charm. *"The bracelet is just symbolic. And it'll be there to remind us that we have each other to lean on, in case we forget once we're out there in the world. And to remind us to keep doing things that make us feel alive."*

Now Liz's eyes were tearing up too.

"Hey, you okay?" Melody asked.

Liz nodded. "Yeah. It's just nice being here with you. Some part of me thought I would never see you again."

Melody visibly swallowed. "I'm sorry."

"It's okay. I mean, no, it's not okay. But, well, it's the past and there's no sense dwelling on things that can't change, right?" Even though Liz dwelled all the time. What she meant was that there was no point in holding a grudge. It did no one any good, least of all her.

A long, uncomfortable silence floated between them. Then Melody suddenly perked up.

"Hey, look at this." She walked over to grab her purse from behind the glass counter and reached inside, pulling out a tiny silver charm.

Liz leaned over to inspect it more closely. "A firework charm? Where did you find that?" she asked with a growing smile.

"It was donated the other day. Well, a jewelry box was donated and I found this tucked inside. I thought it should be added to the bracelet. What do you think?"

Liz laughed. "Yes, it definitely should be added. That is so bizarre."

"Right?"

Liz watched as Melody pried the metal circle of the charm open with her nails and attached it to one of the bracelet's loops.

"There." When she was done, Melody dangled her arm in the air proudly to show off the bracelet's addition.

"Perfect." Liz took a moment to admire the bracelet. Then she turned to look around the store, different and the same as when Jo had run it. "I know you have a big job with this place. What can I help you with?"

Melody shrugged. "Nothing that can be done in one afternoon. I met with Abigail Winslow on Friday. She said that if I wanted to get good market value on this place, I needed to clean it out completely."

Liz shouldn't be surprised that Melody was planning to sell. "I see. Well, I don't mind coming in and helping one day after work. We could go through these things and maybe catch up while we're at it." Liz couldn't believe she'd just said that. She was supposed to be guarding her heart, and instead she was suggesting a girls' night of sorts before Melody disappeared on her again.

"Really?"

"Yeah. I mean, I usually spend my nights being disrespected by my sister these days. And working at my computer."

"I'm glad you're still into photography. Taking pictures was always something you loved to do."

Liz had enjoyed taking photographs of her friends the most. Somewhere in the last decade, she'd run out of people to strike a pose for her and she'd started taking more scenic photos. "So do you want me to stop in one night after work?"

"I won't turn down help," Melody said. "I'll even bring wine."

"In that case, I'll bring some bites from the bakery. Something chocolatey." Liz caught herself smiling. *What am I doing?* She needed to be careful. Melody had been very clear that her intention was to leave Trove again and there was no indication that she'd return, at least not for another decade. And when Melody left, she was gone. From past experiences, Liz knew Mel didn't call or text.

A tiny voice in Liz's head argued that maybe this time they'd keep in touch though, if they reconnected while Melody was here. Perhaps they could message back and forth like Liz and Bri did on a near daily basis. And they could continue passing the bracelet between them. They could add charms the way they were supposed to, filling it up just like Alyssa had intended when they were teens.

"Hey, since you're here, let's pick out an outfit for you," Melody suggested. "I had such a good time shopping earlier. It's your turn. I've got to get rid of all this stuff anyway. You might as well take first pick of what you want."

"Really?" Liz glanced around the store. Now that Melody had cleaned up a little bit, the things were more enticing.

"Yeah. Let's pick out something fun for you."

Liz felt the pull of excitement. "Okay." She nibbled on her lower lip. "But I can't stay long. I don't like to ride my bike after it gets too late."

Melody waved a dismissive hand. "I can put the seat down and fit your bike in the back of my car. I'll drive you home. No need to rush things. We have all the time in the world."

Somehow, Liz doubted that.

An hour later, Liz felt ridiculous and amazing at the same time. She was carrying a bag full of clothes that Melody had picked out for her at Hidden Treasures. She felt a little giddy at the thought of wearing the clingy black dress that Melody had insisted was made for her. When was she ever going to wear a little black dress like that one? She'd also picked out leggings, tight jeans, and fitted tops—some with necklines that plunged lower than she was used to.

She unloaded her bike from the back of Melody's car and then waved as Melody reversed out of the driveway. Liz walked her bike into the garage first and then carried her bag of new-to-her clothes up the front porch. It was almost six o'clock. Rose would be closing The Bitery right about now. Then it was a ten-minute drive here. If Liz was smart, she'd hide these clothes before then because they were so cool that Rose very well might want to take them for herself.

That thought gave Liz another little thrill. Imagine *her* having something that Rose might actually find cool.

Liz dug around in her purse for her house keys, coming up empty-handed. *Oh, no.* Had she left them at the bakery? She groaned before heading over to the flowerpot next to the door. The pinwheel flowers were all half dead. They needed water ASAP. She'd get them water as soon as she was inside.

Liz lifted the pot to grab her hideaway key and frowned.

The key was missing. Of course it was. No doubt Rose had used it and forgotten to put it back.

On a heavy sigh, Liz grabbed a credit card from her wallet and dipped to pick the lock. As she slid the card into the crack of the door, a siren sounded behind her. Liz bolted upright and whirled to look at the cruiser pulling up to her curb. Then she let out a soft breath when she saw Matt step out.

"Breaking into your own house?" A slow grin spread through his dimpled cheeks as he headed up her driveway.

Liz ignored the bump in her heart rate. "I left my keys at The Bitery. And my spare key is missing."

"From under the flower pot? For someone who's so safety minded, that's not the best place to hide a key."

Liz held out her wrists. "Am I under arrest, Deputy Coffey?"

"You do appear to be breaking and entering." His eyes twinkled under streetlights that were starting to come on at dusk.

"Into my own house." She looked between him and her door. "Do you think you can help me get inside?"

He scratched the side of his cheek. "It might be easier if I just drive you up to The Bitery so you can grab the keys from Rose. I was planning on doing a drive-by in that direction anyway." He gestured toward his deputy cruiser. "Come on. I won't make you sit in the back with the criminals."

She looked beyond him to the road. "You have someone back there?"

His laugh brought her back to him. "Just teasing you." He didn't wait for her to agree. She guessed it was go with him or wait for her sister who may or may not show up in a timely matter.

Matt walked to the passenger side door first and opened it for her.

Little butterflies danced around inside her chest as she stepped past him and took her seat, waiting for him to appear in the driver's seat. As he cranked the engine, she gripped the side handle of the door.

Matt's gaze moved to her hand. "I'll drive slow," he said before pulling onto the road and heading toward The Bitery.

The problem with driving slow was that it meant Liz would have more time in a tight space with Matt. The way she felt about him unnerved her. He was handsome and nice. A gentleman. He made her laugh like it was the easiest thing in the world, when some days she didn't laugh at all if he didn't step up to her counter.

But then again, sometimes she also hadn't thought about the accident at all until the moment she saw him. And then her eyes connected with his and there it was. She couldn't separate him from the worst moments of her life.

Matt turned onto Seagull Street and pulled up to the curb in front of The Bitery.

"I'll be right back." Liz pushed the door open, stepped out, and dipped to peer through the passenger window at him.

His gaze was unwavering just like the rest of him. "I'll be right here."

As she turned, she wondered if he was watching her walk away. The thought that he might be usually made her nervous, but somehow it excited her a little bit right now. Who *was* she?

Rose looked up from the counter as the bell chimed over Liz's head, and her expression twisted from indifference to horror. "What are you doing here?"

Liz glanced over to a table full of teenagers. No doubt they were eating for free well past closing time. "Relax. I just need the house keys." Liz walked behind the counter, grabbed a set of keys, and slid the one for the house off. Then she headed back toward the exit.

"Wait. Did you just tell *me* to relax?"

Liz glanced over her shoulder. "Role reversal, huh?"

"You're not mad at me?" Rose asked. "For having friends over?"

"Has it interfered with your ability to serve the actual customers?"

Rose shook her head. "All the real customers left. But I served them perfectly fine when they were here."

Liz lifted a brow. "With a smile?"

Rose's lips curved into a full, beautiful smile. It was almost convincing.

"Good. Then no, I'm not going to yell. See you at home," Liz called behind her. She headed back to the car outside, her heart racing the closer she drew to Matt. She just wasn't sure which reason was to blame. The tiny crush she refused to admit, even to herself. Or the fact that he was her living, breathing reminder that sometimes, in the midst of the best moments of your life, everything crumbled to pieces.

"Got what you need?" he asked as she slid back into the passenger seat.

"Yep. All set." She clutched the door's handle again, holding it tightly as the car began to move. She took a breath and then another, startling when Matt unexpectedly reached out and touched her arm.

"Don't worry, Liz. I'll go slow."

To: Liz Dawson
From: Bri Johnson

Subject: YES!

Liz,

Firstly, and most importantly. You don't need to change a thing.
I love you exactly the way you are.

Secondly. I AM HERE FOR LIZ 2.0! Yes!

Thirdly, if you decrease your hours at The Bitery, tell your mom
I'll pick up the slack. Unless she doesn't want a convicted felon
working for her. I would completely understand if that's the
case. It won't be easy for me to find work once I'm out. I've already been forewarned. My best chance at employment is with
someone I know. At least I know my grandma won't let me be
homeless. If it were up to my parents, I probably would be. I'm
not being bitter or anything, just accepting what's true. I've
learned in my counseling sessions here that accepting the truth
is part of creating a realistic plan for when I get out. I have to do
that for my role in Ally's life too. I might not get legal guardian-
ship of my daughter right away. Or ever. Realistic expectations
will keep me grounded. Maybe keep that in mind when you're
dreaming up Liz 2.0.

B

Chapter Nine

MELODY

Melody hesitated on the text she'd typed out to Christopher. He'd told her she could call or text anytime for any reason. She didn't really like asking for help, especially from him, but she couldn't operate a power tool to save her life. And if she wanted to clean up this thrift store this week, she needed to call in reinforcements.

She pulled her lower lip between her teeth and nibbled softly. To text or not to text?

She re-read the text she'd drafted.

Melody: Hey Christopher! If you don't mind, I was wondering if you could help me hang some stuff at the shop sometime soon?

Was the exclamation point too much? Should she ask how he was doing first? Make small talk? They weren't friends exactly, so she didn't know why she would. She just needed a helping hand, that was all.

Melody read the text one more time and pushed SEND. Then she blew out a breath and busied herself by walking over to some shelves of shoes which ran right along a broken clothing rack that she needed help with. A pair of brown suede flats caught her eye. She placed them on the floor and kicked off her pair of yellow Keds. Then she stepped into someone's used shoes and audibly sighed. The brown suede flats looked almost new and hugged her soles like they were made just for her. That sounded like something Jo would have said. To think someone would bring their old shoes here and that fate would pair them up with their next perfect owner. That was such a Jo thing.

Melody's chest ached. She regretted the lost time between her and Jo, even though Jo would insist that wasting energy on regrets was like throwing money to the breeze. Jo had obviously loved this store. There was so much of her in the little details, like the items she chose to display in the glass case at the register—lockets, charm bracelets, and crystal knickknacks. The stool at the register had a worn candy apple-red seat that Melody imagined her great-aunt sitting on day in and day out as she welcomed her customers with that free spirit Melody remembered.

Alyssa used to say that when you loved something, a little piece of your heart and soul stayed with it. Like the charm bracelet. Alyssa thought wearing the bracelet would be like carrying a little piece of each friend around with her. Maybe a little piece of Jo's heart and soul was still in this store too, Melody thought, glancing around. If that was true, clearing out Hidden Treasures and turning it into something boring would kill off whatever essence of Jo hadn't been cast off in a firecracker.

Maybe, Melody thought, just maybe she could find a buyer who would keep the store as is. Then Jo would live on in some way and Melody's conscience would remain clear.

Her cell phone buzzed in her pocket, pulling her from her thoughts. She glanced at the caller ID and saw her business partner's name.

"Hi, Julie. How are you?" She leaned against the wall and held her cell phone to her ear.

"Hanging in there. How are you?" Julie asked in an upbeat tone.

"Good. Very good." It was an honest answer that surprised Melody even as it tumbled off her lips. She wasn't actually miserable here on Trove Isle like she'd thought she'd be. She was moving at a slower pace than she normally kept, stopping to admire the view, and catching up with people she hadn't allowed herself to think about in years. She was also catching up with herself, if that made sense.

"Great," Julie said. "Next question. You're still planning on returning this weekend, right?"

Melody had told Julie she'd be gone for two weeks, but she'd need longer if she took the real estate agent's advice and cleaned this place out. Selling the store as Hidden Treasures would be easier and allow Melody to get back to her normal life quicker. The only downside was that Melody wouldn't make as much profit.

Melody left the pair of Keds she was wearing on the shelf in place of the brown suede shoes she'd pulled off. "That's the still the plan," she told her partner.

Julie blew out an audible breath into the receiver. "What a relief! I was a little worried you were going to tell me that you'd decided to stay longer. Or worse."

"Worse?" Melody asked.

"Forever," Julie said on a laugh, as if that was a preposterous thought.

"You don't have to worry about that. Not happening." Melody continued walking through the store and collecting lint. "The plan is to leave on Sunday. The real estate agent can do the rest of the footwork to sell this place without me."

"Great plan. This is why you're a fantastic planner and why I need you back at Memory Lane Events ASAP."

Melody stopped walking and glanced at her reflection in the full-length mirror, inspecting the new-to-her shoes and wondering who had worn them before her. Maybe they were

Jo's. Pulling on something that had lived a life before her felt magical in some way, like she was inheriting some small essence of another person. Like she was literally and figuratively walking in someone else's shoes. Maybe they would lead her to her very best friend just like the black ballerina flats that Jo had given her in her childhood had.

"Don't forget, we have the Dunkin's baby shower next week," Julie reminded her.

In truth, Julie could handle an event on that scale alone, but Melody loved baby showers. She'd done the planning for this one from afar, ordering all the decorations and organizing the color schemes. She'd come up with three fun games to play at the event as well. Guessing candy bar types that were smashed into diapers was a special request from the client, who was laid-back and loved to laugh. Melody had also thought up a new activity where guests got to take the baby's last name and come up with a word or phrase for each letter to make an acrostic. Melody had even made an example for all the guests.

Baby Name: DUNKIN
D: Diapers.
U: Undress and redress.
N: Newborn.
K: Kick!
I: Itsy-bitsy, teeny tiny.
N: Nighty night, sweet baby.

Melody was looking forward to all the fun. Half the time her events didn't feel like work once she was in the midst of them and laughing alongside everyone else. At least with her more carefree clientele. The more particular, controlling ones, however, not so much.

"I'll call you once I'm back in town," Melody promised.

"Sounds good. Enjoy the rest of your time at home."

The word "home" reverberated through her. Melody let it bounce around in her brain, pondering whether to accept or reject it. This was her home though. Home wasn't always a purely sweet place. It was bitter too. And Trove Isle was as bittersweet a place as there was for her. "Thanks. I will."

Melody said goodbye and disconnected the call. Then she stood there a moment, admiring the charm bracelet on her wrist. A couple charms had a sparkly sheen to them that she hadn't noticed before. Maybe it was the lighting of the thrift store that made them appear that way.

A tap on her door drew her attention. Christopher waved when she looked his way. *That was fast.* She hurried over and unlocked the door. "Hi. Wow, I wasn't expecting you to drop in so quickly. I just texted you ten minutes ago."

"School is out for the day. I was just leaving campus when I got your message. Your text said you needed a hand?" He looked past her for a moment. From his perspective, it probably looked like her entire store needed a hand.

"Um, yeah. There're just a few things I can't manage on my own."

"No problem." He held up a toolbox. "I'm always prepared. Like I told you at Jo's Celebration of Life, my mom has a never-ending to-do list for me. I never leave home without these."

Melody was relieved. "Thank you." She gestured across the store. "There's a wobbly clothing rack in the back that needs securing to the wall. I don't want it to fall on someone."

"That wouldn't be good," Christopher agreed with a nice smile. So nice that she let her gaze lower to his lips to study them for an awkward moment.

She yanked her gaze back up to his eyes. He was Alyssa's former crush. Melody shouldn't be admiring his nice smile. Or his equally nice eyes, which were a light-colored blue like the sky on a clear day. She nervously tucked a strand of hair behind her ear, needing something to do with her hands.

"Yeah, the last thing I need is a lawsuit while I'm trying to sell this place."

"Right." Christopher tipped his head toward the back of the store. "Lead the way."

"Sure." Melody led him through a narrow path sandwiched with items for sale and gestured at the rack. "I swear, all I did was pull a hanger off and it fell down."

"You sure you weren't doing pull-ups on it?" He eyed her playfully as he placed his toolbox on the floor and hunched over it to locate a tiny screw.

"I wasn't doing pull-ups, but I wouldn't put it past one of the customers." Melody leaned against the wall and crossed her arms, ignoring the little bump in her pulse. "There is never a dull moment in this place. It's kind of like Jo herself. Every time I turn around, I find something interesting. Did you know she kept a box of crystals below the cash register?"

Christopher chuckled as he glanced up. "Actually, I did know that. She gave me one once. Told me to carry it around in my pocket for a month to reset my energy."

"Your energy? Why?" Melody was equal parts intrigued and comforted by all the stories of her great-aunt. She'd missed so much time with Jo, taking for granted that Jo would be here waiting for her when she made her way back to Trove. *If* she made her way back.

"My fiancée had just left town." Christopher straightened to a standing position with his drill and the screw in hand. He put the rack into place on the wall and lined up his drill bit.

"I didn't know you were engaged," Melody said.

Christopher swept his gaze sideward, his blue eyes meeting hers. No, the color was more like the river on a clear day, deeper somehow. "How could you?"

Ouch. "Who was she? Your fiancée."

Christopher cleared his throat. "A teacher at the high

school where I work. She taught math there for a while. We dated and fell hard-and-fast for each other," Christopher explained. Then he stopped talking and drilled for a long moment, securing the rack back into place.

So many questions popped into Melody's brain as she watched him. For some reason, she'd assumed Christopher had never gotten serious with anyone. Otherwise, he'd be married with kids like everyone else they'd gone to school with. He wasn't a band geek anymore though. On the contrary, he was cool. And kind of hot, which she felt weird even thinking.

Christopher lowered his drill and looked around. "Anything else you need me to do in here? While I have my tools."

"You sure you don't mind?"

His gaze swept back to meet hers. "I get daily to-do lists from my mom, remember? I'm a handy guy to have on speed dial."

Melody hedged. "Well, if you're sure, there is a lightbulb that's burned-out in the laundry room. I have a ladder and a bulb. It's a small ladder so I can't quite reach the fixture. Short people problems," she said on a nervous laugh.

"Lucky for you, I'm tall." He headed in that direction and proceeded to change the lightbulb, fix the leaky faucet in the bathroom, and sand out a splintered bookshelf.

"Where did she go? Your ex?" Melody finally asked as he put his equipment away. A good hour had passed since they'd spoken of the woman in Christopher's past, but Melody was still thinking about it. Instead of pushing it out of her head, more and more questions floated around.

Christopher expelled a breath. "Small town life isn't for everyone. She didn't love it here and couldn't see herself spending the rest of her life in Trove Isle." He shrugged as if it was no big deal, but Melody suspected his heart had been broken by this math teacher. "She wanted to move to a big city."

"And you didn't?"

Christopher gave his head a hard shake. "Not a chance. This is my home. My family is here. My friends. My students. My hometown is a huge part of who I am. If she didn't love Trove Isle, she didn't love me. Not fully."

"So you're here to stay," Melody said.

"I am," he confirmed with a nod.

"I love how you included your students. You must be a great teacher."

"Not as good as Mr. Lopez."

Melody laughed unexpectedly. "Mr. Lopez was so boring. Is he still . . . ?"

Christopher folded up the small ladder as they talked, carrying it to its spot between the washer and dryer set. "He may be in his eighties, but Trove High's former senior English teacher is more active than most people half his age. Boring or not, he's doing well."

"That's good news."

Christopher looked around the store. "I can tell you've been working in here. It looks good."

"Thanks. Abigail Winslow said this place will sell better if it's empty, but every time I open the door, a customer walks in. And donations are still being piled up out back even though I have a sign that says we're no longer collecting. Or I had one. It's MIA." Melody grimaced. "Call me crazy, but part of me suspects Jo."

Christopher offered a humorous look. "Sounds like your aunt is scheming beyond the grave."

"Except she doesn't have a grave," Melody said with a head shake. "I still can't get over the whole fireworks thing."

Christopher laughed, the sound low and easy. "Jo was one of a kind, that's for sure. She really loved this place." He glanced around.

"So I hear." Melody looked around too. "And honestly, it's growing on me. I can see why this store was so special to

her." Her gaze locked with his and her breath hitched just
slightly. "It's kind of fun seeing what shows up in the donation box. One man's junk . . ."

"Is another man's treasure." Christopher's eyes seemed to
dance as he completed her sentence. Then he pulled out his
cell phone as if he'd felt it buzz in his pocket. After checking
the screen, he shoved it back into his jeans and looked up.
"My mom's to-do list for today just came in," he said. "I better head that way."

"Well, I'm right next door. Until Sunday, at least. You can
always call me if there's something you think I can do for
her." Melody had always loved Mrs. West when she was
growing up. Mrs. West loved to bake fresh cookies and offer
them to her and Alyssa on the regular. Melody's own mother
hadn't even baked them cookies. "I guess I owe you a favor
for coming to the store today," Melody said.

Christopher rubbed his jaw where there was a light five
o'clock shadow filling in. "You mean that?"

Melody had a feeling she might regret her offer. "Of course.
What do you need?"

"Since my mom is a shut-in, she thrives on company. If
you've got time . . ." He trailed off. "It would mean a lot to
her, to me, if you'd stop in just to say hello. She doesn't get a
lot of visitors other than me, and I'm not the best conversa-
tionalist."

"I don't know. I think you're pretty okay company."
Melody didn't want to like Christopher, but he was such a
nice guy that she couldn't help herself. She also didn't want
to find herself attracted to him. "I'll try to stop in and see
your mom. I'd like that."

"Thanks. She'll like it too." He shrugged. "Who knows?
Maybe you and I can catch up again before you leave town."

Was he flirting? "Yeah. I'd like to hear more about why
you turned down my sister's promposal in high school," she

said. The statement was meant to build back up the invisible wall that Christopher seemed to keep breaking down. "You can list the reasons, and I can tell you how wrong you were." Christopher didn't even blink. "Sounds like a date."

The next day, Melody walked into The Bitery and ordered a cinnamon twist and coffee.

"I'll be over there as soon as the crowd dies down," Liz promised. Her smile had come a lot easier today than it had earlier in the week. She was tolerating having Melody around, which was progress.

"No problem." Melody had her laptop with her and was hoping to start planning a retirement party that Julie had emailed her about overnight. The retiree being celebrated had worked thirty years at a law firm and she wanted a huge celebration this fall.

Melody sat down at a table along the wall, opened her laptop, and tapped her thoughts onto the blank document. By the time Liz came over with their breakfasts, Melody was buzzing with all the possibilities for the event. She couldn't wait to share them with her partner.

"Wow, you look like you're working hard." Liz plopped down across from her.

Melody closed her laptop and placed it back in its leather carrying case. Then she pulled her coffee closer and took a deep whiff of the brew. "I swear this stuff smells as good as it tastes."

Liz grinned over her own cup of coffee. Her gaze flicked to Melody's laptop. "So, what are you working on?"

"A retirement party I've been contracted for. I woke up early and my brain has been buzzing with ideas ever since."

Liz picked at her muffin bite. "You're planning events *and* cleaning out the thrift store?"

"Not exactly. I know it's what Abigail suggested, but I

have a feeling Jo would haunt me until I die if I emptied out her beloved thrift store. In fact, she's already haunting me a little."

Liz furrowed her brow.

Melody waved a hand. "Don't worry. I'm not seeing apparitions or anything. I've just realized exactly how much she loved that place. It feels like a little piece of her is still there. So," she sucked in a breath, "I've decided to clean the store up and find a buyer who wants to operate it as is."

"Someone who wants to run it as a thrift store?" Liz asked, surprise lifting her brow.

Melody nodded. "Yep. I know that's a tall order, especially since I'm leaving on Sunday. The store wouldn't remain open all the time, but there's nothing to say I can't travel back and forth between here and Charlotte and keep it open on the weekends. At least until it's sold. Maybe I won't get as much money off the store, but if Jo's vision is preserved, that's more important, right?"

Liz grinned back at her. "Wow."

"What?" Melody asked. "You're giving me a strange look."

"I'm not looking at you any specific way," Liz argued.

"You are. You're looking at me like I just rescued a puppy or something."

"I'm just proud of you, that's all," Liz said. "And Jo would be too. Hidden Treasures is special and important to the people in town. Whoever takes it over *should* keep it intact. I'm glad you made that decision." Liz nibbled more on her muffin bite and washed it down with coffee. "Well, if you need a photographer to take pictures of the store," she pointed at her own chest, "I'm your woman."

"Noted." It was too bad Liz didn't live closer to Memory Lane Events. There was always a need for a photographer, and Melody would be able to network with Liz.

"Speaking of friends," Liz said, "I'm going to see Bri on Friday. My mom has someone who works days at the bakery when I'm not able to. I contacted her because Rose is in school during the week."

Melody had a feeling she knew where this was heading and she wanted to get up out of this seat and bolt. Liz was the forgiving type. She could never stay mad at anyone for long. But Bri was the type who held a grudge. Her attitude in high school had been legendary, and no one had wanted to land on her bad side. Least of all Melody who avoided conflict when at all possible.

Liz reached for Melody's hand. "Come with me. Or actually"—she chewed her bottom lip for a moment—"maybe you could take me. I hate public transportation."

"You should start driving again then," Melody said, avoiding the question and diverting the pressure just a little bit while she thought of a good excuse to turn Liz down.

Liz pointed at the charm bracelet on Melody's wrist. The metal charms were shiny under the shop's lighting. "You made a promise along with the rest of us. Friends forever. I know you're the one who lost your sister but Alyssa would have wanted you to keep that promise. She wouldn't have wanted you to disappear."

"I know," Melody said quietly. Alyssa would have been adamant that they all remained close, regardless of any circumstances. "I wish I could go back and do things differently."

"You can't change the past. You can change what you do right now though. You're not heading out until Sunday, right?"

Melody nodded. "That's the plan."

"Great. So, go with me to the prison."

Melody looked from Liz to the bracelet, knowing that her friend was right. Liz and Bri had remained close despite the distance between them. Melody was the one who'd messed up the whole pact.

She wanted to say no. She wanted to find any excuse to

avoid this situation. But another part of her wanted to see Bri. She missed her old friend. Being home had made her realize just how much. "Okay. I guess my answer is yes."

Liz looked pleased. "Bri is going to be so thrilled. I can't wait to tell her."

"You talk to her?" Melody asked. "By phone?"

"Not by phone. We send e-messages most days. The prison has some special network that inmates, friends, and family can use. It's a lot like email. Sometimes I think we're closer now than we ever were. Distance doesn't have to be a wedge." Liz gave Melody a meaningful look that Melody thought she understood. When she left on Sunday, it didn't have to be goodbye. And Melody didn't intend for it to be this time. She was glad to have reconnected with Liz. It felt good.

Melody reached for the bracelet on her wrist and slipped it off, dangling it between them. "It's your turn."

Liz's gaze dropped. "You can keep it longer if you want."

Melody shook her head. "It's kind of fun passing it back and forth, and it means we get to see each other more often."

"I agree." Liz held out her arm and allowed Melody to slip it over her fingers to rest on her tiny wrist. She looked at the bracelet for a moment.

Melody leaned in to look at it more closely as well. "Have you noticed that some of the charms have a sparkly finish to them?"

Liz nodded quickly. "I have. They catch the light at different angles."

"Have you thought that maybe some charms didn't shimmer at first and then they did?" Melody asked, feeling a little foolish for even thinking that was possible.

Liz's confused expression told her she hadn't noticed any such thing. Maybe that was just Jo's influence edging in on Melody. And Alyssa's. The longer Melody was here, the more she was reminded of her great-aunt and her sister, and how everything was magical to both of them. Nothing was ordinary. "Never mind," Melody said with a slight head shake.

Liz pushed back from the table. "I need to get back to the kitchen. The bites in the oven will be done in about a minute, and if they're left too long, they burn. Making bites is an art form. It's my mom's art, but I'll have to make another batch if they're not the perfect blend of soft and firm." She stood. "Don't worry about Bri. She'll be thrilled to see you. She hasn't changed all that much from the friend you remember."

"Good to hear," Melody said, even though that's *exactly* what she was worried about.

When Melody had gotten home, instead of retreating to her room down the hall like she'd been doing since arriving in Trove Isle, she walked into the kitchen and got busy cooking a small feast.

In part, it was to distract her mind from the knowledge that she'd agreed to drive up to the women's state prison this Friday to see Bri. The elaborate meal was also an attempt at connecting with her father. She'd avoided meaningful conversation long enough. Jo's letter had been playing through her mind since Friday night. Melody could almost hear the words in Jo's lilting voice.

Don't be too stubborn to forgive. But never forget because forgetting can turn you into a fool. True forgiving though, that lifts you to a level that few achieve. Accept each other and love while you can. Because life is fleeting, and sometimes the things that are lost can't be found again.

Melody's father wasn't the same man who used to sing and dance and be silly in attempts to make his daughters laugh. For some reason, he had loved to sing "I Heard It Through the Grapevine" when he was cooking. Melody missed the man he'd been so much that it hurt to even entertain the brief memories. He was as gone as her mom and sister, and she was left with the lifeless shell he'd been since their passing. Even so, Melody wanted to honor Jo's advice and at least try to have some sort of connection while she was here.

Just in case things got awkward at the table, Melody had a mental script prepared for tonight's meal. As she'd prepared the beans, rice, and grilled chicken—the best she could find in the freezer and pantry—she'd come up with a dozen questions to get the conversation moving.

When had Aunt Jo purchased the thrift store?

How had Jo afforded it?

Did it turn a profit?

Why had Jo left it to Melody?

Then there were other questions that Melody had come up with, mostly about what her father had been doing with his time over the last few years. Melody should know the answers, but she didn't. She'd called far too seldom. She'd run away from everything in life—and everyone. Could her father really blame her for being so standoffish though? After that fight they'd had the last night she was in Trove Isle?

The smoke detector started shrieking just about the time her father walked through the front door. Melody grabbed a dish towel and waved it frantically under the detector's vents. "Shh-shh!"

"Melody?" Her father headed into the kitchen. "What's all this?" he asked, standing rooted in the entryway for a moment as he observed Melody's frantic waving of the dish cloth at the plume of smoke coming from one of the dishes.

"Dinner," she said over the alarm. "Unless I burn your house down first."

He grabbed a towel from a nearby cabinet and together they fanned the smoke until the detectors abruptly stopped shrieking. "You cooked for me?" he finally asked.

"Well, I've got to eat and so do you," she told him with a

nervous shrug. "We might as well do it together, right?" To this point, dinners had been a box of S'mores Pop Tarts that she'd packed in her suitcase before arriving on the isle.

Her father gave her a long look and then assessed the food on the range, lifting his face as he seemed to sniff the air. "It smells delicious."

"Well, don't expect too much. I don't cook very often. I usually get take-out or eat cereal." She didn't explain that it was most often the latter because she couldn't afford the drive-through more than once or twice a week.

Her father looked serious. "A cereal dinner isn't healthy."

"Well, tonight we have a nutritious meal." She forced a smile that felt a little nervous and wobbly. She hoped he didn't notice. "Are you hungry? It's ready when you are."

"I'm starving actually." He tipped his head to gesture down the hall. "I'll just go wash up and be right out."

Nervous butterflies fluttered around in her chest as she waited. She had a lot of questions for her father, but some part of her also just wanted to spend time with him. She was getting used to being okay with the awkwardness and the silence that happened with people you were supposed to know, but didn't anymore.

She prepared them both a dish and brought it to the table. She didn't know his tastes or if he even liked ketchup. But ketchup covered many culinary sins, which she'd likely committed with this meal so she placed it in the center of the table just in case.

A minute later, her father stepped back into the kitchen and looked at the dinner. "This is nice."

She placed a pitcher of sweet tea down and then pulled out her chair. They both sat for a quiet moment.

"I'll say grace," her father finally said, surprising her. Melody's mother had never placed a morsel of food in her mouth without first blessing the food. Once her mother had died though, saying grace had gone to the wayside.

"Oh, okay." Melody watched her father close his eyes. As he began to speak, she did the same.

"Dear Lord, thank you for this food. And for Melody returning home. Amen."

They both opened their eyes and looked at each other. Apparently, he was a man of few words with God too. Good to know it wasn't just her.

He picked up his fork and stabbed at a few beans. Melody did the same. Since he wasn't initiating any conversation, she brought up her mental list of questions.

"So, I wanted to ask you about Jo."

He lifted his gaze as he forked some beans into his mouth. "What about her?"

"Well, where did the store come from? I mean, why did she open it? When?" That was technically three questions all in one, but Melody was eager for answers.

Her father picked up his fork and knife. He expertly cut his chicken and forked a piece into his mouth, chewing quietly and for so long that Melody wondered if he wasn't going to respond. "Jo was a hoarder of sorts. Sometimes people take their dysfunction and make it functional. I suppose that's what she did."

Melody could relate. After her mother died, she'd gotten wrapped up in planning her days. Everything was structured, organized, and in its place. Somehow that was comforting to her. Planning events had evolved naturally from that coping mechanism. "So, she just decided to open a store? Where did the money come from?"

"Mr. Lyme, I suppose." A small grin curved through her father's weathered cheeks. "As you already know, they had a thing, the two of them. Neither was interested in marriage. At least not in this life. I guess, according to her letter, she's open to it in the afterlife." He chuckled dryly. "But Mr. Lyme supported her and she did the same for him." He paused his eating for a moment and looked at Melody. "Your aunt had a special talent. That's what everyone in the town liked to say. When a person walked into her thrift store, she could tell exactly what they were looking for. They might not even know themselves, but Jo knew." He chuckled softly and took another bite of food.

Then he continued to talk without the rest of Melody's slew of questions. He ate and talked while Melody listened, fascinated by every word.

Finally, he paused. Melody wondered if he'd said that much to anyone in an entire year.

"Aunt Jo had something of mine in her thrift store," she said. "The charm bracelet that I shared with my friends. It was lost." Melody withheld mentioning the accident. She and her father had a good thing going tonight, and she didn't want to ruin it. "I'm not sure why she had it or where it came from."

Her father looked at her with interest. "Well, that was part of Jo's talent, I guess. She found things and put them where they were supposed to be. She was waiting for you to return. She always knew you would. I guess you were one of those lost things in her mind. And bringing you back here for the store was her way of putting you right back where she thought you belonged."

Melody wanted to say she didn't belong here anymore, but she didn't want to see the pain those words might inflict on her father's face. And part of her didn't fully believe that was true now. Something inside her, long buried, was coming back to life. She was breathing a little deeper and thinking a little more clearly. "Jo added charms to our bracelet. I guess she was the one who added them, at least." Melody shrugged. "They're random charms that don't seem to mean anything."

Her father picked up his glass of tea, sipping quietly. "Everything Jo did had meaning. Your aunt was a bit . . ."— he hesitated—"peculiar. But she was a good woman. The last time I walked into Hidden Treasures, Jo pointed me to a rack of ties." He lifted the one he was wearing off his chest. "She said this tie would bring me good luck."

Melody assessed the emerald-green neckwear with yellow pinstripes. "Why?"

He dropped the tie back to his chest. "That's just what she told me. It never brought me any good fortune that I could tell though. Until tonight. Perhaps I should wear this tie more often."

Melody chewed her food quietly, feeling the burn of tears behind her eyes. There were a lot of unsaid things in her father's words. If she was listening, he wasn't just talking about wearing the tie more often. He was talking about spending time with her. Maybe she wasn't the daughter he barely tolerated anymore. Perhaps he missed her as much as she hadn't realized she'd missed him. "It's a nice tie," she said quietly. "You *should* wear it more often."

To: Bri Johnson
From: Liz Dawson

Subject: Liz Dawson Upgrades

Bri,

Project Liz 2.0:

Step one: I'm going back to see Dr. Mayer. It's been awhile, and therapy always helped me feel calmer. I don't know why I ever stopped. Life got busy, I guess, and I got tired of talking myself in circles. Nothing seemed to change, but that's mostly because I wasn't fully doing the work. I know that. I want to try again. I want to try harder.

Step two: I've decided that I'm going to talk to my mom when she returns from Ecuador. I don't need to quit the bakery, but maybe I can cut my hours and focus on photography jobs. So, to prepare, I'm going to print some business cards. That's a start. Psst . . . Of course my mom will hire you after I leave. You're family, Bri.

Step three: I can't believe I'm going to say this, and it might take a while to make it happen, but I'm going to get my driver's license. I need to drive in order to take on jobs. Just the thought is making me feel a little breathless. See step one.

xx,

Liz

CHAPTER TEN

LIZ

Liz fidgeted with the bracelet on her wrist and tried not to look as nervous as she felt.

She looked up at Dr. Mayer who sat behind a huge oak desk. Why was his desk so large? Weren't therapists supposed to keep their offices comfortable, with recliners and couches? And why was Dr. Mayer so frustratingly calm? It wasn't normal to be afraid of everything, but was it normal to be as chill and relaxed as the man who sat before her?

Liz took deep, steady breaths. Once upon a time, she used to enjoy coming to see Dr. Mayer. Perhaps she was just having an off day. Or maybe she'd gotten out of the habit of slowing down to discuss the worries and fears that ran circles around her brain.

"Liz?" Dr. Mayer asked.

She blinked and met his gaze, realizing that she hadn't really said anything so far. "I'm sorry. Did you ask a question?"

Dr. Mayer smiled warmly. "I asked what brought you in to see me. It's been a while."

Liz's fingers danced across the charms, trying to determine which was which without looking down at them. The friendship heart. The car. The muffin. The dress. She rolled her lips together. "My parents are in Ecuador for the summer visiting my mom's family. My grandmother had a ministroke, but it sounds like she's doing better."

"That's good news," Dr. Mayer said.

"Yes, it's a relief. Since Rose is in school, my parents left her with me while they're away."

Dr. Mayer's eyebrows rose with interest. He was a dramatic-looking man. All his features were dark against pale, surprisingly smooth-looking skin. "How's that going?"

"Good," Liz said. "I mean, she's immature and hard to handle."

"How old is she now?" Dr. Mayer asked.

"Sixteen. She's driving, and she somehow got her eyebrow pierced without adult permission. My parents won't be happy. Especially my mom."

Dr. Mayer smiled again. "That's a teen's primary goal in life. To make their parents uncomfortable."

"And their older sisters." Liz rubbed the pads of her fingers across the car charm, feeling the rough texture of the glittery finish. "My friend Melody has also come home for a couple weeks. I haven't seen her in nine years."

Recognition crossed Dr. Mayer's face. He had been working with Liz on and off most of her life. Even before the wreck, she'd struggled with anxiety. It had worsened afterward, of course. Dr. Mayer knew everything Liz had been through.

Liz held out her arm. "This is the charm bracelet that was lost in the accident. I've told you about it before."

Dr. Mayer looked at her wrist from behind his glasses. "Yes, I recall. Your friend had it all this time?"

"No. Her great-aunt did. It's a long story, but . . ." Liz lowered her arm back to her lap. "I don't know. The fact that it's been found feels like a sign of some sort."

A little divot formed between the psychologist's eyes. "What kind of sign?"

"I don't know. Maybe it's a sign that Bri, Melody, and I aren't as alone as we thought. That we're still connected."

"Is that what you want?" Dr. Mayer was always asking questions. At one time, Liz had kind of thought it was his job to give her answers, but he never did. She usually found her own answers as she talked to him. He was just very skilled at asking all the right questions that led her to the answers she had difficulty finding on her own.

Liz's fingers moved to the next charm. It was a tiny house. She pressed the point of its roof into the pad of her index. "I think so. Maybe it's a silly fantasy, but I want my friends back. I want us to be the way we once were."

"You know that can't happen though, Liz," Dr. Mayer said.

She nodded, even though she didn't know that at all. Why couldn't it happen? Yes, things had changed, but the one thing that remained was that she, Bri, and Melody were all bonded. Maybe the one thing that tore them apart was also the thing that kept them connected. Maybe the tragedy didn't have to break them. Perhaps it made them stronger when they came together.

Liz talked for another fifteen minutes. Then she stood. "Thank you, Dr. Mayer. This session has been helpful."

"Good. I'm glad," he said. "We'll continue this conversation next week?"

"I'm already on your schedule. See you then," Liz said with a smile.

After leaving Dr. Mayer's office, Liz strolled down the small downtown area where she worked. She wasn't quite ready to go home. She had so much on her mind, a result of all Dr. Mayer's probing questions. They led her to answers she was already well-aware of about herself. She was stagnant in her emotions, her relationships, and her life. Fear was holding her underwater even if she had convinced herself otherwise. The fact that she made it through most days without a panic attack didn't exactly equal progress. It just meant she'd shut herself off enough to deal with what came her way.

Progress was stepping outside the safe confines of her little box—because if she waited for all the fear to go away, she'd never get better.

Liz stopped at the storefront window of The Book Whore and looked at the display. A huge sign was front and center announcing a sale and a complimentary smile. That, in and of itself, made Liz perk up. She decided to go inside.

"Lizzie, is that you?" Danette called from somewhere in the back.

"Hi, Danette. Yes, it's me. I was just out for a walk and thought I'd see if you had any good books for me. I'm going to see Bri tomorrow. I might want to take her one."

Danette seemed to shake from the inside out as she approached. Her head, her arms, her legs all appeared to have a mind of their own, but somehow the parts of her body worked together to get the bookstore owner where she was going. Liz didn't think Danette had any serious neurological disorder. Danette had explained her condition once, saying her nerves were frayed from a life lived haphazardly. At least Danette had lived her life.

Liz swallowed past the dryness of her throat, a result of too much talking in Dr. Mayer's office. She needed a glass of water. Or wine.

When Danette was standing a couple feet away, she straightened her eyeglasses and looked at Liz. "You okay, Lizzie?"

Liz took a deep breath, begging her emotions to get in line. "I think so. I'm just . . ." She paused for a minute. "Have you ever felt like you were sleepwalking through life, Danette?

Then something happens that stirs you awake? Some part of you just wants to go back to sleep, but you can't." Liz's eyes welled with tears that she was determined to keep at bay.

"You're describing my first marriage." Danette chuckled, making her head bob even more. "We married and then I was stuck in this loveless relationship. I didn't want to file for divorce because it felt like too much trouble. All the days blurred together for years."

"What happened?" Liz wasn't sure she had even known that the bookstore owner had ever been married.

"Well, when you're in a state like that, something big has to take place. To shake you." She gave Liz a pointed look. "Or wake you. For me, it was a man. He walked into my store one day. I've never had such a physical reaction to anyone in my life. I felt like every cell inside me lit up. We talked and found out that we had a lot in common. Then he came back every day, pretending to need a new book."

"He liked you too," Liz said, finding herself fascinated by Danette's story.

"Yes, he did." Suddenly Danette's body seemed to calm. The shakiness relaxed just a bit. "There was a moment when I knew I loved him. But, in order to be with him, I had to make the changes I'd been too afraid to before. He was the motivation I needed." She looked at Liz. "So what has finally woken you up? Are you in love?"

Liz folded her arms over her chest and shook her head quickly, the quick motion making her head spin. "No, nothing like that. Just . . . Mel came home. I guess she brought back a lot of memories . . . which reminded me of the reason I've been sleeping through life."

Danette poked her glasses higher on her nose, seeming to scrutinize Liz the way Dr. Mayer had earlier. "If you're looking for a book to help you find the secret to life, it's not here."

Liz already knew that. She'd scoured these shelves and

every self-help title there was. "What about a book of poetry? Bri really loves poems these days."

"Oh, yeah? Well, I do have a small section of that." Danette gestured for Liz to follow. She walked down a narrow
aisle and pointed to the second to bottom shelf. "I can't bend
the way I used to."

Liz squatted low to browse the selection there. As she did,
the charm bracelet slid off her wrist. When she reached to
pick it up from the floor, her hand knocked a book off the
shelf. It landed right at her feet. The cover was a purple color
that stood out among the rest. Liz reached for the book and
read the title. *Dream Weaver: Poems about Following One's
Passion.* Liz wanted this book for herself, not that she read
much poetry, but maybe she'd start. She pulled another book
off the shelf to bring to Bri and stood. "These will do."

"I know Bri appreciates you visiting her," Danette said.
"You're a good friend."

Liz looked down for a moment. *Was* she a good friend? A
good friend might have gone to see Melody in these lost years
of their friendship, instead of feeling sorry for herself and
blaming Melody for leaving. A good friend would have seen
that other people were hurting just as much as she was. Liz
always did the easy thing. The thing that didn't scare her. She'd
stopped driving, so going where Melody was had seemed like
an impossibility. She had called and emailed though. For a
while at least.

Liz looked up at Danette, realization settling over her.
"You're not married. What happened to the guy you fell in
love with?"

Danette's body started to shake again. "Oh, he was just
the impetus I needed to put me on a different track, I guess I
thought I was filing for divorce because of this man, but I
was really filing for myself. This fantasy guy and I had a
whirlwind romance, and then one day he disappeared. I went
looking for him, of course."

"Did you find him?"

"I did," Danette said. "He was married with two kids. He lived in a house with a white picket fence." Her eyes grew shiny for a second. "I guess he was looking for an escape as much as I was."

"I'm so sorry, Danette," Liz whispered.

"Don't be. I stopped sleepwalking through life that summer. I'll always be grateful to him for waking me up. That's worth a broken heart, if you ask me." She turned and walked to the register to ring Liz up. Danette reached for Liz's debit card and swiped it with impressive accuracy considering her condition. "Tell Bri I said hello, will you?" she asked, looking up with a sweet smile.

"I will. She'll love the book of poetry. Thank you for your help. Your bagel is on the house in the morning."

"Oh, happy day," Danette called as Liz headed for the door.

Seeing Dr. Mayer had helped considerably, but in some ways, coming inside this bookstore and talking to Danette had helped even more. As Liz stepped out onto Seagull Street, she stood there a moment and let the sun shine on her skin. Something sparkled below her gaze that made her look down at her wrist. There was a book-shaped charm on the bracelet. Liz blinked. That wasn't there before, was it? Had Melody added it without Liz realizing?

Rose honked and slid their mother's car haphazardly to the curb in front of Liz. The driver's side window was rolled down and Rose poked her head out to look at Liz. "Want a ride?"

Liz stood frozen on the sidewalk for a moment. She thought she was waking up, but maybe she was still dreaming. "You're offering me a ride? Without me asking for one?"

Rose rolled her eyes. "Do you want a ride or not?" she huffed. "I know you had that appointment this afternoon. I saw your calendar. I don't know." She jerked her thin shoulders in a shrug. "I thought you might be tired."

Liz's sister was actually considering her feelings? This was progress. Maybe spending a little time together in their parents' absence would be good for them after all. "Wait. If we're both here right now, who is running The Bitery?"

"I called that temp Mom uses sometimes," Rose said.

"What? Without asking me first?" Liz shook her head.

"You would have said no."

Liz didn't argue. She just headed toward the car. Instead of going to the passenger side, however, she walked around to the driver's side and dipped to talk to Rose. She was tired of letting her fears stop her. If she could drive, she could accept the bigger photography gigs she'd been offered from time to time. She could start pulling in more money from her hobby and chase her dreams like Jo had advised in her final letter. "Can you teach me to drive?"

Rose let her sunglasses slide halfway down her nose and gave Liz an "are-you-crazy" look.

"I'm serious," Liz said. "But I need it to be now before I lose my courage. Please."

Rose's pierced brow arched high on her forehead. "I can't teach you. I just learned to drive myself."

"I have my license. I know what to do." It was true although Liz wasn't sure she actually remembered how to drive. "I need moral support more than anything."

"From me?" Rose's expression twisted further.

Yeah, this probably isn't the best idea. "Slide over," Liz demanded.

Rose hesitated, but then she lifted her body over the center console and into the passenger seat. "Don't kill us, okay?" As soon as she said the words, her eyes widened. "I didn't mean it that way."

Liz ignored the comment, opened the door, and slid into

the driver's seat. She curled her fingers around the steering wheel and began to shake like Danette from the bookstore.

Rose began to speak, but Liz cut her off by holding up a hand.

"Shh." Liz closed her eyes, forcing deep breaths. The more she breathed, the more breathless she felt. Her heart raced so fast that she felt lightheaded. She reached for the charm bracelet on her wrist, hoping it would center her. "I can do this. I can do this," she chanted under her breath.

Rose made a squeaky noise beside her.

"Shh . . . I can do this." Liz finally opened her eyes and looked out the front windshield as the nausea clenched her stomach. "I *can't* do this." Pushing open the driver's side door, she bent forward and vomited on the pavement below.

To: Liz Dawson
From: Bri Johnson

Subject: Friends are good therapy

Liz,

I'm glad you're going back to Dr. Mayer. I think sometimes it helps to talk to someone. I've seen a counselor at the prison a few times. I'm sure Dr. Mayer is a better counselor than the one I saw. I swear that woman was making her grocery list while I poured my heart out to her.

Anyway, you can vent to me too, you know. Always. I can't promise that I'll know what to say. But I'll listen and I won't judge you. That counts for something, right?

Ally sends me messages almost daily. She's having a great time with her father in California. That shouldn't make me upset, but I cry after reading every email (when no one is looking). I want her to have a great time with *me*. I want to be the one to take her places like Sunrise Park and the movie theater. I want to take my daughter on spa dates and get our nails done together. I want to be a good mom.

I want to be a good friend too. I know you need me. I'll be there soon.

B

Chapter Eleven

MELODY

"I'm nervous." The following morning, Melody glanced over at Liz in the passenger seat next to her as she pulled into the parking lot of the women's prison. It had taken thirty minutes to drive there, and the entire way Melody's stomach had been tying itself into tiny knots.

Liz placed a hand on Melody's forearm. "Don't be. You two were as close as sisters once. We all were. Sisters fight, but they never stop loving each other. That's a fact."

Melody offered a smile in Liz's direction. Liz hadn't been the easiest to win over since Melody had been back. Even now, Melody could tell Liz was guarded. The Liz of old wasn't afraid to share her thoughts and feelings. She was an open book. The one sitting next to Melody right now was much more reserved.

Liz turned her attention to the large brick building blocked off by a barbed wire fence in front of them. "It could've been any one of us that ended up in there," she said quietly. "We all handled things in our own way. Bri just had so many injuries and the pain medication they put her on . . . well, it wasn't good."

"I knew Bri was here because she was caught with drugs. I

just wasn't sure of the details," Melody said as she navigated through the parking lot. Melody trailed off because she didn't really need to admit to Liz that she was an awful friend who hadn't kept in touch. Liz already knew that.

"Yeah," Liz said. "Bri struggled after the accident. We all did."

Melody parked the car and pulled the key from the ignition, noticing that her hands were shaking. "I guess I just thought it was none of my business. That I didn't need to know the details of what put her behind bars. But now that I'm about to walk inside and sit across from her, I feel like I should know all of it before I go in." Melody looked over and met Liz's eyes, hoping she would understand.

Liz gave her a small smile. It was getting warmer every time she offered it in Melody's direction. The two of them were becoming closer. Just like friends again. "Okay. Well, Bri was in a lot of pain after her injuries—not only physical, but emotional too. She got to the point where she was desperate to numb it, I guess. Then, a couple years after our accident, she met this guy—Lazer."

"Lazer?" Melody repeated.

Liz rolled her eyes. "He was no good. He had a record and he had all the wrong connections. He helped Bri get more pain medication when her doctor decided it was time she start weaning off."

"He was Bri's boyfriend?" As the question rolled off her tongue, Melody gasped and pulled a hand to her mouth. "Is he . . . Ally's father?"

Liz's entire expression twisted in disgust. "Ew! No. Ally's father is a decent guy from what I can tell. He was a one-night stand for Bri. She met him at a failed attempt at rehab—the first time. From what I understand, Daren has stayed clean."

Melody relaxed a little. "That's good."

Liz nodded. "Anyway, Bri flunked out of rehab and went

back to Lazer. In order to get the pain meds, Lazer started forcing her to be his seller for other stuff. She didn't want to, but an addict will often do whatever it takes in order to get their needs met. Bri swears she never tried any of the other stuff. She was caught once and got off easy. The second time she was arrested, the judge was less forgiving. Bri was sentenced to four years."

Melody swallowed. "Wow. Thanks for telling me. I should have already known the facts."

Liz reached across the console and squeezed her hand. The touch was brief, but welcome. "Have you ever been inside a prison before?"

Melody shook her head, looking up at the building off to their right. "All I know of prisons is based on half a season of *Orange Is the New Black*."

"Then it's a good thing you have me." Liz unbuckled her seatbelt and started to shift around, gathering her things. Melody did the same. Then they stepped out of the car and walked up to the gate where a guard was standing out front. After flashing their IDs, they were let through for further inspection before finally being allowed to meet up with Bri at a picnic table outside.

Bri was already waiting in the visiting area for them. She had long, dark beautiful curls just like she'd had in high school. Instead of wearing her hair down past her shoulders though, it was pulled back in a ponytail.

"Hey, stranger," Bri said with a warm smile that caught Melody off guard. That was not the greeting she'd expected. Not that she'd known exactly what to expect. Maybe a knock against the forehead. She would have deserved it. "I'd get up and hug you, but that's frowned on around here," Bri said, almost teasingly. "A place that discourages hugs. Can you imagine?"

"She wouldn't last a day here," Melody said, pointing at Liz as they took a seat across from Bri at the picnic table.

Liz offered a reassuring smile. "This is true."

Melody fidgeted with her hands below the table. Whereas Liz had always been an open book, Melody had kept hidden any outward signs of her emotion, especially the negative ones. She'd pushed them down and run from them when they'd threatened to consume her. You could only run so far for so long though. At some point, you had to face things head-on.

Melody looked at Bri, took a breath, and put her shaking hands on the table in front of her. "I'm really sorry that I haven't visited you sooner, Bri," she said, still bracing herself for the Bri of old to tear into her and tell her what a horrible person and friend she was. Bri had never been one to pull punches. The night Melody had run away after Melody's mom died, Bri hadn't rushed to give Melody a hug when she'd found her. Instead, Melody had been scared Bri was going to fight her at first.

"You scared me to death!" Bri yelled, anger flaring her cheeks a dark-red color. "I thought you were dead."

"Well I'm not dead. Just my mom." Melody just wanted to be alone. She wanted to disappear.

"If you ever scare us like this again, you're going to wish you were dead because I might beat the crap out of you."

The way she'd said it that night made Melody wonder if she was telling the truth. Bri could be a little scary. She definitely intimidated people when they got in her way.

The Bri sitting across the picnic table right now, however, just shrugged. "I understand."

"You do?" Melody said, surprised.

Bri shared an amused look with Liz. "Well, okay, not really. But Alyssa was your sister so I have no idea what you've been going through. I know it was more than the rest of us though."

Melody lowered her gaze for a moment. Alyssa's name still gave her heart a jolt. They had been true sisters, but Liz was right in saying that she, Liz, and Bri were sisters as well. She hadn't realized how much she'd missed them until returning to the isle.

Melody swallowed hard and looked back up to Bri, who seemed relaxed in her pale-blue jumpsuit. "So, how do you like it here?" It was a stupid question. She knew it as soon as the words had left her mouth, but her nerves had gotten to her. "I'm sorry. That was rude. I didn't mean anything by that question."

Bri cracked a grin. "There's the Melody I remember. You always said the funniest, most inappropriate things that made us all laugh. Do you remember?" she asked Liz.

"I definitely do." Liz smiled as well.

Bri pointed a finger across the table at Liz. "Remember when Melody came to my grandfather's funeral two days after Christmas. And she asked my grandma if she had a nice holiday?"

Liz put a hand over her mouth, muffling the small giggles that erupted. "It wasn't funny."

"But it really was," Bri argued.

Melody listened as the two exchanged stories about her for the next few minutes. Stories that she hadn't thought about in years.

"Do you remember when Melody went through that phase where she was going to be a nun?" Bri asked Liz, barely containing her laughter.

Liz snorted. "What was that even about?"

"Kevin Bailey broke my heart, that's what." Melody rolled her eyes as memories of her seventh-grade year came to mind. "First heartbreaks are brutal, okay? I decided I never wanted to experience one again."

Bri snickered. "You started wearing these long, boring skirts."

"And remember how she cut those awful bangs?" Liz added. "What do bangs have to do with being a nun?"

Melody raised a hand. "I'm right here, you guys." Not that she was offended by the conversation. Instead, it almost felt like she was being re-introduced to herself. Yes, she'd always run from things. She'd shied away from conflict and pain. But she'd run toward fun with just as much determination. She'd run toward fun with these very ladies. They had been her pack, and ultimately, they were the ones who made her realize she didn't want to hide in a convent for the rest of her life. They were the ones who encouraged her to put herself out there and get her heart broken, time and time again. Melody had made acquaintances that resembled friendships in Charlotte, but she'd never found people who knew her the way her Trove friends did.

"I like it well enough here," Bri told her finally, going back to the question. "The wardrobe and the food aren't the best, but . . ." She lifted a shoulder. "I have a few friends that I enjoy hanging out with and a job in the library. I'm making the best of the situation that I've gotten myself into."

Melody nodded as she listened. "That's good."

"So how is life beyond the isle?" Bri leaned forward and propped her elbows on the picnic table. If Melody didn't know better, she wouldn't believe that the woman in front of her was serving time for a crime. She looked relaxed. Happy even. "You're the only one who made it past the bridge. Being locked in prison doesn't count."

"It's . . . well, it's okay," Melody said. The truth was, though, life beyond Trove was lonely. It was surviving, but not living.

"Better than a prison cell?" Bri grinned. Then her gaze fell on Melody's arm and her lips parted. "Is that what I think it is?" She reached out to touch the bracelet, hesitating as if it might bite her.

Melody stretched out her arm on the table. "It's the charm bracelet. I found it in Jo's thrift store."

Bri looked up. "No joke?"

"Liz and I have been passing it back and forth every time we see each other." Melody pulled it off her wrist and slid it across the picnic table toward Bri. "I know you can't have it in here, but you can put it on while we visit. It was meant to be shared, right?"

Bri looked unsure. It took a moment, but then she reached for the bracelet, admiring it first before sliding it over her hand. "I don't understand. How did Jo get it?"

"We don't know." Melody shrugged. "How did Jo get most of the things she had?"

"I could tell you a few ways, but," Bri grimaced, "you'd probably rather not know."

"Dumpster diving. Mr. Lyme told me." Melody suppressed a grin. "Anyway, I think she was waiting for me to come back so that she could give it to me. And since I never returned on my own accord, she gave me a reason by willing me the thrift store."

Bri cracked a smile. "You don't even like used clothes. It's ironic for you to own a store full of old things."

Melody was surprised that Bri remembered that about her. "I'll have you know this outfit is from the shop. Secondhand things have grown on me. But not enough to operate a thrift store for a living. That's why I'm selling it. I'm heading back to my real life on Sunday," Melody said without thinking.

Bri's smile faded and she shared another look with Liz. "I see."

Melody shook her head, guilt swirling in the pit of her stomach. She was so tired of disappointing people. When she was young, it was her job to care for Alyssa, which she'd failed miserably at, even before the accident. Maybe she'd been a glutton for punishment going into her chosen career because, while most were happy, there was always one client who could never be satisfied. "What I mean is, I have events planned and clients who are depending on me."

"Yeah, you wouldn't want to let them down." Bri slipped

the bracelet off and passed it back to Melody. She looked away, her gaze falling somewhere behind them in the courtyard's distance.

"But I'll come back to visit, of course," Melody said, wanting to keep the mood of this visit friendly. "Now that we've found our charm bracelet, I have to, right? So that we can keep passing it between us."

Bri looked at her again. "Our friendship has nothing to do with a charm bracelet, Mel. With or without it, you should have come back."

Melody swallowed. There was the Bri of old. The one who wasn't afraid of a little confrontation. And somewhere inside of Melody, she felt the Melody of old, who was exactly the opposite. Who fled in the face of a fight. "I know. And I'm sorry." What else could she say?

Bri looked at her, long and hard. "Okay, then."

"Okay?" Melody asked, not quite understanding.

"Yeah. You and me, we're good. But if you ever hurt Liz again, we won't be. Because Liz is my best friend, and I don't let anyone hurt her. Not even my other best friend."

To: Bri Johnson
From: Liz Dawson

Subject: Confessions of a Wannabe Brave Girl

Bri,

I'm in the car and trying not to hyperventilate as I send this from my iPhone. It was good to see you just now. I am impressed with how you just handled Melody. I don't know what I was expecting, but you were firm, yet friendly. You were welcoming, yet honest. Frankly, you were amazing. Why am I surprised though? You always are.

Also, there's something I didn't tell you. I asked Rose to support me while I attempted to drive the other day. Before you get too excited, it didn't work out. I threw up before I even cranked the engine. Rose had a field day with that. Now she keeps brown paper bags handy in case I want to hyperventilate or vomit. It's supposed to be a joke, but I'm always halfway tempted to reach for one.

I want to be brave. I want to be bold and fearless. I want to be more like you. It was so nice to see you today. I miss you already.

xx,

Liz

Chapter Twelve

LIZ

Liz couldn't relax in the passenger seat no matter how hard she tried. It didn't matter who was driving. She closed her eyes and took a deep breath, holding it for ten and then exhaling. It was just another trick in her toolbox of self-calming strategies. Then she grabbed her phone and tapped the screen in quick succession.

After a couple of minutes, Melody looked over and asked, "Who are you texting?"

"Eyes on the road," Liz practically snapped.

"Okay. I know."

"Sorry. I'm used to riding with Rose these days. She's still new at this whole driving thing." Liz blew out a breath and forced herself to relax as much as possible.

Melody kept two hands on the wheel along with both eyes on the road. She drove the speed limit, but it was only a couple weeks ago that she'd swerved into Liz's car.

"I'm not texting. I'm sending Bri an email through the prison's system."

Melody glanced over again. "An email? But we just saw her."

"I know." Liz hit SEND and shoved her phone back into

her purse. "This is what we do." Liz saw a smile curve along Melody's face.

"What did you just tell her?" Melody asked.

"That it was nice to see her. And I confessed that I tried to drive yesterday."

Melody looked over again. "You did?"

"Eyes," Liz warned.

"Right. Are you going to try again? With driving."

"Yeah. I mean, that's the plan. If I want to be a professional photographer, I need to be able to drive myself to the bookings, right?"

"Presumably, yeah. You could have asked me, you know," Melody said, looking over again.

Liz had to restrain from ordering her to face forward. Melody probably would have been a better teacher than Rose. "You're leaving Sunday. And I don't think one lesson would have been sufficient."

"I'm not leaving forever though. I'll be back."

Liz wanted to believe that was true. Only time would tell though.

"But since I am leaving, we should totally have a little fun tonight," Melody suggested.

"Fun?" Liz's shoulders tensed again.

"Yeah. It was nice to see Bri, of course, but it was a prison. I wouldn't exactly call that a good time."

Strangely enough, Liz had always enjoyed going to visit Bri. It used to be surreal, seeing women in uniform blue jumpsuits and knowing they weren't allowed to leave. Now, Liz didn't think twice. It was Bri's reality. "Okay, what do you want to do for fun?"

"Well, we should go out on the town. What is there to do for nightlife on the isle these days?"

Liz wasn't sure what to say. "I don't usually go out at night. Night driving is a lot riskier than day driving."

Melody halfway rolled her eyes as she glanced over. She returned her eyes to the road before Liz could say anything.

Liz took a breath, reminding herself that she was still in her twenties. She should act like it once in a while. "Oliver's has dancing and music. It's also within walking distance of my house if we drink."

Melody beat a palm against the steering wheel. "Yes! Perfect. We'll definitely have drinks. A girls' night with dancing and drinks is just what the doctor ordered for both of us. Who knows. Maybe Matt will be there. You like him, right?"

Liz whipped her head to the side, a burn crawling through her cheeks. "What? No. We're just friends."

"You sure? I thought I sensed something between you two after our little wreck the other day."

"You sensed nothing more than a mutual respect for each other."

"I see." Melody nodded. "Then who are you dating? Anyone?"

"No." Liz shook her head, shifting restlessly in her seat.

"Why not? Melody asked.

Liz was growing increasingly uncomfortable with the conversation. "Nosy much?"

"Yes." Melody nodded. "By nature. And out of concern. I want to make sure you're okay. I know I haven't always been here for you, but I want to know what's going on in your life."

Liz sighed, watching the world pass by through the passenger window. "Well, I'm not much of a dater. I have a panic anxiety disorder."

Melody was quiet for a moment. "Yes, I know. And?"

"And it's not exactly easy to be in a relationship with PAD, okay? I've dated in the past and one episode of mine typically sends a guy running. They're gone so quick they can barely mutter a goodbye. It's embarrassing, really."

"Those guys are jerks then. Not all of them will act like that, and you can't spend your life being afraid that they will."

The hypocrisy in Melody's tone was almost comical. "Well, I can't spend it running away either, can I?" Liz asked.

Melody drew back. "Hey, we're talking about you, not me. And you're changing the subject."

Liz grabbed hold of the side door. She needed to hold onto something. "It's not like I have a choice of whether I live in fear. I just do. It's just there. And it won't go away, no matter what I do or who I date."

Melody reached over, her voice lowering, her teasing gone. "I'm sorry. Have you talked to someone?"

"Two hands on the wheel," Liz ordered, trying not to let her emotions escape. She did her best to keep a tight rein on them.

Melody pulled her hand back to the steering wheel, quiet for a moment.

"Of course I've spoken to someone," Liz said quietly. "I've been in and out of therapy for anxiety since I was eighteen. I'm on medication, of course. I've meditated and tried yoga. It might help a tiny bit, but it doesn't fix it. It doesn't fix *me*. This is just who I am now."

The word *now* felt heavy. *Now* that Alyssa was gone. *Now* that we've all grown up and gone in separate directions. *Now* that life was different and would never be the same again. Liz had always struggled with anxiety, even when they were in elementary school, but *now* it was different.

They grew quiet until Melody pulled into Liz's driveway.

"Okay," Liz said, looking over.

Melody turned to her and lifted a brow. "Okay?"

"I'm agreeing to a girls' night. But no guys. We go out together, we come home together."

Melody's grin was back in full force. "I'm not much of a dater either, to tell the truth. I've got commitment issues."

Liz laughed. "Some things never change."

"But sometimes things do," Melody said.

Liz heard the serious note in Melody's voice. She was right. Things did change. People changed. One thing that remained true, however, was this bond between them. There was a trauma bond, yes, but they were bonded before the accident. They were soulmates, not in a romantic sense. Soulmates in the sense that friends could click from the first hello and feel like they'd known one another all their lives. "Thanks for going with me today," Liz said.

"Thanks for making me."

Liz stepped out of the car and waved as she walked inside her home and headed straight to the fridge. She pulled out the orange juice and poured herself a glass half full. After drinking it all, she lifted the mail off the counter and thumbed through bills, pausing on a postcard from Ecuador. The front showed a picture of a large crater lake with the words LAGUNA QUILOTOA at the bottom. Liz paused to admire the beauty of the picture, wishing that she was there. She couldn't even drive a car though. Getting on a plane and leaving the country was out of the question. Not that her parents had invited her on this trip.

Liz quickly turned it over and read her mom's handwriting.

Hello girls!

Mami is doing so much better, and your father and I are having a great time here. It feels so good to be in my family's homeland. Long overdue. We miss you both, of course, but we're sure you're taking care of each other. This summer will be a great bonding time for you both!

Your dad and I can't wait to hear about all the adventures you're having. Mami and the rest of the family send their love. They want you to come with us

next time—because, yes, there will be more visits. This
trip has felt like coming home to me in so many ways.
My heart is with my daughters, but a piece of it is also
here in Ecuador.
  Love,
  Mom

Liz sighed, allowing herself to miss her parents for a beat. Then she hurried about to prepare for her girls' night with Melody. She couldn't remember the last time she'd had one of these. Probably not since before she was old enough to drink.

An hour later, she headed into the kitchen and started to prepare a cup of tea when she was startled by the sound of her front door opening and slamming shut. She was still getting used to the idea that someone else had a key to her house. She'd lived alone for so long that she jumped a little at the sound of her doorknob turning.

Rose walked in and gave Liz a once-over. "What are you wearing?"

Liz looked down at her outfit as well, feeling slightly uncomfortable. She felt good too though. "I'm having a girls' night with Melody. It's our last chance before she heads back to Charlotte on Sunday. Will you be okay here on your own?" Liz asked, suddenly worried.

Rose smirked as she tilted her head to one side. "Who says I'm staying here by myself?"

Liz felt that familiar ping of anxiety in her chest. "Where are you going?"

Rose didn't respond. Instead, she continued to assess Liz's attire. "I like this look on you. But you need a little . . ." She unfolded her arms and stepped closer to Liz, reaching up to mess with Liz's hair.

"Hey!" Liz swatted Rose's hand away too late. "What are you doing?"

"Fixing your hair." Rose reached up again and pulled out the pins that Liz had neatly tucked on the side of her head. Then she rustled Liz's hair before nodding with a satisfied look. "Will he be there?" Rose lifted her expertly tweezed brows. Liz had never gotten her eyebrows done. She thought lying on a table while someone ripped hair off her face would be pretty anxiety-inducing.

"Will who be there?" Liz asked.

Rose folded her arms again. "Oh, come on. It's so obvious. You have a huge thing for Deputy Coffey. And he sometimes plays music at Oliver's on Friday nights."

"I do not have a thing for him," Liz countered although her cheeks felt flushed.

"You do too."

"Do not."

"Yeah, you do."

Liz took a breath, realizing that she and Rose were regressing back to childhood when they'd briefly lived in the same house together and squabbled like toddlers. "And how do you know who plays at the bar? You're not old enough to go to Oliver's."

Rose shrugged, but she didn't answer. Rose wasn't old enough to get a piercing on her own either, but she'd found a way.

"Just tell me where you're going. I'm responsible for you while Mom and Dad are away." Turning, Liz headed into the kitchen to grab a bite to eat. She was tired of verbally sparring with her sister.

"I'm not going anywhere. I'm staying here. Devin is coming over." Rose stepped up to the kitchen bar.

"Devin's still a girl?" Liz clarified.

Rose rolled her eyes. "We're having a girls' night, same as you."

Liz rolled her lips together. "Except my girls' night is strictly friends. No romance."

Rose's brows dived inward. "So is mine. Devin and I aren't into one another. We're friends, duh."

Liz held up her hands. "Sorry. Just clarifying." She reached for a banana from the basket on the counter and unpeeled it. "A girls' night sounds like fun." A night where Liz wouldn't have to leave the house sounded preferable to one that had her riding shotgun in a car after dark. She had to admit there was some tiny part of her that was excited at the idea that Matt might see her in her new clothes.

"So, this Melody person—she's an old friend of yours?" Rose asked.

Liz took a bite of her banana. "Yeah. And look." She held out her arm. "She found the old bracelet we used to share."

Rose stepped over to take a closer look at the bracelet. "That's pretty cool." For once, her tone wasn't sarcastic.

Liz put her banana down and turned the bracelet on her wrist, showing off the few charms that dangled from the links. "Alyssa gave it to us."

"Alyssa is the one who died?"

Liz swallowed past a rush of pain. Even after all this time, it was still hard to imagine that one of her best friends was gone. Rose had been a small child when everything went down. Too young to understand the gravity of the situation. "You remind me of her."

Rose's brow furrowed as she looked up. "Me?"

"Alyssa was a force to be reckoned with. If anyone told her no, she was more determined to do whatever her mind was set to. When she was a freshman in high school, she tried for the lead in the school play. Everyone told her to go out for a small role because the leads always went to seniors. She didn't care. She auditioned as if the main part was already hers."

"Did she get it?" Rose asked.

"Oh, yeah. Alyssa could do anything she set her mind to.

She was fearless, unlike me." Liz let her arm drop back to her side.

"You don't give yourself enough credit. You're not so bad," Rose said.

Liz let out a weak laugh. "I guess that's supposed to be a compliment."

"I mean, you were pretty brave to take me on for the summer."

"Not that I really had a choice in the matter. Mom and Dad were going and you weren't."

The corner of Rose's mouth quirked. "You could have said no. I'd have had to stay with Grandma Sarah though."

The thought made Liz cringe. "You would have been the death of Grandma Sarah. But you're not so bad either."

"That's kind of an insult coming from you." Rose's tone was teasing and almost warm.

Liz laughed out loud. "Well, it was supposed to be a compliment. You're not the easiest roommate, but I think we're finding our groove. Maybe?"

"I don't know. Your rules kind of suck," Rose muttered. "And you're a pain in the butt."

"You're a bigger pain in mine. You've driven me to drink tonight after all."

Rose cocked her head. "I'll come with you if you buy me a Long Island Iced Tea. I'll use my fake ID to get in."

Liz hoped Rose was only joking, but grilling her would ruin what was turning out to be a nice, sisterly moment. "As if."

"Just joking. I don't have an ID. Some of my friends do though."

A prickle of worry niggled in Liz's chest. "Is Devin one of those friends?"

Rose rolled her eyes. "Stop worrying, okay? It's so annoying. I'm behaving and tonight you're going out to relax and stop being so uptight."

Liz's jaw dropped momentarily. "I thought we were making up here."

"Yeah, but all the niceness was a little too much for my comfort level." Rose winked. "You look great. Go have fun, find a guy, and screw his brains out."

"Rose!"

"And before you ask. No, I'm not doing that either. You'll be happy to know that Devin and I are eating popcorn and watching sappy movies on TV tonight. No alcohol and no romance. We're going to plan for prom."

"Prom?" Liz's breath stowed away in her chest. "You're going to prom?" Liz tried to take a breath. How could her parents leave her here to deal with Rose's prom?

Rose looked apologetic. "Devin turned down Jace. We might go stag. Maybe. But maybe not. I don't know. Prom is kind of stupid, if you ask me."

Liz tried not to freak out. She sucked in a breath and held it. Then she looked down at her outfit. Prom was a worry that could wait until tomorrow. "Are you sure I look okay?"

"You look like you robbed my closet," Rose said, waiting for Liz to look at her again. "In a good way."

To: Bri Johnson
From: Melody Palmer

Subject: Guess Who?

Bri,

It's Melody. I know Liz writes to you daily. I hope it's not too late for me to be a better friend. I'm not one to send email and certainly not every day, but I want to keep in touch. Sometimes, the longer you stay away or the longer you keep unsaid things inside, the harder it is. But once you cross that line or say those things, it's suddenly easy.

The point is, I won't stay away for too long. I won't keep from telling you and Liz that you're the best friends I could have asked for. The fact that you both tolerate me now, even after the way I've acted, is the mark of true friendship. Did I thank you for not kicking me under the picnic table during our visit? If I didn't, I should have. My shin thanks you and so do I.

Now I'm off to have a girls' night with Liz. Don't worry. I'll take good care of her.

Melody

CHAPTER THIRTEEN

MELODY

The music was loud and the conversation around them was even louder. Melody thought Liz's smile looked a little too nervous and uncomfortable, and for a moment, Melody wondered if this was a good idea after all.

A waitress stepped up to their table and Melody ordered a Lemon Lime Margarita.

"And for you?" the waitress asked, turning to Liz.

Liz's eyes were wide behind her glasses. Was she going to have a panic attack here at the tavern? Her skin looked splotchy and red. "The same," Liz finally said, her voice a higher octave than normal.

"Hey?" Melody tapped a hand on the table's surface to gain her attention. "Are you okay? Do you want to leave?"

Liz shook her head quickly. "No. It's just, crowds make me a little anxious. And being out after dark makes me jittery too." She looked around, seeming to assess the crowd. "I'll calm down. Promise." She took a deep breath and exhaled as she returned her gaze to Melody's.

"Here." Melody pulled off the charm bracelet and slid it across the table. "Put this on."

Liz hesitated. "It's not magic, Melody."

"Well, it found its way back to us after all these years. It's something in the way of magic. Put it on."

Liz dutifully reached for the bracelet and slid it over her wrist, looking down at it for a long moment. Melody looked at it too, admiring the way the charms sparkled under the tavern's ambient lighting. Then the waitress brought them their drinks.

Melody pulled hers to her. "Okay, here's the plan. Drink every last drop. I'll do the same. Then we're going to dance. If you're not relaxed after one spin on the dance floor, we'll leave. A girls' night can be had anywhere."

Liz looked surprised and also a bit relieved. "I like that plan." She pulled her drink to her, pursing her lips around the straw that protruded out of the pale-green liquid, and started slurping. An hour later, she'd finished off several drinks and was swaying on the dance floor and laughing hysterically at something Melody had said.

Melody was going to have to carry Liz home if she wasn't careful. Liz was petite, but Melody had already had two drinks herself and was feeling a little tipsy as well. The bartender was heavy on the liquor and light on the mix tonight.

"We need a new plan for how we're going to get home," Melody told Liz, leaning in as they danced. "I don't think I can drive after that last margarita. It was stronger than I expected."

Melody expected that Liz would look worried. Instead, she laughed. That's how Melody knew for certain they were both plastered.

"We'll call Rose," Liz suggested.

"Now I know you're wasted," Melody said, making Liz laugh even harder. *What was in those drinks?*

Liz headed off the dance floor and Melody followed, feel-

ing like her body was one step behind her brain. She didn't
drink hard liquor very often. Maybe that was it. "We need
fresh air," Liz called behind her. She held up her cell phone.
"And I'll call Rose."

They stepped outside and the cool air hit Melody's warm
cheeks. Melody watched as Liz tapped her phone's screen
and held it to her ear.

It rang until Melody was certain that Rose wasn't going to
answer. Then Melody heard the faint sound of Rose's voice
on the other line.

"Rose," Liz slurred. "I need your h-help," she hiccupped.

Melody watched, imagining Rose's protests on the other
line.

"Melody and I are stranded on our girls' night. Can you
come get us at the tavern? We're in the parking lot." Liz listened for a beat and then she shook her head. "We're too
flimsy to walk."

Melody grinned. "You mean tipsy. She told us to walk?"

Liz ignored Melody and continued to talk to Rose. "Okay.
Yes. We'll be in the parking lot waiting for you. Bye." Liz dis-
connected the call and shoved her phone back in her purse.
"She's coming to get us."

"That's very nice of her," Melody said sarcastically. She
looked around for somewhere to sit, gathering that it might
be a long wait. She didn't expect that Rose was going to rush
out of whatever she was doing. She sighed and sat on a cement parking block.

Liz blew out a breath as she sat beside her. She moved
slowly and seemed to be off-kilter.

"You okay?" Melody asked, glancing over.

Liz nodded. "Yeah. I'm fine. Better than fine."

There was a slight tremble to her words though that had
Melody taking a closer look. Liz's mouth was moving from

one side to the other as if she was bottling in thoughts or emotions. She'd been giggly inside the tavern, but maybe the cool air had sobered her.

"What are you thinking about?" Melody asked.

Liz shrugged and looked down at the pavement. "Tonight was fun. Today was fun. It's nice to have you back."

"And that makes you sad?"

"No." Liz looked over, her eyes shining behind her glasses. "That makes me happy. Really happy." She lifted her glasses and wiped at a tear below her eye. "I should have warned you. I'm a bit of an emotional drinker." She laughed softly at herself. "I giggle a lot, but I can also start crying in my wineglass."

Melody bumped her shoulder against Liz's. "*Now* you tell me. This'll be good to know for the next time we go out."

Liz's expression became serious. "Right."

Melody could see the question in her friend's eyes. It wouldn't help for Melody to tell her yet again that she would be back after she left. That she wouldn't stay away so long this time. Certainly not for nine years. Melody would have to prove it. She'd have to prove herself. That was fair.

She tipped her face back and looked up at the sky, wondering why she didn't go outside and look at the stars more often. "So, do you think fireworks did the trick? Do you think Jo's up there among the stars, looking down on us?"

Liz tipped her head back as well and nearly fell off the cement parking block they were sitting on.

Melody caught her. "Geesh. You are a true lightweight."

Liz started giggling again even though there was evidence of tears in her eyes. She lifted her face again and they both looked at the sky. "Yeah. I think Jo's up there among the stars. Alyssa too. Because that's where they belong. I have to think that eventually we always get to that place where we belong."

Now Melody felt the burn of tears in her eyes too. She blinked and one slipped free. She tried to wipe it away before Liz saw her, but Liz smiled with knowing eyes.

"Looks like the drinks got to you as well."

"Looks like." Melody blew out a breath and then looked down, her eye catching on something shiny in a scattering of dust and dirt on the pavement. She reached for it and picked it up, holding it in her palm to show Liz. "Look."

Liz leaned over and blinked heavily. "Is that a charm?"

"In the shape of a star," Melody confirmed. She looked up at the sky and back at her palm, chills running over her. "There's no way Jo dropped one of those stars in the sky down in this parking lot for us. That would be crazy."

Liz giggled, but this wasn't one of her tipsy giggles from earlier. It was more of the kind of nervous noise someone made when they couldn't figure out what was going on. "Of course not. It's just a strange coincidence." Liz leaned in to take a closer look and nearly fell in Melody's lap.

Melody steadied her friend, letting Liz prop against her shoulder while they both admired the simple sterling silver charm. What would the message be if Jo had sent it? Which she hadn't. That would be absurd. But if Jo had, maybe she was simply saying hi. Or giving them a wink because she was happy that she'd somehow brought the friends back together. Melody pinched the charm between her fingers. "We should add it to the bracelet. To commemorate our girls' night."

Liz nodded quickly. "The first of many more to come."

Melody attached the charm and inspected the bracelet. A car, a house, a muffin, tiny camera, fireworks, a book, a star. In her drunken state, it all made sense. Or maybe it was just the alcohol talking and once she was sober, the charms would return to being seemingly random.

"There's a story here, in this charm bracelet," Melody said, looking at Liz. "It's our story."

Liz grinned. Then they both looked up as headlights spilled into the parking lot, stopping a few feet short of where they were sitting. Liz nearly tumbled backward again and then groaned when she realized it was Rose.

"You nearly ran us over," Liz said, as she stood on shaky legs.

Rose ignored her. "You're welcome." She flicked her gaze to Melody. "So you're the lady from the other week who ran us off the road?"

Melody froze as she approached the car, which still had scrapes down the side. "Yeah. That was me."

"You're also the one who ditched my sister for like ten years?"

Melody was beginning to wonder if she might be walking home after all. "Nine."

Rose turned to Liz. "You complain about my friends, but look at yours. Seriously." She climbed back behind the steering wheel, calling after them. "Get in the car!"

Liz cast Melody an apologetic look. Melody didn't think it was necessary though. Rose was right. She'd been a lousy friend with nothing but flimsy promises to offer so far since she'd been back. Yes, she'd cut off ties because remembering hurt. Liz and Melody's father and everyone else had pain too though, and they hadn't run away like cowards.

Melody climbed into the back seat, wishing Jo was actually here to offer some words of wisdom. What would Jo say? What would Jo do?

Melody somehow thought she knew part of the answer, and the rest was beginning to come into focus. She couldn't leave on Sunday like she'd planned because she hadn't done what she'd come home to do. Only what she'd *thought* she'd returned for.

She'd thought she'd come home for Jo's thrift store, but the real treasure hidden within Jo's inheritance were the people on Trove Isle that Melody had forgotten when she'd driven as fast as her car would take her over the bridge and far away from her hometown. Her father. Liz. Bri . . . Jo. It even felt like Alyssa was still here in some ways.

If she left on Sunday, she probably wouldn't keep in touch like she'd promised. Two weeks wasn't enough to regrow the shriveled roots to her past. She needed to stay longer. She needed the entire summer.

To: Melody Palmer
From: Bri Johnson

Subject: Countdown to Freedom

Mel,

Remember the time you ran away from home when we were kids? I mean, I'm guessing there was only one time, but for all I know, there were more. I'm talking about when I went to find you and bring you back. I was grounded for two weeks after that because my mom thought I had packed my bags and gone with you.

As soon as I heard you were missing, I knew exactly where you were. We were eleven, right? Your mom had just died and you were struggling. I remembered that you told me about this hunter stand in the woods that you'd found. You said it would be a great place to disappear. I knew that's where you'd be. So I rode my bike as fast as I could pedal until I reached your street. Then I dropped my bike in the woods as I ran inside to find that hunter's stand. At some point, I thought maybe searching for you without telling anyone where I had gone wasn't such a great idea. But you know me. I used to wear those bad ideas of mine like badges of honor.

I also considered going to get you after you moved to Charlotte. But you were eighteen, and I was hurting too. I guess I needed someone to pull me out of my own tree stand in the woods. We all did. Liz's family was there for me and her. They tried at least. Your Great-aunt Jo tried to help us in her own way too. She always said you'd come home. She never lost faith, Mel. Never.

Anyway, it's almost time for me to return to the isle. I don't feel like my bad choices are badges of honor anymore. Now I wish I could hide them. The thing about hometowns is that everyone knows your past. Part of me wants to run away for real when I get out. But I've never been that person. I know it won't be easy, and I wish that Jo was still around to offer her support and Jo-isms. I'm glad I have you, whether it's face-to-face or by email. It doesn't really matter. As long as I know where to find you when I need you.

B

CHAPTER FOURTEEN

LIZ

Liz stumbled slightly as she followed Melody into the kitchen.

"Okay, where is it?" Melody asked.

"Where's what?" Liz felt Rose at her heels. She was a little surprised that Rose was even sticking around instead of retreating to whatever she was doing before Liz had called for a ride. Devin had apparently left early to hang out with some boy. Otherwise, maybe Rose wouldn't have agreed to come pick Liz and Melody up anyway.

Melody whirled. "Girls' night is going to fall flat if we don't get more drinks in our systems."

Liz frowned. "Alcohol was never required at our girls' nights when we were younger."

"That's because we were too young to get our hands on it." Melody offered a sheepish look. "Except for that one time we accidentally found Jo's stash." She swept her gaze toward Rose. "But we shouldn't corrupt your sister's young ears."

"I'm sixteen," Rose argued, putting her hands on her hips. "And you dragged me out to come get you two, so you're not getting rid of me now."

"Well, all I have is wine," Liz told Melody. Liz was always stocked in wine because a glass during a hot bath at night was sometimes just the thing she needed to de-stress after a long day. And here lately, the days had seemed a whole lot longer.

"Wine is perfect." Melody grinned wide and turned back toward the kitchen. "Where are your glasses?"

Liz followed her to the cabinets and pointed. "That one. Second shelf."

"You're getting three wine glasses, right?" Rose asked from behind them.

When Liz turned to look at her, Rose's arms were tightly crossed at her chest.

"Oh, come on. I just want one glass," her sister said.

"No." Liz immediately shook her head. "The legal age is twenty-one."

"That's in public. No one cares what I do in the privacy of my own home. All I want is one drink." Rose tilted her head, flashing puppy dog eyes at Liz. "Would you rather I drink my first sip of alcohol somewhere else with people I barely know? That sounds like a recipe for disaster. I mean, who knows what kind of lightweight I am. Look at you." Rose gestured at Liz as if Liz was a slobbering drunk right now. She wasn't.

Somehow Liz seriously doubted this would be Rose's first sip of alcohol. She glanced over at Melody. "It's illegal to give a glass of wine to someone underage, right?"

Melody seemed to laugh under her breath and grabbed a third wine glass from the shelf. "It's just wine, Liz. Not hard liquor. It'll be fine. Your sister is joining us for our girls' night." Her wide smile flickered for a moment and Liz thought she understood why. Melody's sister had joined their girls' night once. And then twice. And then Alyssa had become a part of their little group of friends.

"This is a one-time invasion of your girls' night, okay?"

Rose said. "It's not like I want to be pals with you two or anything. I have my own friends. I'm just here for the wine." She pointed at Liz. "And you owe me because I picked you up at the tavern. You'd have been walking home if I hadn't come to get you. Something could've happened to you out there. You could've been picked up by some creep and married in Vegas."

Liz rolled her eyes. Maybe she was rubbing off on Rose a little bit with all her safety-mindedness. "Fine. One glass for you." And maybe just one more for her. Rose wasn't wrong. Liz was a lightweight. Who knew what she'd do if she drank too much?

The next morning, Liz cracked her eyes open against the bright morning sun. The world was blurry and her brain was throbbing. One glance at the clock on her nightstand told her that it was just after 6:00 a.m. *Oh, crap!* She needed to get to The Bitery and start preparing muffins and pastries for the morning customers. Otherwise, she'd be serving stale leftovers from yesterday. She couldn't charge for that. Her mom typically gave those out for free.

The aroma of coffee wafting in the air stopped Liz's panic in its tracks. Rose had been living here for weeks now and had never made coffee in the morning so, either Liz had died in her sleep or Melody had done the honors. Liz glanced on the other side of the bed where Melody had climbed in beside her, still wearing her clothes from their girls' night. Melody was gone and the bedding was neatly pulled up.

"Good morning," Melody said cheerily from the doorway. Liz looked in her direction. "When did you get up?"

"A little while ago." Melody answered, looking wide-awake.

"How come you're not hungover?" Liz's throat felt dry and scratchy. Her eyes felt raw.

"Well, I think I've probably had more practice at drinking

than you." Melody gestured at the coffee on the bedside table. "That's for you. I'm heading out. Rose offered to give me a ride to my car at the tavern."

"Really?" Liz sat up stiffly.

"Yeah. I'm going home to freshen up and then open the thrift store this morning. Weekends are prime time for sales, and I've got to push out all the old stuff to make room for the new."

Liz blinked again. If she wasn't a little queasy, she'd be asking Melody a lot more follow-up questions.

"Drink your coffee and take the ibuprofen on the table too. You'll feel better in about an hour."

Liz was still furrowing her brow when Melody turned and left.

"I'm taking Melody to get her car," Rose said from the doorway a moment later. "And before you freak out, I'm going to open The Bitery. I shouldn't even be late. I plan to get all the breakfast items started, so stop worrying."

"Really?" Liz asked.

"Yep."

"Why?"

Rose laughed as she shifted back and forth on two-inch soles that made her miniskirt look even shorter. Liz would have something to say about that if Rose wasn't being so nice offering to take her place this morning. "Because you deserve a morning to sleep off your hangover. And because I can."

Liz was speechless for a moment. This was so unlike Rose that Liz wondered if she was dreaming for a moment. "Thank you," she finally said.

"You're welcome. See you later. No rush."

Liz watched her sister disappear down the hall and heard the front door open and close a minute later. She sat there a moment before reaching for her mug and sipping her coffee. Just a few weeks ago, the thought of Rose opening The Bitery and running it on her own for a few hours would have made

Liz so anxious that she would have dragged herself into the shower and down the street no matter how horrible she felt. Not today though. Rose could handle things. And Liz did deserve a morning off. Since her parents had left for Ecuador, she'd woken at 4:00 a.m. most mornings and had worked full days. It'd been tiresome and thankless, and if Rose was stepping up to the plate for just a few hours, then Liz was going to enjoy her freedom. Or, at least, she was going to try.

She smiled to herself, relishing her French brew. She almost ignored her buzzing cell phone on the bedside table, but picked it up at the last second in case it was Rose alerting her that she'd burned the bakery down in two point seven seconds. She picked her phone up and read the text, her smile deepening. It was from Matt. A few weeks ago, a message from him would have made her anxious as well.

Matt: On a scale from one to ten, how bad is your morning after?

Liz's grin slid away. How did he know she'd been drinking last night? It took a moment for foggy memories to lift to the forefront of her mind. She nearly dropped her coffee mug when she remembered texting Matt once she'd gotten back home last night. *No, no, no.* What had she texted him? She tried to scroll back and look through her message history, but there was nothing. Had she used Melody's phone to send the texts? She vaguely remembered that she had for a reason she couldn't recall.

Liz: I didn't drink that much. I'd say the hangover is a solid four and a half.

Matt: Not bad. Do you need anything from me? I've discovered the secret to cure any hangover. I'll share it with you if you'd like.

She tapped her finger along the screen.

Liz: Oh? We're sharing secrets now. That sounds serious.

Was she flirting? She was hungover and flirting. This was so unlike her.

Matt: The secret is salted peanuts in Dr. Pepper.

Liz's face scrunched up.

Liz: In?

Matt: Pour the whole pack inside the bottle. Then drink up. It sounds gross, but it's kind of good. Salt is good for nausea.

Liz: I'll take your word for it.

Matt: I'll bring you some if you'd like.

Liz tugged her lower lip between her teeth. A couple weeks ago, the answer would have been an immediate *no*. Now the *no, thank you* was coming slower. Maybe things were shifting in her world. To what reason, she wasn't quite sure. Perhaps it was because Melody was home. Or because Rose was living with her, and her life was turned upside down and inside out. Bri would be getting out of prison soon, and she would finally be back in Trove where she belonged. Maybe all of the above added up to a much-needed change.

Liz tapped her finger along the screen.

Liz: Maybe another time.

The dots once again started bouncing as Matt replied.

Matt: Next time, huh? So you're planning to return to the tavern for more drinks? Noted. I'll reserve my Friday nights in case you need me to come pick you and Melody up. I'm glad Rose was able to do the honors last night. But you could've called me.

That text was followed up with a winking emoji that made Liz feel all kinds of sparkly sensations zipping through her body. And that was followed by a roll of nausea that had her getting up out of bed and quickly walking toward the bathroom. Maybe she needed that Dr. Pepper and peanuts concoction after all.

At almost noon, Liz finally made it into The Bitery. The bakery hadn't burned down, but Rose did have the tip jar out on the counter. When she saw Liz eyeing it, she slid it underneath the counter.

"You can keep it out if you work past lunch time. I was

going to see if Melody wanted to grab a bite together. If you can't handle the bakery on your own, though, that's okay."

In response, Rose dipped to grab the tip jar and placed it back on the counter. She looked at Liz. "Devin is working with me this morning. I promised that all the tips would go to her."

Liz glanced into the kitchen. "You hired help for the morning?"

Rose looked at her like she had two heads. "Well, I can't run this place by myself."

"I thought you said you could."

Rose gave Liz a disbelieving look, as if the idea was absurd. "Devin always helps when I work. That's why I put a tip jar out."

Liz considered this. She looked around at all the satisfied customers, and then she turned back to her sister. "Does Mom know about this?"

"No, but I was going to talk to her about hiring Devin when she gets back from Ecuador."

"Good idea." That would line up with Liz discussing her own plans to cut back on hours. "Devin can stay. She knows the rules, right? Wash your hands, wear gloves, all that stuff."

"Of course." Rose looked at Liz as if she she'd grown a third head now.

Liz supposed she wouldn't mind three heads if all of them weren't pounding like her one head was doing this morning. "Great. Well then, I'm walking down to Hidden Treasures. Call me if you need anything. I'll be back at some point." But she wouldn't rush. The freedom of having the morning to do as she wanted felt as intoxicating as the drinks she'd devoured last night.

Liz was smiling wider than she had in a long time as she stepped out into the breezy Saturday and turned toward the thrift store. Her hangover was almost gone. She almost felt like a new person today. What a difference a couple of weeks could make.

She stopped in front of Hidden Treasures to read a sign out front. In pink chalk was an invitation to come inside and stuff a bag for $10. Liz opened the door and stepped into a bustling scene. Everyone had large paper bags in their arms, stuffed to the tops and billowing over with clothing, books, and other items.

Melody sat behind the counter with her laptop in front of her. She looked up and waved Liz over. "Do you want to stuff a bag for ten dollars?" she asked as Liz drew closer.

"Maybe. How could you possibly make a profit that way?"

"You'd be surprised. I've sold at least two dozen bags worth already. And the room out back is full of stuff that needs to be put out front. Jo had devoted people who donated regularly. It's an endless cycle. Business is booming."

Liz couldn't tell if Melody was being serious or sarcastic. "So, if you're this busy, I'm guessing you don't have time for lunch?"

Melody grimaced. "I'm starving actually. Can we order in and eat here? There's a little table in the back room. My customers tend to come in waves."

Liz glanced around at the store full of customers. "The same is true for the bakery. It's kind of weird that way, isn't it?"

"It is. Do you want to call out for our food?"

"Sure. Anything in particular?"

"Surprise me," Melody said, preparing to ring someone up at the register.

Liz headed to the little back room where Melody had a fold-out cot, a small table, and a tiny counter with a sink and dorm-size fridge. She dialed out for a pizza delivery and then headed back up front where Melody was helping a little girl pick out a stuffed bear from a selection of toys along the right-hand side of the store.

"My Great-aunt Jo used to tell me that all the used toys were from the Isle of Lost Toys, waiting to be adopted and taken to a new home. And that being a toy's second owner was even more important than being their first owner because they were lost. She said that helping a toy feel found and loved again was a very important job."

The little girl with braided pigtails nodded as she clutched the bear in her arms more tightly.

"You're up for the task?" Melody asked with all seriousness.

"I am," the little girl said solemnly.

"Well, then that toy belongs to you." Melody looked at the mother. "No charge. Just take very good care of that bear."

"You are just like Jo," the mother said, with evident respect in her tone. "That's something she would have done. Are you following in her footsteps and keeping the store open?"

Melody seemed to hedge. "Through the summer, at least." She looked at the little girl. "So, every time you stop in this summer, you can take one of these lost toys home, okay?"

The girl revealed several missing teeth as she grinned widely. "Thank you, Ms. Melody!"

"You're welcome."

Liz waited for the mother and child to walk away before speaking. "You're staying through the summer?" Liz felt like ever since Melody had arrived, she'd been expecting her to leave at any moment. A day, a couple days, a week. Part of her feared that Melody might even leave without a goodbye the way she'd done the first time.

Melody turned to face her. "After going to the prison yesterday, I decided I want to be here when Bri gets out. That's a huge deal. I don't want to miss it."

"You could come back for her release," Liz said. "I kind of thought you couldn't wait to ditch the isle again."

"That was true. Now I kind of can't wait to stay a little longer. My decision has a little bit to do with you too."

"Me?" Liz asked.

"You can't reverse time, but you can make up for lost time. I think that's what I'm here to do with you. And my dad. Myself. Another month won't kill me."

"Wow. I've been thinking all morning that I barely recognize myself these days, but you're changing too," Liz said. "We must be good for each other."

Melody smiled. "And on that note, girls' night part two is happening this evening. After work, I'm giving you a driving refresher course."

Liz felt her heart thump beneath her blouse. "You are?"

"I am. And then we're creating a website for your photography business while we drink more wine."

"Dr. Pepper for me," Liz said. "With salted peanuts in it."

Melody's expression twisted comically. "That's disgusting."

"Someone told me it was good for a hangover." But Liz didn't plan on drinking tonight. Apparently, instead, she was going to be driving. "I might need one of those brown paper bags after all," she told Melody.

"For the bag sale?" Melody asked.

Liz felt her stomach clench and coil. "For the driving lesson."

To: Bri Johnson
From: Liz Dawson

Subject: Three's a Crowd

Bri,

Three is only a crowd when the third person is my little sister. Rose somehow invaded Melody's and my girls' night at my house. There was wine. It's still a little foggy in my head, but I know that I used Melody's phone to drunk-text Matt, which might be one of the most embarrassing things of my adult life. Of all the people to text under the influence, why him? Don't answer that. Whatever you might or might not say would be misguided. I don't think of Matt that way. Really.

The hangover was short, but the embarrassment might last a little longer. It'll be okay, I guess. Just, note to self, next time I drink, hide my cell phone. And everyone else's around me, just in case.

There'll be no wine tonight. Melody is giving me a refresher course on driving. At least that's the plan. And no matter what, I'm going to do it. Even if I have to wait out a panic attack of epic proportions or vomit outside the driver's side door—again. At some point, I've got to face my fear instead of waiting for it to go away.

Wish me luck!

Liz

CHAPTER FIFTEEN

MELODY

Melody locked up Hidden Treasures after what she would call a successful Saturday Bag Sale. Truly, getting an entire brown paper bag stuffed to the brim with clothes and books was a good deal. One could buy a whole new wardrobe for the cost of a large pizza.

Melody drove back to her father's house and parked in the driveway, prepared to go inside and freshen up before meeting Liz at her house for girls' night part two later. She hooked her purse on her shoulder and closed the driver's side door. As she was making her way down the driveway toward the front door, she heard a woman's voice across the lawn.

"Excuse me? Hello?"

Melody turned and looked around, spotting an older woman with gray hair in the doorway of the house next door. She immediately turned and headed in that direction, knowing it was Mrs. West, who Christopher had said was homebound these days. Melody hadn't asked for specifics on why, but considering that Mrs. West wasn't cutting across the lawn to meet Melody halfway implied that she couldn't. "Is everything okay?" she asked as she hurried to be closer.

"Oh, dear. Is that you, Alyssa?"

Melody stopped in her tracks at the sound of her sister's name. And for a moment, before her mind had processed that Mrs. West was talking to her, some part of her lit up at the thought that Alyssa was actually here, after all this time. "Um, no. It's, um, Melody Palmer. Alyssa's, um, sister."

"Oh, Melody." Mrs. West placed a hand to her chest. "I'm sorry. My eyes aren't as good as they once were." Melody noted that Mrs. West's glasses were perched on the crown of her head instead of over her eyes. "How are you, dear?" the older woman asked.

"Fine." Melody climbed the porch steps toward Mrs. West. "I'm staying with my dad for a little while this summer."

"Well, of course you are. Do you think you can step inside and help me with a few things?"

"Um, sure." Melody stepped past Mrs. West's open door into her cozy home. "What do you need help with?"

"Well . . ." Mrs. West massaged a hand to her forehead. "Let's see. There was something. What was it?" She looked around. Then a timer went off in the kitchen. "Yes, yes, that's right. I'm baking a cake. Can you get it out of the oven for me, dear?"

"Sure." Melody followed Mrs. West to the kitchen where the timer was still chiming. She grabbed a mitt off the counter and opened the oven door. Instead of a cake, she saw a pie.

"Does it look done?" Mrs. West asked.

"I think it does." Melody reached in and pulled it out, placing it on the stovetop.

"A pie." Mrs. West furrowed her brow, looking suddenly upset. "I made a pie, not a cake. Oh, no. Why did I make a pie?"

Melody shook her head. "Pie is good. Everyone loves pie."

"But it's his birthday. You can't have pie on a birthday," Mrs. West lamented.

"Whose birthday?" Melody asked. "Christopher's?"

Mrs. West met her gaze. "No. My husband's. He'll be home soon and I wanted to have a cake to celebrate."

Melody slipped the oven mitts off. Hadn't Christopher told her that his father died? Had Mrs. West remarried? "Oh, well, I'm sure—"

"Mom?" a man's voice called from the front door. "It's Christopher. The front door is open. You okay?"

Melody whirled to see Christopher heading into the kitchen. He stopped short when he spotted her. "Hi."

"Hi," he said. Something about his face seemed to light up as he met Melody's eyes.

"Alyssa was just helping me get the cake out of the oven for your father's birthday." Mrs. West gestured toward the stove and frowned again. "Pie. Your dad doesn't even like pie. Why did I make a pie?"

Christopher stepped over and put his hand on the woman's shoulder. "It's okay, Mom. Pie is fine. I'd love a piece of pie actually."

Mrs. West smiled up at him. "Well, of course, you would. You always did have a sweet tooth. Would your friend like a piece too?"

Christopher turned to Melody. "It's okay if you have something else to do."

"No. I don't. I'd love a piece of pie too."

Christopher looked pleased. "All right then. Can we have two slices of pie? I'll cut it. Would you like some too, Mom?"

"Yes, I suppose so. Although there'll be nothing for your dad when he gets home."

Christopher shared a look with Melody, his eyes regretful. Ah. Melody understood now. Christopher's father was gone

and Mrs. West hadn't remarried. She just wasn't remembering things correctly. Melody resisted the urge to wrap her arms
around Christopher and give him a big hug. Having to deal
with this day in and out must be hard. Moving forward
couldn't be easy when his mom was stuck in the past.

They all sat at a small round table and ate pie. Melody was
a little hesitant at first, but Mrs. West hadn't seemed to forget
how to bake. She'd only forgotten the details of her life, or at
least some of them. When they were done eating, Mrs. West
collected the dirty dishes.

"You'll come to Sunday lunch?" she asked Melody. "Christopher comes every week after church."

Melody hesitated and looked at Christopher.

"Mom makes a delicious spread. You'd think she's expecting the entire town. Sometimes Matt joins us. Liz has been
over a couple times too. You should come," Christopher
urged.

Melody nodded. "Yeah. I'd love to," she told Mrs. West.
"Thank you for the invitation. And for the pie."

"You're welcome, dear. Anytime."

Christopher stood and looked at Melody. "I'll walk
you out."

She waved at Mrs. West and headed back toward the
front. When they got outside with the door closed behind
them, Christopher turned to Melody.

"Sorry about that."

"No, it was fun. I enjoyed catching up with your mom. Is
she . . . okay?"

"Her memory is a little iffy. Some days her thinking is as
clear as mine. Others are like this afternoon. She gets confused and frustrated."

"That's why she's homebound?" Melody asked.

"That and she gets lost on the roads. She used to call me

from random places and not know where she was. It was pretty scary, for her and for me."

"I imagine. I'm sorry." The more time Melody spent with Christopher, the more she saw how wrong she was about him. He had the weight of the world riding his shoulders and he carried it in stride. He made it look easy and acted as if it were no big deal, but Melody knew better than most the toll that kind of selflessness took on a person.

After her mother had died, Melody's dad had checked out mentally. Great-aunt Jo had been amazing, yes, but Melody had also sacrificed to care for Alyssa, disregarding her own needs in the process.

Christopher didn't deserve Melody's hard feelings toward him. He couldn't help that he didn't feel the same way about Alyssa as she had for him all those years ago. It was a silly high school crush that had happened ages ago.

"Fortunately, she's never really liked to the leave the house," Christopher said. "I know a lot of people might wander out and get lost, but I don't worry about that with Mom. She's the most clearheaded when she's at home, and for the time being, she's okay." He tipped his head toward the side of the house opposite of Melody's father's home. "Janet and Larry still live next door. They check in on my mother several times a day. It's a revolving door over here. In a good way."

"That's nice," Melody said.

Christopher nodded. "It's just another reason why small-town living is the best. We take care of each other. We're family."

Seeing Trove Isle through Christopher's eyes was fascinating. Melody hadn't allowed herself to have any positive feelings toward her hometown in years. Now, listening to him, she understood the appeal. "Your mom is a lucky woman."

"And I'm a lucky guy to have her." He cleared his throat,

looking suddenly nervous. "So you meant it when you agreed to Sunday lunch? Because my mom hasn't lost her touch with cooking at all. Her food is the best on the isle."

Melody smiled, feeling like perhaps she was lucky too. "I meant it. I'll come."

A slow grin pulled at the corners of his mouth. "Perfect. I'll look forward to it even more than usual."

To: Liz Dawson
From: Bri Johnson

Subject: Dreams

Liz,

I had a pretty good dream last night. I dreamed that I was home, at last, and everyone was accepting of me. We were at a big festival of sorts and people were coming up to me, excited to see me. Like I was a long-lost friend or something. I kept wondering to myself, *Don't they know I'm an ex-felon? Don't they care?* No one did though. I was just me and everyone treated me as such.

I know that won't be the case for a lot of folks in Trove. I mean, how many ex-felons actually live on the isle? I might be the first. I'm okay with the stigma for myself, but what about Ally? The older she gets, the harder it'll be. She'll be the girl whose mom is the one and only ex-con. How can I do that to her? After my dream, when I woke up in the middle of the night, my thoughts went to dark places. I considered letting Ally move to Cali and be with her father. I thought maybe it would be better to grow up without my reputation haunting her. In the light of morning, I know that's not the solution. My grandma has raised Ally to this point. Ally's home is in Trove Isle. And I'm her mother.

Liz, you might need to talk sense into me, more than once, when I get out. I apologize in advance for all the freak-outs I might have and the midnight calls waking you up.

B

CHAPTER SIXTEEN

LIZ

"Breathe, Liz."

Liz nodded quickly, sucked in a shallow breath, and listened to Melody's voice. She was a much better choice for helping her get reacquainted with driving. Rose would have been short-fused and judgmental. Although, to be fair, Rose had matured a lot lately. She'd proven to be a dependable sister when Liz needed her and a decent employee at The Bitery. Mature and responsible or not, though, she'd still been teasing Liz about their first and last driving lesson together this past week.

"Liz, you're turning a little gray. You've got to breathe." Melody's voice wasn't judgmental at all. Instead, she was calm, gentle, and patient. Melody had every good quality that you could ask for in a driving instructor.

Liz glanced over. She'd only gotten as far as cranking the engine. She was calmer than she'd been with Rose, so that was progress. She wasn't about to have a panic attack or hyperventilate or vomit. Hopefully. "This is me breathing."

Melody didn't look so sure. "All right. Are you ready to drive to the end of the driveway?"

Liz contemplated that question. It was just a driveway.

There were no cars on the street behind them. Not even a pedestrian to witness if she hit the ditch. "I guess so," she said, uncertainty playing in her voice. "Remind me of what I need to do? It's been a while."

Melody tapped the gear. "Press the brake pedal down and shift the gear into drive, lift up on the brake, and let the car roll forward. Tap the brake if the car moves too fast or if you need to stop. Press the brake pedal all the way once you are level with the mailbox. That's a good start for right now."

Liz nodded, more to herself than to Mel. "Right. I've done all this before."

"It's like riding a bike," Melody said.

Liz cast her a look. "No, it's nothing like riding a bike." She blew out a breath. "Put the car in DRIVE," she repeated to herself. "Roll to the mailbox, press the brakes."

"Exactly," Melody said.

Liz looked over. "Are you nervous to be sitting beside such an amateur driver?"

Melody lifted a brow. "We're only going down the driveway. And you have your license, albeit you've barely made use of it."

"With good reason."

"It's not like you're going to speed down the road or drive recklessly. The worst that can happen is that we'll go off into the ditch." Melody cast her a teasing glance. "Then I guess we'll need to call Matt to tow us out. That might work in your favor."

Liz rolled her eyes, although just the mention of Matt's name gave her butterflies. She didn't need butterflies right now. She needed courage. "Okay, here I go." On a deep inhale, she pressed the brake with her right foot and pulled the gear right beside the steering wheel down until it was level with the capital *D* for drive. On an exhale, she lifted off the brake and felt the car begin to roll. Without thinking, she quickly slammed her right foot on the brake and the vehicle jerked to a stop. From her peripheral vision, she saw Melody's body lift forward off the seat and slam immediately backward.

"Whoa! Okay," Melody said. "That was . . . good."

"Liar."

"Well, maybe next time, don't press the brakes so hard. Slamming the brakes is for emergencies only."

Liz wanted to say that the car rolling forward felt like an emergency. Instead, she breathed in through her nose, held it for a minute, and exhaled slowly. "Okay," she said. "Here we go again." She lifted off the brake and the car began to roll once more. This time, she watched through the front windshield as the car continued its roll toward the end of the driveway. Once it was parallel to the mailbox, she slowly put her foot on the brake and pressed down in a calm, controlled manner.

"That's it!" Melody cheered beside her. "You did it!"

Liz laughed out loud, exhilaration running through her body with the same intensity as the fear that had coursed there only two minutes earlier. "I really did!" She leaned across the center console and threw her arms around Melody. She hadn't put the car in PARK, however, and as her right foot came off the brake just slightly, the car began to roll again.

"Whoa!" Melody pulled back from the embrace. "Brake! Brake!"

Liz moved her right foot to the brake pedal and stomped it as quickly as she could. The car jerked to another halt and she saw Melody's body move forward and slam back against the passenger seat once more. "That was an emergency, right?"

Melody sighed. "We have our work cut out for us, don't we? Keep holding the brake pedal down and move the gear back to *P* for park."

Liz did as Melody instructed and then she looked at her friend. "Thank you for this."

"Of course."

"And now you probably want to forget about any more driver's lessons, huh?"

"No way. You made one mistake and everything is fine. No one got hurt. Let's try again. You can reverse to where you were and drive forward to the mailbox."

Liz grimaced. "My neighbors will think I've lost my mind, going up and down the driveway."

"Who cares?" Melody asked. "You're conquering your fear, which is more than most people ever do."

Liz looked down for a moment, steadying her breath and her emotions. "Most people don't have as much fear as me."

Melody gave a humorless laugh. "You'd be surprised."

Liz looked at her friend across the center console. "What's your fear to be conquered?"

"It was returning to Trove Isle," Melody said.

"Well, you did that already. Now what?"

Melody shrugged. "I'm not sure. Now I take this summer one day at a time, I guess. You ready to drive again?"

Liz side-eyed her. "Are *you* ready for me to drive?"

Melody laughed lightly and gripped the handle on the passenger door. "Ready."

On Sundays, Liz had Danette's sister, Sissy, work at The Bitery. Whereas Liz and her mother had once handled the store by themselves, over the last couple of years Liz's mom had hired consistent part-time help.

That was good because today Liz's Sunday was wide-open for whatever she wanted to do. She'd been invited to Mrs. West's home for lunch along with Melody, Christopher, and possibly Matt. She hadn't said yes, but she also hadn't said no. She'd said maybe because she didn't like to be tied down with plans on her one full day off.

Maybe she'd read a book today. Or take a walk and snap some pictures. Or sit in a car and drive up and down the driveway again. The choices and the freedom to choose was nearly intoxicating.

Rose stomped out of her bedroom and looked at Liz. Liz gave her sister a visual assessment, realizing she hadn't necessarily stomped out. She was just wearing boots with a chunky heel over her black leggings that made her sound like she was marching through Liz's home.

"Going somewhere?" Liz asked.

Rose shrugged. "Stores open at noon. I was thinking about going dress shopping."

For prom. That was the only reason that Rose would ever put on a dress. "You're going out with Devin?"

Rose shook her head. "She's busy."

Liz waited as her sister nibbled her lower lip. Liz was the one with anxiety. Rose was always confident, but right now she looked nervous. "Who are you going dress shopping with then?"

Rose's slight shoulders shrugged upward toward large silver hoop earrings. "I was kind of hoping you would go with me."

Liz felt her blood funnel away from her face toward her feet. "Me?"

"Well, Mom isn't here. I mean, I guess I can go alone." There was something vulnerable in Rose's eyes that gave Liz pause. When was her sister ever vulnerable? Never that Liz could remember. "There's just this guy who's going to prom.

We're not going together or anything, but he asked if I'd be there to dance with him. I sort of really like him and I want to look nice. He's kind of preppy and . . ." She held her arms out by her side, "I mean, look at me."

"Preppy?" Liz couldn't hide the surprise in her tone. "You like a preppy guy?"

"And he likes me too," Rose said, a hint of defensiveness in her voice. "Anyway, if you have something better to do today . . ."

"I was invited to go to Sunday lunch at Mrs. West's house," Liz said, clearing a path to say no to Rose. Not because she didn't want to hang out or help her sister, but because this was about prom, and prom was not a topic of choice for Liz. She'd never made it to her own prom. Her life had changed that night. And the thought of watching Rose set off with a dress and corsage in a few weeks sounded like torture.

"Whatever." Rose turned back to retreat to her room. Liz had seen the touch of vulnerability pass across her sister's face right before she'd turned though. This was important to Rose, and it was another moment for Liz to prove to herself that she could resist her fear and do brave things.

"Wait." Liz closed her eyes and took a breath. She reached for the charm bracelet on her wrist before remembering that Melody had it now. Liz didn't need it though. She'd sat behind a steering wheel and had cranked its engine. She'd driven up and down the driveway. Liz opened her eyes to find Rose watching her. "I can cancel lunch at Mrs. West's home. It's not that important."

Rose's face lit up. "Really?"

"Yeah, of course. I can go with you. It'll be fun," Liz lied. It would be the furthest thing from fun that she could imagine doing except maybe driving a vehicle in rush hour traffic.

"Great." A smile flickered on Rose's lips. "Thanks. I mean it."

"Of course." Something warm crawled up inside Liz's chest as she watched Rose turn and walk back to the guest bedroom. Her sister needed her and even though Liz didn't want to go dress shopping this afternoon, she could do it. And she would do it.

She'd found a little bravery behind the steering wheel the other night. She'd faced a fear head-on and it hadn't killed her. So, while it might hurt her heart a little, it was very unlikely that a little prom dress shopping between sisters would be the death of her.

Two hours later, Liz was sitting in a straight back chair with oversized armrests, drinking complimentary lemonade and nodding at the tenth dress that Rose had tried on.

"It looks awful. I can see it on your face." Rose crossed her arms at her chest and poked out a sassy hip.

"It's not really your style," Liz said, taking in the bright orange silky fabric. There was a sash of sequins moving across the front of the dress. Liz scrunched her nose. "You don't usually wear bright colors."

"But bright colors can be cool. Maybe the black dress." Rose turned back to the dressing room. The owner of the store kept bringing dresses and Rose kept trying them on. Finally, Rose growled in frustration and stomped her foot. "None of these are right," she said, on the brink of tears.

"You must really like this guy, huh?" Liz knew that Rose normally didn't care much about things like this. She would've picked a black dress and have been done with it if the guy wasn't someone special.

Rose plopped onto the chair next to Liz's. "He's so cute. I can't even believe he wants to dance with me. Like, some part of me thinks it's a cruel joke and he's really just toying with me, and he'll show up with his real date. And everyone will be laughing about how stupid I was to think he wanted me."

Liz lifted her brows. Maybe she needed to get Rose an appointment with Dr. Mayer. "Wow. You've really been hanging out with me for too long because you sound paranoid. Which is a form of anxiety. Or it can be."

Rose rolled her eyes, but she also laughed a little. "We're from two different worlds, sis. So, do I buy a dress that I would like? Or one that fits his personality? Or something completely different?"

Liz tapped a finger to her chin. "If he likes you, then he already knows your style and likes it. So I say pick something you like. Just be yourself."

Rose slumped deeper into the chair. "Well, I don't like anything in here," she said loud enough to embarrass Liz because she was sure the owner bearing unlimited lemonade had heard her.

Liz cared more about Rose right now though. Her sister needed her support, which didn't happen often. "I think I know where you might find the perfect dress."

Rose looked over, hope glinting in her suspiciously shiny eyes. "You do?"

"I do." Liz nibbled her lower lip. Hidden Treasures was closed today, but she knew the owner. She pulled out her cell phone and tapped off a message to Melody.

Liz: Any way we can have a private showing at your store this afternoon?

The dots started bouncing on the screen as Melody tapped out a reply.

Melody: We're at Mrs. West's house. But say in an hour?

Liz tapped the thumbs up emoji. Then she looked at Rose. "We have one hour to kill before we continue our prom dress shopping. What do you want to do?"

Rose gave her a strange look. It occurred to Liz that, aside from the girls' night the other week, she and her sister had never really hung out for fun. The age gap between them always felt too far to cross.

"Ice cream," Liz decided, standing up. "We'll eat ice cream and then try on every dress in town if we have to." She offered her hand to Rose, who reluctantly took it. Then Liz pulled her sister up to a standing position. "Come on. It'll be fun."

To: Liz Dawson
From: Bri Johnson

Subject: What If

Liz,

All the what-ifs continue to keep me up at night as I get closer
to my release date. I just keep imagining all the worst-case sce-
narios. The best-case ones seem to disappear when I close my
eyes for sleep. You hear about people who get out of prison and
can't find a job or a means to support themselves. They can't
cope. Then they commit crimes just to return to the familiar. I
get why that happens. Don't get me wrong. I want my freedom,
but I'm also a little bit afraid of it. Stupid?

Ally wrote me a letter this week. She's having a blast with her
dad in Cali. What if she doesn't want to come home after spending all summer with him? What if she likes him better? What if I
lose her completely?

B

P.S. Don't worry about me committing a crime to come back to
prison. That's not going to happen. The ex-cons who make that
choice obviously don't have friends like you waiting for them on
the outside.

Chapter Seventeen

MELODY

Melody and Christopher had been the only guests who'd ended up coming to Mrs. West's house for Sunday lunch. Matt had some other obligation and Liz was, of all things, dress shopping with her sister.

"You didn't eat very much," Mrs. West commented, looking over her shoulder at Melody's plate. This afternoon, Mrs. West was in a very different state of mind than she'd been the other day when Melody had seen her. As Christopher had said, she had moments of clarity and others of confusion. Today, she was clear-minded and in good spirits.

"I got seconds, remember?" Melody asked, worried momentarily that Mrs. West was growing confused.

"Yes, that's right. Well, I always have enough to serve thirds when I invite guests over." The older woman smiled warmly as she rinsed each dish and handed it to Melody to load into the dishwasher. She'd aged a lot in the years that Melody had been away. Melody supposed that losing one's husband and suffering from dementia would do that. "Today is the first I've seen you in years. How are you, Melody?"

Melody decided not to mention that she'd actually seen

Mrs. West last week. "I'm good. I live in Charlotte now. I have a job and an apartment."

"Mm. Well, jobs and apartments don't take the place of friends and family, do they? Do you have friends in Charlotte?"

Melody nodded as she took a plate from Mrs. West's hands. "I do."

"And are you happy there?" Mrs. West asked.

Melody hesitated. That was a blunt question—one that no one had bothered or dared to ask since she'd been back to the isle. They'd asked how business was and things like that, but no one had touched on her emotional state, which was neither happy nor sad. It was numb, which is what she'd thought she wanted. "Happy?" Melody repeated, stalling for an answer. "I guess so," she finally said.

"Do you have a boyfriend?" Mrs. West asked.

Melody shook her head. "Not currently, no. I had one. We broke up last year."

Mrs. West looked genuinely apologetic. "I'm sorry to hear that. Break-ups are so hard on the heart, aren't they? If I recall, your first break-up led you to wanting to become a nun." Mrs. West chuckled under her breath.

How could Christopher's mom forget her husband dying, but remember that detail about Melody's seventh grade year? How did Mrs. West even know that detail?

"It was so sad, but also adorable. You were such a good kid." Mrs. West looked at her sincerely. "You deserve love, Melody. I'm sorry things didn't work out with your last fellow."

"Don't be." Melody bent and placed a large casserole dish in the bottom compartment of the dishwasher. "He was lazy. And a bit of a jerk. Not the kind of guy who's nice to his mama."

Mrs. West's lips rounded into a huge O of surprise. "Well, Christopher has always been nice to me," she said then, adding a little wink after her words.

Melody didn't want Mrs. West to get the wrong idea. Melody had spent a little time with Christopher, but there was nothing romantic brewing between them. Yeah, Melody was a bit attracted to him, but she was also attracted to Chris Hemsworth and there was nothing romantic brewing between her and Thor either—unfortunately. "To answer your question, yes, I'm very happy in Charlotte. I plan to return later this summer."

Mrs. West raised her brows and handed Melody another dish. "Why would anyone be in a rush to leave the isle? This town," she said, selling her point with a nod and extended arms, "is perfect. It's safe and there's good food. Good shopping. Good people. You have friends here. And your father is here too, of course."

Melody's father was the only family she had left anymore. "Yes, he is. I'm glad that I'm here for a little while to spend some time with him."

"I suspect he's over the moon, even if he doesn't show it." She patted Melody's arm and continued working.

A moment later, Christopher stepped into the kitchen. Melody's heart gave a little kick. There was nothing romantic between them, she reminded herself.

"You asked me to let you know when it was three o'clock," he told Melody.

"Right." Melody placed the last dish in the dishwasher and dried her hands on a nearby towel. "I hate to rush off, but I'm opening my thrift store to Liz and her sister," she told Mrs. West.

"It's fine, dear. I'm just glad you were able to come. Maybe you'll have Sunday lunch with me again while you're here."

Melody nodded. "That would be nice."

"And bring your father next time," Mrs. West added.

Melody felt an unintended grimace stretch her lips.

Mrs. West laughed heartily and pointed a finger. "He's a stubborn man, isn't he?"

"And his daughter didn't fall far from the tree," Christopher teased. He looked at Melody. "I'll drive you to the thrift store, if you want."

"Oh, that's not necessary. How would I get back? If I don't have a car."

"I'd stay and drive you home afterward."

"You'll stay while I help Rose find a prom dress?" Melody asked.

Christopher shrugged. "Sounds like a fun way to spend a Sunday afternoon to me. Maybe I'll find something to wear to prom too."

Melody cocked her head to one side. "You?"

"I'm one of the chaperones. Only the cool teachers get to chaperone, so it's quite the honor," he told her. "I'm also allowed to bring a date." He looked at her expectantly, as if waiting for her to answer.

He hadn't exactly asked her anything though, which was good because she wouldn't have known how to respond. He'd turned Alyssa's promposal down all those years ago. Even if she wasn't holding that against him anymore, it would still be awkward if Melody went to a prom with him now. Wouldn't it? Since he hadn't asked, she pushed her reservations away and focused on the present moment. "I'd love for you to drive me to Hidden Treasures. Thanks."

After hugging and thanking Mrs. West again, Melody and Christopher stepped out of the house and got into Christopher's truck. Within a few minutes, they turned onto Seagull Street and headed toward Hidden Treasures Thrift Store. Melody spotted Liz standing with Rose outside the shop as Christopher pulled up to the curb and parked.

"You think there's anything in my size?" Christopher asked as he turned off the ignition.

"To wear to prom?" Melody clarified.

"Well, I wear the same boring suit every year. I wouldn't mind finding something with a little more style."

"Anything you could ever want is in that store. I don't know where Jo found all that stuff." Melody's mind flashed to an image of her aunt dumpster diving but she shook it off, preferring to block that part of her aunt's life out. "I'll help you look while Liz and Rose pick through the dresses."

"Sounds like a plan. I wonder if Matt has asked Liz to be his date yet," Christopher said as he stepped out of the truck. He walked around and met Melody beside the truck.

"Matt's chaperoning too? I thought he works for the police department."

Christopher grinned. "This is a small town, Mel. The high school likes to have a good relationship with the PD. The department takes on student volunteers and the school invites officers to all their events. Matt just happens to be the lucky one because he's my best friend and I insist."

Melody smiled. "And what makes you so sure he's planning to ask Liz to be his date?"

"Because he asks her every year. And every year she says no."

Melody wondered again if Christopher was going to ask her. If Liz could turn Matt down, she could turn Christopher down. And she should. He was a nice guy and all. Handsome too. But even without the added weirdness of his history with Alyssa, she wasn't staying in Trove.

"Thanks for meeting us," Liz said as they approached. "Rose didn't like anything at the Classic Woman Boutique."

Rose huffed. "I mean, just think about the title of that store. I'm not classy, and I'm not a woman. There was never going to be anything for me in there."

Liz shook her head and looked at Melody. "There were lots of overpriced, beautiful choices. But maybe there's something even more special here."

Melody pulled the keys to the store out of her pocket, found the one to the front entrance, and poked it into the lock. Then she turned it and the door sprung open. "If you find the perfect dress, it's yours. Jo's gift to you."

Liz smiled warmly, her gaze bouncing between Melody and Christopher. "I hope I didn't interrupt anything."

"Not at all. We were finished eating with my mom. We needed the distraction. Otherwise, my mom would have handed over a lengthy to-do list for me to complete. She always does."

"It'll wait until tomorrow," Liz said with a laugh, her gaze trailing after Rose. "I better go help her."

"And I'm going to help Christopher." Melody pointed to a small section of men's things. "Your next prom wardrobe awaits."

Christopher headed in that direction and she followed, watching as he went through the racks. Two funky purple suits caught his attention.

"Those are dreadful," Melody said as he held one up. Maybe he hadn't outgrown his nerd phase after all. "And why are there two?"

Christopher shrugged as he lowered the suit and held it against him. "I don't know, but it's my size. The other will fit Matt, I'm pretty sure. I'm going to buy both."

"You're going to wear a purple suit to prom?"

"It's cool." Christopher cast her a teasing grin. "We'll be the only ones there with suits like this."

"With good reason." Melody leaned against the wall beside the rack. "He might not agree."

"Oh, he'll agree." Christopher checked the tag. "Fifteen dollars each."

"I said it was all on the house."

"Maybe for Rose, but not for me and Matt. I'll pay. Now we just need to find you a dress," he said, turning to her. "That is, if you'll go to prom with me?"

"Oh, I-I'm not sure," she stammered.

"Why not? You've decided to stay for the summer. What's keeping you from saying yes?"

Her hand absently went to the bracelet. She looked at the purple suit in Christopher's hands instead of at him while she considered which choice to make. It was just a dance, that's all. She'd never made it to her own prom so maybe she was overdue to see what the big fuss was about. What was keeping her from saying yes? "Do I need to wear a matching purple dress?" she finally asked, looking up at him. "Because that might be hard to find."

"In my opinion, it's better if our attire clashes. I love to give the kids something to roll their eyes at."

Melody smiled at this. "Okay," she said, still holding onto the bracelet at her wrist. "I guess I need to join Rose in looking for a dress."

To: Bri Johnson
From: Liz Dawson

Subject: Okay

Bri,

You will be okay. Everything will be okay.

This is short, but I fully expect you to read that line over and over again until you believe it.

xx,

Liz

Chapter Eighteen

Liz

Liz felt clammy. She'd been sitting in a chair outside the dressing room at Hidden Treasures for half an hour now, smiling plastically each time Rose stepped out with another dress. Rose had tried on at least two dozen today between all the shops they'd been to.

"This one!" Rose said, stepping out of the dressing room.

Liz looked up, speechless for a moment. Her little sister looked gorgeous in a fitted bubblegum-pink dress with a tiny frill that fanned out just above her knees. The dress had two tiny shoulder straps on each side and only dipped to show the smallest amount of cleavage. The back, however, plunged below her shoulder blades. Even though the dress was pink, it wasn't girly at all. It was kind of an 80s punk rock dress that Madonna might have worn in one of her music videos back then. "It's perfect," Liz agreed. "Wow. That dress."

"It's vintage, which is so cool right now. I love it," Rose went on. "This is for sure the one."

Melody stepped over to them and assessed Rose in her dress. "You're right. That's definitely perfect for you. I don't think I've ever even seen that dress. Where did it come from?"

"The rack over there with all the others," Rose pointed.

"Hmm." Melody looked over at Liz, her smile fading. "You okay?"

"Yeah. Yeah, I'm fine." Liz tried to swallow, but her mouth was too parched. "Actually, can I have a glass of water?"

"Sure. I'll get you one," Melody said. "Be right back."

Liz's hands were shaking. She placed one over the other to try and anchor them to her lap. Rose's gaze was heavy on her. "Are you going to have . . ."

"If you say a freak-out," Liz warned.

"I was going to say an anxiety attack." Rose came and sat beside her, laying her hand over Liz's.

Liz blew out a breath. "I'm trying not to think about where you're going to wear that dress. Perfect as it is. Or the drive to where you're going to wear it." She sucked in a breath. She'd rode down the street where they'd had their accident many times before, of course. She usually closed her eyes and pretended it wasn't happening. When Jo was alive, she'd kept a little wooden cross tamped down in the dirt on the roadside in Alyssa's honor. Liz guessed it was still there, serving as a reminder. She'd never needed to be reminded though. Alyssa and the accident were always lingering in her subconscious.

Melody reappeared with the glass of water and placed it in Liz's hand. "Here you go."

"Thanks." Liz drank it gratefully. "I'll be okay," she finally said, looking between her sister and Melody. "Everything is okay." She'd just e-messaged those very words to Bri. It was something she said to herself all the time. Sometimes that was all it took. Just a reminder that the world wasn't ending and just being okay was enough.

"If you're this upset about the idea of me going to prom," Rose said, "then I won't go. I'll stay home."

Liz looked over at her sister. She couldn't believe Rose would say something so selfless. "No. You should go. It's a once in a lifetime experience."

"Well, twice," Rose said. "There'll be a senior prom too."

Liz smiled. "A twice in a lifetime experience. I want you to go. It's just going to take a few extra deep breaths for me to handle it. And I might be hyperventilating in a bag as you set out on your way there. It'll be fine. I promise."

Rose nodded. "Okay."

Liz looked up at Melody. "Maybe you and I can hang out that night. You can be my distraction."

Melody rolled her lips together, hesitating before responding. "Actually, I just agreed to go to prom."

Liz frowned. "What?"

"With Christopher. He and Matt are chaperones, and I kind of said I'd be one too. But I can walk back my yes and stay with you that night if you need me to," Melody said quickly. "Christopher will understand. I just thought it might be a full circle moment. I never went to prom. None of us did. Maybe this will be healing in some way." She shrugged a shoulder.

Liz couldn't imagine how doing the thing that had almost gotten them all killed, that had killed Alyssa, would be healing. It sounded traumatic to her. Like one big anxiety attack that lasted a full night. "I see. No, you should go. If you think it might help you, you have to. I'll be okay. I'll just watch TV or read a book to distract myself."

"Maybe . . ." Melody hedged.

Liz shook her head. "If you're going to suggest that I go to prom too, you can stop right there. There's no way."

Melody nodded. "Right. Sorry."

Liz lifted her glass of water, her hand shaking so hard that she had to steady it with her other hand in order to not spill it all over herself. She drained the last drop and handed it back to Melody. "We'll take the pink dress."

"Like I said, it's on the house. Courtesy of Jo." Melody smiled. "Check out the shoes on the far wall. Maybe you'll find the perfect pair to go with it," she told Rose.

Rose stood, leaving the chair empty for Melody to slide in beside Liz.

"You're sure you're okay?" Melody asked.

Liz blew out another breath. "Yeah. So you're going with Christopher, huh? Will it be a date?"

Melody looked toward the store where Christopher was perusing the men's items. "I'm not exactly sure."

"But you aren't opposed?" Liz found that focusing on other people eased her tensions.

"I'm not opposed," Melody agreed. "He's cute. And nice." She returned to looking at Liz. "Is it weird that I want it to be a date? Because he was Alyssa's guy. She was crazy about him."

"He never returned the crush though. And that was ages ago," Liz said. "It's not weird at all. Christopher is a hot commodity here on the isle, you know? All the single women have tried to catch his eye."

"Really?" Melody hadn't known that. "But he's not a stud or anything."

"Maybe not, but the pool of single men isn't that big in Trove. You should know that. And a nice guy like Christopher is hard to find. Maybe he's not a stud, but he is handsome."

"You don't have a thing for him, do you?" Melody asked, suddenly looking worried.

Liz laughed, the tension further dissipating. "He's more like a brother to me."

Melody's gaze stuck on her again. "And you have a thing for Christopher's friend, Matt?"

Liz wanted to deny that question too. Instead, she looked down at the empty glass in her hand. "I'm not really looking for anything romantic."

"You may not be looking," Melody said, "but sometimes romance finds you when you least expect it."

*　*　*

Liz was alone in her home. Right after getting home from dress shopping, Rose had gone off with a couple of her friends. That was good because Liz fully expected to have some kind of mini panic attack. She was waiting for it actually. After helping her sister pick out a prom dress, there was no way she wouldn't be crying, hyperventilating, or pulling out her hair tonight.

Except, she wasn't. On the contrary, she felt pretty good. Maybe getting started back with Dr. Mayer was helping. Or facing her past and Melody. *Something* was helping.

Liz stood and walked to the living room window that overlooked her street. It was a nice evening. Darkness hadn't yet descended. She supposed she could take her bike out if she wanted. Her gaze moved to her parents' car in the driveway. Rose had gone off with her friends in Devin's car.

Liz waited for her heart rate to quicken at just the idea that she might get behind that wheel right now, on her own, with no one helping. She waited for the tight chest and sweaty palms. It didn't happen. In fact, a little zing of excitement zipped through her pulse. Without giving herself time to second guess this impulse, she went into the kitchen where the keys were kept in a small dish on the counter. She picked them up and jingled them for good measure. No fear, just excitement.

Liz walked out of the house toward the car, her breaths coming evenly. *I can do this.* She could back out to the mailbox and drive up to the house. Then repeat, just like she had with Melody the other day. Not only could she do this, she *wanted* to.

Liz opened the driver's side door and dipped inside. When she realized she wasn't panicking, she closed the door behind her. With a shaky hand, she placed the key in the ignition and twisted. A satisfying rev came from the engine and then a steady purr of the motor.

Liz blew out a breath. Working on autopilot, she pressed the brake and moved the gear into REVERSE. Then she eased up on the brake and felt the car slowly roll backward. Her gaze flicked to the rearview mirror, making sure she didn't hit anything. She was moving painstakingly slowly, but she was moving and she was doing this all on her own. When she reached the mailbox, she pressed the brakes again and moved the gear into PARK. Then she expelled a heavy breath. "I did it!" she squealed. "I did it!"

Someone knocked on her passenger window and she nearly passed out from the startle. Matt was standing there, peering into the window at her with a perplexed look in his eyes and a smile at the same time. Then he opened the passenger side door and dipped inside.

"What are you doing?"

"I'm driving," she said, oozing pride from every cell in her body. "I drove. On my own. And I didn't hit the mailbox."

Matt chuckled. "Good job."

"Thanks." She blew out a breath, feeling so alive in this moment. "What are you doing here?"

"I was out walking Mr. Beast and saw you miss that mailbox by a solid inch." He grinned. "I thought I might check on you and make sure you were okay."

"Better than okay," she said, beaming at him.

Matt nodded. "Good. Where are you going to next?"

Liz nibbled at her lower lip as she contemplated. "Back up the driveway, I guess." That's as far as she'd gone when she'd driven with Melody on their second girls' night.

"Or," Matt said with a growing grin, "I can stay in the car with you and we can go down the road."

"Down the road?" She waited for the panic to consume her. Where was it this evening? All she felt was exhilaration. "Yeah. Let's go. Close the door and buckle up."

Matt's grin flatlined. He suddenly looked unsure. "I was only halfway serious."

"Well, I'm fully serious."

"I do have Mr. Beast with me," he said, gesturing to his little Chihuahua.

Liz loved dogs. She certainly didn't mind one coming along for the ride. "He can ride in the back seat. Hurry before I lose my nerve." Because this wasn't like her at all. This felt amazing. She felt free and uninhibited for the first time in years.

Matt placed his little dog—the most unbeastly creature she'd ever seen—in the back seat and closed the door behind him.

Liz didn't waste any time. She moved the gear out of PARK and slowly started backing onto the road.

"Easy. Easy does it," Matt said as she guided the car out of the driveway. "Whoa!"

Liz slammed the brakes as she nearly hit the mailbox across the street. Her heart jumped into her throat. "Sorry."

Matt looked unfazed. "No problem. You've got this," he said. "Deep breaths."

She nodded. Then she blew out a heavy breath. "Okay. Here we go." She pressed on the gas pedal and guided the car down the street, rolling slower than her bicycle would go, but she didn't care. When she got to the STOP sign, she glanced at Matt before checking both ways. Not another car in sight, which was perhaps for the best.

"We can circle around," he said. Their street was one big loop. "We can go in circles as many times as you want. Or we can turn on another street."

Liz shook her head slightly. "Baby steps is fine by me." She circled around their street and ended up back in her driveway. Then she put the car in PARK and glanced over at Matt. "That was . . . amazing." She resisted leaning over and giving him a hug. "I can't believe I just did that."

"I can." Matt's gaze was unwavering. "Want to do it again?"

Liz did. She wanted to do that simple loop of driving all night. "Hell, yeah," she said, putting the car in REVERSE and backing out of the driveway again.

"I think you missed the mailbox by a good two inches that time," Matt joked, giving her a wink as she glanced in his direction. "That's progress."

To: Bri Johnson
From: Liz Dawson

Subject: Brave

Bri,

You'll never believe what I just did! I drove down my street! I mean, we didn't leave the neighborhood, but I actually reversed out of the driveway, without hitting the mailbox, and navigated around the block. It was the most exhilarating moment, maybe in my entire life. Isn't that crazy? Sometimes you can work yourself up about something to the point where it seems like a mountain. And in one instant, one breath, the mountain crumbles. *My* mountain crumbled. I know, I know. It was just one street, but being behind the wheel without panicking is half the battle. I know, in time, I can do more.

You were the first person I wanted to tell because I knew you'd get it. Now, I'm going to call Melody and tell her. Maybe I'll rope her into driving us to see you next week. Or better yet, maybe I'll drive us there myself. Just kidding. I'm not ready for that— yet.
xx,

Liz

CHAPTER NINETEEN

MELODY

The fridge was empty. Melody had hoped to make dinner for her father tonight, but short of a trip to the grocery store, that wasn't happening.

The front door opened and her father stepped in. He placed his briefcase on the floor beside the couch as always and greeted her with a quiet smile.

"Hi, Dad." The D-word still felt foreign from all the years where Melody had so infrequently said it.

He looked up. "Good evening. How are you?"

"Hungry, actually. I was thinking, maybe we should go out for dinner tonight."

He straightened and seemed to hesitate. Then he offered a small nod. "Where to?"

"Anywhere. Let's just go have a nice meal together that someone else prepares. It'll be fun."

He gestured down the hall. "Let me just change into something less stuffy first."

"Sure. I'll change as well."

Melody headed to her room and scanned the closet, which was now full of items she'd chosen for herself from Hidden Treasures. There was also a pale-blue prom dress hanging in there. She still couldn't believe she'd taken it or that she'd said yes to being Christopher's date. She pulled a soft-yellow sundress out of the closet and some strappy sandals with rhinestone accents. Perfect for a nice restaurant or something more casual.

Five minutes later, she met her father in the living room.

"You look handsome," she said. "Maybe you'll catch the eye of one of Trove's single ladies tonight."

He chuckled unexpectedly. "I don't think so. All I want to do is spend time with my beautiful daughter. Shall we?" He opened the front door for her.

"We shall."

Melody let her father drive. He was more familiar with where to go on the isle these days. He drove her to the west side of town to a little hole-in-the-wall mom-and-pop place.

"I come here alone sometimes. They give me a quiet corner off to myself," her father said as they got out of the car and walked up to the front entrance.

"Alone? You don't mind sitting all by yourself?"

Her father held the door for her. "No, I'm used to it by now. And I like the quiet when I'm eating. I like to sit and eavesdrop on the folks around me too."

Melody laughed softly. Who knew her father had a sense of humor? She was rediscovering him and realizing maybe she'd never known him at all.

"Oh, Mr. Palmer. You brought a guest this time," the hostess said. It was a young woman with long blonde hair and brown eyes.

"This is my daughter," Melody's father told the woman, his voice full of pride. Melody felt the opposite of pride. The fact that she'd left town and her father had had to sit at restaurants all alone made guilt swell in her ribcage, closing in around her heart.

The hostess led them to a table in the back corner where her father said he was normally seated. "Here you are. Enjoy your dinner and company," she said before heading back to the front entranceway of the restaurant.

Melody's father sat and looked across the table at her. "Today I don't need to eavesdrop. I'll just talk to you."

Melody felt oddly nervous. "So, what do you order when you come in?"

"The special, of course."

"Always?"

"Always," he confirmed.

"But what if you don't like it?"

"Food is food. I'll like it."

Melody closed her menu. "Okay. Then I'll have the special too. I just hope it's not frog legs or something like that."

"That's only on Tuesdays," he said. "Since today is Thursday, you should be fine."

Melody couldn't tell if he was joking or not. She certainly hoped so. Fortunately, the special turned out to be roasted lemon chicken and asparagus sautéed in an alfredo cream sauce. It was delicious and the conversation was equally appealing.

"You don't have to pay," Melody said at the end when her father placed his debit card on the bill tray and handed it to the waitress.

"You're my only date in over a decade. This is on me."

Melody fidgeted nervously with her napkin. "Thank you."

"Of course."

Once they'd left the restaurant, they returned to her father's vehicle. She thought they were going back to his house, but her dad made a detour to a flower shop on Seagull Street.

"What are you doing?" she asked.

"I'm getting two bouquets of flowers, if you don't mind. I typically stop here once a week to get some flowers for your mom and your sister. Maybe you'll come with me this time."

"To the cemetery?" Melody was surprised by this information. "Sure. I guess so."

He stepped out, walked into the shop, and returned within five minutes with two bouquets of wildflowers.

"You really go to their graves once a week?" Melody asked as he veered back onto the road and drove in the direction of the town's main cemetery.

"I try to. I might miss a week if it's storming or if there's ice on the ground."

"That's really nice, Dad."

"You sound surprised."

She was. Her father didn't even have photographs of her mom or Alyssa out in the house. She'd assumed he had forgotten about them or more likely, that he didn't want to think about them. But he hadn't forgotten any more than Melody had.

A few minutes later, her father parked again. Melody pushed her car door open and walked around the vehicle to catch up to her father. The sun-dried grass crunched beneath their feet as they walked through the cemetery. They stepped onto the sidewalk and followed a path that Melody hadn't been down since she was eighteen years old.

"Here." Her father handed her the bouquet. "You put these on Alyssa's grave."

Melody held the wildflowers in her hands. Reflexively, she tipped her nose into the bundle and breathed them in. She'd brought flowers to Alyssa on the opening night of a high school play that Alyssa had starred in. Alyssa had acted like Melody had given her a thousand bucks. She'd practically crushed the bouquet in the middle of the hug she'd given Melody.

"*You're the best sister ever!*" she'd said, on a rush of theatrical adrenaline.

"*You say that now. Just wait until the next time you're mad at me.*"

Alyssa laughed and shook her head. "*Sisters get mad at*

each other, but it never changes the fact that we're family. Family sticks together. You're stuck with me, forever."

Forever.

Who knew how short that would be?

Melody approached the granite headstone. It was simple, which just felt wrong for Alyssa. Nothing about Melody's younger sister had ever been simple. Alyssa was complicated and dramatic. She was bursting with color and energy—even at night. Melody remembered that her sister would toss restlessly in bed, having difficulty winding down because she was go-go-go all the time.

Alyssa would whisper across their dark bedroom to Melody, *"Psst. Are you awake?"*

"I am now," Melody would groan. *"I have school tomorrow. So do you. Go to bed."*

Melody had taken on a bit of a motherly role after their mother died. They'd had their Great-aunt Jo to step in sometimes, but Jo didn't live with them. Melody was the one who'd been there when Alyssa had gotten her period. No way their father could have ever handled that well. He seemed clueless about raising girls. Melody had taught Alyssa about tampons and shaving her legs. At least Jo had done the honors of telling them both about sex. Jo had waited until Melody was sixteen though, and unfortunately high school sex ed class had beaten Jo to the punch.

Melody's father had taken a shot at that lesson too. His only words on the matter were: *"Just don't have it."*

Melody bent and placed the flowers on Alyssa's grave now and stood, memories tossing around like ocean waves. Her father was standing beside her so it was awkward. They both just stood there quietly. "Is this what you do when you come here?" Melody finally asked.

"No. I usually talk to them."

Melody glanced over. "You talk to them?"

He looked a bit sheepish as he shrugged. "Yeah. I think

they hear me. I've been over to Sunrise Park too and I've spoken to Jo."

"You have?"

Her father chuckled. "You think I'm crazy now?"

"No. Just sentimental. Who knew?"

"Well, an accountant has feelings despite what some might
think." He cleared his throat. "A father does too." He hesitated for a long moment. Melody remained quiet because she
could feel something heavy weighing on his thoughts.
"Melody, your mother's death destroyed me. I didn't think I
had any heart left to break after that, but then—" He took a
shallow gulp of air. "Then Alyssa—" His voice cracked and
Melody could see that he was fighting off tears.

She reached for his hand, covering it with her own. "It's
okay, Dad."

"No," he said quickly. "It's not okay. That's what I'm trying to tell you. It was not okay for me to blame you for what
happened to her that night. It wasn't your fault. You need to
know that I never thought it was."

Melody's eyes flooded with unexpected tears and her mind
brought back memories of that last night in Trove Isle before
she'd left town. Her father had asked why Alyssa was the one
who was taken. Why her? Melody had taken that to mean:
why not Melody? She'd interpreted those words as her father
wishing she was the one who'd died instead. She shook her
head. "You were just upset. Distraught. It's understandable.
You lost a daughter."

"But you lost a sister." He held her gaze, allowing his tears
to cloud his vision. "Melody, I can blame my emotions, but
that doesn't make how I acted okay. I have regretted the
words I said to you ever since they left my mouth. That regret
has held me prisoner. It kept me from reaching out so many
times after you left. What right did I have to keep you as a
daughter after the way I acted? I was ashamed of myself."

Melody swallowed. "It's okay, Dad."

He squeezed her hand. "Don't do that, Melody."

"Do what?" she asked, furrowing her brow.

"Accept my apology before I've even given it to you. You've always done that. You forgive so easily after someone has hurt you."

"Isn't that a good thing?" She offered a half smile in his direction, not understanding what he was saying.

"Not in this case. You need to think about whether my simple apology is enough. It's okay if it's not. It's okay if you need more time." He nodded. "I just needed you to know, it was never your fault."

Melody was overcome with an emotion she couldn't quite pinpoint. The feeling washed over. She waited to speak until she knew she wasn't going to break down. "I'm sorry too, Dad. All this time I thought I was justified in leaving and not coming back, but maybe I was just immature."

He pinned his gaze on Melody's mother's headstone. "We all have regrets, Melody. No one gets out of this life without them."

"Except maybe Alyssa," Melody said. "She died too young to have real regrets. Maybe she's the lucky one."

Her father reached for Melody's hand and held it. "All I know is that I'm glad you're here with me now."

"I've missed you so much," she said, stepping toward him and throwing her arms around him now. She didn't think, she just followed her compulsion to hug him.

"I've missed you too, Melody. So, so much," he whispered in her ear. Finally, Melody pulled back and wiped at her eyes. "Do you think Mom and Alyssa are watching us right now?"

"And Jo too. They're probably dancing up there. The three of them."

"Alyssa is singing," Melody said with a wide smile, imagining the scene.

"With her beautiful angelic voice," her father agreed.

"She would have been a star."

"She already was in my eyes. You too."

Warmness moved through Melody's chest as her father looked at her. She wasn't sure she'd ever felt so much warmth radiating off him.

"You ready to go home?" he asked, reaching for her hand.

Melody swallowed. *Home.* She was well past ready to be home and only just now realizing it.

Last time Melody had come to the women's prison, she'd been on edge and nervous to see her old friend. Today she was just excited. She and Liz took a seat and waited for Bri to join them.

Melody put her arms out in front of her on the picnic table, the bracelet catching the bright sunlight and making it sparkle slightly. "I can't wait to show Bri the new charms we've added," Melody told Liz.

"I can't wait to let Bri wear it once she's out. It's not right that she hasn't gotten a turn yet."

Melody glanced over. "Want to drive on the way back?"

Liz's eyes rounded comically. "On the highway? No, I don't think I'm ready for that."

Melody smiled as she fidgeted absently with the charms. Then Bri was standing at the head of their table. She'd snuck up on them without them seeing her.

"Hey, you two. What are you chatting about?" She plopped down on the bench across from them.

"I was asking Liz if she wanted to drive back," Melody said.

Bri looked at Liz. "Really? I thought you were just sticking to your neighborhood right now."

"I am." Liz rolled her eyes. "Baby steps, okay? I'm not driving home."

Melody shared a look with Bri. "How are you?" she finally asked.

"Counting down the days. It's less than thirty now." Bri

tipped her face up to the sun, closing her eyes for just a moment. She sucked in an audible breath. "Ah, I can practically smell my freedom."

"And your lifetime supply of free bites from The Bitery?" Liz asked.

"Mmm. So, how are you two doing? What is it that you're not telling me in our daily messages?" Bri's gaze bounced between them.

"Well," Melody said, "I'm going to prom."

Bri straightened into a more upright position. "What?"

"Christopher West is chaperoning the high school's prom like he does every year, and he asked me to join him," Melody clarified.

"Like on a date?" The corners of Bri's lips curled into a small smile. "You're dating Christopher?"

"No." Melody quickly shook her head. "I mean, I guess it's kind of a date. But it's also me helping out with chaperoning the kids."

"Of all the people to choose to chaperone, they ask a person who doesn't even live in Trove anymore? No. Not buying that." Bri lifted a brow and looked at Liz. "You're going too?"

"Oh, no way. You couldn't drag me to prom with a bribe of a million dollars. Not happening."

"Why is that?" Bri asked, her dark brows furrowing, making a little divot between her eyes.

Liz's expression wilted. "You seriously have to ask?"

"Because of what happened to us?" Bri asked. "That's why you're not going?"

Liz nodded. "Isn't that enough of a reason?"

"I thought you were facing your fears this summer," Bri pressed. "You're driving. You're going to tell your mom you don't want to run The Bitery once she's back in the country. You're making plans for your own photography business."

"Going to prom is different." Liz looked down at her interlocked hands.

Bri gestured at Melody. "I don't know. Melody's going."

Melody bumped her shoulder against Liz's. "It's not too late. We can find you the perfect dress in my shop."

"Your shop?" Bri asked.

"Hidden Treasures."

Bri grinned widely now. "Wow. From wanting to get rid of it to calling it yours. That's new."

Melody shook her head. "I mean, the store is mine right now. Until I sell it."

Bri clasped her hands in front of her, looking between Melody and Liz. Then her gaze fell on the charm bracelet. "Oh. I almost forgot. I have something for us." She reached into the front of her shirt and pulled something out of her bra. "Sorry. I don't have pockets." She slid a charm across the picnic table.

"Wow. Where'd you get this?" Melody asked.

"I work in the library here. The librarian had a bookmark with a charm attached."

"You stole it?" Liz's jaw dropped.

Bri frowned, looking annoyed by the question. "No. She said I could have it. She *gave* it to me."

"Oh. Sorry," Liz said sheepishly.

Bri shook her head and pointed at the charm. "It's a wave. I want to add it to the bracelet. And when I'm free, one of the first things I want to see is the ocean. It's been years. That's my dream."

Melody picked the charm up and inspected it. Then she looked up at Bri. "We're going on a beach trip as soon as you're free. I love that idea."

"Perfect way to end the summer," Liz agreed.

Melody used her fingernails to pry the metal circle attachment open. Then she attached the wave charm and pinched the circle shut again. "There." She handed the bracelet to Bri to admire.

Bri turned the bracelet around, looking at every charm for a moment. "It's getting full. I can't believe after all this time, we're finishing what we started with this bracelet. It feels like a full-circle moment." She handed the bracelet back to Melody.

Melody tipped her head to the side and gestured at Liz. "It's Liz's turn."

Bri handed it to Liz instead. "Here you go."

"And once you're out, it'll be your turn." Liz slipped the bracelet onto her wrist.

"You should consider going to prom," Bri said, returning to the previous subject. "That feels like a full-circle moment too. If I were out, I'd go for sure. Just to prove that I can. And for Alyssa. I think she would want us all to go, seeing that we never got a chance."

Liz looked suddenly pale. Her hand moved to the bracelet on her wrist, turning it around and around. She seemed to pull in a shaky breath. "I don't need to prove that I can. Because I know for a fact that I can't. That's one thing I can't do." She shook her head. "Ever."

CHAPTER TWENTY

LIZ

Liz caught herself fidgeting and stopped. She wasn't anxious exactly. It was just a bad habit. Okay, maybe Dr. Mayer still made her a little nervous. He kept writing notes on his pad of paper, which always made her a little paranoid. What was he writing?

"I'm glad to hear you're feeling good behind the wheel. That's quite a milestone for you," he said.

"Well, I didn't drive here today," Liz pointed out. "I rode my bike." But she'd wanted to drive. She'd contemplated it. "My friend, Melody, is chaperoning the high school's prom in two weeks."

Dr. Mayer gave her a steady look. "Oh?"

"She's going with Christopher West, a teacher at the school."

"And how do you feel about that?" Dr. Mayer asked.

Liz could have predicted that question. "Irritated," she answered honestly.

"Irritated that she would feel okay going after what happened to you and your group of friends?" Dr. Mayer asked.

"No." Liz shook her head. That wasn't it at all. She was happy for her friends. "I'm irritated that I'm not able to go too. I don't feel comfortable. The idea makes me sweaty and nauseous." Even talking about this right now had her palms damp. "I should be okay by now, shouldn't I? I mean, it's been years. Melody is fine to go. Why aren't I?"

Dr. Mayer's gaze was steady. "You tell me?"

Liz shrugged as she searched for some deep answer. There was only one explanation for why she couldn't bring herself to go to prom too. "Because I'm not as strong as she is."

Dr. Mayer gave her an unwavering look. "I don't think that's true. I see you as a very strong woman, Liz. Look at all you've overcome."

Liz didn't feel like she'd overcome anything. She'd just been surviving, living one breath and one day at a time.

"What would happen if you did go to this prom?" Dr. Mayer asked.

Liz squirmed in her chair. She uncrossed her legs and re-crossed to the other side, still not feeling comfortable. Was his office usually this hot? "What do you mean?"

"Exactly what I said. What would happen?"

"Well, my chest would feel tight. I might have a heart attack. I'd definitely have a panic attack."

"You've had panic attacks before. You know what to do. You know how to calm yourself when you're having one. And you have a support system who could help you if that were to happen," he said.

Liz swallowed past a tight throat. "We could get in a car accident on the way. Just like we did that night."

"That could happen next time you're a passenger in the car with someone though, couldn't it?" he asked. "Didn't you say you just traveled to the women's prison with your friend? And you arrived back home safely."

Liz was fidgeting again. She didn't even try to stop herself this time. She uncrossed her legs and folded them underneath her this time.

"What would happen if you said yes and went to that prom and proved to yourself that you were strong? It's not about proving that to anyone else. Everyone who knows you already knows that's the case."

Liz blinked, trying to calm the burn of tears in her eyes that was clouding her vision.

"What's the worst thing that could happen?" Dr. Mayer pressed.

Liz could feel her heart beating harder. She could hear the sound of her pulse in her ears. All of this just because she was thinking about going to the prom. "I could die, I guess," she finally said.

"You could die sitting here right now."

Did he think that would make her feel calmer?

"Now, what's the best thing that could happen?" he asked, leaning forward over his desk.

Liz shook her head, her fingers running over the charm bracelet on her wrist. Her fingers felt each one, trying to name them in her head as she moved from one to the other. A dress. A butterfly. The newest one—the wave, representing Bri's dream of going to the ocean. "I guess the best thing would be that I wouldn't die. I'd live."

"You'd live," Dr. Mayer repeated, the smallest hint of a smile on his mouth.

Liz wasn't sure she'd ever seen him smile before. He always looked so serious and contemplative. "Yeah. I'd live and I'd be proud of myself, I guess. It'd be like I passed some impossible test."

"I'm guessing that would be an amazing feeling," Dr. Mayer said. "Doing something that is hard. That you feel incapable of doing."

Liz's heart was still beating fast, but it wasn't solely from fear anymore. There was a spark of something more. Possibly excitement. "Yeah."

"What if you just thought about it for a couple of days? What if you devoted some time to picturing yourself in a dress and high heels. Picture your friend picking you up and driving you to the high school. Imagine that the trip is uneventful and you feel calm all the way there. Then you arrive and go inside and you're still calm. Do you think you could work on imagining that?"

"Visualization?" Liz asked.

"It's a very effective tool that's always available to you. Prom is two weeks away, you say? Visualizing yourself there every day for two weeks might make it a reality."

Liz looked down at the bracelet. Her fingers were still resting on the wave charm that Bri had added. "So you think I should go?"

"If there's something a person can do to make themselves feel a sense of pride, to overcome a fear, or something they can hurdle that will advance them leaps and bounds instead of setting them back, I always think they should take a chance and do that thing."

Liz was surprised that Dr. Mayer was fully smiling at her now. "I'll think about it. And visualize it."

He leaned back in his chair, a satisfied look on his face. "Good. Let me know what happens."

She nodded and unfolded her legs to stand. "I will."

Later that evening, Liz sat on her front porch swing, letting the forward and backward motion carry her thoughts to and from various places. Rose was working at The Bitery tonight with her friend Devin helping out. Liz was certain that Rose probably wasn't dressed appropriately for running the counter, but Liz wasn't Rose's mother. When their mother got back, *she* could try to reign in Liz's unruly, outspoken, vibrant, and courageous sister.

Liz's gaze traveled to the brightest star in the sky tonight, which made her mind go to Jo. "Hey, Jo. Hey, Alyssa," she said quietly, blowing out a breath as the swing screeched in its upward motion. "Do either of you have any advice for me?" As soon as she uttered the words, movement on the street caught her eye. She blinked the figure into focus, realizing it was Matt walking Mr. Beast past her home. She flicked her gaze back to the star. "You never were very subtle," she told Jo, wondering and hoping her late friend could hear her.

Matt stopped walking when he seemed to notice her sitting there. Then he lifted his hand and waved.

She waved back, feeling a jolt of something in her heart. A tiny lightning bolt of energy. A spark.

"It's a beautiful night," he called across her lawn. "Care to join me on my walk?"

Liz started to say no, but the word came out all wrong. "Sure." She stood on wobbly legs and headed down the porch steps. Then she walked across the grass to where he was standing. Mr. Beast ran over to sniff her shoes.

"Complete honesty here," Matt said, looking at her, "I was pretty sure you were going to turn me down."

"Me too." She turned her body forward and took a step, waiting for him to walk with her. It was just an evening stroll under the stars with a guy who made her heart skip. No big deal, she told herself.

"How was your day?" Matt asked.

Liz considered the question, deciding to follow Matt's lead and go with complete honesty too. "I had an appointment with my psychologist."

"Yeah?"

She listened for any hint of judgement, but there was none. No one had ever judged her for seeking help. It was her own paranoia and self-judgement that made her shy away from talking about things with people. "Mm-hmm. He thinks I'm a strong person."

Matt cleared his throat. "Well, he sounds like a smart guy. For the record, I think the same thing about you."

Liz glanced over. "You do?"

"Hell, yeah. The strongest woman I know."

Liz took a shuddery breath, feeling the little bump in her pulse. "He wants me to visualize myself going to prom. And consider going for real. Just like Melody."

"Wow," he said quietly. "What do you think? Is that something you're ready for?"

"I don't know."

Matt was quiet for a long moment. "I'm not a psychologist. I'm just a cop. But, in my book, you're strong regardless of whether you decide to go. You could decide to shut yourself inside your home and never get behind a steering wheel again, and it wouldn't make me think you were weak."

Liz kept her gaze forward. She couldn't look at Matt right now. She might break. "Thank you for saying so."

"I'm just saying what's true. Do you want to go to prom?" he asked.

They stopped walking so that Mr. Beast could lift his leg on a mailbox post. Liz finally looked at Matt.

"No, I really, really don't want to go," she said. She wasn't sure, but she thought she saw disappointment flash in his eyes. "But . . . somewhere deep inside I feel like I need to. Does that make sense?"

Mr. Beast tugged on the leash that Matt was holding and they began to walk again.

"When I was a kid, I was scared of the dark." Matt chuckled softly beside her. "Like, I was really scared. I had a night-light, a flashlight, you name it. My mom said it was okay to be afraid of something, but then I went to stay with my dad and he belittled me. He said no son of his was going to let fear win out."

"You were just a kid," Liz said softly.

Matt nodded. "Yeah, my dad was a first-class jerk on a lot of levels. He didn't let me have my nightlight or flashlight. He took the bulb out of the ceiling fixture so I couldn't have light at all. Those first couple nights were the longest of my life." He looked over at Liz. "I would never be the person to tell you to do something just because it scares you." His jawline bunched and released. "I will say, after that visit with my dad, I was never afraid of the dark again. I was never really afraid of anything much again." He looked at her. "Except maybe a pretty woman. Those always scare me."

Liz wanted to look away, but she couldn't. Was he talking about her? Was he calling her pretty? "So, what you're saying is, if I force myself to face my fears and go to prom, I'll never be afraid of anything again?"

Matt shook his head on a smile. "No, I'm not saying that at all. But I am offering to go with you, if you want me to."

Liz's heart melted at the offer. Matt had asked her to go to prom with him every year for the last five. It was always a casual invitation that she didn't think twice about turning down. "He went about it all wrong, but I think your dad was just doing what he thought was best."

"Loving me in his own way." Matt nodded. "I know. So? What do you say?"

Liz felt shaky and weak. "My doctor told me to visualize going. I haven't really been able to picture it in my mind. I can't imagine wearing the dress or walking into the gym. It's like my brain refuses to go there."

The sound of Mr. Beast's paws against the pavement ahead punctuated the quiet of the night. "I understand," Matt said after a moment.

Liz shook her head, knowing Matt didn't understand. "I haven't been able to visualize going until right now in this moment. I can imagine going with you. Kind of." She laughed nervously. "I mean, it's a blurry vision. But I'm there. With you. It doesn't feel as scary with you beside me."

Matt grinned at her, his eyes seeming to sparkle as they reflected the stars. "Then we should go—together. I can be your nightlight."

"I would like that."

To: Liz Dawson
From: Bri Johnson

Subject: Grounded

Liz,

There's something so comforting about doing what's familiar. I love working in the prison library. I love it, and the thought of not having this job to go to once I'm out makes me feel breathless and panicky. Once I leave this building, I won't have any of the familiar things that I've come to rely on these last few years. You're probably thinking, "you'll have me." But even you aren't familiar because I'm used to turning to you with an e-message. I'm not used to seeing you face-to-face all that often. I'm not the adventurous girl I once was, who loved the idea of what was new and exciting. I've changed. We all have. And now I'm faced with having to change again because I can't be who I've become in this prison out there in the real world. I just can't. And I can't go back to who I was before I got here either. Anyway, I guess what I'm trying to say is, don't be surprised if I continue to email you once I'm free. Our e-messages might just be the one familiar thing that keeps me grounded.

B

CHAPTER TWENTY-ONE

MELODY

Melody was waiting impatiently. What was taking Liz so long? Melody had hung a half dozen dresses inside the tiny dressing room of Hidden Treasures for Liz to try on. Surely one of them fit.

"Liz?" Melody listened as movement rustled behind the closed door. "Liz, are you okay?"

Finally, the door opened and Liz appeared wearing the same clothes she'd stepped into the room wearing.

"You didn't try on any of the dresses?" Melody asked.

"I did. I tried all of them on. None of them felt right." Liz blew out a breath.

"Well, that's okay. I'll find more. There are dozens more dresses here and if they don't work, then we'll go shopping somewhere else." She forced a smile, trying to convince Liz. She really didn't want to give Liz any reason to second-guess her decision to chaperone prom with Matt. This was a huge deal—for all of them. "Want to keep looking?"

Liz lowered her head. "No. I think I'm done for tonight. Maybe this weekend. I was considering going to take photographs of Sunset Park at sunset."

"Oh? Are you riding your bike over there?" Melody asked. Sunset Park was several miles away.

Liz rolled her lips together. "No. I'm driving." She scanned the store and Melody had the distinct impression that her friend was holding something back.

"I'm not sure you're ready to drive solo just yet."

"That's true." Liz slid her gaze to Melody. "Matt is riding shotgun."

Melody felt her eyebrows lift. She pulled her hands together at her chest, pressing her fingertips together. "A date?"

"No." Liz shook her head quickly. "Not a date. It's just . . . we're just friends. He wants to help me practice my driving, and I want to take photographs of the sunset. For my business."

Melody noted the slight blush rising on Liz's cheeks. "Well, I think that's wonderful. I want one of the prints after you take them. I'll hang it on my office wall."

"Your office wall?" Liz asked.

Melody nodded. "In Charlotte."

"Right." Liz looked away again.

Guilt layered in Melody's gut. She had a right to have a life outside of Trove Isle, didn't she? A career? "Maybe I need two prints so I can keep one here in my room at my dad's too. Since I'll be coming home so often now."

Liz's smile was wobbly. "Anyway, I need to go. Matt is meeting me at my house."

"Have fun. I'll keep an eye out for the perfect dress for you. It'll show up, I promise," Melody called to Liz's back. She watched Liz leave and then she continued to stand there for a long moment trying to decide what to do with herself. As she pondered, a tall, dark, and handsome man appeared on the other side of Hidden Treasure's door.

Everything inside of Melody lit up. Her reaction to seeing Christopher took her off guard a bit. She'd known she had a growing attraction to him, but she hadn't realized just how much it had grown in the last few days.

He opened the door and stepped in, his eyes trained on her. "I was in the area so . . ."

Melody grinned. "Oh? What were you on Seagull Street for? Bites from The Bitery or books from The Book Whore?"

Christopher rolled his eyes playfully. "I can't believe Danette gave her store that name. But no, I get my books from the library. I can't bring myself to shop at a place called The Book Whore."

Melody mocked a pout. "But it's Danette. And supporting small-town businesses is crucial to keeping their doors open."

Christopher stepped closer. "I didn't realize you were so passionate about small-town things. Now that you're a city girl and all."

Melody enjoyed the flirty banter between them as he came closer. She leaned against a circular rack next to her, ready to spout off something witty—hopefully—when the rack rolled under the weight of her arm. Instead of coming off witty and charming, she fell toward the ground clumsily.

"Whoa!" Christopher reached for her arm, but she was too far gone on her trip toward the floor. Instead of catching her, she pulled him down along with her. It wasn't at all like one of those romantic scenes in a rom-com featuring Sandra Bullock or Kate Hudson. No, this was less romantic and more awkward.

"Ow," Melody moaned, trying to pull her arm from under Christopher's weight.

"Are you okay?" he asked, lifting himself off her. He stopped though when he realized her charm bracelet was snagged on his necklace. She'd never realized he wore a gold chain. He must keep it tucked in his shirt.

"Oh, sorry," she said. "Let me see if I can—"

Christopher hovered over her as she tried to disconnect their jewelry.

"This bracelet has a mind of its own. This is the second time it's done this to me." Melody's hands were shaking too much to free the jewelry.

Christopher grinned at her. "You're talking about it as if it's a living, breathing thing."

Melody noticed the charm on Christopher's necklace. "What is that?"

He looked down at his chain. "It was my dad's. He wore this every day. When he died, I assumed he'd be buried in it, but my mom gave it to me after the funeral. Dad told her he wanted me to have it. I kind of feel like he's with me somehow, when I'm wearing it."

Melody's eyes were suddenly burning. "That's beautiful."

He looked at her for a breathless moment. "You're beautiful."

Her first impulse was to pull away, but she was kind of stuck to him right now. "Um . . ."

"Sorry." He shook his head and then attempted to disconnect the charm bracelet and his chain himself. "I shouldn't have said that."

"No, it's okay. Thank you. That's nice to hear. You don't have to apologize."

Christopher looked at her again, his gaze roaming from her eyes to her lips. Then the jewelry seemed to release on its own. He rolled onto the floor and sat beside her, running a hand through his dark hair. "Well, that was interesting."

Melody laughed nervously. "And I'm going to have a bruised butt tomorrow."

He side-eyed her and cleared his throat. "I probably shouldn't be thinking about your butt."

Melody burst out laughing. "Sorry."

"I, uh, know I wasn't your favorite person when you arrived in Trove this summer, but I'm glad we're getting closer," he said earnestly.

"Me too." She picked herself off the floor and offered a hand down to help him up.

He looked skeptical. "You're not scared I'm going to try to get payback and pull you down like you just did to me?"

She laughed some more. "I guess I would deserve it."

He placed his hand in hers and she used her body weight to pull him upward. She wasn't fooled. He stood on his own. And when he did, he was standing closer than she'd expected. Her heart thumped in her chest. Falling for him was an epically bad idea. She wasn't staying, and she'd hurt enough people in Trove Isle already. She was making amends with the people here. Getting involved with Christopher opened the door to potential hurt feelings and heartbreak. Remaining just friends was best.

"Is your, uh, butt okay?" he asked.

Melody grimaced. "I thought we agreed you shouldn't be thinking about my, um . . . backside."

"You started it." His voice dipped low as he leaned in.

"Yes, it's fine." She shrugged. "I mean, I guess ice cream would make it better."

Christopher grinned. "Then, by all means, I should take you to get some. The only question now is one scoop or two?"

"After that fall, I definitely deserve two," she said, not completely talking about the fall on her store floor. It was her heart that was taking the biggest fall this evening.

The next day, Melody opened the thrift store and headed back to the counter to sit and work on an event that Julie had emailed her about overnight. It was easy enough to work the counter while jotting down ideas.

The event was for a client's debut book release. Melody had never planned a book release before, but she was excited. She had all kinds of thoughts about a cake that looked like the book itself, a photo booth to insert people's faces into the book's cover, a karaoke sing-along to the author's playlist inspired by the book. The ideas were coming to mind faster than Melody could jot them in her little notebook.

A bell jingled as the door to the store opened and a customer stepped inside.

Melody looked up and smiled at Mr. Lyme. She expected him to head in her direction, but instead he walked over to the far side of the room where there was a bookshelf. He stopped and looked over the selection for a long moment and then continued perusing the store like any other customer.

Melody thought he looked a bit sad this morning. Or maybe he looked lost.

He stopped and touched a selection of silk scarves that were hanging next to the display of shoes. "This one looks like something Jo would have kept for herself," he said, turning to talk to Melody over his shoulder.

Melody stood and walked around the counter, heading in his direction. "It's nice to see you, Mr. Lyme. Are you looking for something in particular?"

"Not really," he said on a soft sigh. "I was just doing a little shopping and thought I'd stop in." His smile wilted a little at the corners. "Actually, I was just missing Jo and thought I'd come by and see if I could feel her somehow." He glanced around. "I like what you've done with the place. I guess you've decided not to sell it?" There was a hopeful lift to his words.

"I'm still selling. But I've decided to sell this place only to a buyer who intends to keep it open as a thrift store."

Mr. Lyme nodded, his eyes glistening. "I think that's good. Jo would have been pleased to know that."

Melody watched him for a long moment. "Do you feel her here? Right now?"

Mr. Lyme sighed as he continued to glance around. Then he pointed to the corner where all the donated toys were.

"She loved to take the old dolls that were left here. They'd be marked up with Sharpies and their hair would be cut off by their previous owners. Your aunt would spend all day sitting behind that counter scrubbing them clean. She'd even out their haircuts and make them bows to cover the bald spots." He chuckled to himself. "Those dolls would be like new or better by the time she was done."

Melody looked at the current selection of dolls in that corner. She hadn't touched them up the way Jo apparently had. The ones for sale right now were obviously used and well loved. "Sorry. I guess I'm not making Jo proud with the condition of these toys right now."

Mr. Lyme turned to her. "On the contrary. She'd be very proud of you, Melody. She always was. Do you mind if I just walk around for a little longer?"

"Not at all. Take your time." Melody gestured to the counter. "I'll just be up there working."

"What are you working on?"

"An event in Charlotte."

"Ah. That's nice." Mr. Lyme nodded. "I hear your friend Brianna will be having a homecoming soon. Maybe you'll plan an event for her."

Melody hadn't even considered that, but of course she should. "I wouldn't even know who to invite."

"The whole town, of course. She's one of us after all. Doesn't matter how long she's been away. Home is home." He gave her a meaningful look. "Go ahead and work. Don't mind the sentimental old man walking around."

Melody squeezed his shoulder. "Let me know if you need something."

"I will."

Melody returned to her stool behind the counter, but she couldn't focus on the event for her author client anymore. Now her thoughts were on Jo and Mr. Lyme, and all the time they'd lost. On the dolls and Jo's Isle of Lost Toys. On Bri's homecoming event, which had to happen.

Ten minutes later Mr. Lyme came to the counter holding a doll without any clothes. Its hair was matted and someone had taken a purple marker to give it eyeshadow. That or a black eye, Melody wasn't sure. He held it up. "I'd like to purchase this please."

Melody held up a hand. "Take it. No charge."

Mr. Lyme hesitated as if he was debating whether to argue with her. "I'll bring this back once I've given her a Jo-worthy makeover."

Emotions knotted at the center of Melody's chest. She hoped she'd be here to see the results. "Sounds good. Have a good rest of your day, Mr. Lyme."

"You too." He tucked the doll under his arm like a football and turned to walk out.

Once he was gone, Melody wandered over to the toy section as well, scanning over the selection until she finally picked up a little wooden dollhouse that had seen much better days. She wasn't all that crafty but she knew how to work a paint brush. She carried it to the counter and placed it on the floor beside her stool. Then she picked up her notepad and turned the page away from the one for the author event. At the top of the fresh page, she wrote: Bri's Homecoming Event.

To: Bri Johnson
From: Liz Dawson

Subject: Familiar

Bri,

I think some things stay familiar even when you haven't experienced them in years. The heart has memory, maybe a better one than your brain. The familiar doesn't need your yesterday or last week to be relevant. You'll see. Once you get home, everything will feel true and right, almost like you never left. And if that's not the case, and you really need to, of course you can email me, day or night. I'll always reply.

xx,

Liz

CHAPTER TWENTY-TWO

LIZ

The photographs from Sunset Park were displayed on Liz's computer monitor. Everyone in Trove Isle had probably seen a sunset over the park, but these photographs—hopefully—captured the magic of it. Because it was magical, especially when spent with Matt Coffey.

Last night's drive had started rocky, but had turned out to be okay. She'd driven ten miles below the speed limit all the way to Sunset Park, but Matt hadn't said a word—not even when the car behind her had honked and passed them. Liz had taken deep breaths, kept her hands on the wheel, and she'd gotten them to their destination without incident. Matt had done the honors of driving them back to her house afterward because it was late and Liz wasn't ready to drive in complete darkness.

He was gentle and thoughtful, understanding, and handsome. In a word—perfect.

A knock on her office door got her attention. "Yeah?"

"When are you coming out?" Rose asked.

Liz would have guessed that Rose would want Liz to stay in her workroom indefinitely. They'd grown closer lately though. They'd come to an understanding that Liz still didn't quite understand. It was nice. Her mom was right, this summer was good for them. "When I'm finished," Liz responded, realizing she sounded a bit sarcastic. If there was a single sarcastic bone in her body, it was Rose's influence this summer. On a sigh, she turned and opened the door. "Now. I'm coming out now. Is there something you need?"

Rose furrowed her brow. "No. I was just, well, you're always trying to get me to have dinner with you so . . ."

Liz checked the time on her cell phone. "Oh. I didn't realize it was so late. Are you hungry?"

"A little." Rose lifted a shoulder. "I can help. If you need me to. And, um, well, Josh is here."

The preppy guy? "He is? Why?" Liz asked.

Rose looked taken back. "Because he's my boyfriend."

"Boyfriend?" This was news to Liz. "Since when?"

Rose shrugged a shoulder. "I wouldn't expect you to know this, because you're kind of oblivious to the dating world, but people don't actually ask you to be boyfriend or girlfriend anymore. It's not like I can tell you the exact moment it was official. We like each other. We don't want to hang out with anyone else. At least not romantically. That makes him my boyfriend."

"Makes sense," Liz said, overlooking the slight dig at her own personal life.

"So, Josh is here. And . . ." Rose nibbled on her lower lip, "he's hungry too."

Liz wanted to laugh. "Are you asking me to cook dinner for you two?"

"Not just for us. For you too," Rose said. "I kind of thought it'd be nice if we all got to know each other."

"Oh." It would have been nice if Rose would have given her a heads up. Liz wasn't even sure she had anything to cook. "Well, let me check the fridge and see what I can whip up."

"You're okay with this?" Rose asked as an afterthought. It

was still nice that she asked at all. "You're not going to start breathing real weird or anything, are you?"

"I wasn't planning to. But I can if you want me to embarrass you in front of your guy friend." Liz grinned, loving this new, more playful version of herself that was surfacing now that her anxiety was taking a back seat. It was still there, but it wasn't driving her life.

"No. That's okay." Rose smiled back at her.

"So where is Josh?" Liz asked.

"In the living room. Watching TV with Matt."

So much for keeping her anxiety in the back seat. "Matt? He's here?"

Rose furrowed her brow. "I thought you knew he was stopping by. He said he had a free night and wanted to see if you were up for another driving lesson."

That was sweet. He was always thinking of her. "Where is he now?" Liz asked, suddenly worried that she looked like a complete and utter mess.

"He's sitting on the couch. I told him you were in the bathroom and you'd be out to see him in a minute." Rose grimaced.

Liz's breathing grew shallow. "You told him I was in the bathroom? For how long?"

"Like fifteen minutes now, I guess. I left him there a while ago. Sorry."

It was too late for apologies. "Well if your boyfriend is staying for dinner, looks like I'll have a chance to embarrass you too."

Rose held up both hands. "I'll go tell Matt I was mistaken. And invite him to dinner." Her lips curled in a barely smile. "It can be like a double date."

Liz shook her head. "Matt and I are just friends," she said reflexively, but even she wasn't buying that line anymore. She had feelings for him. Feelings that were getting harder and harder to ignore.

"Great." Rose turned back and started walking before Liz could protest any more. "I'll tell your *friend* that he's welcome to stay for dinner with us."

Half an hour later, Liz placed a lasagna at the center of her table. She'd already had one prepared in the freezer and had only needed to pop it in the oven. She sat down nervously beside Matt.

"For someone who said she had nothing to cook, you sure know how to pull together something delicious," he commented.

"You haven't even tried it yet." Liz cut him a slice and placed it on his plate.

"If it tastes as good as it smells, it's the best I've ever had," Matt said.

"No wonder you're still in the friend zone. You're trying to win my sister over by lying to her," Rose said, sarcastically.

Matt didn't even blink. "I'm not lying. I'm building her up whenever and wherever possible. The world does a decent enough job of tearing people down. Any guy worth his salt will guard against that."

Liz noticed that he didn't argue that he wasn't trying to win her over. She placed a square of lasagna on Rose and Josh's plates too. Then she placed some on her own plate and sat down. "Well, let's taste and see." She picked up her fork but waited for someone else to take the first bite.

"Mm. Delicious," Josh said, sharing a glance with Matt.

Matt grinned. "There you go." He looked at Rose. "You might have yourself a keeper there."

"She's only sixteen," Liz objected. "She's not allowed to have a keeper yet."

Rose tasted the lasagna. "He's right. This is pretty decent."

"You're my sister. You don't have to worry about losing or keeping me," Liz said.

"No, but I do want to build you up. And besides, it's true. It's better than Mom's if you ask me. But don't tell her I said so."

Liz took a bite now and nodded. "Mm. Actually, you're right. It is better than Mom's," she said—because there was nothing wrong with building herself up either.

The next day, Liz was trembling from head to toe. She'd shaken the entire drive from Trove Isle to the women's prison. Pulling into an empty parking spot, she put the gear into PARK. Then she turned the key in the ignition and turned the car off, finally releasing a breath. "I did it!"

Melody laughed beside her. "Yes, you did." She blew out a breath too, gaining Liz's attention.

"You were nervous too?" she asked.

Melody grimaced and held her fingers an inch apart. "Just a tiny bit. You're a new driver and we weren't on backroads anymore. That was a tough drive. I'm proud of you."

Liz shook out her hands. "I'm proud of me too." She handed the keys over to Melody. "But you're driving us on the way back home. That's enough for me for one day."

Melody dropped the keys in her purse. "And enough for me too." She pushed her car door open and stepped out. "Let's go see Bri."

Liz pushed the driver's side door open and stepped out as well, meeting Melody around the hood. Then they headed toward the expansive building in front of them. Liz had the bracelet on today. Melody had slipped it on her wrist before they'd set off.

"For luck," she'd said.

It had given Liz a certain confidence during the drive over. She'd found herself glancing at it every time she felt her nerves getting the best of her. Then she'd taken a breath and continued forward.

"I can't wait to tell Bri that I'm the one who drove us

here." Liz picked up her pace, matching Melody's. They were both eager to see their friend. And soon they wouldn't have to drive an hour just to visit with her. Soon Bri would be free and home where she belonged.

After checking in at the front and being led to an open area outside, the two of them sat down at a picnic table and waited for Bri to appear.

Liz rested her arms in front of her, letting the sun's rays bounce off the charm bracelet.

Melody elbowed Liz. "Here she comes."

Liz straightened and looked up, watching Bri draw closer. As she approached, Liz noticed the dark bruise around Bri's left eye. "What happened?"

Bri's smile was slow in coming. "It's nothing."

"It doesn't look like nothing to me." Melody leaned in closer to get a better look at Bri. "Did you get in a fight or something?"

"Or something." Bri took a seat in front of them. She blew out a breath. "Another inmate has a problem with me. Now that I'm on the short rows. Sometimes folks around here get jealous and start picking fights." Bri gestured at her face.

"Oh, no. I'd hoped people would be happy for you," Liz said.

"Most are." Bri shrugged. "Anyway, I'm just hoping this doesn't push my release date back."

"What? Are you serious?" Melody's voice rose a notch. "It wasn't your fault. You didn't start the fight."

"No, but it's my word against hers. I'm lucky I even got to visit with you two today."

"That's not fair," Liz said.

This made Bri smile. "In case you haven't learned that lesson yet, life isn't always fair."

Liz lowered her gaze and looked at her bracelet. "Well, I'm confident you're still getting out when you're supposed to.

Our luck is turning up." She looked at Bri. "In fact, I just drove here, and I didn't stop to vomit or breathe into a paper bag a single time."

Bri's lips parted. "Are you messing with me?"

"Nope. She's telling the truth," Melody said. "And . . ."

"There's more?" Bri looked between them. "What else?"

Liz rolled her lips together. "And I'm chaperoning the prom with Melody, Christopher, and Matt."

Bri pulled her head back, her eyes subtly rounding. "You're going to prom? And you have a date with Matt?"

Liz shook her head. "No. We're just going as friends. It's not like that." Even though some part of Liz wanted it to be—a small, suppressed part.

Bri had a huge smile on her face. "Same as Melody and Christopher. Well, this is great news. I wish I was going to be out in time to see that."

"Me too." Liz reached across the picnic table and squeezed Bri's hand. "Next year."

"You're already planning to go again next year? This is a pretty big deal." Bri looked around the prison courtyard and withdrew her hand. Liz knew it was because physical contact was discouraged. So many things had been stripped away from Bri. It wasn't fair. Maybe Bri was right that life wasn't always fair, but sometimes it was. It could be. That was a lesson that they all needed a refresher course in.

When it was time to leave, Liz stood up. "Less than a month. Hang in there."

Bri nodded. "I can get a lot of black eyes in a month's time. No backing out, okay?"

Liz knew she was talking about prom. "Okay."

"I'll make sure she doesn't," Melody said.

Bri gave Melody a long look. "Thanks."

Liz and Melody were quiet as they left the prison. Melody took the driver's seat this time.

"It's hard to leave her here," Melody said, her shoulders rounding toward the steering wheel.

"It always is." Liz watched Melody start the car and reverse out of the parking lot. Then they drove home.

"So," Melody said after several non-starter conversations, "you're wearing the bracelet. What are you doing that scares you and makes you feel alive?"

"Driving to the prison today doesn't count?" Liz asked. "Because that was pretty terrifying."

"Only in your head," Melody said. "You actually didn't seem all that scared. You were calm. You were ready."

Liz turned to watch the world buzz by through her passenger side window. Melody was right. Facing her fears was scary, but worth it. Her fingers felt along the bracelet as she considered Mel's question. Finally, she looked back at Melody. "I'm driving. I'm going to prom. I'm planning to tell my mom I don't want to work indefinitely at The Bitery. I'm going to pursue my own photography business. Everything is changing. Can I just earn my next charm by living?"

Melody glanced over. "That is the point of the charm bracelet. To prove we're alive. Not just zombies."

Liz laughed quietly. "Alyssa had a way with words, didn't she?"

"She did. I think she'd be happy for you. You're taking a lot of huge steps here lately."

Liz's fingers found the muffin charm, her skin trailing the textured frosting. "I'm not sure what scares me more. Going to prom or talking to my mom about The Bitery."

"Well, the bracelet stays on your wrist for both."

"Are you sure?" Liz was hoping to wear it longer, but she didn't want to monopolize it.

"I'm positive. You need it more than I do. And I just promised Bri that I wouldn't let you back down. I don't want to go back on that commitment. I won't." Melody shook her head.

Liz reached over and squeezed Melody's arm.

"Can we stop by Hidden Treasures on the way home?" Melody asked. "I just need to take the donations inside. It looks like it might rain."

"Sure. I'll help. I don't have anywhere to be. Rose has taken to bringing her boyfriend back to my house so I don't mind delaying being a third wheel."

Melody cringed. "I guess that means she feels comfortable at your place."

"Yeah. She's not hiding in the guestroom or leaving every chance she gets anymore. We've made progress. It's nice. And I actually like the guy. I think he's good for her."

"You trust him to be alone with your sister?" Melody asked.

Liz thought for a moment. "Not really, but Matt gave him his seal of approval. And I don't need to trust him. I trust Rose." Which was progress. Liz and Rose had come a long way in their relationship this summer.

Melody stopped at a red light and looked over at Liz. "If you're wondering, I give Matt my seal of approval for you."

Liz suppressed a sigh. She was tired of protesting that she and Matt were anything more than neighbors and friends. Thunder clapped overhead and Liz noted the way Melody stiffened. She pressed the gas and the car's speed picked up. Liz grabbed the handle on the passenger door, squeezing gently and reminding herself that she was safe. What were the odds of getting in two car accidents with her best friend in this lifetime?

"You okay?" Melody asked. "Do I need to slow down? I just don't want any donations to get ruined. I'm still going below the speed limit."

Liz inhaled deeply. "I'm fine. It's okay." She exhaled and noticed the slight sprinkle that began to hit the front windshield. "You can even go a little faster if you need to. I think as long as you're less than five miles per hour above the speed limit, you're safe."

"Five above the speed limit?" Melody grinned. "Who are you and what have you done with Liz Dawson?"

To: Liz Dawson
From: Bri Johnson

Subject: Score one for the home team!

Liz,

Good news! The fight that won me this black eye isn't going to add any prison time to my sentence. I didn't start the fight and I didn't even fight back. Witnesses backed me up on that. I was a bit surprised because Tilly, the one who gave me the shiner, has a way of getting people to say and do what she wants. Not this time.

Anyway, I just wanted you to know. The countdown is still on!

B

CHAPTER TWENTY-THREE

MELODY

When Melody opened the back door to the thrift store three days later, she paused and gaped at the large pile of donations. She wasn't sure if it was from one person or if the entire town had decided to do their spring cleaning all at once and drop their possessions behind Jo's store. *Her* store.

Melody didn't move for a moment. Did Jo get this many donations all the time? No wonder the store was so popular here among the locals. All the reason to keep it running as a thrift shop. She'd spoken to Abigail Winslow about her terms earlier today. There must be someone on the isle who would want to run this place.

Bending, Melody picked up several boxes and carried them inside. She repeated the process until everything was toppled over in her back room, ready for her to go through, clean, and tag.

A silky piece of lavender fabric stuck out from the middle of the pile. There were simple clear-colored rhinestones attached to the hem that made Melody's heart quicken. She'd been keeping her eye out for the perfect dress for Liz, just knowing that it would magically show up. Maybe it was silly of her to think that Jo was arranging for used items to be dropped off to Hidden Treasures that were just Liz's size and in like-new condition.

Melody didn't breathe as she reached toward the silk piece.

"Need help?" someone asked from behind her.

Melody nearly jumped out of her skin, whirling to face Christopher. "How did you get in here?"

"You left the front door open. I just walked in. I thought you heard me enter."

Melody shook her head as she drew a hand to her chest. "No."

"Sorry to startle you. I was just stopping in on my way to the post office. I'm shipping some things out for my mom." He grimaced. "She's gotten into online shopping. I'm returning a few hundred-dollars' worth of stuff she doesn't need. Like a lava lamp. She has no idea what a lava lamp even is."

Melody smiled. "Well, if she really wants one, I have one here that she can have."

Christopher chuckled. "Probably a lot cheaper too. Do you need help with this stuff?"

Melody sighed. "No. I just pulled it in from out back. I'll go through this stuff little by little. The sign out back—or the one that was out back—doesn't seem to deter folks from donating." She gestured to a box of flashlights that had been dropped off. "Got any use for these?"

He leaned against the counter that ran along the wall. "We could use them at prom. Instead of looking for dark spots to make out with our dates, we'll be the ones shining flashlights on those dark spots and telling the kids to break it up."

Melody gave him a small laugh.

"You think I'm kidding? These kids are way more advanced than we were at their age. They know things that I'm still not quite sure I know about even now."

This made Melody laugh. It also made her wonder more about Christopher's love life. "Liz said you're a hot commodity around the isle."

"A hot commodity?" he repeated, lifting his brows.

"Handsome, single guy. With a job. Those are all very important to thirty-somethings."

"Well, you're a beautiful, single woman. With a job. Two jobs actually. At least at the moment. Are you a hot commodity in Charlotte?"

Melody shrugged. "I don't have a whole lot of time for dating. At least I haven't in a while. I can't say I miss it. It's not all that fun in my opinion."

"Then you're not doing it right. Or the shmucks who've been taking you out haven't been doing it right." His gaze hung on hers for a moment. If she were staying any length of time, she might wish Christopher would show her how dating was done right.

Melody looked down at the pile of clothes in front of her. "I was actually about to look at one of these donated items that caught my eye." She pulled the clothing that sat on top of the silky lavender fabric and set it in a second pile. Then she lifted a long gown with simple rhinestone accents that decorated the chest. "It's breathtaking," she finally said.

"Yes, it is. It would look amazing on you."

Melody lifted her gaze, flattered by the compliment. "It's not for me. It's for Liz." She checked the size on the tag. "It's a perfect fit for her." *Thank you very much, Jo.*

"I still can't believe you got her to come with us," Christopher said.

"It wasn't me. It was your friend Matt. I can't believe it either. It'll be good for us though. A full-circle moment."

"Those are the best." He dipped and pulled a He-Man figurine from the pile, seeming to inspect it thoughtfully as he continued talking. "You going with me to chaperone prom feels like one of those moments. I had such a thing for you back in the day. I wanted to ask you out, but I didn't want to be rejected."

Melody's cheeks flushed hot. "I had no idea."

"That's why I couldn't say yes to Alyssa. I didn't want to hurt her, but I only had eyes for you."

Melody wasn't sure how to respond, bewildered that she had totally missed his affection during their teenage years. She had never given Christopher any thought back then because she'd known how much Alyssa liked him. You don't go after your sister's crush. It ultimately never would have worked between Alyssa and Christopher though. Alyssa was destined for Hollywood and Christopher was committed to Trove Isle.

"I've made things weird, haven't I?"

"Only a little," she teased. "I honestly didn't know. You hid it well."

"Yeah? Am I hiding it now too?"

She shook her head as she laughed quietly. "Not so much." Her heart fluttered around in her chest. Needing to redirect the conversation, she gestured toward the figurine in Christopher's hand. "I think the castle got donated too. I carried it inside."

"Are you trying to sell me Castle Grayskull? Jo would be proud of you for that." He set the He-Man doll back in the pile. "Some kid will happily take it off your hands. As for me, I need to get to the post office before it closes. And hope my mom doesn't decide to order more stuff she doesn't need while I'm away." He shook his head. "I don't think she'll be able to live alone much longer. She likes her independence, but I'm thinking I'll be moving in with her soon. I'll keep my own place, of course." There was something delicate in his eyes. A pain he couldn't hide.

"So we'll be neighbors again," Melody said.

"At least until the end of the summer." He looked at her for a moment. "You're staying until then, right?"

"That's the plan, at least. I think it'll probably take a while to sell this place." That wasn't the only reason she wanted more time in Trove Isle. She was working on rebuilding relationships. And perhaps creating a new one with Christopher. Was that foolish? Ultimately, she wasn't planning to move back. Anything she started with Christopher was destined for heartbreak. Right?

The bell above the front entrance jingled as someone else stepped inside the store.

Christopher glanced in that direction. "Looks like you've got a customer. See you later, Mel."

"Bye." She watched him walk out the door. Then she carried the lavender dress toward the front counter and carefully folded it, placing it next to her purse. She couldn't wait to take it to Liz and see what she thought. Melody took a seat on the stool behind her counter and watched the woman who'd stepped into the store. The woman was probably in her mid-to-late fifties. She was tall and blond, towering over the racks of clothes as she aimlessly weaved through. "Do you need help finding something?" Melody finally asked.

The woman beelined in Mel's direction. "I heard this store is for sale."

Melody sat up straighter. "Oh. Yes, it is. It was my great-aunt's thrift store. I'm looking for a buyer to keep the store operating as is. Are you interested?"

The woman really didn't look like she belonged among the used items. She was well-dressed in clothing that was likely all brand-new. "This storefront would be perfect for my boutique," she said.

Melody shook her head. Maybe the woman hadn't heard her correctly. "I'm seeking a buyer who agrees to run this building as Hidden Treasures Thrift Store."

The woman's lips pinched tightly. "Is that even legal? Once someone purchases a storefront, they're free to do with it as they please. It's their property."

"I guess legally that's true." Melody shifted uncomfortably on her stool. This woman obviously wasn't a good prospect for taking over Jo's store. She didn't even look like she belonged here standing in front of the glass case. "I guess the agreement would be in good faith."

The woman set her purse on the counter. "I will pay over your asking price. It's not about money for me. This piece of real estate is gold. I can make you an offer you can't refuse."

The arrogance of this woman! Melody had no intention of selling Jo's beloved store to the likes of this lady. Taking a calming breath, Melody smiled back at the potential buyer. "I'm sorry, but if you don't intend to run this store as is, I'm afraid I am refusing."

The woman leaned closer. "Thirty thousand over asking."

Melody felt like the breath had been knocked out of her. Surely she had heard that wrong. "What? You don't even know what my asking price is."

"Of course I do. The store is for sale. It's public knowledge and I do my homework. So?"

The offer was a lot of money. Melody wouldn't have to worry about covering her expenses for a long time. That kind of money was a down-payment on a house.

"You heard me." As if it was already a done deal, the woman extended her hand to shake.

Melody stared at the woman's hand. "I . . . I'm not sure what to say." She swallowed past a suddenly tight throat. She needed a glass of water. She needed time to process. "Can I . . . can I think about it?"

On a huff, the woman withdrew her hand. "Fine. You have until the end of the week. Then my offer drops to ten K over asking price. No one else is going to give you that. Note to the wise, take the offer and run, honey."

Run. All the thoughts racing through Melody's brain skidded to a sudden stop. She was done running though. Wasn't she?

* * *

At four o'clock, Melody turned the sign in the front window to CLOSED and stepped out of the store, carrying a bag and the lavender dress for Liz. She glanced down Seagull Street toward the pink polka dot awning, hoping Liz was still working The Bitery. She couldn't wait to give her the dress. She also needed to tell her about the offer on the store. It really was an offer she'd be hard-pressed to turn down.

"Melody!" Liz was grinning ear to ear as soon as Melody pushed through the front entrance of The Bitery. "I'm so glad you're here."

Melody approached the counter, wondering at her friend's good mood. "What's going on?"

"I sold two photographs." She gestured toward the wall where her work was displayed and for sale. "And one of the buyers asked if I could be a photographer for their upcoming anniversary party. And I said yes!" Liz was practically jumping up and down behind the counter. "I can drive now, so there's nothing holding me back. Except the fact that I'm using my parents' car and when they return, I won't have consistent access."

"You definitely need a car of your own," Melody agreed. "But we can totally figure that out. You're doing amazing, Liz. I'm so happy for you."

"I couldn't have done this without you," Liz gushed. "If there wasn't a counter between us, I'd hug you so hard. I'm just so . . ."

"Happy?" Melody supplied.

"Yes. That's the perfect word for how I'm feeling." Liz laughed giddily. "This is going to go down as one of the best days ever for me. Nothing can ruin it."

Melody's stomach tied itself into knots. Her news about the potential sale of the store might ruin it. Maybe she should save that tidbit for another day. "Well, here's some more good news for you." She lay the bag on the counter.

"What's that?" Liz asked, her gaze flicking between the bag and Melody.

"A present. Kind of. Look and see."

Liz pulled the bag toward her and peeked inside, her breath audibly catching. She reached inside the plastic covering and pulled the dress out, holding it up against her body. "It's . . . wow. This was donated?"

"Mm-hmm. It's perfect, right?" Melody asked, unable to contain her own enthusiasm.

Liz looked up with tears glimmering in her eyes. "It couldn't be more perfect. Thank you."

Melody shrugged. "I didn't really do anything except pull it from a donation pile."

"Who would get rid of this beautiful dress?" Liz wondered out loud, smoothing her hand over the fabric.

"I don't know, and it doesn't matter. It's yours now."

Liz folded the dress back up and placed it inside the bag again. Then she placed the bag below the counter. "Best day ever," she beamed.

Yeah, the information about the store could wait. Melody wanted to think that Liz would be happy for her, but something told her it was more complicated than that.

To: Bri Johnson
From: Liz Dawson

Subject: Tonight's the night

Bri,
I have my dress on and it's a perfect fit. I feel like Cinderella, which probably sounds stupid, but I do. I'm all dressed up—I barely recognize myself—and just like Cinderella, I feel like there's this ticking time bomb over my head, ready to implode this whole happily ever after. I know that's my anxiety talking, and that's probably not the case. I know that in my head, at least. I'm not sure my heart will ever fully realize that though. I think a heart is like an elephant. It remembers and doesn't forget. Anyway, I'm wearing a beautiful dress, my hair is curled, and I have the charm bracelet dangling on my wrist. This is a momentous occasion for me. I'm going to try to enjoy it—one breath at a time.

xx,

Liz

Chapter Twenty-four

LIZ

"Breathe. Just breathe, Liz." Liz leaned over her knees and covered her face. She was breathing heavily and talking to herself. This was not a good start for the night.

"Liz? . . . Liz, you okay?" Rose's voice carried past the locked bathroom door followed by a knock. "Liz?"

"I'm okay," Liz said, managing to sound convincing enough. At least to her own ears. Liz's mother would have been able to hear the slightly shrill note playing in her words, but probably not her sixteen-year-old sister.

"It's just, you've been in there a while. Josh is going to be here soon, and you said you'd take photographs."

Liz sat up and closed her eyes, inhaling and exhaling deeply. "I will. I just have a touch of an upset stomach."

"Ew. TMI, sis."

Liz almost laughed. "It's probably the burgers from last night. I'll be out in just a second."

"Okay. Good thing you have two bathrooms because I need to touch up my face." She scrunched her face. "And I don't want to go in that bathroom after you."

Liz stood on shaky legs and walked over to the mirror to

inspect her reflection. She barely recognized herself. Rose had done her hair and helped with her make-up. She was wearing her favorite stud cubic zirconia earrings that perfectly complemented the rhinestone neckline of her dress. "You can do this," she whispered to herself. "You've got this." Turning toward the door, she opened it and found Rose standing there, wearing the dress she'd gotten from Hidden Treasures. It had been beautiful on the rack, but it was even more gorgeous tonight, hanging off Rose's shoulders like it was made just for her. Her hair was swept off her neck in an updo, secured by pins accented with black rhinestones. The look was dressy, but also perfectly Rose. "I thought you went to the other bathroom," Liz said, overwhelmed by a sudden outpouring of her emotions.

Rose shrugged. "I was going to. But something told me to stay. In case you needed me. Do you?"

Maybe their mom wasn't the only one who could read Liz's cues.

Liz sucked in a breath. "I'm not going to lie. It's a hard night for me."

"I know that," Rose said quietly. "But I'm hoping it'll also be a wonderful night. For both of us."

The doorbell rang and Rose's entire face lit up. She didn't move to go answer it just yet though. She looked torn between staying with her sister and racing to the door where her boyfriend was waiting.

Liz forced a smile. "Go ahead. I'll get my camera."

"Thank you." Rose reached for her hand and gave it a squeeze. Then she squealed softly and hurried toward the front of the house.

Liz took another deep breath and then went to retrieve her camera from her bedroom dresser, noticing that her hands were shaking. She wanted this to be a good night. She did— for Rose's sake and her own. Tonight was a milestone for her, just like when she'd driven with Melody and then Matt. She was making progress, little by little. Turning, she walked out of her bedroom and down the hall. "Hey, Josh," she said as she entered the living room. "You look handsome in that suit."

Josh looked down at what he was wearing and then gestured to Rose. "I don't look half as great as Rose does. Or you," he said, looking at Liz.

"Aww, that's nice of you to say." Liz liked Josh, which surprised her. "You're going to drive the speed limit tonight, right?" she couldn't help but ask.

"Liz." Rose folded her arms over her chest.

"Sorry. I just need some reassurance for my own sanity." Liz looked at Josh expectantly.

"I will drive the speed limit, make sure Rose is buckled up at all times, and only take the main roads. No backroads."

Liz's lips parted. This guy was impressive. "Matt's right. He's a keeper, Rose."

Rose intertwined her arm with Josh's and leaned in to him. "Okay, take your pictures so we can be on our way."

Liz lifted her camera to her eyes and directed the happy couple on where to stand and how to position their bodies. After a dozen or so pictures, she lowered her Canon and made a shooing motion with her hands. "Don't do anything I wouldn't do."

Rose rolled her eyes playfully. "That's not too hard to accomplish."

Josh opened the front door and then paused. "Liz, your date has arrived," he said, shaking Matt's hand.

Liz imagined that she lit up in the same way that Rose had ten minutes earlier.

Rose pointed a finger at Matt. "Don't drive over the speed limit. Make sure you both buckle up whenever the vehicle is in motion. Take main roads, no backroads. And don't do anything we wouldn't do," she said, gesturing between Liz and Matt.

"That shouldn't be too hard to accomplish," Liz said, impersonating Rose's level of sarcasm.

Rose offered back a smirk. "See you two at the prom. Take good care of her," she told Matt.

Matt glanced over at Liz and everything inside her warmed. "Roger that."

Liz lifted her camera and took photographs of Josh leading Rose out to his older model Mustang. She snapped pictures as they reversed out of the driveway and drove away, suppressing the urge to cry. "I can't help thinking about the night that me, Alyssa, Melody, and Bri set out," she told Matt quietly.

"I'd worry about you if you didn't think about that on a night like this one."

She turned to face him. "You would?"

"Of course. You don't need me to validate your feelings tonight. It's okay to feel any way you want to. And you don't have to hide it from me."

Liz breathed a sigh of relief. "Just hearing that makes me feel a little bit better."

Matt nodded. "Then I'm doing something right."

Liz held up her camera. "Can I take a few photographs of us? I have a tripod and a timer."

"I gotta warn you, I might break your camera. I'm not very photogenic," he said.

"Somehow I doubt that." She punched a playful fist into his shoulder, the touch zinging through her. Stepping away, she placed her camera on its stand and set the timer. "You'll see the red light flashing. Just be ready to smile."

"Got it."

Liz stepped up beside him, keeping a couple of inches of distance between them. As the red light began to flash, Matt pulled her closer and wrapped an arm around her shoulders. Everything inside Liz came alive. Every single cell. Then the camera flashed for an extended moment and Liz's mind leaped to another place and time.

It was her prom night and she, Bri, Melody, and Alyssa were posing for pictures excitedly, standing in Liz's parents' living room. Liz felt beautiful, maybe for the first time in her life. Her aunt had come over to do her hair and makeup. She'd just gotten her driver's license that afternoon and she was doing the honors of chauffeuring their little group of friends to their high school gymnasium.

"Smile!" Liz's mother had said, taking the hundredth photograph.

Alyssa swept her arm around Liz's shoulders and the charm bracelet that she was wearing snagged on Liz's dress. "Oh, no!" Alyssa tugged, but Liz reached out and grabbed her wrist.

"You'll break it. Hold on." Liz attempted to free them from each other as her mom's camera continued to click and flash. Apparently, Liz's mom thought the moment was worth remembering.

"I think this bracelet has a mind of its own," Liz said.

"It's magic, if you ask me." Alyssa grinned. "It's telling us we belong together. Friends for life."

Liz finally freed her dress. "Got it! There. Phew!" She looked up at Alyssa. "We can still be friends for life, but I don't think you want to go to the bathroom with me every time I need to pee tonight."

Alyssa's laughter was contagious. "To the bathroom together, yes, but I don't want to be in the same stall."

Liz's mother's camera clicked again.

"Mom." Liz turned to her mother. "You don't need to capture all the moments."

Her mother sniffled. "Prom night is one of the happiest of your life. You'll never forget it."

"Especially with all the pictures you're taking," Liz said,

sarcastically. Sarcasm wasn't really her thing, but sometimes she caught herself sounding a lot like Bri.

"Liz?"

Liz opened her eyes and looked at Matt as she struggled to take a breath.

He placed a hand on her shoulder. "Hey, you're okay. You're safe. You're at your house with me. I'm not going to let anything hurt you."

She blinked. "I don't want to fall apart tonight. I really, *really* don't."

"Listen, if you're not up to this, I get it. I can call one of the other deputies that I know and ask them to chaperone in my place. I can stay with you if that's what you need."

Liz wished she could pull the plug on this night and take that option. She'd never forgive herself if she backed out now though. This night needed to happen. "No, I want to go. I need to. I can do this."

Matt gave a slight nod. "Yeah, you can. I'm with you one hundred percent of the way."

"Thanks." She blew out a shaky breath. "I hope these photographs turn out great," she said, trying to lighten the mood that she pretty much just ruined.

"Like I said, I'm not very photogenic. But if you're in them, I'm sure those pictures are going to be amazing."

"Such a charmer." She smiled sincerely now. "Okay, let's go." She placed her camera back in its bag and looped it over her shoulder. She wasn't the prom's official photographer tonight, but Christopher had mentioned that she could submit candid pictures to the school's yearbook. Liz stepped out the door and heard Matt pull it shut behind her. Then he walked her over to the passenger side of his truck and opened the door for her.

"Hold on. I forgot." He dipped inside and pulled out a pale-yellow corsage. "For you," he said, straightening back to a standing position in front of her.

"Aww. You didn't have to. This isn't actually a date, so . . ." She trailed off, noting the brief glint of disappointment in Matt's eyes. Who was she kidding? This night had all the makings of a date, including the sparks. "Um, thank you for the corsage. It's beautiful."

"It goes on your wrist. You don't have to wear it if you don't want to. I know you have your charm bracelet, which is way more important. I just know a lot of the kids get them for each other at prom, and I thought you should have one."

"I want to wear it." She held out the wrist that wasn't wearing the bracelet. "Will you do the honors?"

Matt looked almost embarrassed, which struck her as odd. And sweet. He slid the flower on her wrist and met her gaze. "There you go." Gesturing toward the passenger seat, he said, "Your chariot awaits."

Liz reminded herself to stay in the moment as she stepped into his truck.

"Here we go," Matt said as he got behind the steering wheel and cranked the engine.

"You do realize that this ride is going to be way worse for me than a driving lesson. That I might freak out, as Rose puts it, or throw up or . . ."

He reached out and touched her arm. "I know what I'm getting myself into, Liz. I always have." With that, he faced forward and reversed out of her driveway.

What did he mean by that? By saying he always had.

As if hearing her thoughts, Matt glanced over and smiled. "It's no secret that I like you. I don't eat all those muffin bites for my health."

Liz's heart raced. "You don't eat them all anyway. You give them away."

"I eat half of them." He grinned. "And I've always known my chances with you are slim. Like I said, I know what I'm getting into."

"And what's that?" she asked.

"A strictly friends relationship that I'll always wish was more."

Liz clutched the side door, heart racing, thoughts completely on Matt as he drove. "Any other guy probably would have moved on by now, and asked someone else out."

Matt was driving exactly the speed limit and keeping both hands on the wheel. Liz suspected he was working hard to make sure she felt safe. He always made her feel safe, ever since the accident. "Call me an eternal optimist, but I believe one of these days, you're going to look at me and see the man of your dreams."

Liz understood that he was joking. At least she thought so. "Or, one of these days, you're going to realize I'm not the woman of yours."

"Nope." He slid his gaze over for just a moment before returning his focus on the road. "One thing about me is that I know what I like and I never stray from it."

"So, you like petite woman with brown hair. Glasses. The nervous type." Liz slowly released her grip on the door's grab bar. She pulled in a shallow breath and then another, keeping her attention on him while he kept his eyes straight ahead.

"I like the *you* type."

He was laying it all out for her on this ride. Part of her wondered if it was just a distraction technique to keep her mind off the road and where they were headed. If so, it was working.

"I like you, too," she confessed. Maybe she was working hard on distracting herself as well. "I don't think you realize just how hard it would be to date me though."

He glanced over. It was just for a moment and then he returned his gaze forward. "Dating me wouldn't be a cakewalk either, trust me. I like to think the good outweighs the not-so-good though. I think that's probably true in most relationships. And just so you're aware, I'm not afraid of hard things."

Liz felt a little flutter inside her chest. "Good to know." She was glad he was facing forward so he wouldn't see just how hard she was working to hold back a giddy grin. How could she be grinning at a time like this? She was on her way to prom, the very last place she would ever want to go.

Finally, he pulled into the parking lot for the high school gym and cut the engine.

He released his seatbelt and looked over. "We made it," he said in a near whisper.

She rolled her lips together, wondering if she should ask the question on her mind. "Did you, um, mean what you said? Or were you just trying to distract me?"

"Did I distract you?" he asked, pulling his hand back and straightening in his seat.

She remembered to breathe. "I guess what you were saying did keep half my thoughts on you. Was it true though?"

Something about him looked suddenly vulnerable. It was a rare look for him. "Does it matter?"

"It matters to me."

He reached for her hand, lifted it to his lips, and pressed a kiss across the back of her fingers. "I've always liked you, Liz. I don't think that's a secret. If we were to date, I would know exactly what I was getting into. I know you." He smiled quietly at her. "Come on. Let's go inside."

Liz felt a whirlwind of conflicting emotions right now. She pushed her truck door open and stepped out onto the pavement, her legs akin to wet noodles in heels. In a quick second, Matt was beside her just like he'd promised he'd be tonight. Music could be heard coming from the gymnasium. The parking lot was mostly empty. Prom didn't officially begin until seven-thirty. Chaperones were arriving first.

When Liz stepped through the gym's door, Melody rushed her with a huge hug.

"You're here!" she said, pulling back from the embrace to look Liz over. "And you look amazing!"

Liz looked Melody over as well. "So do you."

"How was the trip here?"

Liz glanced over at Matt who was talking with Christopher. He'd told her he always liked her, which wasn't a huge revelation but it was still nice to hear. "It was . . . well, we made it. I guess that's all that really matters."

Sadness flashed in Melody's eyes. "We both made it this time."

Liz looked down for a moment, pulling a deep breath into her lungs. They'd never made it to the first prom. Just the fact that they'd both gotten here felt like a small miracle. She looked back up at her friend and then around the room. "You really outdid yourself. The gymnasium looks fantastic."

Melody smiled proudly. "It does, doesn't it? I can't help thinking about what I would have done differently if I were planning this event. A fairy tale theme has so much potential."

"Maybe you'll plan next year's prom." Liz looked at Melody hopefully. Some part of her was still hoping Melody would stay in Trove Isle. Her mind knew better than to hope for such things. Her heart couldn't seem to help it though. It felt good having Melody home, like a long-lost piece of her had been put back into place. That would imply that Liz was broken without Melody, which wasn't true. She was definitely better with her though.

"It would be difficult to plan a prom from a distance. I mean, I could if someone here was helping me carry out the decorating." She looked at Liz. "Like you."

"Me?" Liz laughed. "I'm not a decorator. I could perhaps volunteer to be the prom's photographer next year. Maybe Bri will be your wingman."

"Wow. Bri will be out this time next month." Melody sighed as a happy smile enveloped her face, making her look even more beautiful tonight. "We'll all have to come here together next year."

There it was again. Melody was talking about being in Trove Isle. Liz knew it was just to visit, but there was a thread of something more there. There was just enough hope to keep Liz hanging onto her fantasy that all her friends would be together, just like the old days. All but one.

CHAPTER TWENTY-FIVE

MELODY

"Care to dance with me?"

Melody looked at Christopher's outstretched hand. Prom had been going on for about thirty minutes now. The gymnasium was full and loud. "Are chaperones allowed to dance? Shouldn't we be watching?"

"We are watching. There's no rule against watching while dancing." He wiggled his fingers in a come-hither gesture. "Come on. Dance with me."

As if on cue, a slow song started up through the speakers. It was a familiar tune that Melody couldn't quite put her finger on. She turned to look for Liz to make sure she was okay. Liz was standing near the refreshment table talking to Rose and her date.

Finally, Melody slipped her hand into Christopher's. His skin was warm and inviting against hers. They stepped onto the dance floor and Melody leaned in to his warm body as he drew her closer. She had the urge to lay her head on his chest, close her eyes, and disappear into the moment. They weren't like that though, even if some part of her wished they were. Maybe in some other reality where she and Liz and Bri, and Alyssa, had actually made it to their own prom. If Melody hadn't left Trove Isle when she was eighteen. If Alyssa had lived and her crush on Christopher had moved on to some other guy.

Christopher dipped his head to her ear so she could hear him, his breath tickling her exposed neckline. "What are you thinking about?"

She tipped her face back and looked at him. They were dangerously close. "What might have been, I guess."

"You know what they say."

She wrinkled her brow. "They say a lot of things. Which thing are you referring to?"

"Don't look back. You're not going in that direction."

Melody smiled. "I haven't heard that one before." She paused. "Thanks for taking me here tonight. This is great."

"You say that now. Last year, the kids spiked the punch and several prom-goers passed out. A couple barfed. Being a chaperone is not for the weak."

Melody laughed. "I think I'm up to the challenge."

His voice dipped low. "I know you are."

They swayed for a few more seconds. Then Melody tuned-in to the song. She recognized it now. It was a classic.

"Did you request this song?" she asked, searching his eyes.

"Mm-hm. You and I were never an item. Only in my imagination. But," he shrugged, "this song used to play all the time when we were in high school. And every time I heard it, I thought of you."

"You did?" Melody swallowed. Her throat was dry. Her heart pattered. She listened to the words, trying to place the singer. "It's by Chicago?"

"One of my all-time favorite bands. There are perks to being a chaperone. I requested a few songs that these kids have probably never heard of. Maybe it'll turn into one of these couples' songs." He grinned before starting to sing quietly along.

Tears burned behind Melody's eyes. She blinked them

away, feeling too much in this moment. She wanted to disappear. Run away. Stay exactly where she was and never leave. She wanted all these things at once. "Christopher," she said, the word coming out as a plea.

"It's just a song, Mel. And it was just a crush that I had. Those first crushes are brutal though. You feel everything one hundred percent."

"That's how Alyssa felt about you back then."

There was something sad in Christopher's eyes. "When one crushes that hard, it's rarely ever reciprocated. Two people crushing on each other at the same time is like lightning striking. When it happens though, I think it's probably pretty special."

Melody was having a hard time pulling in a deep breath. "We're probably too old for that kind of crush now."

He lifted his finger and brushed a lock of her hair off her cheek. "Speak for yourself. I'm not sure I'll ever get over my first crush."

She opened her mouth to speak, but no words came out. What could she say? She wasn't staying in Trove. She couldn't. Wasn't it enough that she had come home for a visit?

Her cell phone rang out from the tiny purse she kept along her shoulder. "Oh. I thought I turned that thing off." She hadn't turned it off though because she'd wanted to make sure Liz could call her if she was having difficulties. Melody dug through her purse and pulled her phone out, seeing Candy North's name on her screen—the woman who wanted to buy the thrift store. Melody owed her an answer by tomorrow. "I have to take this." Melody looked back up at Christopher. Then she stepped back and gave him an apologetic look. Truly, the call could probably be returned later in the evening, but her instinct to run overpowered her when she was presented with the excuse to slip away.

Christopher didn't seem to mind. "I should probably sample that punch and make sure history doesn't repeat itself.

Spiking the beverage seems to be a rite of passage at these types of things."

Melody broke into a small laugh, relieved at how easygoing he was. "Were we ever so rebellious?" she asked.

"Not me." He feigned an innocent look that made a fluttering sensation in her chest. "Save me another dance later?"

"Of course."

Melody turned and hurried toward a door, hoping she'd find privacy on the other side. The phone had stopped ringing. She tapped the screen to re-dial.

"This is Candy," a woman's voice answered.

"It's Melody Palmer, returning your call."

"Yes. Melody, hi. I hope I didn't catch you at a bad time."

Melody wasn't sure if the timing was good or bad. Part of her wished she were still swaying in Christopher's arms. "You didn't."

"I'm calling to see if you have an answer for me. I gave you a timeline and I meant it."

Melody closed her eyes. She could still hear the music from just beyond the door. The slow song had stopped and a faster tempo was thumping through the speakers in the next room. "Have you reconsidered keeping the store as my great-aunt's thrift store?"

Candy cleared her throat. "I don't sell used things. I sell new and unique women's clothing. I want to run a boutique, not a secondhand mess."

Melody flinched as tension gathered in her chest. Did the woman have to be so rude? "Can I have a little more time to consider?"

"I'm sorry. I don't have time to waste," the woman said bluntly. "I can find another place."

Melody pressed a hand to her chest. The thrift store was Jo's dream, but Jo wasn't here anymore. And neither was Melody's mom. Or Alyssa. She'd lost so much in this town, and tonight just seemed to bring all the emotions to the surface. She'd enjoyed dancing with Christopher, but the desire to run away hadn't been this strong since the first day she'd arrived a couple weeks ago. She felt conflicted and lost. "Okay," Melody said quietly.

"Okay?"

"I'll sell the store to you at the price you mentioned. No conditions. If you don't want to run it as Hidden Treasures, that's your choice." Melody just wanted to swipe things off her plate. She wanted to cut the cord keeping her here any longer than she needed to be.

"Wonderful!" Candy said enthusiastically into the receiver. "My real estate agent will be in touch."

"Okay." Melody disconnected the call and stood there, feeling hollowed out and running over with emotions all at once.

"I thought you said you wanted to keep Jo's store in place," a woman's voice said.

Melody turned toward Liz, surprised to see her standing there. "Liz. Are you okay?" Her friend's pink lips were vibrant against her pale complexion.

"You said you were keeping it as Hidden Treasures. That's what Jo would have wanted. I thought you wanted the same thing."

"Liz." Melody stepped toward her friend.

Liz took a step back and held up her palm. "Some part of me still believed you would end up staying in Trove. That you would realize what you left behind and decide you couldn't leave us again. Some part of me thought you meant it, all of this." Liz gestured toward the charm bracelet on her wrist. "You were never planning to stay though, were you? For all I know, you're not planning to come back either. It's all a lie." Liz's voice shook. "And I am such a fool because I believed it. Everything you said." She shook her head and Melody saw the glisten of tears on her cheek.

"It's not a lie. Liz, I'm just selling the store. I was always planning to sell the store. I never promised anything different."

"You did though. You said it would remain Hidden Treasures."

"You don't understand. This woman offered above the asking price," Melody said, as if that really mattered. Money was nice, but they both knew that wasn't why Melody had taken the offer so quickly. "The kind of money that's not easy to turn down."

Liz frowned. Then she looked at the charm bracelet on her wrist and slid it off.

Melody watched her. "What are you doing?"

Liz sniffled and took an audible breath. Anger sparked in her eyes when she looked up again. Her jawline tightened and she pulled her arm back and forcefully threw the bracelet at Melody's feet. "So take the money and leave, Mel. And take the bracelet with you when you go. I don't need it anymore. Or you." She turned on her heel and charged toward the door.

Melody hurried after her. "Liz? Wait. You're overreacting. Liz?"

The door slammed behind Liz, leaving Melody alone in the room. She didn't want to go out into the gymnasium just yet. She needed a moment to catch her breath. Tonight was turning out to be an emotional roller-coaster ride. Liz was just being emotional as well. That's what that was. Tonight was triggering for her too. People lashed out when they were triggered. They shut down. They pushed people away. They accepted real estate offers. And apparently, they also threw charm bracelets.

Melody whirled to go and retrieve the discarded piece of jewelry. She didn't see it immediately so she walked deeper into the room, looking around the furniture that was stored there. This appeared to be an area for unused desks and podiums.

The bracelet wasn't there. She couldn't see it. Tears clouded her vision and then it was impossible to see anything at all. All she wanted to do was leave, but that would be running away, wouldn't it? And Melody Palmer didn't run anymore. Did she?

To: Liz Dawson
From: Bri Johnson

Subject: A night to remember

Liz,

I'm on my cot tonight, thinking of you and Melody, and imagining you two having the times of your lives. I don't need to be there. Just knowing that you both have this chance to redo history in some way, and fix some small piece of it, is enough. I can't wait to hear every detail. I want to see pictures because I know you're taking them. It will be a night to remember!

B

Chapter Twenty-six

LIZ

Liz was too angry to cry. She needed space. She needed to get out of this place. "Hand me your keys." She held out her palm to Matt.

"What?" He was in the middle of a conversation with two students who looked guilt-ridden, as if Matt had just caught them doing something they shouldn't be.

"Hand me your keys. I need to, um, get something from your truck."

"Oh." He looked concerned, but he was also half distracted by the teenagers standing in front of him. He dug into his pocket and pulled out his keys, searching Liz's gaze. She didn't look at him directly. She just snatched the keys and muttered a thanks. Then she walked as quickly as she could in heels out of the gymnasium, gasping for air when she finally stepped outside.

What am I doing? Did she actually think she was going to get into Matt's truck and drive away? Her thoughts were spinning in circles in her mind as she unlocked the driver's side door and yanked it open. Maybe she'd just cry here and wait for Matt to come back out at the end of the night.

No. He'd eventually come looking for her and then he'd

either persuade her to go back inside or offer to take her home. When his commitment was here. *So, leave, it is.* She jammed the keys in the ignition as tears rolled down her face. Her hands were shaking. Her entire body shook with a force that frightened her. She wasn't used to driving by herself, especially not in the dark.

Just do it, Liz, she told herself. Then she slammed an open palm on the steering wheel, accidentally honking the horn. The sudden noise startled her enough to dry up her tears momentarily. She straightened and glanced around the parking lot to make sure she hadn't drawn attention to herself. No one was out there though. Everyone was inside the gymnasium having the time of their lives.

Taking a steadying breath, Liz shook her head as more tears threatened to rise. "I can't do this. I can't." She started to lay her head down on the steering wheel when someone knocked on the passenger side window. Liz startled upright again.

"Let's get out of here," Rose said, climbing into the passenger seat and sniffling quietly.

"Why aren't you inside?" Liz asked. "You're supposed to be enjoying your prom."

Rose folded her arms over chest. "Josh is acting like a jerk. He got us a hotel room when I told him in no uncertain terms that this dress was not coming off tonight."

Liz's jaw dropped. "He what?" she practically yelled. She'd liked this Josh guy. She'd trusted him.

"I'm so upset." Rose's voice quivered. "Please, just take me home."

Liz understood that home right now was Liz's guestroom. She sat frozen for a moment, unsure of what to do. Encourage Rose to go back inside and have fun or drive when Liz wasn't sure she was up for it. "Do you, um, want to drive?" she asked.

Rose glanced over, tears rolling off her lashes. "I drank the special punch."

"The special punch," Liz repeated. "What was special about it?"

Rose rolled her eyes. Then the tears started falling harder. That was all the motivation Liz needed. She turned the key in the truck's ignition and cranked the engine. "Buckle your seatbelt," she ordered. Then she slowly steered Matt's truck out of the parking lot.

"Josh said that he doesn't expect us to *do* anything," Rose said as she sniffled some more. "He said we would just cuddle."

"No one books a hotel room and expects to just cuddle." Liz clutched the steering wheel with both hands.

"That's what I said," Rose cried. "I mean, I shouldn't have to feel like I have to have sex with him if I don't want to, right?"

Liz kept her eyes pinned to the road ahead. "You should never feel pressured."

Rose reached for a tissue from a pack in Matt's center console. "I want my first time to be with someone I love."

Liz took that information in. So Rose was still a virgin. At least Rose hadn't lost her virginity on Liz's watch this summer.

"This night is awful," Rose said, miserably. "Prom night is the worst." As if realizing what she'd said, she gasped quietly.

From her peripheral vision, Liz saw Rose looking at her.

"I'm sorry. Your prom night was way worse than mine. I'm so self-absorbed."

"No, you're not," Liz said. "You're human. You have every right to be upset. I'm upset on your behalf," Liz said. "But, on the other hand, I do want to point out that most guys consider the possibility of taking their prom date's dress off. It doesn't make Josh a bad guy, as long as he respects your boundaries." They were almost to Liz's house. Liz relaxed her grip on the steering wheel.

Rose pulled in an audible breath. "Prom is a lot of pressure. There's hair and the dress. The nails. Everything has to be perfect. I guess when Josh told me about the hotel room, I kind of lost it." Rose dabbed the tissue beneath her eyes. "He probably hates me now."

Liz reached over and touched Rose's shoulder. "Well, at least you didn't steal his ride. I stole Matt's truck and now he's stranded at the prom."

Rose laughed softly. "Why were you sitting in Matt's truck anyway? Did he book a hotel room too?"

Liz pressed her lips together. "I'm not upset with Matt. It's Melody."

"Uh-oh." Rose angled her body toward Liz's. "What'd she do this time?"

Liz shook her head. Just thinking about their argument made her want to start crying. "I don't want to talk about it. All I want to do is climb under my covers and drink a hot cup of tea."

Rose was quiet for a moment. "I'm sorry, Liz."

"You can't apologize for Melody."

"I'm not. I'm apologizing for myself," Rose said. "I guess I never really understood all that you went through that night. And after that night. It makes my small dramas seem so stupid."

Liz glanced over.

"Eyes on the road!" Rose ordered, teasingly.

Liz whipped her gaze back to the front windshield. She pulled up to a STOP sign and then turned onto her street, slowing to turn into her driveway.

"Maybe I overreacted. Josh is a really nice guy." Rose looked out the front windshield as Liz parked. "Cuddling would have been nice."

Liz laughed. "I think you could have probably told him how you felt and it would have been fine. You should text him," Liz said. "Tell him that he can pick you up here and that he can drop you off here no later than midnight. No hotel room."

Rose looked relieved. "You should text Matt and tell him to catch a ride home with Christopher tonight."

Liz nodded. "That's a good idea."

Rose's phone rang in her lap. She stared down at it. "It's Josh."

"Answer it," Liz said.

Rose hesitated and then connected the call, holding her phone to her ear. "Hey . . . mm-hmm. I know. I believe you." Rose locked eyes with Liz as she listened to what Josh was saying. "So, um, do you want to come pick me back up at my sister's house and start the night over?" Rose smiled at whatever he said next. "Okay. I need to be home by midnight though. Are you good with that?"

Liz was happy for her sister. Her disappointment was temporary and could be resolved easily. Liz's wasn't.

"Okay. See you soon." Rose lowered the phone and disconnected the call. "Josh is coming to get me. Unless you need me to stay with you instead."

Liz was grateful that Rose would be willing to pass on one of the most important nights of her young life. "No need. I'm just going to sleep."

"I'll wait here then."

Liz nodded. Then she pushed the truck door open. "Have fun," she called over her shoulder. Closing the truck door, Liz headed toward her house. She couldn't wait to get these heels off. And this dress. She climbed the porch steps, unlocked the door, and stepped inside, breathing a sigh of relief. The momentary feeling dissipated when her phone began to ring. First Melody. Then Matt. "Go away," Liz muttered. She wanted everything to go away right now, especially the slight headache that had begun to throb at her temple. She didn't respond to Melody, but she owed it to Matt to let him know she was okay. She tapped the screen, sending off a quick text.

Liz: I'm home safe and sound. I'll call you tomorrow. Right now, I just need to go to bed.

To: Melody Palmer
From: Bri Johnson

Subject: Making memories

Mel,

I won't lie. I'm a little jealous that you and Liz are at prom tonight—even though it's not ours. A person can't turn back time. If they could, everyone would be doing it, and we'd all be in a bigger mess than we are right now. Probably. Anyway, take pictures. I'm sure Liz has that covered. Have fun. And try to remember as much as you forget. I think that's key in moving on. Fifty-fifty remembering and forgetting. Add in some fun and a whole lot of love. And a few hard-earned charms.

B

CHAPTER TWENTY-SEVEN

MELODY

It was gone. For the last thirty minutes, Melody had crawled around on her hands and knees looking for the charm bracelet. It was as if it had disappeared when Liz had tossed it to the floor. Melody needed to get up and return to chaperoning the prom. It was something she'd committed to, and looking for the charm bracelet any longer was pointless.

Melody walked to the door that led to the gym and paused, listening to the music on the other side. Before she'd come in here with her call, she'd been swaying in Christopher's arms. Tonight her feelings were all hanging out on the surface where she couldn't control them. It was risky putting herself in a situation where she might say or do something she'd regret. Like leaning into Christopher for his support after her fight with Liz.

Was Liz in the room beyond this door? Would she cool down enough to let Melody explain things in a rational manner?

The door opened from the other side and Christopher peeked through the opening. "There you are. You okay?"

"Yeah, I just . . ." Melody glanced over shoulder. "I lost the charm bracelet in here, and I can't find it."

Christopher's lips set in soft line. "It can't have disappeared. I'll take you back here tomorrow. I have a key. We'll find it together."

Melody nodded, feeling a little better with a plan in place. "Okay. Sounds good."

"Ready to come back out here and chaperone with me? The kids are starting their shenanigans. I could use some backup."

"What about Liz and Matt?"

Christopher shrugged. "Liz took off. Not to worry. Rose went with her and took her home. She's fine and doesn't want anyone checking on her. Matt is on the case."

Guilt spiraled inside Melody. This was her fault. She'd ruined everything. Christopher didn't seem to know that yet though.

He held out his hand. "Come on. I'll get you a plate of cocoa bites. They're sure to make you feel better."

The Bitery was one of the local businesses to donate to the prom's spread of food and beverages.

"I'm not really hungry." In fact, she wasn't in the mood to do anything right now except go home and hide under her covers. But she'd made a commitment and she would keep it. She stepped toward Christopher, forcing a smile that felt like one big lie. *She* felt like one big lie. As they stepped back into the gymnasium, Melody's gaze scanned the room, and she spotted Rose dancing with Josh. In quick strides, Melody walked across the room until she was standing in front of Liz's little sister. "How is she?"

Rose pulled her arms away from Josh. "She's hurt. I don't know what you did to her, but she's pretty upset."

Melody took a breath. "I didn't do anything."

Rose frowned. "Of course you did."

"I just . . . I just agreed to sell Hidden Treasures. I was always going to sell the thrift store though. Liz knew that. I don't know why she's so mad."

"Maybe because she believed in you." Rose shrugged. "Liz has always believed in me, even when I disappointed her. Liz finds the best in people. She probably realized she was wrong to do that in your case."

Ouch.

"So I'm the bad guy just because I have a life somewhere other than this town? I was never going to stay here. Never." Melody caught movement from the corner of her eye and turned to look at Christopher. He looked disappointed too. "What?" she asked, throwing her hands out to her sides.

He shook his head and averted his gaze. "Nothing."

"Someone made me an offer I can't refuse. They don't want to run the store as a thrift shop. They plan to open a boutique instead. That wasn't my original plan, but I think Jo would have liked the idea."

"No, she wouldn't have," Christopher said, the letdown evident in his expression.

"You don't know that. Jo loved fashion and clothing." Melody forced a smile. "This is good news. We should be celebrating." She looked between Christopher and Rose, neither of whom seemed to be in the celebratory mood. "It's just a store."

"Wow," Christopher finally muttered. "I kind of thought you would eventually change your mind. Maybe you'd stick around."

"That was never the plan," Melody reiterated quietly. "You know that."

Christopher's gaze lowered to the floor. "I guess. But it was also the plan to maintain Jo's shop as a thrift store." He looked back up and met her gaze, searching her eyes. "What happened?"

"I can't rearrange my whole life to make Jo happy. She's not even here." Melody blew out a pent-up breath. "What would you do differently if you were in my situation?"

Rose stepped closer. "You left for like, ten years, and never looked back. Not once. I never would have done that to people who I claimed to love. There's no excuse, not that you gave anyone a good reason anyway."

Melody had thought everyone had moved past this. "I lost my sister. The only sister I'll ever have. I was hurt, okay?" Melody felt the rush of tears to her eyes.

"Bri was hurt too. So was Liz. Everyone was hurting. You should have come home sooner. Liz needed you. She still needs you," Rose said. "And you're packing up to leave and, in her mind, you're not coming back for another ten years. Is she right about that?" Rose put her hands on her hips.

Melody blinked past her tears and one slid down her cheek. "Of course not."

Rose lifted her chin a notch, looking down at Melody through her lashes. "Why don't I believe you?"

There were two long hours before the prom was over. Melody stayed near the refreshments table, trying to fulfill her commitment to chaperone the students. When the clock struck midnight and all the students had left, she climbed into the passenger seat of Christopher's truck so that he could drive her home.

"I seemed to have ruined this night for everyone," she said. "I'm sorry."

Christopher glanced over. "Don't be so hard on yourself. Talk to Liz tomorrow. She'll come around. She's pretty understanding in that way."

"Is it really so wrong of me to sell Jo's store?"

"I guess it's your prerogative. You can do whatever you want with it."

Melody could tell he didn't approve, though. "This woman is ready to pay a lot of money. I mean, a lot. I can't just reject it."

Christopher was quiet for a long time.

"It's easy to say it's not about the money when it doesn't affect you," she went on, feeling a bit defensive.

"I didn't say that, did I?"

"No, but you were thinking it." She watched the darkened landscape go by through her window, wishing she were already home. Coming out tonight had seemed like a good idea, but in hindsight, it was a mistake. Maybe she never should have come to town at all. She could have had the paperwork for the will faxed to her and handled it from Charlotte.

Christopher finally pulled into her driveway. Melody placed her hand on the door's handle, ready to bolt as soon as the vehicle came to a stop.

"I'm not judging you, okay? I'm not trying to, at least. Only you know what's right for you, and ultimately, it's you who has to live with it." He shrugged. "All I know is I'm glad you chaperoned the prom with me tonight."

The compliment nearly broke her. She needed someone to affirm that she wasn't an awful person right now. "Really?"

"Oh, yeah. Maybe it went a little sideways—"

"More like upside down," she cut in.

"Yeah. Well, before it did, it felt good being with you. Makes me wish things had been different."

"I wish that all the time. About everything." Melody sighed. "Thanks, Christopher. You're a good guy. Some nice girl in Trove Isle will be lucky to find you." One that intended to stay and not break his heart like his ex-fiancée had. Melody wasn't that woman though. For one, she wasn't staying, and secondly, she wasn't all that sure she was nice. "Goodnight."

"Wait." Christopher pushed his door open. "The least I can do is walk you to your front door. Don't worry, I'm not going to try to kiss you."

Melody smiled half-heartedly. That was less assuring than he might think. "Okay."

The next morning, Melody woke to the smell of bacon wafting down the hall. There was also the aroma of coffee, which had her getting up and moving a lot faster than she probably would have otherwise.

When she entered the kitchen, she found her father standing in front of the stove.

"Morning," he said, turning to offer up a small smile. "How was last night?"

Melody groaned. Then she headed toward the cabinet where the mugs were kept, grabbed one, and poured herself a deep cup of dark brew.

"Hungry?" he asked.

"Starving." Melody sat down at the kitchen table, opting to drink her coffee black just so she could have it faster. "The prom was a disaster," she said after a couple minutes and several sips of coffee. "Liz is upset with me."

Her father slid a plate of food in front of her. He placed his own plate on the table beside hers and sat down. "I'm sorry to hear that."

"Me too." She grabbed a slice of bacon and bit into it, receiving a satisfying crunch.

"Whatever happened between you two, I'm certain you can repair it today," her father said.

Melody wasn't so sure. She rolled her lips together, wondering if she should rip off the Band-Aid and disappoint him as well. "She found out I'm selling the thrift store."

"You've always been planning to sell it, though," he said, looking up.

"I guess she thought I wouldn't. I'm not sure." She forked some mounds of eggs into her mouth and chewed.

"There's a history between the two of you. Leaving town to go back to Charlotte isn't just a casual thing to her. You left for ten years." He set his fork down. "It's not a casual thing for me either."

"But I've told you that I'll be back. It won't be like the last time. Things have changed."

"I know," he said quietly. "At least I'm trying to know it. I suspect neither me or Liz or anyone else will know it, including you, until that actually happens. History has a way of repeating itself."

She wasn't very hungry anymore. She continued eating, but she could barely taste her food because she was thinking about what her dad had said. "I'm going home this coming week. That's still the plan. But I won't stay away this time. I promise."

He gave her a grateful smile. "You know where to find me. I'll always be here. This is your real home, Melody."

"Thanks for meeting me here." Melody fidgeted nervously with her hands as Christopher unlocked the door to the high school's gymnasium later that morning.

He glanced over, his blue eyes twinkling under the rim of his ball cap. "It helps to know people in high places, huh?"

"High places?" She laughed at the absurdity of that statement.

"They don't just give anyone a key, you know?" The door opened and he gestured for her to go inside.

She took a step in and then froze. "You're sure we won't get in trouble? I don't want the police to show up and think we're breaking in." Getting tossed in the county jail would put a wrench in her plans to head back to Charlotte.

Christopher nudged her forward. "It helps to know a police officer in town too. It's the charm of living in a small town. Yes, I'm sure we won't get in trouble. I told Principal Blevins we were coming. He thinks we're cleaning up after the prom, but that's not a complete lie. We are looking to take away one item from here, right?"

"The charm bracelet." Melody blew out a breath, hoping it would turn up somewhere this morning. She'd felt sick last night when she hadn't been able to find it. Losing it again after all these years would be awful.

It was special. Meaningful. It was part of what had brought Melody, Liz, and Bri back together after so many years. "I lost it in the room off the side of the gym."

"Then that's where we'll go." Christopher stepped ahead of her now and led the way through the dimly lit gymnasium. He hadn't flipped the lights, but the entire gym had windows just shy of the ceiling bringing in a good amount of natural light. Christopher opened the door to the adjoining room for Melody and waited for her to step by him. She looked around, scanning the floor. There were only so many places the bracelet could have gone. The room was full of unused school-related furniture, but the floor underneath was clear, polished to a shine that implied very few people had walked across it.

Melody felt increasingly panicked as her eyes scanned the area, making quick sweeps at first and then moving slower as if the bracelet would suddenly appear. It was magical in a way. It could happen. "It's not here," she said, deflating to the point that her body felt like it was folding in on itself. "Where could it have gone?" She glanced up at Christopher, some part of her hoping that he could see it even though she couldn't.

He shook his head. "You said Liz threw it at your feet?"

Melody flinched at the memory. "Pretty much. She was standing exactly where you are now."

His gaze moved past her to the floor. "I doubt anyone has been in this room since the prom. The school has been closed. The custodians don't work the weekends. You and I are probably the last to leave and the first to enter this area."

Melody sighed, turning in a full circle before looking up at him again. "Bracelets don't just disappear into thin air."

Then again, that's exactly what this particular bracelet had done on the night of the accident when she was eighteen. Tears burned behind her eyes, blurring Christopher's image. "I guess this is my sign."

His dark brows lowered. "What sign?"

Melody swallowed thickly. She really didn't want to break down in front of Christopher right now. "That I've overstayed my welcome. My sign that it's time to leave."

"Or . . . maybe you're just reading into this and rationalizing what you want to do anyway. Justifying it."

Melody lifted her chin a notch, allowing herself to lean in to her knee-jerk defensiveness. Getting mad was better than crying. "I don't need to justify anything. I have a life and a job to get back to. I'm not doing anything wrong by going home."

He shook his head. "No, but Liz and I aren't doing anything wrong by wishing you'd stay. Are we?"

Melody swallowed, wanting to pull her gaze from Christopher's but she couldn't. She lowered her voice, softening her tone. "It probably wouldn't last between us anyway, you know. If I stayed."

He gave her a long look before responding. "Guess we'll never know, will we?" Then he tipped his head toward the door that led back to the gym. "Come on. We'll lock up and leave. Before the police get here and arrest us."

Melody followed behind him, barely able to keep up with his brisk pace. "You're teasing, right?" She didn't feel like joking around. Inside, her heart ached. It throbbed like a sore tooth—the kind that kept one awake at night. The bracelet was gone. Her renewed friendship with Liz was strained. And the could-have-been with Christopher would never be because she couldn't stay in Trove Isle indefinitely. She had to go, and she had to do it now.

To: Bri Johnson
From: Liz Dawson

Subject: Prom night and other natural disasters

Bri,

Don't ask. It wasn't as awful as our first prom night, but it wasn't pretty. The short story is that Melody sold her store and she's leaving town. We fought, I threw the charm bracelet at her, and we're probably never going to see each other again. I'm not even exaggerating. It was truly disastrous. I'll give you the long story next time I see you.

xx,

Liz

CHAPTER TWENTY-EIGHT

LIZ

The phone stopped ringing. A moment later, it beeped, signaling that the caller had left a voicemail.

Liz stared at it. She hadn't checked the last three voicemails from Melody—two on Sunday and one yesterday—and she didn't plan to check this one either. She was still upset, disappointed, hurt.

Her phone lit up again and started ringing. This time it wasn't Melody. Instead, it was her mother. Liz quickly picked up her phone and connected the call. "Hello?"

"Lizzie! How are you, mi corazón?"

Mi corazón meant my heart in Spanish. Her mom had been using that term of endearment for Liz since she was a baby. "I'm good. Are you at the airport?"

"We are. We'll be home sometime tonight. Tell Rose she can stay in her own room tonight."

Liz would have thought she'd be jumping for joy at the thought of her little sister returning home. She'd gotten used to having Rose down the hall though, and Liz wasn't sure she was ready to return to living alone. Her life had twisted and turned upside down this spring. Sometimes returning to normal wasn't a good thing. "I'll tell her."

"I know you'll be glad to get her out of your hair. Rose can be quite a handful. I really appreciate you allowing her to stay with you while we've been away. Thank you, Lizzie."

"Of course. She's my sister after all. It's no big deal." She swallowed down a thick lump that kept rising in her throat. It'd been there since Saturday night at the prom.

"Maybe you'll come over this weekend for Sunday dinner," her mom suggested. "Then you and Rose can tell your dad and me all about everything we missed. And we'll tell you about our adventures in Ecuador."

Would that be a good time to also inform her mom that she didn't want to continue working at The Bitery full-time? "I'd like that."

"Good. I'll look forward to it."

After a quick goodbye, Liz disconnected the call and put her phone back on the counter next to the register. There were a few customers in The Bitery this morning, but it was mostly quiet. Liz was thankful for that.

The bell above the store's door jingled and Liz looked up at her incoming customer. Her stomach clenched painfully.

"Hey," Melody said as she drew closer.

"I thought you'd left town by now."

Melody shook her head. "Without saying goodbye? I wouldn't do that."

"You did one time before," Liz pointed out, avoiding Melody's gaze. She knew it wasn't fair to continue throwing the past in Melody's face. They'd moved past that, or at least, Liz had thought they had. Her hurt feelings had never fully resolved though. They'd just gone into hibernation. "Would you like a coffee or something to eat?" she asked, treating Melody like any other customer.

"Both." Melody glanced over her shoulder as if checking to make sure there was no one behind her. Then she faced forward.

Liz felt Melody watching as she prepared her drink. "When are you leaving?"

"Tomorrow. I have a few things I need to wrap up before I go."

Like selling Hidden Treasures.

Liz turned and slid the coffee across the counter to Melody. Then she grabbed a square of parchment paper and tongs to retrieve a cinnamon twist. She already knew what Melody wanted. Then again, she'd thought that about the sale of Hidden Treasures too. "Here you go." She placed the wrapped twist on the counter and began to ring Melody up. When Melody handed her debit card over, Liz's gaze dropped to her wrist. It was bare. She glanced at the other one.

"I tried to find it," Melody said as if reading her thoughts. "After you threw it at me."

Liz cringed slightly. Not her finest moment. "What do you mean you tried to find it? You couldn't?"

Melody shook her head and shrugged. "I practically crawled around on my knees, in my prom dress. I don't know what happened to it."

Liz felt like the wind had been knocked out of her. That bracelet was special. It had survived all this time, and in some way, it had brought Liz and Melody back together. "You have to find it."

"Even Christopher looked. We returned to the gym on Sunday and we both went through that room with a fine-tooth comb. No trace of our bracelet."

Liz steadied herself against the counter, feeling dizzy.

"I'm sorry, Liz. I know how much it meant to you."

"To me?" Liz blinked and looked up. "Right. It didn't mean anything to you. You were just here for what? To ease your guilty conscience and then return to Charlotte and forget about everyone here again."

"That's not true."

"The bracelet is gone. This little back and forth deal we had with sharing it is done. Just like our friendship."

Melody's eyes subtly widened. "So, we can't be friends anymore just because I'm selling the store? Like I always planned to do. That makes no sense, Liz."

Liz was typically slow to anger, but the emotion was suddenly bubbling up inside her. "You lied, Melody. You said you were going to keep the store as Hidden Treasures and I believed you. I can't believe I honestly thought you were serious."

"I was," Melody insisted.

"Maybe you were lying to yourself too, then. The thing is, if you lied about this, who's to say you aren't lying about coming back to Trove after you leave? About maintaining our friendship." Liz nudged the cinnamon twist in the parchment paper closer to Melody. "Have a nice life, Melody."

"Liz? Wait," Melody said.

Liz turned her back to her old friend. Maybe she was being irrational, but she couldn't seem to help it. The fact that Melody was allowing the store to be sold this way was just further proof Melody couldn't be counted on or trusted.

"Liz? I told you I would maintain our friendship this time. I meant it. We moved past all this," Melody called after her.

Liz turned to look at her, anger and hurt swirling around in the center of her chest. "Maybe you did. I guess I didn't." A bell dinged from the kitchen. "The bites are ready. I need to get them out of the oven. Have a safe trip *home*."

That evening, Liz rode her bike in the drizzling rain. She could drive now, but she didn't have a car. Rose had taken their mom's vehicle back to their parent's house. That was fine because Liz needed the exercise to clear her head. By the time she turned into her driveway, her clothing was soaked through. She didn't notice Matt until she pushed her bicycle toward her garage. She left it under the shelter of the open garage door and sprinted through the rain toward the cover of her front porch.

"Hey," she finally said. "What are you doing here?"

"Waiting for you." He was sitting on the front porch swing. "I saw your parents arrive in town earlier. I figured Rose would be back there tonight and you'd be here alone. I wanted to check on you."

Liz stepped over to one of the rocking chairs near the swing and sat down. "That's sweet. But I'm fine."

"I would have given you a lift home from work if I'd had any forethought."

"I like to ride my bike."

"It's raining. Next time call me, Liz."

She looked at him for a long second. "Do you ever get tired of being so nice? So noble?"

This made Matt laugh. "No. Helping others is a selfish pleasure. It makes me feel better about myself."

"Selfish? I don't think so." Liz blew out a breath. "Do you want to come inside?"

Matt looked past her toward the front door. "Do you want company?"

She shrugged. "I didn't think I did, but now that you're here, yeah. I can change clothes and cook dinner."

"I don't want you to go to any trouble."

"Like you said, it's selfish on my part. I want to feel better about myself too." She rolled her lips together, barring the tears that wanted to come. "Melody and I kind of had another argument today. It was all my fault this time."

"I'm sorry." Matt's gaze was steady.

She shrugged again as if it were no big deal, but it was. Losing Melody all over again was going to really hurt. She stood and jingled her keys. "These wet clothes are making me cold."

"Can't have that." Matt stood as well.

Liz felt him step up behind her as she turned the key in her lock and pushed open the door. She stepped inside and turned to face him as he stepped in after her.

"Why are you looking at me like that?" he asked.

Liz wasn't sure what she was doing. For so long, she'd been uncomfortable around Matt because he reminded her of the accident that she desperately wanted to forget. She already struggled with anxiety. Dating someone who was a reminder of the worst day of her life seemed like a bad idea.

But now she was seeing things differently. He was the calm in that storm. He had pulled her out of the accident. He was the ray of hope when there wasn't any, and he was still that ray and so much more to her.

She didn't want to push Matt away; she wanted to pull him closer. More than anything, she wanted Matt to hold her tonight. She stepped toward him.

"I thought you were cold and wet," he whispered.

"I am. And if you wrap your arms around me right now, you're going to get wet too."

He opened his arms for her to step into. "I don't mind."

Liz buried her head in his chest. She could hear the steady thump of his heart, lulling her to a calm she didn't know existed. Lifting her face, she looked at him, willing his mouth to dip to hers. He didn't move.

Fine, she'd do it herself. Going up on her toes, she pressed her lips to his. His mouth was warm. His hands moved to the sides of her arms, bracing her.

"Wow," he said once she had pulled away. "What was that for?"

She touched a finger to her mouth. "I've been wanting to do that for a long time."

"Me too." He smiled. "Well, am I any good at kissing?"

Liz laughed at the unexpected question. "You could use some practice. It's the least I can do since you helped me with my driving."

"Nice of you," he said quietly, his lips curling up at the ends.

Liz offered a slight nod. "So, I'm going to change clothes. Then I'm going to cook dinner for you." She rolled her lips together. "And, so we're clear, I'm considering this a date."

Matt looked surprised. "In that case, I'm going to the local florist while you change and cook. Call me old-fashioned, but a date deserves flowers." Concern swept over his expression. "Will you answer the door when I come back?"

Liz planted another kiss to his lips. "Yes. See you soon."

Matt stepped back toward the door. "I won't be gone long."

"Okay." She watched him step back out into the rain. Then she closed the door behind him and pressed her hands to her face. Who was she and what had she done with Liz? She was a different person these days, and she liked the new and improved version of herself. Melody was partly to thank. Rose too. She should call Melody back. She wasn't ready to let go of her anger just yet though. It wasn't exactly focused on Melody. Liz had been angry over a lot of things. Lost time and what-ifs. She wasn't going to lose any more time pushing Matt away. What if tonight changed things between them? What if they became more to each other than neighbors and friends?

She hurried down the hall toward her bedroom, eager to peel off her damp shirt and pants. After pulling on dry clothes, she stepped into the bathroom and turned to look in the mirror. She took a breath and stared herself in the eye. "You better answer that door when he comes back," she said. Then she blinked. Rose was barely gone a day, and now she was talking to herself. All the reason to answer the door to Matt when he returned. Plus, she really wanted to kiss him again. He'd asked if he was any good and she'd kept that answer to herself. The truth was, she'd never quite been kissed like that, in a good way—the best way.

To: Liz Dawson
From: Bri Johnson

Subject: On the bright side

Liz,

I'd like to say it's probably not as bad as you think, but it's not really helpful when people say that, is it? What I do know is that things will get better. Eventually. Hopefully, Melody won't stay away forever, but if she does, just know that you're stuck with me no matter what.

B

CHAPTER TWENTY-NINE

MELODY

Hidden Treasures had come a long way since Melody had arrived in town. She glanced around the shop now, waiting for her real estate agent to arrive and make her acceptance of the buyer's offer official.

Jo had never been one to keep things tidy necessarily. That wasn't her way. When Melody had inherited this place, it'd been a mess. Melody thought that was likely the appeal to some—digging through the mounds of donations to locate the one perfect item for an individual. She'd found quite a few items here herself, including the shoes she was currently wearing.

Melody glanced down at her feet, clicking her heels together like Dorothy in *The Wizard of Oz*. There's no place like home. Where even was home for her?

A knock on the glass door got her attention. Abigail Winslow waved from outside. Melody made a gesture to invite her inside. The door was unlocked even though the sign was turned to CLOSED today.

Abigail looked around as she entered. "You sure about this?"

Melody exhaled a breath. Her mind told her she should be

sure, but her heart begged to differ. Even though Jo hadn't had this store when Melody had lived in Trove Isle, this place was sentimental to Melody. She could feel Jo's presence here. Letting go of the store felt like losing Jo all over again. "I'm sure," Melody lied. Selling was the most rational thing to do. She didn't live here and the buyer was offering a lot of money.

Abigail nodded. She laid a briefcase on the glass display case and leaned against the wall. "The buyer's agent is bringing the paperwork. I'm just here as moral support to make sure you understand exactly what's going on. If you have any questions . . ."

Melody nodded. "I'm just ready to get this done." And get out of town. As soon as Melody signed the paperwork, she intended to drive to Charlotte. She'd already told her father goodbye for now.

A knock on the door got both of their attention.

"Speak of the devil," Abigail said with a frown. "I know her. Be glad I'm here. This woman is the Cruella de Vil of real estate."

Melody hesitated, but waved the woman inside. She wasn't surprised that Candy had hired a hard-edged agent.

"Well, hello there." The woman looked at Abigail. "Abby," she said, lifting her chin a notch and looking down her nose at Melody's agent. "Good to see you again." Her gaze flicked to Melody. "You must be Melody Palmer."

"I am," Melody said, watching the woman approach.

"I'm Wendy Mattis." The woman stepped closer and offered her hand.

Melody shook hands with the woman, already disliking her. There was a clear look of distaste on her face. "Nice to meet you."

"You as well." Pulling her hand back, Wendy made a point of assessing the store. "This is some place," she finally said in a tone that implied that she didn't mean anything good by that comment. "You know my buyer doesn't want any of this stuff, right?"

Abigail rolled her eyes. "We're well aware of that, Wendy."

Wendy offered a plastic smile, keeping her gaze fixed on Melody. "It's all going to be thrown out. If there's anything you want, best to take it."

Did she have to rub it in that all these things, these treasures, would be taken out like trash? Jo was probably rolling over in her grave, or wherever she was. Melody would do her best to get the things inside Jo's store donated some place. Maybe Christopher could help.

Wendy rubbed her hands together. "Okay, then. Let's sign and get this deal done, shall we?" she said, looking between Melody and Abigail.

Abigail gave Melody a pointed look and lowered her voice. "Are you ready?"

"Yes." Melody led the two women to the small table in the back room and gestured for them to have a seat. "Can I offer either of you some coffee?"

"No time for that." Wendy placed a pen on the table along with a stack of papers. "There are Post-Its marking where you need to sign." She sat back, crossed one leg over the other, and folded her hands over her knee.

On a nod, Melody pulled the stack toward her and picked up the pen. It felt abnormally heavy, along with her heart. *This is just a thrift store. I never even wanted it to begin with.*

"Sign right there, sweetie," Wendy said, tapping the paper. "Do you see the line?"

"She sees it," Abigail said, giving Wendy a hard stare. "We're in no hurry. Take your time, Melody."

Melody nodded and then continued. Her hand shook as she scrawled her name. Once she got started, she just kept going, barely taking a breath. *Just get this over with. Sorry, Jo!* Finally, she exhaled and set down the pen. "Done."

Wendy smiled. "See? Quick and painless." She collected the stack of papers, dropped them in her briefcase, and stood. "I'll see myself out. I'm serious. Keep whatever you want in here. My buyer doesn't want any of it."

Melody didn't get up to see Wendy to the door. Abigail waited until after Wendy left.

"You okay?" Abigail asked as she stood.

"Yep," Melody said, even though she wasn't sure that was the truth. "Thank you for your assistance. I really appreciate you meeting us here this morning. I'm not sure I would have wanted to be here alone with that woman."

Abigail laughed. "Of course. Call me if you need anything else. You have my number."

Melody nodded. "I will. Thank you."

Abigail grabbed her briefcase and saw herself out as well.

Melody sat there numbly, waiting to hear the jingle of the bell up front, announcing that both women were gone and she was once again alone. She considered remaining at the table and crying. That's what she felt like doing. What good would that do though? It would just make for red, puffy eyes as she drove to Charlotte in a little bit. Taking Wendy's advice, she decided to walk around and see if there was anything she wanted to keep. She'd been the one to put all the items out on the shelves. If there was something here that she wanted, she would have found it by now. Even so, she walked around, perusing clothing, shoes, well-read books, and toys. Finally, she stopped at the glass case below the register. The photograph of the little child was there along with Jo's pink broach. Melody slid the case open and took those items out. They didn't belong in the trash. The broach really wasn't her style, not by a long shot, but she pinned it to her purse anyway. Then she looked back down into the glass case and gasped. Were her eyes deceiving her? *How did it get here?*

She quickly reached inside the case and picked up a charm bracelet. Her hands were shaking so much she could barely get a good look at it. There was the muffin charm. The dress. The little car and the shooting star. The wave. The butterfly. They were all here. This was her charm bracelet! Hers and Liz's and Bri's. What was it doing here? Liz had tossed it at her feet at the high school and it had been lost. She'd thought it was gone for good.

Tears rushed to Melody's eyes. Who cared about them being red and puffy later? The charm bracelet wasn't lost. She slipped it over her wrist, savoring the feel of the cool metal against her skin. "I don't know how you did this, Jo. But thank you."

She had to tell Liz. Liz would never believe this.

Hurrying toward the door, Melody stepped out onto the sidewalk and locked the shop up behind her. She turned toward the pink polka dot awning a few stores down and practically jogged all the way.

"Welcome to The Bitery," a woman's voice said as Melody stepped inside. It wasn't Liz. "Are my eyes deceiving me? Melody Palmer, is that you?"

"Yes, it's me. Hi, Mrs. Dawson." Melody approached the counter.

"Lizzie told me you were back for a little while, but I didn't dare hope I'd get to see you before you left town. How long are you staying?"

Melody was supposed to be leaving today. Right now. But she desperately needed to do something first. "I'm not sure. Is Liz here?"

Mrs. Dawson shook her head. "She doesn't work here anymore, you know?"

Melody's jaw dropped.

"I guess you didn't know," Mrs. Dawson said on a small laugh. "Lizzie quit. Well, I mean, she'll still help out around here until I can hire Brianna in a few weeks. I still can't believe Brianna is finally coming home. You four were like sisters." Her smile faded. "I know you miss your sister."

"Yes, I do." More than she'd allowed herself to realize all these years. "If Liz isn't here, do you know where she is?"

"She's working a photography gig today. Oh, she was so excited. I even let her borrow my car to get there."

Melody blinked back tears. "She drove? By herself?"

"She did. I go away for one summer and everything changes. For the better, of course." Mrs. Dawson leaned over, her elbows on the counter. "The event she was working should be over soon. Knowing her, I'm sure she'll go straight home to start editing the photographs. If you want, you can wait for her there."

"That's a good idea," Melody said. "Thank you. It's nice to see you."

"You, too! Don't be a stranger, Melody!" Mrs. Dawson called after her.

Melody left The Bitery, got in her car, and drove the short distance to Liz's home. She pulled in the driveway and got out, deciding to wait on Liz's front porch. The weather was nice today. Perfect for making up with a long-lost friend.

Melody glanced down at the charm bracelet encircling her wrist. This little piece of jewelry had defied all odds to get to her and Liz again. Yeah, she knew it was just a bracelet. It wasn't magical or anything, but it had been lost—twice! How could she explain that without entertaining some divine intervention?

"Melody? Is that you?"

Melody blinked and noticed Matt walking up the driveway with his little dog on a leash. "I'm just waiting here for Liz," she said.

His brow furrowed. "Does she know you're coming?"

Judging by his tone, Liz had told him about their quarrel. Of course she had. "No."

"Should you maybe text or call instead?" he asked.

Melody didn't blame him for being overprotective. "I have. She won't respond. She's ignoring me."

Matt stopped walking when he was a few feet away from the front porch. His little dog sat at his feet, its tail wagging. "Can you blame her?"

Melody was taken off guard by his directness. "I understand that she's upset, but the offer on Hidden Treasures was a lot of money. If Jo had wanted the thrift store to remain a thrift store, she should have known not to leave it to me. She could have left it to Mr. Lyme. Surely, he would never sell that place."

Matt shielded his eyes with his hand. "I don't think this is about whether you sell that store, Mel. That's not why Liz is upset with you. I think you know that."

Melody swallowed. "She doesn't trust that I'll come back. But she's always known I'd leave."

"You didn't even tell her when you got the offer on the store. You kept it a secret. The thread of trust you'd built back with her is gone."

"I was going to tell her."

"When?"

"After prom. It was an important night. I didn't want to ruin it. But it got ruined anyway." Melody sighed and looked down at her bracelet. "I signed the paperwork to sell the store this afternoon." She blew out a breath. "I don't know. I thought it was the right thing to do, but maybe that was just my emotions talking. The prom hit me harder than I expected it to. It wasn't our prom so I didn't think it would matter, but my emotions just rose to the surface. I sold the store and just planned to get back to real life in Charlotte."

"But?" Matt asked.

Melody shrugged. "But now I'm second-guessing that decision."

"Guilt?" Matt asked.

Melody looked up and considered his question. "No. Regret. Maybe that place meant more to me than I realized." Tears surfaced in her eyes. They were quick and unexpected.

"Maybe Charlotte isn't real life. Perhaps it's just the fake life I've created to avoid real life." She swallowed hard. She'd only wondered that thought, but saying it out loud, she knew it was the truth. "I've got to go."

"Thought you were waiting for Liz."

Melody hurried down the steps. "If you see her, tell her that . . . tell her . . ." There were so many things that Melody wanted to tell her. But they had to be said in person. "Just tell her that I'll be back."

Melody got into her car and reversed out of the driveway. She didn't like regrets. She'd had too many in her life, and if selling Hidden Treasures made her feel even an inkling of remorse, she was going to do whatever it took to un-sell it.

To: Melody Palmer
From: Bri Johnson

Subject: Get it together

Melody,

You can't come back if you're going to just run away again. I thought we were clear about that. Liz needs you. I need you. But what we don't need is a repeat of losing you for the next decade. I never cared about a lost charm bracelet. I cared about a lost friend. Alyssa, yes. But also you. And I know that I'm one to talk because I got myself locked up and left Liz as well. I guarantee, once I'm released, I'm not leaving her again. You can live in Charlotte. That's not what this is about. It's about being here for one another. Through texts, calls, emails. Just don't disappear. Friends forever, no matter what.

B

CHAPTER THIRTY

LIZ

Liz wasn't holding her breath about the possibility that Melody would stop by tonight. Matt had told her that Melody was on her porch earlier, but that was hours ago. Melody wasn't dependable. Liz couldn't pin any hopes of a friends forever kind of relationship on her. If one good thing had come out of Melody's return, it was that Liz was moving on. She'd driven to a photography gig today and had left that job with two more requests for her to take pictures at local events. She'd stopped by The Bitery on the way home and she'd checked in with Rose, who asked if she could spend the night at Liz's house this coming weekend.

Life had shifted in the last month. Liz stared at her computer's screen and focused on the fine details of the photograph she'd taken at this morning's event. She adjusted the tone and cropped until the image was just slightly off-center, which was what she was aiming for. She did the same for each photograph, one by one, getting lost in the work. It was a welcome distraction from Melody who, for all she knew, had already left town.

A text message came through, making her phone buzz. She

glanced at the screen, smiling at Matt's name. He was patrolling tonight, which meant she wouldn't be seeing him.

Matt: Can we see each other next weekend?

Liz picked up her phone and smiled. Then she tapped off a response.

Liz: Yes, please. Fair warning, though. Rose is spending the night this weekend.

Matt: That's nice. Has Melody been by?

Liz: No.

Matt: I'm sorry. I saw Christopher earlier. He hasn't heard from her either.

Melody had likely gone back to Charlotte. Liz couldn't exactly hold it against her that they hadn't said a proper goodbye. She'd been ignoring Melody's calls and texts. It was just easier this way for Liz. Somehow her anger protected her from getting hurt.

Matt: I'll check in later.

Liz: Okay.

She stared at her phone for a long moment, wishing she could see Matt right now. He would be a welcome distraction for her as well. Getting up from her desk, she stretched her arms overhead, hearing her back make a series of satisfying pops. Then she headed into the kitchen to prepare herself a cup of herbal tea.

Her doorbell rang and she spun to stare into the direction of the front of the house. Matt was working. Rose was at their parent's house. It could be Melody, which both excited and made her nervous. What could Melody possibly say to make things better between them? In all honesty, Melody hadn't really done anything wrong. Liz had just realized she still didn't fully trust that Melody wouldn't hurt her again. Yes, Melody lost her sister, but she'd once told Liz they were sisters as well. Not the blood kind, but the kind you make with your heart.

The bell rang a second time. This time Liz started walking in that direction. She didn't have to open the door. Or, if she did, she didn't have to allow Melody inside. She checked the peephole and, sure enough, it was her.

"Liz?" Melody called from the porch. "If you're listening, please open the door. Please."

Liz inhaled. She was anxious, yes, but there was no panic attack lingering. She twisted the deadbolt and turned the knob, staring back at Melody through the screen door.

"Can I come in?" Melody asked.

Liz hesitated. "I'll come out there." Because if she allowed Melody in her home, they might end up sharing a mug of tea or a glass of wine. Liz wasn't up for that. If Melody was just going to disappear again, she wanted to keep her walls up. She stepped out onto the front porch. "You can have the rocking chair. I'll take the swing." Without waiting for Melody to respond, she crossed to the far side of her porch and sat down. The swing swayed in an easy back and forth motion.

"Liz, I didn't sell the thrift store," Melody said. She didn't budge from where she was standing. "I mean I did, but then I realized it was a mistake."

Liz's lips parted. "I hope you didn't change your mind on my account. You should do whatever you want."

"That's just it. I don't want to get rid of the store. It's part of Jo. Part of this town. And this town is part of me."

"You don't have to feel guilty for leaving, Mel."

Melody finally walked over and sat down on the rocking chair in front of the swing. She held out her wrist, showing Liz the bracelet.

Liz gasped and leaned forward to check that it was indeed their bracelet. "You found it? Where?"

Melody shrugged. "I can't take credit for finding it. It was in the glass case at the thrift store."

Liz furrowed her brow. "How'd it get there?"

Melody lowered her wrist. "The only answer that makes sense to me is that Jo found it. I know that actually doesn't make sense at all, but . . ."

Liz's eyes burned with tears. She couldn't decide if they were happy or sad. Maybe both.

"You said it was lost like our friendship, but I don't think either of those things was ever truly lost. I think we were the lost ones—because of what happened."

Liz blinked and one of the tears in her eyes came free, trailing down her cheek. "I've really worked to move past my fears this summer. I guess my fear still won out when I realized you were selling the store for real. I let myself believe that you were going to leave and never come back, and I just can't go through that again."

Melody reached for her hand and gave it a squeeze. "You won't have to. I didn't just decide to keep the store. I also decided to stay."

Liz's eyes widened. "What?"

"In Charlotte, I have a job that I love and a few friends. In Trove, I have a father, a store, a best friend and another on the way home soon. I have a guy who wants to date me. I have a history here that I don't want to forget anymore. I want to remember it." She shrugged. "Turns out, the thrift store is a great spot for planning events and there are several things going on here that require a good event planner."

"I can be your photographer," Lis said excitedly.

Melody smiled. Then she slipped the charm bracelet off her wrist and handed it over. "It's your turn to do something wild and crazy."

Liz laughed as she took the bracelet and looked at it, spinning it on her wrist to admire every charm. Then she wiped at a tear, stood, and opened her arms.

Melody stood as well and stepped into the hug that Liz offered.

"You're really staying?" Liz asked when she finally pulled away. She didn't want to get her hopes up, even though they were practically soaring.

"I am. And you know what, the thrift store is pretty spacious. I was wondering if, while I'm running my event planning business, you might want to run your photography business from there. We could sell treasures while pursuing our passions."

"Run the store together?"

Melody shrugged. "It's just an idea."

"I love the idea." Liz laughed out loud. "And when we get hungry, we'll go visit Bri at The Bitery. My mom has already agreed to hire her."

A grin spread through Melody's cheeks. "Sounds like a good life."

"The happy ever after we always wanted. Although different from the one we thought we wanted. You wanted to travel."

"I did and it got me nowhere. This is the happy ending we always deserved," Melody said.

"Or the happy new beginning." Something shiny caught Liz's eye. She looked down at her feet and gasped. "Where did that come from?"

Melody lowered to pick up the small metal charm and stood, holding out the palm of her hand to show Liz.

"A raindrop?"

Melody shrugged. "This outfit is from Hidden Treasures. It must have fallen out of the pocket. Maybe."

Liz reached for the charm and held it up to look at it better. "If we add it to the bracelet, it would need some kind of meaning. Right? What does a raindrop mean?"

"That we've weathered a lot?" Melody grimaced. "I know, that's probably a stretch."

Liz shook her head. "No, I like it. And without the rain, there'd be no rainbow."

Melody lifted a brow. "Wow, we're really getting cheesy in our old age, aren't we?"

Liz just stared at the charm in wonder. It was too much of a coincidence that another charm would find its way at their feet. "You don't think . . . ?" she asked, trailing off.

Melody's lips parted as she seemed to understand exactly what Liz was wondering. She looked beyond the porch and up toward the clouds. "Thanks, Jo," Liz heard Melody whisper.

Liz reached for Melody's hand and gave it a squeeze. There was probably a perfectly reasonable explanation, such as the charm falling out of Melody's pocket. It made sense. But who wanted to believe in reason when it was just as easy to believe in the things that defied it? Like love and forever friendships that endured the greatest hardships. Like the charm bracelet.

Epilogue

Nerves bound Liz's chest tightly. Bri would be here any moment.

Melody had volunteered to the do the honors of driving up to the prison to pick Bri up while Liz stayed back to make sure the event of the century went off without a hitch.

It was supposed to be a surprise party, but Melody and Liz had both decided that was maybe too much for Bri right now. Sometimes even happy surprises could be stressful, and knowing what was just around the corner was preferable. Bri had argued against the party, at first, but then she'd agreed on just a small homecoming with Liz's family, Melody, Christopher, Matt, and a few others, including Danette Rhodes. Mr. Lyme was going to stop by as well.

"The car just pulled in." Matt turned from the window and caught Liz's eye.

Liz's insides lit up, half from the anticipation of Bri walking through the door, half from Matt himself. They were dating these days, double dating with Melody and Christopher some of those days.

Matt flicked the switch to turn the lights off.

Liz was about to object. That wasn't part of Melody's plan. Since Bri knew they were here, there was no reason to hide. Before Liz could say anything though, the door opened and Bri stepped through.

"Surprise!" Matt and a few others said.

Bri's smile was hesitant, growing warmer as she glanced around the room.

When she finally looked in Liz's direction, Liz grinned. "Surprise," she mouthed.

Bri laughed quietly. Freedom looked good on her. Her skin was glowing and her eyes were bright. "All this for me?" she asked, gesturing at the decorations that Melody had hung around the room. There was a table of gifts as well.

"Why not for you?" Danette asked, her head bobbling as usual. "You deserve it."

"I deserve it because I made it out of prison?" There was a note of sarcasm in Bri's voice.

"No, because you're you. The same you who grew up around here and the you you'll always be. The one we know and love," Danette said.

"Words of a wise woman," Christopher said with a nod.

Danette's smile dropped. "Are you calling me old?"

"I wouldn't dare, Danny," he said with a laugh.

Liz just watched, soaking up the moment. She'd wished for this moment for years and she'd never thought it could be like this, with all of them together again. Almost all of them at least.

Bri hugged each person as they stepped forward. Then, when all the hugs had been doled out, Melody directed folks to the tables that were set up. One might think today was a graduation ceremony or retirement party of some sort. It was fancy, yet simple. Perfect in a word.

Melody walked toward Liz. "Aren't you going to sit down?"

"Yeah. I was just taking a few pictures to document the afternoon."

"If you spend the whole time behind your camera lens, you'll need those pictures to know what happened. Come on," Melody said, reaching for Liz's hand.

As they reached the table where Bri was sitting, Mr. Lyme stepped up as well.

"Bri, glad to have you home."

Bri nervously twisted the charm bracelet on her wrist. Liz suspected that Melody had handed it to her as soon as Bri had walked out of the prison. There was a lot of making up for lost time to be done. "Thank you. Glad to be home."

Mr. Lyme reached into his jacket pocket. "Jo gave me something to give you once you were out. She had clear instructions that you should have it immediately." He handed Bri a small black box with a blue bow adhered to the top.

"What is it?" Bri took the box and looked down at it, not moving to lift its lid just yet.

"Well, you'll have to open it to see." Mr. Lyme chuckled. "Jo would have a fit if I ruined the surprise before you laid eyes on it. Go on."

Liz noticed how Bri's hands shook as she grasped the lid and lifted it up. Then a soft gasp tumbled out of her.

"It's beautiful."

Liz leaned over to see what the gift was, and she gasped as well. "A charm."

The charm was of a teacup. It was gold with amber stones accenting the top.

"Jo always told me we'd share a cup of butterscotch tea when I got out." Bri wiped at a tear, dangling from her lower lash.

"Butterscotch tea was Jo's go-to for any occasion. Not sure if you knew, but her cup always had a little something extra." Mr. Lyme winked.

They all laughed.

"Jo must have known we'd find the bracelet in her shop," Melody finally said.

Bri shook her head. "She was one of a kind."

"That she was," Mr. Lyme agreed. "Anyway, welcome home. When is Ally getting here?"

"Tomorrow," Bri said. "Her father is putting her on a nonstop flight from California. I can't wait to hug her."

"Give her a hug from me as well." He offered Bri his hand and squeezed.

After he'd walked away, Bri took the tiny charm in her palm and looked at Melody. "Can you add it to the bracelet?"

"Of course."

Liz watched as one more charm found its link. The bracelet was filling up quickly.

"What's next?" Bri asked once it was attached.

Melody lifted a hand to answer that question. "We eat and then we have our own little private celebration. Just us."

Liz nibbled at her lower lip. "And the guys. But we can make them disappear for a while."

Bri grinned. "I like the sound of that."

The night was chilly, even though when the sun had been shining just a few hours earlier, the temperature had climbed into triple digits.

Melody glanced over at her friends. This day had felt like it would never arrive and now that Bri was here, sitting on the ocean shore, it felt like it had always been just like this. Time was relative.

"Hey." Christopher stepped over to Melody and plopped down beside her. "You look like you're lost in thought. Care to share?"

Melody leaned her shoulder to his. "I'm just happy, that's

all." She pulled in a breath and released it into the night, tipping her head back to look at the stars.

Christopher's hand found hers, covering it with his warm palm. "Me too. Not everyone likes the small-town life, but you really can't beat a night like this. Good view. Good friends. Good drinks."

Melody glanced over. "I like this small-town life."

"Well good, because I like you." He leaned in, brushing his mouth to hers in a sweet kiss.

"Eww, guys. Come on," Bri whined. "I just got out of prison. Spare me the PDA at least on my first night." She was just teasing, of course. Bri seemed happy and carefree, for the most part. "Besides, Liz and Matt are coupled up. Mel and Christopher are making out. I'm the odd woman out. It's making me consider going back to lock-up."

Liz laughed. "No, you are not. We'll find you a date, if that's what you want."

Bri frowned. "Don't threaten me like that. All I want tonight is a glass of wine. Do you know how long it's been?"

Melody leaned forward and grabbed the basket with wine and glasses inside. "Too long, my friend."

Matt shared a look with Christopher. "You ladies pour your wine. Christopher and I have business to take care of."

Christopher stood, avoiding Melody's inquiring glance.

"I wonder what that's about," Liz said when it was just her, Melody, and Bri sitting together at the end of Sunset Pier.

Melody shrugged. "Guy talk. That's okay because we can have girl talk." She pointed at the bracelet on Bri's wrist. "When you wear that, you have to do something wild and crazy, something you would never do, in Alyssa's words, to prove that you're not just a zombie."

Liz shook her head. "Okay, maybe we should change the purpose of this bracelet. Obviously, we're not zombies. Not anymore, at least."

Melody nodded. "Good point. Maybe we just wear the bracelet and remind ourselves not to forget any of it. Alyssa. Jo."

"Prison," Bri said quietly.

"Panic attacks and fear over everything," Liz added.

"Charlotte." Melody leaned back on her arms with her legs extended in front of her. "When we wear the bracelet, we remember those things that made us who we are. They're not good or bad, they're just part of us."

"And we remember each other too," Liz said. "I never want us to lose each other again."

Bri leaned forward over bent knees, wrapping her arms around her shins. "I like this new pact. It's fitting."

Liz draped an arm around Bri's shoulders from her left side. Melody did the same from the right, sandwiching their newly free friend. "Do you think Jo and Alyssa are smiling down on us right now?"

Melody swallowed past the thick lump in her throat. "I'm pretty sure."

A pop rang out, puncturing the night, followed by fireworks lighting up the sky of stars. Red. Blue. Yellow. Orange. One splash of color after another. Melody's lips parted. "Do you think the guys are behind this?" she finally asked.

Liz laughed. "I'm pretty sure."

Melody grabbed the bottle of wine and popped the cork. Liz grabbed the glasses, offering up one at a time for Melody to fill. Then, once all three of them had glasses in hand, Melody raised her glass. "A toast."

Liz and Bri raised their glasses as well.

"To long-lost friends and newly found direction," Bri said.

"To remembering to remember," Liz added, clinking her glass to the other two.

"To us," Melody finally said. "All of us." She clinked her glass to theirs and then her gaze caught on the newly added teacup charm on Bri's wrist. It was as if Jo was toasting them as well, and maybe she was. Another splash of brilliant color erupted across the black canvas of the night sky. On a happy sigh, Melody brought her wine glass to her mouth and took a grateful sip, savoring this moment and looking forward to all the ones to come.

ACKNOWLEDGMENTS

I first got the idea for this book years ago when I was having a mini writing retreat with my critique partner, Rachel Lacey. I immediately fell in love with the idea of writing the story of childhood friends who were ripped apart by tragedy and brought back together in adulthood. This story has been a long time in the making, but I am so thankful to finally have it out in the world! I have so many people in my life to thank, starting with Rachel Lacey who shared my excitement for this story and encouraged me to write it.

I would like to thank Kensington Publishing and my editor, Shannon Plackis, for making this book possible. Thank you, Shannon, for sharing my vision of this story and helping me mold it into what I always knew it could be. I have enjoyed collaborating and working with you this past year. Thank you to the amazing art department for an absolutely gorgeous cover! I am also appreciative of Jane Nutter and the rest of the PR department for helping *Charmed Friends* find its readers.

I would also like to thank my amazing literary agent, Sarah Younger, who also believed in these fictional friends. Sarah helped me mold the story and find its forever home.

Everyone's expertise and talent is appreciated and recognized. I am honored to be working with such a wonderful team of professionals.

I also could not have completed this book without the rest of my critique partners: Tif Marcelo, Jeanette Escudero, and April Hunt. You ladies inspire and amaze me every day. Tif, I cannot thank you enough for taking time out of your busy schedule to read an early copy of this book and give me invaluable feedback. You are an incredible friend, and I'm so lucky to have you in my life.

I've said it before and I'll continue to say it: Kimberly Bradford Scott, you are so appreciated. I don't know how I did this writing business before you. You are so much more than a writing assistant, you're a good friend and a valued reader. Thank you!

To my own childhood friends, Trisha McMillan and Susan Spears. Childhood friendships are so special. Knowing you was fundamental in forming who I am today. Even though people drift apart—such is life—you will always have a special place in my heart.

Last, but never least, I want to acknowledge my family. I recognize the sacrifices you make every day to help me meet my deadlines. You all have also been so wonderful in making sure I "fill my well" and keep the creativity flowing. Sonny, Ralphie, Doc, and Lydia, YOU are what inspires me on a daily basis. I love you deeply. Thank you for supporting me.

DISCUSSION QUESTIONS

1. *The Charmed Friends of Trove Isle* focuses on four childhood best friends torn apart by tragedy. Did you have a close group of friends when you were growing up? If so, are you still close or did you drift apart after graduation?

2. The main character, Melody Palmer, returns to her hometown of Trove Isle after being gone for a decade. Do you think the saying "you can't go home again" is true? Or do you believe that home is a place that one can always return to?

3. In the story, Liz's character struggles with anxiety and panic attacks. Her fears hold her back from chasing her dreams. Have you had a similar experience where fear kept you from going after something you wanted? How did you deal with that?

4. When Liz sees Melody for the first time since Melody's return to Trove Isle, Liz is torn between welcoming her long lost friend with open arms and being angry at her for abandoning their group of friends when they needed her most. How would you feel if you were in Liz's position?

5. All the friends feel guilt over the death of their friend in high school. Alyssa was Melody's younger sister and Melody was supposed to look after her. Liz was the one driving. Bri encouraged Alyssa to come with them that fateful night. Do you think any of the friends is more guilty than another? Do you think that a friend

could ever fully get over the guilt of an accident like this one?

6. A recurring theme in this book is friendship. The characters were friends in the beginning and then lost touch. After a tragedy and years apart, they reconnect as very different people. Do you feel that friendship can survive anything? Do you have a friendship that has endured despite hardships?

7. In the book, the friends all share a charm bracelet with special meaning to them, passing it around with the intention of doing something out of the normal. Something to prove they aren't just "zombies" as Alyssa put it. Have you ever had an object that you felt inspired or empowered you in some way?

8. Each of the three friends handled their grief in different ways. Melody ran. Liz shut herself off and became imprisoned by her fear. Bri self-destructed and found herself in a literal prison. Which friend do you relate to the most and why?

9. Even though Aunt Jo was deceased at the start of the book, she was very present in the story. Did Aunt Jo remind you of anyone in your life? What was your favorite aspect of Jo's character?

10. Liz's attraction to Matt was difficult for her because he was the one who pulled her from the wreckage after the fatal accident that killed Alyssa. Liz was afraid to fall for him because he reminded her of the worst day of her life. Do you think you would be able to fall in love with Matt if you were in Liz's shoes?

11. If you inherited a thrift store from your Great-aunt Jo, would you run it as a thrift store or turn it into something different?

12. Discuss this saying: One man's junk is another man's treasure.

13. In addition to the theme of enduring friendship, what other themes did you identify in this book?

Visit our website at
KensingtonBooks.com
to sign up for our newsletters, read
more from your favorite authors, see
books by series, view reading group
guides, and more!

BOOK **CLUB**

BETWEEN THE CHAPTERS

Become a Part of Our
Between the Chapters Book Club
Community and Join the Conversation

Betweenthechapters.net